SUDDENLY THAT SUMMER

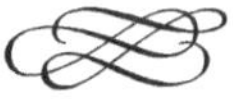

LORI HANDELAND

AUTHOR'S NOTE

You may notice that some of the song titles I've used at the beginning of each chapter were actually written or released after the events in this novel take place. I will claim artistic license as some of these songs of protest were just too perfect to resist.

I have also placed civil rights activist, Bayard Rustin, at a rally in Madison, Wisconsin, during the Summer of Love, 1967. This rally did not happen; Mr. Rustin was occupied elsewhere that summer fighting for civil rights and authoring many articles on the same.

I would like to give grateful thanks to.
Colonel Merline Lovelace, USAF (Retired) not only for her twenty-three years of service, but for graciously reading this book and sharing with me both her experiences in Vietnam (at Tan Son Nhut Air Base and in Saigon) as well as being one of the first women to attend Princeton University.

Any mistakes are, as always, my own.

CHAPTER 1

Jay

"Billy Don't Be a Hero"

Willow Creek, Wisconsin—March–May 1967

Billy shoved the leash of his shaggy, multicolored mutt into Jay's hand. "Ringo's yours now."

In the gray light of dawn, his words gave Jay a shiver she couldn't quite shake.

"He's *yours*," Jay insisted, though she *had* been the one to find the puppy curled up in the alley behind the café. Jay had a knack for finding the lost—be it keys, shoes, or furry things. "He'll always *be* yours."

Momma, chatting with the driver of the big white bus that would take Billy away, glanced in Jay's direction.

Jay swallowed, and something just south of disgusting slid down her throat. "Right?" she asked more quietly, and Momma turned back.

"Sure." Billy ran his hand over Jay's long, tangled hair, then tugged on the ends the way he always had, the way she was going to miss more than she'd ever missed Daddy. "He's mine, but while I'm gone, he can be the mascot of the Four Musketeers."

Which was the unoriginal name Billy had given to Jay and her three best friends: Mags, Ronnie, and Helen.

The driver strode past. "Say your good-byes, kid."

Billy was so excited to get started on the path he'd been dreaming of since . . . forever, the path that would mold him into the man he wanted to be, the man their grandfather *expected* him to be, that he practically bounced.

He hugged Jay, and she clung to him. She was scared in a way she'd never been before. What if he didn't come home?

"I'll be fine," Billy said as if he knew what she was thinking. Sometimes she wondered. "This is something I have to do."

"You didn't have to. Not yet. You wanted to."

He'd practically *begged* to.

"If I don't enlist, eventually I'll be drafted. Being dragged *to* the war isn't the way to *go* to war. Especially when I believe in the war."

Billy planned to save the world toot sweet from yet another threat on democracy. Jay wasn't sure democracy was worth it.

"Gramps has been training me for this since I could walk."

Momma, who hovered nearby, muttered something that sounded very much like *fucking old man*, except Momma never used the F-word. Ever.

Because of his only son's desertion, as well as his refusal to enlist despite military service being a Johnson family tradition, Gramps had pushed Billy to be stronger, quicker, smarter, better, *more* than the father who had come and gone before.

As a result, Billy could track any animal in the forest by the time he was eight. He'd received his first rifle on his tenth birthday. By twelve, he was the best shot in the county. Not that he'd actually killed anything yet.

"Deer look like Ringo when they're dead," he'd confided to Jay.

What the hell was he going to do in Vietnam? Dead people had to look like . . . dead people.

Nevertheless, Jay put on a happy face when Billy climbed on that bus; she kept it on as the bus pulled away, and Ringo tried to follow—the leash he had never needed before suddenly made sense. But once the bus was history, Jay's smile died.

* * *

Months passed while they waited for a letter that would explain what would happen to Billy next. Would he come home? For how long? When? The only communication they received was an odd, worrisome note that arrived with the clothes he'd worn the day he'd left.

Dear Momma and Jay,

Here are some things I no longer need. I have arrived at Fort Polk in Louisiana and I am fine.

With love, your son and brother, Billy Johnson

See? Worrisome.

On the first day of summer vacation, Jay stared down the road where her brother's bus had disappeared as she'd done every day since. She didn't know why. She was only wasting her time and getting a reputation for being strange. Something no seventeen-year-old really wanted.

Ringo whined, and Jay dropped to her knees, and threw her arms around his neck. "No matter how much we try to pretend otherwise, boy, nothing's ever going to be the same again, is it?"

He licked her nose, then returned his gaze to the empty road.

The day had dawned clear and cool. Late May should be summer, despite the calendar's insisting it was spring. However, May in Wisconsin often insisted on acting like winter.

As Jay and Ringo wandered toward Maple Avenue, the main

drag of Willow Creek—other streets within the city limits known by the oh-so-unique names of various trees in the Wisconsin tree almanac—the wind nipped at her bare knees with teeth of ice. The sun would warm everything by noon, it would warm her, but right then, Jay shivered with both cold and nerves.

She contemplated the fluffy white clouds drifting across the blue-blue sky. Could they travel from here to Fort Polk? Would Billy see tomorrow the clouds she had seen today? Even if he did, soon he would not. Clouds from Wisconsin did not make their way to Vietnam.

Billy was gone from here, going over there, and the idea that she might never see him again . . . she put it out of her mind. There was a reason she hadn't slept the night through since he'd enlisted.

Jay nearly walked past the boy sitting on the bench outside of Reitman's Bakery/Liquor. If it hadn't been for Ringo pausing to snuffle at his Adidas sneakers, which were nearly as white as his T-shirt, she would have.

Jay stopped, startled, then wasn't sure what to say.

He scratched behind Ringo's ears and accepted kisses with surprising ease. Ringo's huge head, huge body, massive paws, and equally massive jaws full of teeth often caused those unfamiliar with his sweet disposition to cross the street at the sight of him.

"Hi, I'm Paul."

He was beautiful—blond, blue-eyed, already tan—and she'd never seen him before in her life. That didn't happen often in Willow Creek, and when it did, it was cause for great curiosity.

Why was he here? How long would he stay? Unfortunately, Jay couldn't manage to voice those questions any more than a greeting. But Paul didn't seem put off by her stupidity as most boys would have been.

"Who's this?" He tilted his head toward the dog.

"Ringo." Jay's voice cracked; she wanted to die.

"That must be why he likes me."

Jay stared at him blankly.

He pointed to himself. "Paul." Then to the dog. "Ringo. Get it?"

She tried to say something clever, gave up, then nodded.

"Hey, Ringo, you're the best."

Ringo grinned, agreeing that *yes, he was the best*.

Paul smelled like heaven, if heaven smelled fresh and clean with just a hint of lime. Jay drew in a lungful, then let it out reluctantly. What was wrong with her?

Sure, she was seventeen, but she was a young seventeen, raised in a small town where everyone knew her and she knew them. She didn't get many chances to talk to a new boy. In truth, he was her first. New boys in Willow Creek were as rare as a warm spring day.

"What's your name?"

"Jane Josephine Johnson," she said, then wished she hadn't. Jane was so plain, Josephine so old, and Johnson so boring. "Everyone calls me Jay."

"They should call you Three-J." He made the peace sign. "That would be groovy."

Jay wanted to say *you can call me that*, but she couldn't seem to get the words out of her mouth.

"I've . . . uh . . . seen you around." He whirled his hand, hunched his shoulders, seemed at a loss for what to say next, which made Jay feel less like a dork, until she thought about where he might have seen her, what she might have been doing. Like staring down the road after that long-ago bus and talking to Billy's dog.

But he didn't say, she didn't ask, and the silence stretched until he finally blurted, "Is it weird to have the same last name as the president?"

Jay shrugged. "There were Johnsons in Willow Creek long before anyone ever heard of Lyndon B."

"Interesting."

Was it? Jay didn't think so.

"I just moved here," he continued, "from San Francisco."

"Why?"

"I'm seventeen." Paul spread his hands. "My parents made me. My dad is the new assistant dean of liberal arts at the university."

Jay wasn't sure what an assistant dean did; she wasn't exactly sure what liberal arts were, but she kept it to herself. She already looked moronic enough.

"Willow Creek must be a big change from San Francisco."

Paul stood, taller than Jay's embarrassing five-foot-ten by at least two inches. She couldn't think of another guy her age that was.

"A big change was the idea. My parents thought San Fran was getting wild. You heard about the Be-In?"

Jay could only shake her head, wide-eyed. Whenever Momma caught her watching the news, she'd snap off the television and order Jay to do her homework, clean her room, walk the dog, or Jay's particular favorite, *find something better to do before I find it for you.* As a result, all Jay knew about San Francisco was that it was cooler than Willow Creek. Was there any place on earth that wasn't?

"You didn't?" Paul seemed almost as surprised by that as Jay had been to discover a new boy in town. "In January, over twenty thousand people gathered in Golden Gate Park wearing costumes, playing music, burning incense." Paul glanced around, then lowered his voice so she had to lean in. "Smoking dope."

Jay hadn't thought her eyes could go any wider. She'd heard about dope but hadn't seen any yet, and she kinda wanted to.

The San Francisco Paul described sounded exotic, foreign, hip, and happening.

"I had to sneak out, but it was"—he lifted his gaze to a sky as brilliant as his eyes, and Jay held her breath—"disappointing."

Her breath gushed out. "Wait. What?"

"I thought there'd be more action. There was a lot of sitting, talking, drugging. Not a lot of doing."

"Doing what?"

"Protesting."

Jay stiffened. "The Be-In was a war protest?"

"Not really. It was meant to be a peaceful opposition to oppression—of Negroes, women, whoever. But people were more interested in turning on, tuning in, and dropping out like Timothy Leary. Jerry Rubin's speech, though, was outta sight. He wants to organize a protest march on the Pentagon. Can you imagine?"

Jay could, and she didn't like it. Someone who wasn't over there, complaining over here about something he didn't, couldn't, wouldn't understand.

What a scuzz bucket!

"You're against the war." Jay's skin, which had been pleasantly warm since she'd met him, went clammy and cool.

"Isn't everyone?"

"No." Jay snapped her fingers, and Ringo stopped snuffling Paul's shoes to return to her side. "My brother's shipping out soon."

She didn't know how soon *soon* would be. But Billy would be headed to Vietnam eventually.

Paul frowned. "Why would you support a government that drafted your brother and a war that will probably kill him?"

Jay winced.

"Sorry. I get worked up about Johnson's lies."

The president was lying? Since when? About what?

Wait a second. Why was she listening to someone who was against everything Billy was for?

"My brother volunteered. He understands, like everyone else

in this town, that we have to stop communism faster than we stopped the Nazis. You want Hitler in charge of Southeast Asia?"

"Hitler's dead."

"There's always another nut ready to take over the world."

"You think Ho Chi Minh is going to take over the world?" Paul asked.

"If we let him."

"There's no way that'll happen."

"Exactly, because my brother is headed to Vietnam . . ." *Along with thousands of other guys.* " . . . to make sure it doesn't."

She was repeating the words of her gramps, but they were what Billy believed, and if she didn't believe them too, what did that make her?

Someone she did not want to be.

"Is his life worth it?"

Silence fell with the shock of a brick through a glass window, and the next thing Jay knew, she was running, Ringo on her heels.

"Three-J! Wait!"

She didn't. Instead, she ran until she reached the sidewalk in front of her house. Her chest hurt; she was breathing too fast. She couldn't figure out if she was more upset over Paul's question or over what had popped into her head in response to it.

No. Her brother's life was not worth stopping Ho Chi Minh. Nothing was worth that.

Jay glanced over her shoulder. No Paul. At least he could take a hint.

Ringo trotted ahead, ears pricked, paws prancing as if they had a visitor, though no one stood in the yard; no one sat on the porch. What did was a jumble of papers pinned to the center of the welcome mat with a rock. Where had they come from?

Even before Ringo snuffled the pile with true devotion, knocking the rock aside, forcing Jay to chase the stack across the plank floor, snatching one sheet after the other just before the wind took them away, Jay knew they were Billy's. The creamy pages had to have been torn out of a sketchbook similar to all the other sketchbooks he'd ever sketched in.

Billy could draw better than anyone, and even though Gramps had sneered at his "sissy hobby," Billy kept on doing it. Jay admired that. Gramps could be a real ass sometimes.

As always, Billy's drawings made Jay feel amused, curious, uneasy, apprehensive but most of all closer to him.

CHAPTER 2

Billy
"Fortunate Son"

ort Polk, Louisiana—March–May 1967

Billy stared straight ahead as he left everything he'd ever known and loved behind. He told himself he would only look forward from now on. That's what a man did. In truth, if he watched Willow Creek, Momma, Jay, Ringo disappear—maybe forever—he thought he might cry, and if he started crying before he even got to basic, how would he ever become a standout star in Vietnam? Gramps had been disappointed in Billy for most of his life. That ended now.

Several hours later, Billy reached Chicago, where he made his way off the bus and onto a southbound train. He wasn't in his seat for more than a minute before a colored recruit climbed on. Even though old Lyndon B. had passed the Civil Rights Act in 1964, there was still a lot of "seat taken," "saved," and other comments as he made his way down the aisle. Not a one of them wiped the smile off the guy's face.

Billy started to wonder if he was slow in the head. Except, if that were the case, how had he ended up on the train to Fort Polk?

It made Billy mad how people were behaving, so when the fella stopped next to Billy's seat and lifted his eyebrows above the big, black Buddy Holly glasses, Billy moved to the window.

"Thanks, man. I'm Terrell. Terrell Jones."

"Billy Johnson."

"BJ!" Terrell smacked his palm against Billy's, then drew it back slow and flicked his own hand away. "That's how us Negroes say howdy. Gimme some skin." He did the palm slap, draw, flick motion again.

Since Terrell called himself *Negro* instead of *colored*, Billy figured he'd best do the same, if he had to call him anything but Terrell, and why would he?

Terrell had an Afro as big and messy as Jimi's. It was hard, at first, for Billy to keep his eyes off it.

"You wanna touch my fro, bro?"

Billy did, so bad he sat on his hands to keep from doing it. Touching someone's hair was weird and would probably earn him strange glances, though they were already getting a few that he couldn't figure. So what if he sat with Terrell? No one else had wanted to.

"You always this quiet?" Terrell nudged Billy with a bony elbow. "Still mad about being drafted? I don't think I'll ever get over it."

"I enlisted."

Terrell shoved his long fingers into the center of all that hair and scratched. "Why in hell would you do that?"

"To stop communist aggression."

Terrell laughed so hard everyone gawked.

"He . . . he . . ." Terrell managed to get his breath. "Enlisted."

Eyes widened in faces both white and black. Billy's face flamed red.

At least Terrell didn't continue the conversation until the rest of the guys stopped staring. "You believe that propaganda?"

Billy wasn't sure what propaganda was, but he didn't let on.

"If we'd have stopped Hitler," he began.

"Not the same."

"Little man, big, bad dreams. People dying."

"Not our people, BJ."

Every time Terrell called him BJ, Billy wondered if he was supposed to call Terrell TJ, but he didn't have the guts. His gramps always told him *no guts, no glory*, but Billy would rather not lose the only friend he had here by reaching for glory he didn't need.

"We're goin' to a country where the trees different, the bugs different, the language different. You foolish enough to think everyone's gonna be happy to see us? I hear they hate us, and they only gonna hate us more as time goes on."

"But we're trying to save them."

Terrell shook his head. "You crazy."

In New Orleans, they got off the train, then waited for a bus to take them to Fort Polk, several hours away. Right outside of town, Billy fell asleep to the sound of Terrell's voice. He awoke to just-before-dawn darkness and the same sound. Had Terrell been talking the entire time?

"You know basic used to be twelve weeks?" Terrell peered through the window at the silent camp where no one seemed to have noticed they'd arrived. "But they cut four weeks 'cause they need bodies in Vietnam too bad to waste time. Guess that ole communist aggression is really gettin' aggressive."

For a minute, Billy worried about losing those four weeks, but just because he'd never shot a living thing didn't mean he couldn't; it wasn't like they were going to fire at live targets here anyway.

A man appeared at the front of the bus, tall and wide in the shoulders, with hair so short it was hard to decide if it was white or blond. His face a constant shade of fury, his mouth opened so wide words seemed to erupt from an endless cavern of teeth.

"Off your ass and on your feet! Move it, move it! Vacate this goddamn bus right now!"

Everyone jumped up at once, stepping on toes, cursing. After a lot of pushing and shoving, they managed to reach the ground.

"Asshole to belly button!" the big man shouted. "Asshole to belly button! Today!"

Guys bumped into one another, then bounced back like bumper cars as they tried to understand what *asshole to belly button* meant. Finally some recruits in front figured it out and lined up so close that one man's zipper pressed between another's back pockets. That close, it was easy to tell they'd been traveling for days.

Pee-ew!

"I am Drill Sergeant Garrett. You will call me Drill Sergeant. You may think of me as DS to save brain space, even write it to save paper space, but I had better never hear those letters uttered in my presence. Are we clear?"

Men nodded, mumbled, shuffled.

"If you are clear, answer with 'Yes, Drill Sergeant!'"

Enough of them did, so DS Garrett moved on. "To the barracks, double time."

They found it pretty difficult to double time with their zippers pressed between a stranger's pockets. Several guys stumbled. One even fell, which slowed everyone down. Eventually they made it to the nearby buildings. Inside, bunk beds ran up one side and down another.

"Form a line. Alphabetical order! Now!"

This wasn't as simple as it seemed. Hardly anyone knew anyone else's first name, let alone their last. Add to that they were tired, scared, and it took a half hour to decipher where everyone belonged. But by the time they were in alphabetical order, Billy could have recited nearly all the names from memory.

Getting to know you, US Army style.

Terrell and Billy shared a bunk—Terrell on top and Billy on the bottom.

"How's that for luck?" Terrell had climbed up to check out his bed, then had to climb right down, double time. Everything was double time, unless it was ASAP.

They finally got to take a shower. Hallelujah! But before they could greet the soap and water, DS Garrett told them to—

"Grab your ankles."

Billy had no idea what their drill sergeant could possibly be searching for in a place the sun didn't shine, but Terrell did.

"You bring any Mary Jane, they gonna find it now."

"Mary Jane?"

"Pot. Weed. Grass. Dope. Mari-jew-ana. Where you from again?"

Billy didn't figure anyone would be dumb enough to stick *that* where they were searching, but he was wrong.

"We have a winner!" DS Garrett held up a plastic bag filled with what appeared to be moldy, dried grass, then he kicked the pothead in the butt so hard he fell on his face.

"What a dummy," Terrell whispered. "There are enough drugs in-country that no one needs to bring their own."

"Why would anyone do drugs? We'll have rifles, grenades. We need to pay attention."

Terrell shoved his glasses up his nose and called Billy *choirboy*.

The shower was exactly like the ones taken after high school phys ed—a room full of naked guys trying hard not to glance at one another and get labeled *queer*, but many still sneaking glances, especially at those who were so different from them.

Afterward, they dressed in their newly issued army-green uniforms—fatigues—and black leather combat boots, which made everyone look a lot the same, then marched to the barbershop. When they came out, they looked more the same than when they'd gone in.

Billy thought Terrell might cry, and since Billy's desire to do so had lessened once he'd met Terrell—Terrell's constant chatter sure helped—Billy blurted the first thing that came to mind, hoping to erase his friend's weepy expression.

"Guess I shoulda touched your fro when I had the chance."

Terrell's dark-brown eyes narrowed behind his big glasses, and for a second, Billy thought Terrell might slug him, then he grinned, looped his arm around Billy's shoulders, and rubbed his knuckles along the top of Billy's almost-bare head. "Guess you shoulda."

A couple of white guys gave them the side-eye, and one sneered. "Too bad you won't get mistook for Jimi no more, spade."

Billy took a step in the fool's direction, but Terrell laughed. "I guess that's good since I can't carry a tune to save my soul, and my hands . . ." He held them out for all to see, large and wide and not very nimble at the end of such skinny arms. "Well, they just too clumsy to ever play guitar."

The idiots frowned, then wandered off.

"Why didn't you pop him?" Billy asked. "I'd have backed you up."

Not that Billy had ever been in a fight—except with Jay, and she'd kind of kicked his ass— but he should probably start. What would he do when he had to fight hand-to-hand if he'd never even punched someone once?

"If I lose my temper, it'll be open season on teasing the Negro, and the only one who'd end up in the stockade is me. That's how this world works."

"Why is everyone such an asshole?"

Terrell slapped Billy on the back. "We ain't."

Morning after morning, the army woke them with the bugle call of reveille, but it was nothing like the jaunty way Gramps had sung it—*I can't get 'em up, I can't get 'em up, I can't get 'em up this morning; I can't get 'em up, I can't get 'em up, I can't get 'em up at all!*—whenever Billy and Jay had stayed overnight at his dairy farm.

Every time he heard the melody, Billy missed Gramps just a little. And Jay, Ringo, Momma too. Something he could never let slip. Confessing he missed Mommy might be as bad as smuggling weed in his back end.

"What time is it?" asked a short, dumpy recruit one morning, patting what was left of his dark hair.

He'd introduced himself as Robert from Alabama, and he always seemed to need a shave, even after he just had one.

"It is 0500, Alabama Bob!" DS Garrett announced.

From the twitch of several recruits' lips, the nickname was gonna stick.

"Aren't you overjoyed to greet this fresh new day?"

Alabama Bob's pale-blue eyes slid to the black-velvet sky beyond the windows. Billy could almost see his thoughts appear in a bubble above his head like a cartoon: *Isn't it still night?* At least he had the sense to say, "Yes, Drill Sergeant!"

"You got two minutes to fall out, or you'll be doing up downs till you puke."

Because they were sleeping alphabetically, Negroes were all mixed up with white guys, and there were some scuffles as everyone scrambled to get dressed and rush outside. One glare from DS Garrett stopped that nonsense.

"In 'Nam, everyone bleeds red. Got that?"

"Yes, Drill Sergeant," they shouted, but Billy didn't think everyone got it.

Like those dirtballs that muttered *nigger lover* whenever he walked by.

Billy ignored them. What else could he do? Momma always said: *Ignorant can be fixed, but stupid is forever.*

"You're gonna need to get yer heads on straight," DS continued. "Have one another's backs no matter what goddamn color that back is. You wanna live through Vietnam, you need to be as color blind as VC bullets."

"He's right, Beej." Terrell had already shortened the two-syllable BJ to Beej, and since Billy had also heard *blow job* coughed out a few times as he passed, he didn't mind. "We all soldiers now, we gonna have to stick together or else we'll just come apart."

Terrell had a way of looking at things that got to the heart of the matter. His words reminded Billy of Jay and her pals.

All for one and one for all.

CHAPTER 3

Jay
"What's Going On?"

*W*illow Creek—June 1967

Jay lifted her head. Had that been a cry, quickly muffled?

The house slept—silent, still. Momma had gone to bed long ago. Nothing new. She owned the only beauty salon in Willow Creek, spent her days on her feet with her fingers buried to the knuckles in bleach, hair dye, and perm solution. No matter how many times Momma smoothed on lotion, her hands still resembled monkey's paws.

She'd pulled the weight at their house, even before Dad had taken one look at his brand-new baby girl and booked.

Probably not true. While there was undoubtedly more to Dad's departure than the sight of her face, the timing was suspect.

Jay had tried to sleep, but every time she closed her eyes, she saw Billy's drawings. Finally, she turned on the light and pulled out the illustrations, as worn and thin after so much handling as Billy's last letter, which had arrived a few days ago and made Momma blink back tears. Because at the bottom of a very short note, Billy had scrawled: *Leave canceled. Shipping out. More from Vietnam.*

The first sketch was a portrait of a young man—her brother's chicken scratch across the bottom named him *Terrell*—eyes lively behind his thick glasses, his Afro at least three inches high, his smile big and bright. Jay liked him right away.

The second was also a portrait, or maybe a caricature—a word she'd learned from Billy. The soldier—*Drill Sergeant Garrett*—appeared angry, from the tip of his crew cut to the bottom of his square chin. His mouth stretched wider than humanly possible, an echoing cavern full of teeth from which orders and insults spewed. Jay disliked him as fast as she'd liked Terrell.

In the third sketch, a bunch of guys in rumpled civilian clothes stood beneath a forlorn crescent moon, lined up so close there wasn't an inch of space between them. From the set of their shoulders, the position—*asshole to belly button*—was mighty uncomfortable.

A second cry split the night—this time she was sure of it— and Jay shoved the drawings under her pillow. She hadn't shown them to anyone, not even her mother, and she wasn't sure why.

She crept along the hall. Momma's door was open. Jay couldn't recall a time it hadn't been.

Her mother slept on her back, dark hair splayed across the pillow, one arm thrown out. The moonlight spread from the window and over her bed, over her, highlighting lines around Momma's mouth and eyes that Jay didn't remember seeing before. She told herself they were a trick of the silvery light, but she knew better. Momma was worried and so was Jay.

The pain of missing Billy was a constant lump in Jay's throat, like she'd taken a too-big bite of something, and it'd gotten stuck. No matter how many times she swallowed, that lump never went away.

Jay hovered, unwilling to wake her mother in case she'd stopped dreaming whatever had induced the sharp, pathetic cries—Jay had a pretty good idea what it was—then she heard them again. From Billy's room.

Ringo stretched across the mattress, head on the pillow where it had always rested next to Billy's. Jay's brother would spoon his dog, arm thrown over Ringo's barrel chest. The steady, peaceful in and out of Ringo's breathing had no doubt lulled Billy to dreamland. Now the dog's legs twitched, and he whined as if someone were breaking his heart.

Someone had.

"Hush," she whispered the way Momma did whenever Jay cried, the way she had when Jay's heart had broken too as that bus drove away with her brother. The word didn't help Ringo any more now than it had helped Jay then.

She lay down and placed her arm where Billy's had always gone. Neither she nor Ringo managed much more than a doze all night. Either the dog would whine and wake Jay, or she'd start and wake him.

When the sun rose, the shower went on, and Jay hurried to her room so Momma wouldn't know she'd spent the night in Billy's bed, with Billy's dog. She'd think Jay wasn't handling things well.

She wasn't, but she didn't want Momma to know that. She didn't want anyone to.

Jay threw on her clothes—no problem wearing shorts; the weather had at last turned to summer—then hid Billy's drawings behind her winter boots. She and Ringo were out of the house and on their way to the clearing before her mother had finished washing her hair.

Jay had happened upon the place deep in the woods when she was twelve, and it had become a spot where she and her friends could talk about anything because no one would over-hear them. One where they could do anything too—no one would see them. The clearing was theirs alone. Jay hadn't even told Billy about it.

Once there, the silence—broken only by the babble of water from the creek—made Jay think again of Billy. He'd always needed more peace and quiet than anyone else. How was he doing in a country that hadn't seen peace, or quiet, for decades?

Even though Gramps encouraged Billy to be a doer, Billy was more of a thinker, and if he thought too much over there, he was gonna get killed.

Ringo barked once, and Jay jumped, though she knew from the way his butt wiggled who would emerge from the trees.

Ronnie "the Tomboy" Frederick, her unfortunate red hair plastered to her head despite the balmy morning, lifted her shirt tail to wipe sweat off her face, revealing pale skin covered with freckles. Ronnie had tons of them. Everywhere.

"How many miles?" Jay asked.

"Five." Ronnie scrubbed behind Ringo's ears, just the way he liked it. "No, six."

While her legs might be short, her endurance was as epic as her stubbornness. Ronnie was going to compete in the Olympics or die trying.

"Better you than me."

"I . . . um . . ." Ronnie started picking her cuticles, a habit they'd spent the last year training her out of. "Saw Mags the other day."

Mags, or as Ronnie referred to her, *The Princess of All She Surveys*, hadn't shown up at the clearing since school had let out, and no one seemed to know what she was doing instead.

"She was with Susan Grant and some of her friends."

Susan was a cheerleader. Did not deign to talk to the likes of them. And really, they didn't want her to. Susan was mean.

"She looked right through me as if I wasn't even there."

"Sounds like Susan," Jay muttered.

"I meant Mags."

"Mags didn't say hi, wave, nothing?"

Ronnie continued to stare at her hands. She'd already picked one finger bloody. "She pretended she didn't see me."

"Maybe she didn't."

Ronnie just shook her head.

That explained why Mags had been MIA. She'd found some friends who cared as much about hair color and makeup application as she did. Mags was going to be Miss America one day, a life goal that horrified her math-professor mother.

"If Mags wants to have her hair combed by those bitches," Jay said, "let her."

It felt good to curse. Jay kinda understood why people did it. Some of the anger inside seemed to come out through the mouth and disappear.

"What do you care anyway?"

Ronnie and Mags were oil and water. All they ever did was fight.

"Why wouldn't I?" Ronnie's confusion seemed genuine. "All for one, one for all, right? Now and forever."

Momma always said the four of them would probably grow apart. Beyond age, they had little in common. Jay hadn't believed her, but now she wondered.

"You know, it's the *Three* Musketeers," Jay said. "We'll be all right." Though it made her sad that Billy's name for them was fading away. What else about Billy would fade away?

Ronnie's sigh reminded Jay of Ringo's whenever he looked into Billy's room and found him gone.

"My mother's visiting Gramps on Sunday night." Usually Jay went along too, but Momma was still annoyed with Gramps because of Billy, and Jay suspected she planned to ream him out. "We should have a sleepover."

Ronnie perked up. "First sleepover of summer, all right! But . . . what if Mags doesn't come?"

"Then we won't have to scrub off mascara."

They'd promised Mags at the next sleepover she could do makeovers. They didn't want makeovers, but they had to throw her a bone, and who knew? Sometimes the thing you wanted to do the least was the thing you wound up liking the most. Jay doubted that would happen in this case, but she would keep an open mind.

She should have kept her mouth shut because Ronnie's perk had suddenly unperked.

"I found a bottle of schnapps in Billy's closet," Jay blurted. Where he'd gotten it since he was only old enough to buy a beer in a bar and not hard liquor anywhere, Jay had no idea.

"Really?" Ronnie seemed as intrigued as Jay had been.

"We can try it at the sleepover."

"Far out!" Ronnie jogged toward the path that led to the creek. "I'm gonna cool off."

She disappeared an instant before Ringo grumbled—not a growl, not really—then Mags emerged from the forest, light-brown hair perfectly styled and sprayed so not a single strand had blown out of place. Instead of the cutoff denim shorts and T-shirt Jay wore, Mags had donned pink gingham culottes with a white eyelet, boat-necked, sleeveless blouse.

How did Jay know such things? Because Mags often narrated her outfits as if she were on the runway in Paris.

Mags looked Jay up and down. "Why do you insist on hacking off your old blue jeans?"

"Because I can. Why do you insist on wearing something you could wear in school when you don't have to?"

The Willow Creek School System had yet to allow girls to wear pants, let alone shorts. Culottes were acceptable. Lord knows why. Attach shorts to a skirt and they miraculously became . . . not shorts.

"How we dress reveals who we are," Mags said. "Sometimes who we want to be."

Jay rolled her eyes. "How I dress reveals what's lying on my floor that morning."

Mags wrinkled her nose and crossed the dew-damp grass carefully in low-heeled white go-go boots, which she'd been desperate to own ever since she'd seen the dancers wearing them on *Hollywood a Go-Go*. She cocked a knee. "I bought these in Milwaukee."

"Well, la-ti-da."

Shopping in Milwaukee was something they'd always made fun of. Something the prissy, rich, cheerleady girls did.

Aha! Jay suddenly had no problem asking the question she'd been avoiding. "Did Ronnie see you with Susan Grant?"

"So?" Mags patted Ringo's head and rubbed his nose. He was ecstatic at the attention. Usually, Mags told him to go away and stop snotting on her.

"You ignored her as if you didn't even know her."

"That's not true."

From the way she wouldn't meet Jay's eyes, it was *so* true.

Before Jay could tell Mags that she didn't need to stay, that they were just fine without her, Ronnie returned with Helen, who must have walked in from the creek instead of town. Ronnie ran ahead, laughing and holding a book out of Helen's reach.

"Give it back!"

Jay couldn't recall a day since Helen "the Brain" Murphy had learned to read—at the age of three, the overachiever—when Helen's nose hadn't been in a book for the majority of her waking hours.

"This is *Macbeth*." Ronnie waved her prize like a flag.

"I'm reading Shakespeare this summer."

Ronnie snorted. "Why?"

The blue eyes narrowed behind glasses that were as much a part of Helen as her curly black hair. "Summer's when I get my pleasure reading done."

"I haven't read Shakespeare, Brain, but I'd bet money it isn't a pleasure."

"You'd lose."

Suddenly bored with the game, Ronnie tossed *Macbeth* into Helen's outstretched hands. "I'll bring snacks for the sleepover. To go with the schnapps."

Mags stopped petting the dog. "What schnapps?"

"I found peppermint schnapps in Billy's closet. But don't feel you have to—"

"When?"

Ronnie and Helen seemed so happy Jay couldn't tell Mags to take a hike. Who knew? Maybe the Susan Grant episode was a one-time thing, or a two-time thing considering the shopping expedition. Maybe Mags had decided that she liked the Musketeers better. Otherwise, why had she come to the clearing? To show off her go-go boots? No one cared about those but her. And Susan Grant.

"Five o'clock Sunday," Jay said.

"I'll be there."

Ronnie cast Jay a concerned glance as if she didn't believe it either. They'd just have to wait and see how *all for one and one for all* Mags still was.

They spent the rest of the day together, giggling and chattering as they always had, and for a while, it seemed that everything was back to the way it should be. Jay even told her friends about Billy shipping out.

As they walked back to town in the late afternoon light, the strains of "Groovin'" by the Young Rascals flowed from the transistor radio in Mags's ever present white macramé purse. The matching sunburn on the tips of their noses gave Jay a feeling as warm as the grass in the clearing. The world changed, they changed, but a lot was still the same, and it was comforting.

In the town square Mags went one way, Helen another. Ronnie and Jay walked on together.

"My mom asked if I was a lesbian."

"What?"

Ringo yipped. Jay had said that pretty loud.

"It's when a woman—"

"I know what it is! But why would she ask that?"

Ronnie swept her hand down her stout, boyish body.

"I don't get it."

"You know my mom."

Mrs. Frederick had been Willow Creek Holiday Fair Queen, prom queen, homecoming queen, and second runner-up in the Miss Wisconsin Pageant. The only explanation for her cranky disposition was that she was still ticked off about the last one.

"What did you say?" Jay asked.

"That I didn't know yet."

Ronnie's expression . . . Jay couldn't figure it out, then Ronnie shrugged.

"I wanted to mess with her. Don't tell anyone else, okay?"

"Okay," Jay agreed, though she wasn't sure why it mattered. Ronnie's mom said plenty of flaky things.

As they passed Reitman's, Ronnie paused to scoop something from the bench. After a glance, she handed it to Jay.

Rally! shouted the magazine's masthead. Up one side of the cover and down the other ran article titles.

"Haight-Ashbury—The Rock, The Roll, The Drugs!"

"LSD Ice Cream. Recipe Included."

"Should Men's Hair Be Longer than the Beatles?"

"Hanoi and the China/Russia Connection."

"It's the Summer of Love! Are You Going to San Francisco?"

The headlines reminded Jay all too much of a recent conversation. In front of this bakery. With Paul.

Coincidence? Probably not.

"See ya Sunday!" Ronnie hurried in the direction of home, and Jay did the same.

Inside, Jay closed her bedroom door and flipped the lock. She didn't think Momma should see her with *Rally!* No way.

In Willow Creek, patriotism was as much a religion as religion. Which only made it the same as any small midwestern town. Billy wasn't the first or the only boy to join up. He wouldn't be the last.

While waiting until you were called up—a.k.a. drafted—wasn't loudly discouraged, it *was* frowned upon, at least by the men who'd fought in the Great War, like Gramps, or WW2, like a lot of fathers, or the Korean "conflict," like a lot of uncles and older brothers. The draft was something new for Vietnam, and no one was quite sure what to think about it. No one was quite sure what to think about a lot these days, and it made them say and do odd stuff.

For instance, every previous summer the Musketeers had ranged free—night, day, whenever—all over Willow Creek. But this summer they had a ten o'clock curfew. So did a lot of other kids.

"You're nearly an adult now." Momma had fixed Jay with one of her serious looks. "You don't need to be hanging out on street corners in the dark like a hippie."

Lately, too, every unacceptable behavior was labeled "hippie." Sure, Willow Creek was pretty square, but come on! How could doing what they'd been doing since forever become anything other than what it had always been?

Fun.

Nothing ever happened in Willow Creek—nothing—and all the adults wanted to keep it that way. Jay would have liked to see the police chief use his siren just once. The man literally had the easiest job in the world. Ronnie's dad liked to complain that the city should start paying him based on how many crimes he dealt with. Ronnie's mom had pointed out that he wouldn't be able to feed his family if that were the case. He wouldn't be able to buy a Coke.

Jay opened the magazine.

More hippies stream into San Francisco every day, lured by Scott Mackenzie's voice telling them to wear flowers in their hair, Grace Slick crooning about the white rabbit, and the promise of Janis Joplin singing anything.

Jay paged forward, then back. When she could no longer avoid the article on Vietnam, she breathed in, then out, and began.

Will the increase in boots on the ground, which nearly doubled at the end of 1966—from two hundred thousand to three hundred and ninety thousand—lead to twice the number of American casualties? As last year's death toll stands at just over six thousand, the principals of mathematics point to twelve thousand more dead Americans by the end of this year.

"Goddamn Lyndon B," Jay muttered.

In the latest polls, the percentage of Americans who think the war is a mistake has increased to 37 percent, up from 24 percent in 1965 before the troop escalation began.

Was any of this true?

The idea of a journalist lying was almost as upsetting as the president doing so, but if only half of the article was based on fact, the protests Jay had glimpsed on the news made a lot more sense. Jay had believed the chanting, marching masses were troublemakers—what Momma, Gramps, and Billy had called them. But now . . .

She wasn't so sure.

CHAPTER 4

*V*ietnam—June 1967

When the advanced infantry training instructor told Billy he was shipping out early and without leave because several transports delivering new recruits to their platoons in Vietnam had been shot down before they even got where they were going, Billy made the mistake of asking about the ship. He should have understood by then that the army didn't choose its words based on any kind of truth.

"Ships take too damn long. Army only uses them if the air base isn't secure, and Tan Son Nhut has been secure since 1959."

"I bet the army's idea of secure and everyone else's a little different," Terrell murmured.

After that, it seemed like they'd no more than blinked, and they were in San Francisco.

"Hippies be gatherin'." Terrell pressed his nose to the

window of the bus taking them to Travis Air Force Base. "Protest the war, the man, the establishment. Whatever."

Billy had never been sure who *the man* was exactly, but he didn't say so. There were a lot of things about the world that confused him, and if he kept quiet, he learned. If he spoke up, he looked like a dimwit.

He'd done as well as he'd hoped in basic and earned the admiration of not only his superiors but his friends and non-friends alike, so Billy tried not to do or say anything stupid that would make those admiring eyes roll. Seeing that expression of disdain hurt even more now than when Gramps had done it.

There'd been a night not long ago when he'd woken from a strange dream of hands clutching a rifle. Those hands were pale, grasping, desperate.

Useless.

Only when the word whispered through his head did Billy understand that those hands were his, and the voice was his grandfather's.

They arrived at the air force base without ever seeing a single hippie, and Billy was glad. How could they protest a war they didn't understand? Because if they *did* understand, they wouldn't protest. They'd cheer.

He kept those thoughts to himself too. They put him in the minority, and being a minority was not fun. People stared, whispered, said mean things straight to your face. Just ask Terrell.

The army jammed nearly 250 troops onto a specially designed civilian charter plane; they flew first to Guam, then Manila, and finally to Vietnam.

At Tan Son Nhut Air Base, their plane sat on the tarmac in the steaming heat; the soldiers shifted, impatient to escape after spending nearly twenty-six hours elbow-to-elbow.

"We wait here, we wait there, we wait and wait everywhere," Terrell said.

"You should send that to Dr. Seuss."

"Who?"

Sometimes he and Terrell seemed to have grown up on different planets.

When the plane's door finally opened, it wasn't to let them off but to let several South Vietnamese officials on. Before anyone could figure out why, the men sprayed the cabin with a fog of—

"Fucking DDT." One of the guys headed back for another tour waved a hand in front of his face.

"They worried we might bring in bugs?" Terrell asked.

"Yep." The second-timer grabbed his gear from the overhead rack. "Why would we when they got plenty of their own?"

The instant Billy stepped onto the rollaway stairs, the heat hit him, along with a tingle of fear. Would he leave Vietnam the same way he'd come or make the return trip in a coffin?

"Move it." Terrell poked him in the back, and Billy moved it.

On the tarmac, troops gathered under the shade of the wings. The distant whine of engines built to an ear-rattling rumble as a trio of small two-engine cargo planes roared past. One after another, they lifted into the sky.

"Those are C-123s." A sergeant, who appeared to be a lifer from the lines on his face and the rack of stripes on his sleeves, arrived with a clipboard. "In Vietnam, you call all birds by their numbers—*DC-8* or *C-123* or *C-130*. You'll learn which is which soon enough."

"Where they goin' in such a hurry?" Terrell's face tilted up; the sun bounced off the lenses of his glasses as he watched the C-123s disappear.

"Defoliant mission." The man pointed his pen to a long line of barrels marked by an orange stripe. "The jungle is a monster, full of sneaky, moving teeth. If we don't control that monster, it will devour us. Understand?"

"Yes, sergeant!"

"Fall in!" He frowned at his clipboard while everyone got in line. "I'm sure you're aware of the individual rotation system in Vietnam. This war ain't like World War Two where troops served from the day they wore their first army boot until they defeated those assholes Hitler and Hirohito. Here, your tour in-country is one year. Start checkin' off days on your calendars."

Billy had seen a few guys on the plane with handmade calendars. One had a notepad where he'd written *365* on the first page, then counted down a number on every page after until he reached his DEROS, or Date of Expected Return from Overseas. Billy hadn't planned to make a calendar; it seemed like something someone who *didn't* want to be here would do. But he'd gotten bored and found himself scribbling 365 numbers on the last page of his sketchbook.

"Troops reach their DEROS every day," the sergeant continued. "They gotta be replaced. You will be sent to different units all over Vietnam in an attempt to bring everyone closer to full strength. But first there's processing at the replacement battalion." He motioned for them to follow him to nearby buses.

Long rows of concrete revetments sheltered various aircraft. A side apron was crowded with choppers.

"Lookit all them birds," Terrell said. "Army sure is nuts about 'em."

Billy recognized some from basic training. Each one seemed to have a different name—the Huey, the Chinook, the Sea Knight, the Hare, the Huskie, the Hound. Soldiers were supposed to use those names just like they were supposed to refer to planes by their letter/number designations. It wasn't easy. The names didn't make any sort of sense.

The bus trip was uneventful. Though the windows, encased in steel mesh, hinted this wasn't always the case. Their quarters at the replacement battalion resembled those at Fort Polk, with two-story barracks and bunks. They spent almost a week filling

out more forms: next-of-kin notification, life insurance benefi-
ciaries.

"Makes ya feel all warm and gooey, don't it?" Terrell asked.

They received Geneva Convention ID cards, ration cards, exchanged any money they carried for MPCs—military payment currency. Possession of a greenback was a court-martial offense. However, considering the need for soldiers in-country, Billy doubted anyone would be convicted. They learned how to send letters home—write *FREE* on the envelope —and to another unit—write *IN-COUNTRY*. They swallowed their first dose of large, orange malaria pills.

"Failure to take yer horse pills can result in being charged with Article Fifteen—fine and reduction in rank," the sergeant said.

After sharing that little ditty, the army promptly promoted all Private E-2s to Private First Class.

"We get more money!" Alabama Bob grinned.

"Where you gonna spend it here?" Terrell spread his big hands, and Bob's grin died.

The day arrived for assignments. The sergeant began shouting names, pointing to where each soldier or group of them should stand. It didn't take long to figure out he was reading down the line in alphabetical order, and Billy crossed his fingers behind his back, hoping that wherever the division came between going here and going there, it would not separate him and Terrell. They'd been together since basic, along with Alabama Bob, though Billy wouldn't mind seeing him sent somewhere else.

In the end, he got one wish and not the other as all three of them were assigned to the Fourth Infantry, Ivy Division—a play on the Roman numeral IV—stationed in the Central Highlands.

Terrell's eyes went wide. "Central Highlands is where the shit done hit the fan a long time ago."

"You think we were gonna have desk jobs in Saigon?" Billy asked.

In truth, he felt almost as shaky about their assignment as Terrell. Billy wanted so badly to do well he feared nearly every second that he wouldn't.

"Naw, sir." Terrell stood up straighter, lifted his chin. "I'm ready. And I know you ready. You been talkin' about endin' that ole communist aggression for months. Now's your chance." He curled one hand into a fist and punched upward.

Billy had thought that gesture meant *right on*, but Terrell said it was more like *Power to the People*. Terrell probably knew better than Billy did, but sometimes Terrell punched the air when *Power to the People* made no sense at all.

Not too long after, the three of them, along with several other guys, were herded into the open side hatch of a UH-1 by a flight engineer in a baggy flight suit.

"I hope it's not far," Alabama Bob shouted over the *whap-whap-whap* of the Huey's rotor blades as they lifted from the ground, then he shifted like a four-year-old. "I gotta take a piss."

Terrell rolled his eyes. This was not the first time they'd heard that.

Pleiku wasn't as far from Saigon as San Francisco from Louisiana, but it wasn't close either. Not to mention they had to drop other soldiers at different locations on the way.

At one of the stops, a deuce and a half waited to haul recruits wherever it was they were going, the truck bed covered in sandbags, a soldier perched behind an M60 machine gun—referred to as an MG or M60—mounted on top of the cab, a mound of ammo curled at his feet.

"Guess the army can't afford seats," Terrell said.

"Sandbags keep you from getting your balls blown off if that truck hits a land mine."

Billy hadn't seen the soldier parked in the rear of their transport. Since both Terrell and Bob started at the words, they hadn't either. Covered in dust, the guy had blended into the shadows.

"The way the enemy creeps around, you never see 'em until they bite you on the ass."

As the Huey took off, banking low over the jungle, Billy imagined teeth snapping in the middle of all that green, and he shuddered.

A noncom named Bullock met them upon their arrival at Camp Enari, twelve klicks outside Pleiku. His gaze flicked over the names sewn on their utility uniforms, and he frowned, which made Billy wonder if he'd even known they were coming. The longer Billy was in the army, the less impressed he was with their record-keeping.

"Grab your gear. Follow me." Bullock strode away while they scrambled for their duffels.

The strains of "Nowhere to Run" by Martha and the Vandellas filled the air as they hurried after Bullock. Was that someone's idea of a joke?

The tents had been hammered by the sun and wind and rain so long they weren't army green anymore but a ghastly puke gray, about the shade of his best friend Harold's face, and Billy's too, after they'd drunk a twelve-pack of beer when they were fifteen.

Billy never did much drinking after that. The schnapps Harold had given him as a going-away present sat unopened in his closet. They'd use it for a toast when he got back in one piece. If it weren't for Terrell, Billy would miss Harold somethin' awful.

With a lift of his chin, Bullock indicated the sandbags stacked halfway up the sides of the tents, which were perched on rickety planks set a few inches off the ground. Gramps would call them *half assed constructions*.

"If there's a rocket attack, those keep flying shrapnel outside instead of in. They also keep the water from drowning us in monsoon season, which doesn't end until October."

"Looks pretty dry to me." Alabama Bob scratched his blue-black stubble.

"It'll rain tonight, hell, every night, a lot of the days too. Canteens get filled by siphoning rainwater that collects on the roofs of the tents both here and in the field."

Alabama Bob made a face, and the NCO laughed. "Yeah, tastes like dust, but everything does. Add Kool-Aid. It helps. You'll have to haul a lot of water into the bush and don't forget to take your salt pills so you retain some of it. Still, you're gonna sweat like you never sweated before no matter where y'all hail from."

"If you got sandbags, why you need the tents on skids?" Terrell asked.

"Snakes." Bullock continued walking.

"Is he serious?" Alabama Bob whispered.

"He ain't the jokin' type." Terrell hustled to catch up.

Soldiers stared at them as if they were the enemy.

"Three FNGs?" one shouted. "Give us a break."

Trying to figure out the meaning of *FNG* caused Billy to stumble over the toe of his boot.

"Ah, hell. That one can't even walk and chew gum."

Laughter ensued, interspersed with repeated mentions of FNGs said with such derision Billy couldn't summon the courage to ask what it meant.

Bullock motioned them inside a more permanent structure with wooden sides protected by more sandbags and a ridged, metal roof. The supply sergeant handed over lightweight jungle fatigues—he called them *fatikees*—undershirts, shorts, and a towel, along with an M16, ammo, and a green nylon rucksack with an aluminum frame. The duffels they'd arrived with, along with their utility uniforms, were put into storage until their tour was over.

"If ya don't want a case of rotcha-crotch-off," the man said around his cigarette, "don't bother with the shorts in the boonies. Use that towel as a drive-on rag, wear it 'round ya neck to soak up sweat. Lose the undershirt too."

Billy waited for Bullock to nix that, but all he said was, "Sleeves are required unfolded and down at night. Mosquitoes carry malaria, so take your goddamn pills. I'll show you where you'll bunk."

"Snakes, floods, malaria, and what is *rotcha-crotch-off?*" Alabama Bob asked as they tried to keep up with Bullock, always several paces in the lead. "You think it's VD?"

The NCO paused; Alabama Bob's voice had been pretty loud. "Probably want to take care if you go to Sin City, just outside Pleiku. Army doctors check the whores for VD, trying to keep it from running through the ranks." He lifted his face to the blistering sun. "Have to say, it isn't working that well."

Billy had danced with the idea of losing his embarrassing virginity in Vietnam, but the idea of Sin City made him take a personal vow of chastity. From Terrell's expression, he had done the same. Unfortunately, Alabama Bob was practically panting. Sometime in the next few months he'd no doubt catch a lovely case of the clap.

The sergeant flicked a finger toward the tent where they'd bunk. "I've been told we'll replace these at base camps soon with tropical wood structures since the canvas rots in this climate, but for now, we make do. Before you're assigned to a platoon, there is a required three-day training course."

"We've already trained for months," Billy said.

"Nothin' I can do." The man lifted a hand and walked away.

The three of them hovered just outside the entrance of the tent.

"Take the empty racks, dipshits." The speaker was a tall, stringy fellow with bad acne. His attention remained focused on a cassette recorder, which must have been the source of the music they'd heard upon arrival. He pressed the button, and "Nowhere Man" streamed out. He was definitely messing with them.

Still, it was nice to hear the Beatles, Billy's favorite, though it made him long for Ringo—the dog, not the drummer—more than ever.

Two of the empty racks—singles, not up-and-downs like they'd had before—were next to each other with the third on the other side of a narrow aisle. Without consultation, Terrell and Billy took the side-by-sides, and Alabama Bob headed for the single.

"You two queer or somethin'?"

Terrell stilled. "What you say?"

"Ah, leave 'em alone, Flash." A guy who appeared to be Mexican but didn't have an accent ducked inside. "They might have your back one day."

"You think so, Deus?" Flash looked them up and down. "I don't."

Deus held out his hand for a shake, and Billy stepped up, probably shaking too enthusiastically, thrilled that someone wanted to welcome them.

"My name's actually Jesús." Deus pronounced it *hay-soos* instead of *gee-zus*, with the accent on the second syllable. "But everyone has a nickname here, so I'm Deus. Latin for God." He appeared embarrassed by that; who wouldn't be? "How 'bout you?"

"Billy Johnson."

"I call him Beej. And I'm Terrell Jones."

"Then you're Teej?" Deus asked.

"Sure." Terrell winked at Billy. "We rhyme. This is Alabama Bob."

Their friend had tried to get people to call him Robert, but that hadn't happened in the States, and it wasn't ever happening now.

"What's this training the sergeant mentioned?" Billy asked.

"We call it charm school, and it's the same chickenshit you already learned at basic. They'll show you an AK-47, which is what the gooks have." Deus tilted his head. "I wish we had some. Even the bullets are bigger for those things. Be thankful the training's down to three days instead of the five it used to be. You want a tour?"

Alabama Bob shifted from foot to foot. "Can we start with the latrines?"

Deus laughed. "You bet."

They were about as foul as everything else, just a hole in the ground over a buried metal drum. And if the drum was full . . . ugh. That was something Billy would never write home about.

Deus led them past the mess hall, the officer's quarters, and the watchtowers placed around the perimeter.

"We're as secure as you get out here. Bunkers for defense if the dinks are stupid enough to attack."

"Dinks?" Alabama Bob's face scrunched. "I thought they were gooks."

"Dinks, gooks, gunkies, slants, slopes. Guys come up with new ones every day."

"Wouldn't it be easier to just call them Vietnamese?" Billy asked.

"Technically they are, but there's a difference between the ones we're fighting and the ones we aren't."

"Can't *see* much of a difference," Terrell said.

Deus lifted one shoulder. "I found out quick it was easier to do what I had to if I wasn't shooting a person."

"But you *are* shooting a person." And Billy was worried about that.

What if he wasn't able to fire on the enemy same as he hadn't been able to fire on a deer? Then not only would he die, but his friends might too. He'd understood war in a distant way, because he'd been distant, but he wasn't anymore. Now the war, what he might have to do—what he *would* have to do—was about to become very real.

"I'm shooting a gook, a slant, a dink. See what I mean?"

Billy nodded slowly. A mind trick. Did it work?

"Why would they have to be stupid to attack?" Terrell asked.

Deus pointed to three rings of barbed wire surrounding the camp. "Land mines buried between the wires along with a nifty invention we call Fou Gas. Fifty-gallon drums of napalm. Blasting caps hooked to a detonator. If we set those off, you got flying liquid flame. Breaks up a ground assault like no one's business. It's a sight to see."

Billy swallowed the thickness at the back of his throat as he imagined that sight. He wasn't sure he ever wanted to see it.

"Any other questions?"

"Um . . . well . . ." Alabama Bob scuffed the toe of his boot across the dirt. "What's an FNG?"

"Fucking New Guys. You're a menace."

"Hey!"

Deus held up a hand. "Fact is, new guys get killed. New guys get *us* killed. And in Vietnam, there's a constant stream of new guys."

"How do we get to be old guys?" Billy asked.

Deus slapped him on the back. "Follow the men who've been here. Do what they do, walk where they walk. Don't be a self-starter. That usually leads to stepping on a mine or worse. Got it?"

The three of them nodded, but as Deus walked away, Alabama Bob whispered, "What could be worse?"

"I don't wanna know," Terrell said.

The next three days they were taught to do things they already knew, getting very little sleep because of the random bursts of mortar and rifle fire, artillery and flares shot off every night at a nearby firebase in an attempt to demoralize the enemy. Instead, the Harassment and Interdictory Fire, in army-speak H & I Fire, caused sleep deprivation in FNGs. Everyone else slept right through it.

"The theory is that anything moving outside the camp is an enemy," Deus explained. "And if one of those random shells falls on them . . ."

"Yippee," Terrell muttered.

"The army . . ." Deus lips twisted ruefully. "It's complicated."

Deus, who was on his second tour and seemed to know everything, became their main source of information. He had patience to spare.

"The only stupid question is the one that gets you killed because you didn't ask it."

"Okay," Alabama Bob said. "Why are the VC called Charlie?"

"Who ca—?"

Deus threw Terrell a silencing glance. "It's simple. The Vietnamese Communists call themselves *Việt Nam Cộng-sản.*" Deus pronounced the foreign words as well as he did just about anything. "The Americans, who are always in a hurry, shortened that to Viet Cong. The army, in an even bigger hurry, used VC, and in radio speak VC is Victor-Charlie. Voilà, we have Charlie." He fixed them with a dark, intense stare. "And man, do we have Charlie. He's everywhere. Remember that."

"Seems more complicated than simple," Alabama Bob said.

"Just like the army."

Bright and early on the morning of their fourth day, they were assigned to the same platoon as Deus and Flash, who were at base camp because they'd received minor wounds a few weeks before. Everyone climbed aboard a Slick, a Huey used for transport with no weapons on the outside, just two door gunners at doors that had been removed. They flew over rice paddies; the Vietnamese working in them resembled black bugs dotting the water.

Deus pointed to the purple smoke curling out of the jungle in the distance. His mouth formed the letters *LZ.*

Landing Zone.

They gathered their gear as the pilot circled lower and lower. The door gunners' gazes scanned the trees for landing-zone watchers—enemy soldiers that hung around LZs hoping to ambush a chopper or the GIs getting off or going onto one—reminding Billy that he was here and not on leave because the last FNGs had died doing exactly this.

His skin prickled, and he got dizzy, but he shook it off. No time for any of that now. No time for any of it anymore.

The Slick touched down gingerly in a small clearing, and they jumped out. As their boots hit the earth, the pilot lifted and zoomed away. The instant the backwash of air from the rotors disappeared, the insects swarmed so thick Billy could hardly see.

The elephant grass shimmered. Terrell lifted his M16, so did Alabama Bob. Billy's hands were so sweaty he nearly dropped his own. What if he died without ever firing a shot?

GIs emerged from the brush. Their uniforms hung in scraps, and they had scratches to rival their bug bites.

"Three cherries? Three?" One of the guys smacked himself in the forehead right below the word *Boom-Boom* written in magic marker on the green side camo cover of his helmet. Dirt rained down, either from his face or his fingers, it was hard to tell.

Billy wasn't sure if *cherries* was more or less insulting than FNGs.

"Six more hands is six more hands." Deus pointed to each of them in turn. "Beej, Teej, Alabama Bob."

They nodded and smiled and must have resembled morons considering the eye rolls that were their only welcome.

"Let's get out of the open," Flash said. "I'm getting the willies."

Billy'd had the willies since he'd climbed off his first chopper. Any more he always felt like someone was watching him, as if the jungle not only had teeth but eyes.

"Move it, Cherry." The guy closest to Billy gestured to the jungle with the barrel of his rifle.

They followed the rest of the squad into a dense thicket, but the guy at point—called Monk, no one said why—seemed to know where he was going. Every so often he drew a machete, then hacked at a particularly thick chunk of bamboo.

"Stuff grows like weeds," Monk complained in an accent that spoke of swamps and alligators and heat. "Hack it down one day, and I swear it's back up just as high the next. Only thing that kills it, even for a minute, is napalm. Where napalm goes, nothin' grows."

Alabama Bob peered upward as if he expected napalm to arrive at any second, but the tree canopy was so thick only slivers of sky peeked through.

"When we're deep in the shit, can't hack at it like this," Monk continued. "Cong'll hear all y'all. Then ye just gotta crawl. Takes forever."

Everything Billy didn't know swarmed him like the mosquitoes; the sharp bite of nerves prickled along his skin.

Camp wasn't much more than a second clearing occupied by a few tents, a larger one in the center.

"Report to LT." Deus aimed them toward a tall, broad-shouldered, fair-haired man having his cigarette lit by Flash.

As they approached, so did another soldier. His helmet cover read *Sparky*.

"Sir, I've fixed the Prick."

Bama choked, and LT flicked a set of amazingly dark eyes, considering his pale hair, in their direction. "That would be the PRC-25, called the Prick by RTOs everywhere. I hear it's like humping a case of Coke on your back, plus a six-pack weight for the battery."

"Close enough," Sparky agreed. "We're good to go at 0500."

LT nodded as if he'd expected nothing less. "Welcome to the

Central Highlands. I'm Lieutenant Welch. You know Flash, fastest guy in the platoon, and Sparky is obviously our RTO."

The radiotelephone operator swooped one finger outward from his forehead, both hello and good-bye, before he walked off.

"I hear you're Beej, Teej, and Alabama Bob."

"Don't you wanna know our real names?" Alabama Bob asked. "What if . . . uh . . . you know we . . . uh . . . how would you let our parents know we'd . . . uh . . . ?"

Flash snorted, and LT cast him a glance, which stopped whatever Flash had been about to say and impressed the heck out of Billy. He didn't think anyone could get Flash to shut up, ever.

"You can say die, son. You should probably get used to sayin' it." LT tapped Alabama Bob's dog tags, and they rattled. "I can find out all I need to know right here."

"Oh, yeah. Right. Sir."

"Tape those together. All of you. I hear tags clacking together in the bush, you can bet the enemy does. I goddamn guarantee if that happens, you'll wish the VC had shot you once I'm through with your ass."

Alabama Bob wrapped a fist around his tags, and Flash hooted. "You're redder than a baboon's behind."

Alabama Bob thrust out his chin. "How would you know what a baboon's behind looks like?"

"Plenty of them out there." Flash waved at the jungle. "Haven't you heard 'em screechin' at night when they get killed by the tigers?"

"There are tigers?" Terrell appeared more shook by that than he'd been by anything so far.

"Sure are." Flash hauled up his pants, which were centimeters away from falling down. "Just waltzin' around out there with Charlie."

"You're so full of it," Terrell said.

"You'll see for yourself." Flash sauntered toward another group nearby.

LT drew on his cig, letting the smoke trail out on another sigh. "I wish I could say he was making that up."

Billy and his friends went wide-eyed.

"We're without a sergeant for the time being. I'm waiting on orders from our CO. A replacement. Something." LT took another drag, letting that one trickle out his nose. "Get settled. We leave at 0500 on search and destroy."

The three of them blinked, exchanged glances, and LT sighed. "Our platoon is assigned a village tagged as VC sympathizers. We go to that ville, we search everywhere, and then we destroy it."

Billy pressed his lips together to keep the *why* from popping out. The army didn't like why. In fact, the army hated it.

"Okay?" LT asked.

It didn't sound okay. It sounded like bad news. But Billy and the others said, "Yes, sir!" and managed not to salute. According to their recent training, VC loved to waste officers.

That night Terrell spoke softly across the darkness between them. "You think their sarge went home?"

"Sure," Billy answered, though he didn't.

When the sun was just a hint on the horizon and the air actually felt cool, they marched out of camp. Didn't last. By the time they left the jungle and started down a road, sweat dripped into Billy's eyes so fast that if it hadn't stung, he'd have thought it was raining.

When Monk tore a strip of cloth from the tail of his shirt and tied it around his forehead to keep from being blinded, Billy and his friends did the same. The raggedy appearance of the old-timer's uniforms suddenly made a lot more sense.

As the morning wore on, the three of them had a harder and harder time keeping pace with the rest.

"Think we'd be in better shape after basic." Terrell scowled at the butt end of the guy in front of them.

"I see why they look like they took a vacation at Dachau," Alabama Bob said. "No breakfast, then double time in this heat."

"We gonna look like them soon enough." Terrell shoved up his glasses. They slid right down his sweat-slicked nose again.

All Billy could think of was his momma's face when she saw him next, or what was left of him.

Sudden gunfire erupted, and everyone dove away from the sound and into the ditch. Billy was the last one to land. Lying there, his too-quick breaths seemed very loud.

"Son of a bitch!" LT snuck a glance at Sparky, who lay where he'd fallen in the road, PRC-25 still attached to his back. "How are we gonna get support without the goddamn radio?"

No one answered. They were too busy returning fire into the thick hedge that concealed the enemy. Only Billy remained frozen, his silent M16 clutched in his hands.

Sparky's foot twitched.

Bones, the medic, scrambled out of the ditch and crawled toward the RTO. The dirt kicked up near him, but he wasn't hit.

"Ain't it against the rules to shoot at folks wearin' that Red Cross patch?" Terrell reloaded.

"Commies don't have rules." Alabama Bob smacked his M16 with the flat of his hand, though the rifle appeared to be firing just fine.

"VC always go for the RTO and the gunner first if they can," Deus said. "Take out the comms so we can't get help, take out the MG so they have a fighting chance."

Bones tugged on the RTO's arm but couldn't move his dead weight. He tried to lift Sparky, radio and all, and failed. Bones was skinnier than most. Had he been nicknamed *Bones* because of that or because of his job?

Billy shook his head to make the nonsense thoughts go away, but when they did, his brain only filled with others not so foolish. The fear that he would fail here, that his dreams of becoming the man Gramps wanted him to be, that *Billy* wanted to be, would die in disgrace, that he would die in disgrace, that all those he was supposed to protect would die because of him.

Return fire from the VC seemed to be retreating around the dogleg up ahead, and several members of the platoon scooted along the ditch in that direction, careful to keep their heads below the sight line. Only a few troops remained to cover Sparky and Bones, sitting ducks in the middle of the road. Why hadn't the VC picked them off by now?

A rifle barrel parted the elephant grass directly across from Billy just as Terrell dropped his M16 and leaped free of the ditch, running toward the fallen RTO and medic. The barrel of the AK tracked him; behind it, Billy caught a flicker of movement.

A shot rang out. The whole wide world seemed to still, then a Vietnamese soldier tumbled clear of his cover, a neat hole in the center of his forehead.

Everyone stared at Billy.

"Holy fuck, what a shot!" Deus lifted Billy to his feet and smacked his shoulders.

Billy flinched, waiting for one or both of them to die, but nothing happened. The only gunfire came from around the corner where the rest of their platoon, and apparently all the VC but one, had gone.

Terrell punched Billy's arm. "Thanks for saving my life, Beej."

Billy wasn't sure what had happened. He'd been paralyzed by his thoughts, his fear of failure making him fail; he hadn't fired a shot. Then Terrell had made himself a target, and Billy had reacted. Gramps had always told him he thought too much, but Billy hadn't been sure how to stop. A single AK-47 pointed at his friend seemed to have done the trick.

Maybe he *could* become the standout star he'd hoped to be.

A few guys dragged the dead soldier into the road.

Billy glanced at the body, then just as quickly away as thoughts he didn't want to have poked at the corners of his now carefully emptied head.

"Set your boot on his chest." Flash pulled a Polaroid camera from his rucksack. "Everyone gets a picture with their first kill."

Billy hesitated. A picture seemed—

"Come on!" Flash motioned impatiently with the hand not holding the camera. "I don't got all day."

Expectant faces turned in Billy's direction, waiting for him to be the man they thought he was. What choice did Billy have but to step forward and plant his boot on the dead man's chest?

CHAPTER 5

Jay
"For What It's Worth"

Willow Creek—June 1967

On Sunday, Momma had just left when Helen and Ronnie knocked on the door. Jay'd had to find Momma's keys again. They'd been in the junk drawer, same as the last time.

"Mags here?" Ronnie asked.

No one had seen her since the clearing.

"You're early. She's always late."

"Good point." Ronnie looked at her shoes. "Think she'll show up?"

"If she doesn't want to come, she shouldn't come."

"Why wouldn't she want to?" Helen's eyes were big blue balls of hurt.

Hell.

"You're right. Why wouldn't she?"

Silence fell. All three of them fidgeted.

"We should probably drink the schnapps right away." Helen blushed, but they were all anxious to try it. "Make sure we're done before your mom comes home."

Jay stepped into the kitchen and grabbed the first glasses she put her hands on. Then all three of them sat around the geometric-patterned wood coffee table, eyes on the schnapps in the center. When the doorbell rang at five, they jumped.

"No way that's her." Ronnie grabbed the bottle by the neck and shoved it behind the gold couch cushions.

Jay opened the door. "Why are you on time?"

"It's rude to keep people waiting." Mags waltzed past, ignoring Ringo the way she always used to.

"Since when do you think it's rude to keep people waiting?" Ronnie asked.

Mags flipped her hair—noticeably blonder despite her mother's having forbidden Miss Clairol—and sat on the burnt-orange, crushed-velvet chair without answering.

Susan, or one of her cohorts, must have taken issue with the constant tardiness of Princess Mags.

Helen unearthed the schnapps from behind the couch cushion. Jay poured generous helpings and handed them around.

"Cheers!" Ronnie lifted her glass.

"All for one and one for all." Helen sounded nervous, but Helen sounded nervous a lot.

She was the scarediest of scaredy cats, thanks to her two brothers—near replicas of their father, all skinny with scraggly dirt-brown hair, underbites, and no ambition. They delighted in making Helen's life as difficult as possible. One of the reasons she got spooked so easily was that "the morons," as she called them, spent most of their time figuring out ways to torture her.

Brothers do that, she'd said, but Billy would never. At least on purpose.

Nevertheless, Helen continued to hope that someday, somehow her brothers would stop being assholes.

Jay didn't think assholes ever stopped being assholes, especially assholes like those.

Everyone tapped their glasses together and drank. Helen choked; Ronnie coughed. Mags and Jay did neither, but their eyes certainly watered. No one said anything. Eventually it became awkward.

"Um . . . you want to do makeovers?" Helen asked.

Ronnie immediately shook her head. Mags didn't appear too excited either.

Jay tried to think of something, *anything* to do. They'd never had this problem before at a sleepover. Maybe it had to do with the half a Fred Flintstone jelly glass of schnapps they'd each swallowed.

Mags and Ronnie sighed like two leaky tires losing air.

"I wonder sometimeshhhh . . ." Helen blinked—once, twice, again—then continued without the slur. "If I'll ever get out of this town."

"Will any of us?" Ronnie asked.

"I will," Mags said.

Ronnie rolled her eyes. Once upon a time—like last week—this would have started the two of them arguing. Instead, Mags didn't notice. Why did this seem worse than the arguments had?

"Have you seen the new guy?" Mags asked. "His name's Paul."

Ridiculous jealousy flamed, followed by a flare of annoyance. Jay certainly didn't want anything to do with Paul. Mags could have him.

"His dad works at the university too. He moved here from California!" Mags sounded almost as excited about that as she'd been about Twiggy's white eye shadow. "We should invite him over."

"What?" Jay yelped at the same time Helen and Ronnie said, "No!"

"Why not? He's new. He doesn't know anyone, though he said he met Three-J." Her gray eyes shifted.

Jay had never noticed before how much like a cat's they were —not in color but expression.

"I assume he meant you."

"Ringo fell in love with his shoes, and I talked to him for a sec. No biggie."

Mags's cat eyes narrowed. She'd seen a canary, was considering if she had the energy to pounce. Well, let her. Jay had nothing to hide.

"Another drink for everyone!" Ronnie reached for the bottle, and someone tapped on the door. Her hand jerked, knocking over a Flintstone glass, spilling a thin trail of schnapps. The syrupy scent of peppermint filled the air. "Shit."

"It's your mom!" Helen's whispered words wavered.

"My mom doesn't knock." Jay yanked open the door.

Harold, Billy's only friend for as long as she could remember, stood outside.

"Hey, Jay." Harold's gaze settled on the others. "Ladies."

They stared at him wide-eyed.

"Everything okay?"

Helen hurried to get a dishrag to mop up the spilled schnapps. It was still pretty obvious what it was, considering the smell and the bottle in plain view.

"My mom's not home."

"Duh," Mags said, and Jay wanted to smack her, but Harold only smiled.

His smile—thanks to years of braces, something neither Billy nor Jay would ever see—was the second-best thing about Harold; the first was his devotion to Billy.

Harold wasn't a handsome young man. His nose was too long, too thin, his chin too big, his dark eyes too large—though always kind—and his dishwater hair had already started to thin. Momma said he'd make some woman a great husband one day, as if that were the top of the mountain for any man. Considering Dad's behavior, for her it probably was.

"Your mom stopped by for gas on her way out of town, which is why I'm here now." He shifted his shoulders beneath the blue-gray service station uniform.

The job had once been Billy's, but Harold, home from college for the summer, was working there now instead.

"I need to borrow Jay for a minute." He took Jay's elbow and drew her onto the porch. "Carry on." The door closed, and Harold released her.

"Everything okay?" he repeated.

It wasn't, of course, but Jay tightened her lips so that nothing in her head—the Musketeers falling apart, Ringo crying in his sleep, Momma's worry, Jay's fears, the sketches—would tumble out of her mouth.

"About Billy—" Harold began.

"Is he alive?"

"He was when he sent this." Harold lifted a smudged and tattered envelope with a hand marked by oil and Lord knows what. "If something happens, Jay, they come to your door."

"Okay." Jay had no idea what "they" did, and she didn't want to find out.

"Billy sent me more drawings." Harold rubbed a thumb over the envelope, leaving another smudge. "He told me to let you see them if I thought it was a good idea. I am definitely *not* supposed to show your mother."

"You left the others?"

"Well, yeah. I said that in the note."

"There wasn't a note."

Harold's frown made his chin appear bigger, if that were possible. "I left it on top, then set a rock there so nothing would blow away."

"Ringo knocked the rock loose and . . ." Jay wiggled her fingers to indicate papers fluttering across the porch. "I thought

I saved everything but . . ." Obviously, she hadn't. "There were three sketches?"

Harold nodded, and Jay relaxed a bit. Losing the note was one thing. Having one or more of Billy's sketches disappear forever . . . She didn't know how she'd deal with that.

"I'm not sure it *is* a good idea for me to show you these. What he drew is . . ." Harold took a deep breath.

Jay curled her hands into fists so she wouldn't snatch the envelope away. Billy's drawings. She wanted them.

His breath rushed out. "You have to promise not to show your mother. Did you give her the last batch?"

Jay shook her head. She'd felt bad about that, but maybe it had been for the best. Momma wouldn't expect to see any sketches if she didn't know they existed in the first place. From Harold's expression, his behavior, the ones he held were not portraits of friends or amusing caricatures of anyone.

"I promise I won't show Momma." Jay held out her hand again, curling her fingers inward.

After another second's hesitation, Harold gave over the envelope. "Billy sent them to me because he didn't want them lost or ruined, though . . ." Harold chewed on his lip. "I can see where some of these, in the wrong hands, might cause trouble."

Causing trouble? So not Billy. Everyone, lately, seemed to be someone they hadn't been before.

"You want them back?"

"I do not want to be responsible for your mom seeing what Billy doesn't want her to, but . . . well . . . What if these are the last drawings we ever get from him? You should have them."

Billy's last drawings ever? Jay's eyes burned.

"Hi, Three-J!" Paul flashed the peace sign as he sped past on his bike.

Paul's voice was so light and breezy; *Paul* was so light and breezy, so opposite of everything else right now, Jay nearly forgot she was mad at him and waved.

"Who's that, *Three-J?*"

"New kid."

Paul rode into the sunset, his tie-dyed T-shirt as brilliant as the colors in the sky.

"You probably want to be careful with him and others like him."

"Like him how?"

"The peace sign, the tie-dye. He's a hippie. Probably a radical war protestor."

"You can tell that from a T-shirt and two fingers making a *V?*"

"These days, yeah. What would Billy think if he knew you were hanging out with someone who was against everything he's risking his life for?"

He'd think she'd betrayed him, and Jay couldn't let that happen.

"I met Paul once. He put down the war, and I haven't seen him since until right now."

Harold peered into her eyes the way Billy used to when he was trying to determine if Jay was lying. And like Billy, Harold gave a sharp nod when he decided she wasn't. That look, that nod made Jay miss her brother more than ever.

"I know the war's messed up," he said. "The country's messed up . . ."

America or Vietnam?

"But we have to keep in mind what's important."

"Billy."

"Always."

Harold hugged her. He'd never done so before, and Jay ended up smacking her nose into his chin. Smooth. If she ever tried to kiss a guy, she'd probably knock out his teeth. And why was she thinking of kissing a guy after hugging Harold? *Ick!*

Harold stepped away and punched Jay's shoulder.

That was more like it. She punched him back, and Harold headed for home.

Jay opened the envelope and removed the drawings.

The first depicted a pair of hands holding a rifle. Why wouldn't Billy want Momma to see this? Except the longer Jay looked at the way the hands clutched the weapon, the more the sketch bothered her. She shoved it behind the others.

The next showed a massive truck surrounded by a dense, dark jungle. Soldiers sat on piles of sandbags in what would have been the dump bed of a dump truck, if it had been a dump truck, but according to the caption along the bottom, it was a *deuce and a half*. High and lonely above the cab sat a machine gun, ammunition trailing down, twining into a coil that resembled a cobra. It wasn't so bad until she noticed that the jungle had teeth and several of the trees had eyes.

The next one had to be less . . . less . . . what? No idea. Maybe what the next one had to be was *more*.

More like Billy.

It wasn't.

CHAPTER 6

Billy
"Gimme Shelter"

Vietnam—June 1967

Flash handed Billy the Polaroid as some others rolled the body of the VC sniper into the ditch.

"Beej, you want his AK?" Terrell asked.

Billy couldn't tear his eyes from the picture. In it he appeared older, stronger, better—a man to be admired not a boy to be pitied, someone he badly wanted to be. None of the others seemed aware that he hadn't fired a shot until this one, and he planned to keep it that way.

"Earth to Beej!" Terrell pointed to one of the Negroes—was his name Sugar Bear?—holding the sniper's AK-47 in the air.

Gramps had told Billy stories of soldiers who'd taken Lugers or Gewehr 88 rifles from dead Germans and died because of it.

Never go into battle with an unproven weapon.

Billy had been training with the M16 for months—he'd

heard it might jam when he most needed it not to, but he'd yet to see evidence of it—so he shook his head.

The soldier *whooped* and began looting the body for ammo since AKs took a different bullet than M16s. What happened if you got into a firefight and ran out? You couldn't use your buddy's, so you died, and he probably did too. Billy didn't plan to be that dumb.

His eyes were drawn back to the Polaroid as if attached by a string.

"Lemme see." Alabama Bob snatched the snapshot from Billy's fingers. He stared at the photo as if it were a pinup. "You're so lucky."

"Unlike that guy." Flash jabbed a finger at the ditch and snickered.

"That wasn't luck." LT set his hand on Billy's shoulder. "Why didn't you tell me you'd had sniper training?"

"I . . . uh . . . didn't." Billy took the Polaroid away from Alabama Bob. He'd scored pretty high on his rifle qualification in basic, but that was as far as things had gone.

"Shit." Flash's laughter vanished as quickly as it had appeared. "Whole thing was a fluke. Better keep that picture so you can prove you actually did somethin' while you were here besides take up space."

"Tell him!" Alabama Bob blurted so loud several soldiers ducked and snapped "Shh!" before hefting their M16s and scanning the dense thicket on both sides of the road.

"It's no sin to admit to a lucky shot, son."

Except LT's voice kinda hinted that it was.

Billy stood proud. "My grampa fought in World War One. He taught me how to track, and he trained me to be the best shot in the county."

"Where you from again?" Flash asked. "Lameville, USA?"

"Beej is from Wisconsin where they hunt deer like no one's business," Terrell said. "How many you shot, Beej?"

"I—"

"Deer aren't people," Flash interrupted.

For once Billy was glad of Flash's tendency to be an asshole, which turned the attention away from a question he shouldn't answer. Regardless of how many deer he'd shot—none—he'd done his job today, and people were alive because of it.

"Your grandfather must be proud of you," LT said.

"If he ain't, he will be now." Terrell punched Billy in the shoulder. "Right, Beej?"

Billy tucked the Polaroid into his ruck. He knew just what he was going to do with it. "Right."

LT checked on Sparky, who, it turned out, wasn't dead but only knocked silly by an AK round to the helmet.

Deus joined them. "That's why I keep my bucket on even when it feels like my brain is cooking."

"I've seen more guys' brains go splat from a bullet to the steel pot than not," Flash, ever-cheery, put in.

"Any resistance helps." Deus winked at Alabama Bob, who quickly put on the helmet he'd been holding.

"Saddle up!" LT called low, yet still they heard.

"Are we going back to camp?" Alabama Bob asked.

"We got a ville to search and destroy, man." Flash appeared happier about that than he should've been.

"But . . ." Alabama Bob's gaze cut to the dead VC.

Flash gazed heavenward, then took up his former position at tail-end Charlie.

"If we ran back to camp every time we engaged the enemy, we'd never get anything done." Deus joined the flank, which connected point and tail-end.

"Okay if you have our six?" Terrell asked, and Billy nodded.

Sometimes Billy swore the army was populated by half-wits, then other times they'd come up with something like *have your six*, which was a darn clever way to talk. Basically if the jungle was a clock, and Terrell stood at twelve, then whoever stood at six—in this case Billy—had his back.

Before they'd moved out that morning, they'd been given their assignments at the village. The FNGs would watch the back trail while everyone else came in hot.

"Snatch up every male not in diapers," LT ordered. "*Zip-zap*, before they have a chance to dive into any tunnels or arm themselves with hidden weapons."

Once they reached the village, the operation went down fast and slick. In no time, dozens of Vietnamese men, bound hand and foot, sat in a circle guarded by Boom-Boom and Flash. Other soldiers tore through the huts, tossing things, breaking things as several old women followed, wringing their hands and shouting what must have been Vietnamese obscenities.

"I need to learn me some Vietnamese," Terrell said, dark eyes solemn on the dwellings.

"Why don't they take more time, make less of a mess?" Billy asked.

Monk—turned out he'd earned that name by carrying a pocket Bible everywhere, though no one had seen him actually read the thing—held his Zippo to the thatch that covered the nearest roof, and the hut went up like he'd used napalm.

"Why be neat when it's all-a-gonna burn anyways?" Monk winked. "How y'all likin' your first Zippo raid?"

Billy didn't much care for it. There was engaging an enemy that was trying to kill you, and then there was this. Kids shrieked; old folks cried; women tried to rush back to the huts as everything they owned in the world went up in flames. Some of the soldiers herded them into a huddle at the edge of the village.

"So many huts, only one Zippo," Terrell said.

"Not just one." Alabama Bob indicated at least five other guys with Zippos and a mission. "I need to get one of those."

"What we gonna do with . . .?" Terrell lifted a chin toward the Vietnamese. "We can't just leave 'em here, can we?"

"Hell no," Alabama Bob said. "They'll turn VC."

Wouldn't you? Billy thought, but he said nothing. He was thinking too much, and he needed to stop, be on the lookout, make sure he didn't freeze again like he had before.

In the center of the village, where they'd dropped their heavies earlier, LT interrogated captives with the help of a former VC that had defected to become a scout for the United States.

"I don't trust that Kit Carson son of a bitch," Terrell said.

The marines had bestowed the name in honor of the famous Indian fighter who'd recruited scouts from the enemy tribes of those he hunted. In Carson's own words, he would "use a thief to catch a thief."

"I heard 'em called tiger scouts." Alabama Bob's eyes watered as smoke blew into his face.

"How about we just call him traitor?" Terrell asked.

LT beckoned, and Billy lifted his hand, then started that way. "He *is* helping us."

"If they turn on one side, they'll turn on another." Terrell spat into the dirt.

As Billy approached, the scout let out an angry stream of Vietnamese and kicked what appeared to be a teenager, though it was hard to determine age with everyone so skinny and their teeth so bad. He kept kicking until the guy inch-wormed—the only way to move with his hands and feet bound—over to join several villagers in a second huddle nearby.

"Keep an eye on the perimeter." LT gestured to the scout. "Win seems to think there might be a few gunkies missing from the party. I don't need them interrupting."

"You gonna assign perimeter to a cherry?" Boom-Boom banged his palm against his steel pot.

Had the soldier rattled his own brains with the constant

head smacking, or had something rattled them for him, leaving behind the nickname-bestowing tick?

"The kid sees the field like"—LT drew on his ever-present cigarette, then blew out the smoke on a smile—"Bart Starr."

Billy didn't mention that while his eyesight *was* excellent, what had happened that morning was as much a feeling as a seeing. Though Bart Starr might explain his uncanny goodness the same.

"He can QB any perimeter I'm inside," LT continued. "You got a problem, Boom-Boom, take it up with management."

"But"—Boom-Boom's face scrunched—"you're management."

"Then I guess you're fucked. Shut up." LT's eyes flicked to Billy. "Why are you still here?" He indicated the jungle that surrounded them. "Walk it."

"Roger that."

As Billy went past, Boom-Boom muttered, "Watch out for booby traps, Cherry."

Two other guys, whose names Billy didn't know yet, laughed. Why did everyone laugh at stuff that wasn't funny? So they didn't cry at the stuff that was?

Billy walked the perimeter, running the booby traps they'd been briefed on in basic through his mind.

The snake pit he dismissed since that involved an open, seemingly empty rucksack, which concealed a venomous bamboo pit viper. No rucksacks around here but their own.

The idea of the punji trap, however, made Billy slide his boots along rather than step lively as he scanned the ground for signs of a camouflaged hole containing sharpened sticks covered with feces or urine. Any GI that stepped into it and had his foot punctured might come away with a lethal infection.

The tiger trap and the mace consisted of a huge plank or a heavy ball covered in spikes; when activated by a trip wire, they would swing down from above and impale the unlucky. The thought of those contraptions slowed his pace even more. Should he keep his attention on the ground searching for a trip wire or on the sky so he could duck rapidly approaching, horrible death?

"What the hell are you doing?" LT approached, moving fast, not looking anywhere but at Billy.

"They told me to be careful of booby traps, so I . . . uh . . ." He motioned at the ground, the sky. "Punji traps and mace and—"

LT set his hand on Billy's shoulder before leaning in and lowering his voice. "They probably aren't gonna put those this close to a ville and risk some dumb kid setting them off."

"Oh yeah. Right."

"I'm not saying you shouldn't keep an eye out but keep it more there"—LT pointed to the trees—"than there." He pointed down. "I know they filled your head with a lot, but sometimes you just gotta let that go and figure things out on the ground."

"Yes, sir."

Billy started to move again, gaze on the trees; every time some bit of info tried to worm its way into his head, he shoved it out. When he'd managed to walk the perimeter once without being blown to bits, Billy wiped the sweat from his face and walked the exact path again. Deus had told them to *Follow the men who've been here. Do what they do, walk where they walk.* It was good advice, even when the one you were following was you.

By the time LT and Win had determined over a quarter of the men in the village were VC, Billy had worn a muddy strip in the damp grass, and he hadn't seen anything in the jungle but bugs.

"*Dừng lại!*"

Billy spun, finger on the trigger of his M16.

"*Dừng lại!*" Win shouted again as the captive he'd kicked sprinted for the swaying bamboo on the far side of the village.

How had he gotten loose?

"Shoot him!" LT snapped.

The guy scurried behind the huddle of villagers, and Billy hesitated. What if he shot one of them by accident? Should he? Shouldn't he? Before he could decide, the boy darted into the thick, swirling smoke.

"Shoot!" someone—maybe Flash, maybe Monk—shouted.

Billy's finger tightened, then Deus strode out of the gray cloud, right where the kid had gone in, and Billy lowered his weapon.

LT shot him an unreadable glance.

"What happened?" Deus asked.

"You see a gunky run by?"

"I couldn't see my own hand in front of my face in that direction." Deus jabbed a thumb over his shoulder. "I sure didn't see no gunky."

The look LT shot Billy then was easily understood, but he snapped an order just the same. "Find that little SOB."

As Billy plunged into the smoke, Deus's voice followed. "I was the last one out."

Which meant anyone in there shouldn't be.

Billy hadn't walked ten steps when his rifle barrel bumped something. He ended up blasting a hole in a flaming hut.

"Be cool, man, be cool." Sweat dripped off his nose.

Cheers erupted outside the smoke, back where people could see, and even though they had no idea that he'd shot a wall, their applause helped Billy continue with more confidence.

He could do this. He *would* do this.

The crackle of flames warred with Billy's own labored breathing. His chest had begun to burn as painfully as his eyes. The desire to get out of there—now—threatened to overwhelm him.

Billy banged into what was left of another hut. At least he managed not to kill it. Embers rained down, burning tiny holes in his uniform, in him, but he pushed on, faster still when the smoke cleared a bit and a wash of jungle green flickered ahead.

He hurried toward it and nearly fell into a hole. For an instant, he couldn't see straight with the fear that he'd nearly stepped on a spikey, infectious stick. But this hole loomed black and seemingly endless.

He'd heard stories of the VC appearing out of nowhere. Like *shazam*, and the point got sprayed with gunfire. Then *poof*, the enemy would rabbit into an escape hatch concealed in a hill or a thicket or a village.

"Found something," he shouted, eyes and rifle fixed on that hole as he waited for someone to pop up and try to kill him.

LT and a few others emerged from the smoke, their faces shiny with sweat and filthy with cinders.

"Tunnel entrance must have been hidden under this." LT kicked a toppled cook pot out of the way. "You see him go in?"

"No, sir."

"Where else would that dink asshole go?" Flash asked. "Everything's burning."

"We have to clear it regardless. Alby, you're up."

Alby, who maybe weighed a buck twenty soaking wet and wore a perpetual sunburn even in the rainy season, blinked eyes nearly as colorless as his hair. "Me?"

"He's got short-timer disease." Flash clapped his hands behind Alby's head, and Alby hit the dirt, proving his point.

When a soldier's DEROS ticked down to less than sixty days, he became a short-timer. As the date approached, their attention sometimes wandered ahead to a place called home or became so fixed on not dying right there that they died right there, or someone else did. Another example of too much thinking and not enough doing. Often, short-timers were put on noncombat duty but not Alby. Not yet.

"Short-timer's disease, my ass." LT scowled. "Somebody smoke that hole!"

"Got it!" Flash pulled the pin on a frag grenade—labeled such because the explosives inside caused the shell to shatter into fragments—then tossed it into the hole. A muffled *thonk*, and dust rose through air holes twenty feet away, then floated off with the still-billowing smoke.

LT handed Alby a sidearm, which looked like a .38 instead of their issued .45, and Alby crept toward the hole. Billy inched back so Alby could tentatively peek over the edge and—

Bam!

"Fuck me," LT said as Alby fell to the ground.

CHAPTER 7

Jay
"Chain of Fools"

Willow Creek—June 1967

Fire *whooshed* upward—twisting, dancing. Despite the lack of color in the third penciled sketch, heat pulsed.

Not so bad until Jay peered closer and realized that the flames were composed of faces—women, children, old people, young. At first, she thought they were only Vietnamese, but here and there flickered the uniform of an American soldier.

Jay placed her fingertips atop the phrase scrawled at the bottom of the last drawing—*Where Napalm Goes Nothing Grows*—then she watched the same sun set in the west that would soon rise on Vietnam. That, even more than those words or these illustrations, brought home the distance between her and Billy. Billy lived in the future.

If he still lived.

Tears threatened, but Jay refused to let them fall. Was she going to feel scared and lost every minute until Billy came home, dead or alive? She couldn't. She *wouldn't*.

Instead, Jay would believe her heart, which said her brother had to be alive, because if he wasn't, she'd know. Yes, that belief was foolish, but right now . . .

"It's all I got."

"What was that?" Mags emerged from the house.

Jay whipped the drawings behind her back. "Nothing."

Helen and Ronnie shuffled into view, half asleep, maybe still half loaded. Jay felt completely sober. Nothing like guns and fire to kill a buzz.

"Keep talking to yourself and people will think you're stranger than they already do." Mags skipped down the porch steps, missing the last one and almost falling on her nose. Apparently, *she* still had a buzz, or she was in a great big hurry to get out of there.

"This is a sleepover," Ronnie said.

"I have something to do in the morning."

Ringo circled once and collapsed at Jay's feet. "Then leave in the morning."

"Thanks for the schnapps." Mags hesitated as if she'd say more. Maybe the truth about why she was going?

She smiled at Jay the way she used to, and Jay smiled back. "You should pluck your eyebrows."

Jay's smile froze.

"Quit being weird," Ronnie snapped, angrier than she should be over Mags being . . . well, not exactly Mags, or at least not completely Mags.

She was New Mags. *Their* Mags. And Ronnie's anger made a certain kind of sense.

"Well . . . uh . . . see ya!"

"Tomorrow?" Helen asked.

"Sure!" Mags hurried away, turning the corner and disappearing into the descending dusk faster than ever before.

"Do you think she—?"

"She's off to meet her shiny new friends." Ronnie huffed through her nose like an annoyed Angus bull. "Probably sleep over at their place."

"Why can't you be nice?"

"Because I'm not nice."

"She left because of you." Helen seemed on the verge of tears.

Ronnie sighed. "She wasn't ever going to stay. She came for the schnapps. She didn't even bring a bag."

Helen spun and disappeared into the house; Ronnie followed.

Jay shoved Billy's sketches down the back of her shorts, arranged her shirt over the top, and joined them. Two bags sat inside the door—Ronnie's and Helen's—why hadn't Jay noticed that before?

Ronnie poured everyone another half inch of schnapps. Jay drank hers in one swallow the way she'd seen the bad guys do at the saloon on *Gunsmoke*. She choked. Her throat burned. She thought she might die.

Ronnie pounded her on the back. "That's more a sipping drink, Jay."

"Right," she managed, a little hoarse. While she regained her breath, the others finished, and Jay gathered the sticky glasses and the bottle. "I'm gonna put this stuff away before my mom comes home."

She set the glasses in the sink where she filled them with warm water and dish soap so Momma wouldn't smell the peppermint—there'd be no explaining that—then she hid the bottle and the drawings in her closet with *Rally!* By the time she got back, Ronnie and Helen lay, foot-to-foot, on opposite ends of the couch.

"What did Harold want?" Ronnie waggled her eyebrows. "You?"

"Me?" Jay repeated, mystified both by the question and Ronnie's eyebrows.

"You hugged."

Helen pantomimed gagging herself with a finger. Jay had to agree.

"He's like my brother."

"Brother. Right." Ronnie didn't sound convinced.

Harold? The thought had never crossed Jay's mind. Not like the thoughts that had crossed it since she'd met Paul.

And why was that? He was a hippie, maybe a war protestor . . . but didn't he have that right?

The questions gave her a headache. Or maybe that was just the schnapps.

What was it about Paul that made her think about him more than she should? The bluest of eyes, the blondest of hair, the tan arms, his biceps bulging, then releasing within the confines of his T-shirt, the fineness of the hair on his legs, the—

"Jay?"

The images of Paul went *poof.*

Helen and Ronnie waited for an explanation of Harold's visit. Jay wasn't sure how to tell them or even *if* she should tell them about the drawings. Harold had said not to tell Momma but—

"What are you girls up to?"

Jay and Ronnie jumped; Helen's indrawn breath sounded more like a shriek. Even Ringo gave a startled yelp as Momma suddenly appeared in the hall. She must have come in the back door, and they'd been too engrossed in their conversation—or looped—to notice. What was Ringo's excuse?

"We're just talking," Jay said.

"That's right," Ronnie agreed.

"Talking," Helen echoed.

Momma toddled to the crushed-velvet chair and kicked off her shoes. Momma's feet always hurt, even on Sunday. "Talking about what?"

Jay's friends sat up. They appeared stumped. They'd never been any good at lies. Not like—

"Mags had to leave," Jay blurted.

"Leave?" Momma appeared as confused as they had been. She frowned at the darkness that now pressed against the front window. "Why?"

"She had something to do in the morning."

"Well, hell." Momma got to her feet, groaning when she put weight on them. "Now I gotta call and make sure she's home."

As Momma limped to the phone in the kitchen, Jay sat on the arm of the couch and whispered, "Don't say anything about Harold."

"Why?" Helen asked in her regular voice.

Slugging Helen? Suddenly appealing.

Jay continued to whisper, hoping Helen would take the hint. "Because I asked, okay?"

Ronnie nodded. Helen's forehead crinkled, but she nodded too.

It hadn't occurred to Jay to be worried about Mags, and it should have. Sure, nothing ever happened in Willow Creek, but sooner or later, something probably would.

Momma dialed, waited, spoke. "Hi, Peggy, it's Laura. Mags left the sleepover, and I wanted to make sure she got home all right." Momma frowned. "Okay. Thanks." She hung up, then stared at the phone and bit her lip.

"Should we look for her?" Jay asked.

"No." Momma returned to the chair, put her feet on the coffee table, and wiggled her toes. "According to Mrs. McBride, she's at a sleepover tonight, but it isn't yours."

"Told you so," Ronnie said.

Helen sniffled.

"Sorry, girls. You three run along to Jay's room. Have fun." Momma glanced at her watch. "But I want you to stay there. Got it?"

"Yes, ma'am."

They followed Ronnie, who detoured first to grab the bag of Cheetos and Chips Ahoy! Momma had left on the kitchen counter.

"I hate this stupid curfew," Ronnie muttered as soon as the door to Jay's bedroom shut behind them.

In the past, they'd done their share of racing around town, spying on boys they liked or girls they didn't, even TPing houses. Though the last wasn't easy to accomplish without getting caught in a town this small, they'd still managed it enough for a few fond memories.

"Do you feel like climbing out the window and running through the dark?" Jay sat on the floor, rested her back against the closed door, thought of what they might see if they did just that, and concluded, "I don't."

Helen stared at the darkness pressing on the glass; her shoulders hunched. Helen did not like the dark. If someone was with her, sure she went, but being alone out there was another story.

Ronnie fell onto the bed and scowled at the ceiling. "Why does she want to hang around with that bitch?"

"What bitch?" Helen perched on the edge of the mattress.

"What other bitch is there? Susan." Ronnie shoved a handful of Cheetos into her mouth; orange dust coated her lips. "Sometimes, Brain, I worry about your mind."

"You think Mags—?"

"I *know* Mags."

"Who cares?" Jay demanded.

"Right," Ronnie agreed. "Who cares?"

From Helen's expression, she did, but instead of saying so, she ate a Chips Ahoy! with a nervous, ratlike nibble.

The number of things they weren't saying was starting to bother Jay.

Since sleepovers weren't about sleep, they were about how little sleep you got—even if they didn't sneak out—they stayed up late snacking, talking, laughing, basically pretending this night was the same as any other night they'd slept here, or there, together. Helen conked out first. She always did.

"I think carrying around that huge brain wears her out." Ronnie, cocooned in a sleeping bag on the floor, spoke quietly so as not to wake their friend.

Jay's smile at the familiar tease faded when Ronnie spoke again, quieter still. "You saw the bruises?"

Jay's gaze flicked to Helen's wrist, where three semicircles the shade of a rotten grape marred her pale-pale skin. "What did she say this time?"

"Same as last time. She's clumsy."

Jay didn't think anyone was that clumsy.

The bruises had started showing up a few months ago, enough to be noticeable, enough to be worrisome. Especially if you considered that there might be bruises they didn't see.

There *probably* were bruises they didn't see.

"You know how we hardly ever go to Helen's?" Ronnie didn't wait for an answer. "And if we do, it's always when no one's home."

"She's scared of the dark."

"Yeah."

Ronnie didn't mention how they also went to Helen's only in the light if no one was home either, and whenever they went there, Helen couldn't sit still. She constantly looked out the window, and if any of her family showed up, she practically dragged the Musketeers out.

They figured she was embarrassed. Even though Willow Creek didn't have any railroad tracks, Helen still came from the wrong side of them. But lately, Jay wasn't so sure.

"What should we do?" Ronnie asked.

"What can we do?"

Family stuff was private, secret, off-limits. No one asked Jay about her dad. No one asked Ronnie where her oldest sister had gone last summer or how, when she came back, her nose was a whole lot smaller. No one asked Mags what was going on when her mom screamed at the top of her lungs and threw plates against the wall.

People might whisper, they might wonder, but they didn't meddle.

"I don't know." Ronnie sighed. "But shouldn't we do something?"

These were questions they'd asked before, and like before, they had no answers.

Next thing Jay knew, rain pattered against her window; the light was murky and gray. Both Helen and Ronnie stared at her.

"What time is it?"

"Half past the time when I usually eat," Ronnie said. "I'm starving."

"Since when don't you help yourself to whatever?" Jay headed to the bathroom, then detoured through the kitchen, returning with a box of Pop-Tarts.

"All right!" Ronnie held out her hand.

Pop-Tarts were a new breakfast treat, too expensive for every day, too expensive for *any* day, at least in Jay's family. She was shocked Momma had bought them.

"What are we gonna do all summer?" Helen took the pastry Ronnie handed her without looking at it, let alone trying it.

"Ride our bikes, play games, swim in the creek, watch TV, hang out at the clearing." Ronnie swallowed. She'd already eaten half her Pop-Tart. Had she paused to savor the strawberry goodness? "The usual."

"I don't know about you"—Helen took a tiny bite; she hadn't even reached the filling yet—"but I'm over the usual."

Ronnie shot daggers with her eyes. "You sound like the princess."

"Someone has to."

"No, someone doesn't. We just got rid of her. We don't need you becoming her."

A more accurate description would be that Mags had gotten rid of them, not the other way around, but if Ronnie wanted to pretend it had been their choice, let her. Maybe she could convince Helen.

Helen handed Ronnie her barely touched Pop-Tart and began to roll up her sleeping bag, face scrunched into an expression Jay knew well. She was thinking about something that excited her more than anything had since they'd added Advanced Geometry to the curriculum.

"What?" Jay asked.

"I'll let you know." Helen stood.

"I'm confused," Ronnie said.

"And she worries about my mind." Helen shut the bedroom door behind her, and an instant later, the front door closed too.

Ronnie spread her hands; Jay shrugged. Sometimes Helen was like that. Her brain operated on a level at least two or three higher than anyone else's.

Not long after her second Pop-Tart was toast—ha—Ronnie left as well.

Jay was bored all day. At least until Momma came home, the mail in one hand, her other waving a letter from Billy. They read it right away.

Dear Momma and Jay,

Vietnam is different from anything I ever thought it would be. Sure, summer in Louisiana and summer in-country are about equal in sweaty, steamy days and nights. Add to that the trouble getting a shower, and as my friend Terrell likes to say, "Everything just nasty."

One day it rained so hard a few guys pulled out their soap and started to wash. Of course, it stopped raining before they could rinse, which was funny, but not to them because soap can really itch if you don't get it all off, then there's a rash and . . . well, that's just nasty too.

Sometimes the beauty of Vietnam surprises me. I imagined a moonscape, cratered and ugly. Instead, it's all blue and green, brown and yellow. Flowing, peaceful, the mountains are amazing.

Which makes me glad for the colored pencils you sent. I haven't used them yet, but I'll try to so I can send along in my next letter some sketches I've made with them. Thanks for the package of candy from the Ben Franklin too. With so many different kinds, I felt like I was standing right there in the store. I shared it with a few others. Their moms aren't half as good as mine, or their sisters neither.

I keep the picture of Ringo in my ruck. Though I don't get to pull it out much, I like knowing it's there. Send me a picture of the two of you, please.

Don't worry about me. I was the best shot at basic, just like I was at home. Even my DS—that's drill sergeant—who didn't seem to like anyone, liked me. He said I was the most gung-ho individual he'd ever seen. I was made for this job, thanks to Gramps. Jay, I hope you are visiting so he isn't always alone.

Without Billy here, the idea of going by the farm was . . . well, Jay had been glad Momma hadn't made her come along when she had.

"You don't have to visit if you don't want to. Last time I was there he . . . we, well I . . ." Momma took a deep breath. "I said some things. He won't be expecting me soon, if ever. I know when the two of you stayed with him, he was only interested in your brother."

Momma's parents had passed before either Jay or Billy had been born, and like Dad, she had no brothers or sisters. She'd wanted her children to have a relationship with their only living relative. But Jay thought Momma wished, lately, she hadn't bothered.

"I found stuff to do," Jay said.

She'd played with the calves, the kittens, even the farm dogs

—though they weren't very playful—picked vegetables, swept the kitchen, then lay in the grass and watched the clouds until the men came back. You know, what women had done for centuries.

Momma stuck the sheet of paper into the envelope. "I wish he'd write longer letters."

Jay wasn't sure longer would be better. She had a pretty strong feeling Billy wasn't telling them everything. In fact, he didn't seem to be telling much of anything.

In words. The sketches were another story.

Jay spent a lot of the time she couldn't sleep staring at them, which only made it even harder to rest. Whenever she closed her eyes, she saw what Billy had drawn and more—not in black and white like those sketches but in living, moving color. Every time she looked at them, she wondered: Was the boy she knew becoming a man she didn't?

And how on earth had she ever thought he might not?

CHAPTER 8

*V*ietnam—June 1967

Billy didn't realize he'd stepped over Alby's body and fired his M16 into that hole until the rifle *clicked* empty. In the resulting silence, the crackle of the flames seemed very loud.

"Should I get Bones?" Deus asked.

Flash made a derisive sound. "What for? Half his head is somewhere else."

Billy took Flash's word for it as he was having a hard time tearing his gaze from the entrance. Lucky DS Garrett had made them reload, over and over, in the dark so they could do so without looking, as he was doing now.

Pride filled him at his quick reaction. If he could do something instead of nothing, even when he'd been standing right next to someone who wasn't standing anymore, then maybe, just maybe, everything would be all right.

"Helluva way to go." Hammer, a Negro whose hard, massive fists hit like one, contemplated the body.

"Didn't see it coming. One second here." Boom-Boom smacked himself in the forehead. "Next gone. Worse ways to go."

"Jesus!" LT took a step toward the hole. "That tunnel still has to be cleared."

"No." Deus grabbed his arm.

"I'm not sending another man to die today."

"We're already down a sergeant, we don't need to be down an LT too."

"I heard there's a tunnel rat squad in the First Infantry," Boom-Boom said. "Like Green Berets but all they do is run tunnels."

"Well, they aren't here so we make do with what we got— guys who survived it a few times." LT took another step toward the opening.

Deus blocked his way. "That's more than you can say. You're too big to squeeze through anyway. That's why the small guys do this."

Billy risked a quick look-see into the hole. No one shot him, so he dropped his M16, snatched up the fallen .38, a better idea in tight quarters, then scrambled in. He was taller than Alby by a lot, but he was skinny. Still, he dislodged dirt with his elbows and boots as he made his way down the shaft. The others kept talking; no one seemed to notice he was gone.

"If LT wants to go," Flash said, "let him."

"You wanna be in charge?" Deus asked.

"Maybe."

"Like hell—" Hammer began.

"Where's Johnson?" LT snapped.

The air belowground pressed hot and close against Billy's sweaty face. It smelled off, like the barn at his grandfather's farm after a long winter. His feet touched down where the grenade had exploded, scattering earth and rocks and roots outward from a small circle of light and into an area where darkness reigned. No blood, so whoever had shot Alby had been smart enough to stay out of range of the grenade Flash had dropped, then hightailed it out of there before Billy's gunfire erupted.

"Goddammit! Get up here!"

Hunched nearly double—the tunnels had been dug for VC, and they weren't anywhere near as tall as most Americans, definitely not as tall as Billy—he retrieved his flashlight with the hand not clutching the .38 and flicked the light around the perimeter. A dirt passageway, maybe three feet tall and two feet wide, led off in the direction of the air holes that had spouted dust.

Billy wasn't sure what had possessed him to climb down, but now that he had, he'd finish the job before he climbed out. As long as he kept moving forward—doing, not thinking—he wasn't scared. Maybe scared was all in your head, and if you didn't let it in, then you didn't have to kick it out.

Billy went to his knees and shone light into the tunnel. He was going to have to use his elbows to pull himself along since he'd have a flashlight in one hand and the sidearm in the other.

"Dammit," LT said again. "Keep an eye on the ceiling for two steps. Gunkies like to hide 'em in a stick of bamboo."

"Does he even know what a two-step is?" Deus asked. "Beej, those are poisonous snakes. If they bite you, you only last two steps before you die."

Billy swept the ceiling with his light, then exhaled. Just dirt and roots, the latter brushed against his steel pot with a creepy, *swooshy* sound. Despite the stifling heat, he shivered.

"You should be able to smell 'em, even if you can't see 'em."

"They'll be able to smell him too." Deus's voice became fainter as Billy moved farther away. Soon Billy wouldn't be able to hear anyone anymore, maybe forever. "He hasn't been eating *khoai mì.*"

Billy wasn't sure what that meant, and he didn't have time to worry about it because something smelled even worse than the manure perfume he'd been breathing so far. Could VC reek that bad?

He spun to the side, leading with the pistol, shoving with his boots, and tumbled onto the floor of a larger, cleared area. Lifting the light, he scoured the four-foot-high ceiling—no bamboo sticks, just a few bats that ruffled their wings when the yellow beam passed over them.

Billy slowly gained his feet—he didn't want to startle the bats—then nearly dropped his flashlight when he saw the dead man. The corpse was ripe enough to make his eyes stream, so he moved on slow and sure, crawling when he had to, dragging himself too, half-standing whenever he could, illuminating the ceilings, the corners, the floors.

Every inch of the way his skin prickled as if someone was watching him, just out of sight, prepared to launch forward and kill him before he could fire a shot. His heart beat so loudly he wouldn't have heard any warning, even if there'd been one.

Billy discovered another five dead, but he didn't find the runaway who had started it all. Maybe he hadn't come in here. Maybe he'd run into the jungle, found a VC patrol, and was right now bringing them back to ambush Billy's platoon.

But if the kid hadn't come down here, who'd shot Alby? Maybe whoever Billy continued to feel up ahead hovering in the dark? How far was he supposed to go? Tunnels could range for miles.

His stupidity at blazing forward with something he knew so little about suddenly hit him hard. What had he been thinking?

He hadn't been. On purpose. Thinking too much had made him hesitate; the kid had gotten away; Alby had died. The only way to make up for that, even a bit, was to make sure no one else met the same fate because Billy Johnson thought too damn much and acted too damn little. He'd come to Vietnam to fight communist aggression, sure, but he'd also come to prove he was a man to be proud of. He wasn't, yet, but he could be.

Billy's lead elbow hit air, and the flashlight revealed an area he could stand in, though he had to hunch a bit to avoid dragging his pot along the ceiling. Several doorways opened into sleeping quarters, with crudely built bunk beds, three high, extending from the room's entrance to a dirt wall six feet away.

Through another sat bloodstained rough plank tables; an earthen bowl cradled three M16 bullets, also bloodstained. Woven baskets held torn strips of cloth, some clean, some far from it. In a bag that looked far too similar to the one Bones carried—army green canvas stamped with the two snaked, winged staff bookended by the letters U and S—Billy found a jumble of knives, scissors, what appeared to be a knitting needle. None had been cleaned very well. Understandable without running water, soap, peroxide, alcohol—things he did not find a trace of any more than live VC.

In the final dugout, the escaped kid hung from the long bamboo pole that must have smashed forward with incredible speed and force, the trip wire still caught between his bare, dirty toes. The boy was so skinny several of the foot-long spikes that had gone into his chest stuck out his back.

If Billy had shot him when he had the chance, the kid wouldn't be hanging here now reminding Billy of the way Gramps and his friends hung their kills from the trees to drain the blood. The deer would twist in the wind and darken the dirt below so deeply that sometimes the maroon splotch was still there in the spring when the snow melted.

Billy's gaze lowered and caught on a similar splotch that wasn't ever going to melt away either.

What difference did it make how the guy had died? He was the enemy. Right?

"Shh," Billy said, and the sound echoed in the empty chamber.

The runaway was dead because he'd been in too much of a hurry to check for booby traps. Billy wasn't so foolish. Where there was one, there was probably another.

Instead, he uncovered what had once been the exit. Would still be if someone—most likely the US Army—hadn't already blown it to smithereens, leaving behind a heap of dirt, rocks, debris, and . . . was that a hand? The more Billy stared at that pile, the more he thought he knew where everyone had gone.

He returned the way he'd come, doing his best to step where he'd stepped before, crawl where he'd crawled before, rechecking every corner, every curve, as well as the ceilings, holding his breath past the bodies he'd already found. Not thinking beyond doing and, in that way, he made it back alive.

Time had slowed while underground, but it had moved on quickly above. The sun that had shone down the shaft when he'd entered was gone.

"Hello? Anyone out there?"

Billy inched away from the opening, hovered close enough to the tunnel to dive in if his answer was a barrage of Vietnamese words or bullets, maybe even one of their homemade grenades.

"Get your insubordinate ass topside double time," LT roared.

Maybe he should stay down here.

Billy contemplated the dirt, smelled again that smell, thought of spending the rest of his life in a place like this, and double timed his insubordinate ass topside.

The instant his head cleared the ground, LT cuffed him in the ear just like Gramps always used to when Billy did anything really stupid. "Get out of that hole!"

Billy stepped out.

"I should send you straight to LBJ."

"Sir?" Why would LT send him to the president? And how?

LT closed his eyes. His mouth moved. He was counting to ten as if Billy were a three-year-old kid. Here, that's just what he was.

LT's eyes opened; they looked so very, very tired. "Long Binh Jail, near Saigon. Military stockade."

If Billy wound up in the stockade after less than a week in Vietnam, Gramps would not only never speak to him again, but he'd refer to him forever after with the same words he used for Billy's father.

Worthless. Useless. Irresponsible. Loser.

"Don't get all worked up, son. If I did that, I'd be down another man I can't afford."

"Hallelujah, you're alive!" Terrell hit Billy broadside, hugging him so hard his ribs cracked.

"Johnson! Jones! Fuck! I hate alphabetical grunts. You!" He pointed at Terrell. "Get out of my way. I am not done reaming him a new asshole."

"Yes, sir!" Terrell's grin was so infectious Billy fought a mighty struggle to keep from returning it.

"I can't tell if you have shit for brains or if you're the smartest goddamn idiot I ever met."

"Bravest," Terrell murmured.

"Shut the fuck up!"

The eye-burning cloud had disappeared. Tiny gray tendrils curled here and there, ghostly above the blackened earth.

The rest of the platoon milled around nearly a football field away—smoking, chatting, casting glances in Billy's direction. Flash flipped him the bird with both hands, then guffawed so hard he had to bend over.

"Where are the villagers?" Billy asked.

"The villagers aren't your business. Neither was that tunnel."

"Someone had to do it."

LT's hand twitched as if it wanted to smack Billy again. "That someone should have been me."

"We need you."

"We need *you*," Terrell said.

LT scowled and pointed in the direction of the platoon.

Terrell dragged his feet the entire way.

"I assume it was a cold hole." At Billy's blank expression, LT rubbed his forehead. "No VC."

"There were VC."

LT dropped his hand.

"But they're all dead."

"How many?"

"At least seven, including the kid from the ville. Pole with spikes got him."

"Bamboo whip booby trap. Horrible way to go. What do you mean 'at least seven'?"

Quickly Billy explained the rooms with the beds, the hospital, and the pile of dirt and rocks decorated by a hand.

"The VC hide their dead in the tunnels so we can't count 'em." LT extracted a small notebook and pencil from his pocket and scrawled the date, the coordinates, and the number seven. After short consideration, he added a plus sign. "Fucking war of attrition."

"Sir?"

LT returned both the notebook and the pencil to his pocket. "You've seen the body counts on the news?"

Billy nodded.

"The success of this war is measured not in territory gained but in bodies counted. If there are more dead on their side than ours, we're winning."

Billy's doubt must have shown because LT snorted. "Exactly. The big brass believes eventually we'll hit a tipping point where we've killed more slants than they can replace. Then they'll surrender." LT lit a smoke; his hand had seemed naked without one. "I find that hard to swallow, but no one's asked me. I follow orders, and I count bodies."

"We don't know that kid was the enemy. Maybe he was just scared."

"If they're dead and they aren't American, they get counted."

"But—"

LT held up a palm like a crossing guard. "Ours is not to reason why, ours is just to do or die."

"Shakespeare?"

LT's lips curved. "Tennyson, or close enough. Maybe the army should start tattooing that on everyone's ass. It would make my life a lot easier."

Tennyson. Huh. It made Billy wonder what the man had been doing before he'd come here.

LT set a hand on Billy's shoulder in a way that was becoming familiar and welcome. "You okay?"

"Yes, sir."

Even if he wasn't, Billy would never say so. He'd learned that the first hour he'd spent at his grandfather's farm. Men did not whine; they didn't cry or complain. Men were *always* okay.

LT lowered his voice. "Just between us, thanks. That was incredibly brave." LT stepped back, and his hand fell away. When he continued, his voice was loud enough for everyone to hear. "That was stupid! I'm going to give you a pass because you're a fucking new guy, and I don't want to see an even newer fucking guy tomorrow after I send you to the stockade tonight." LT cuffed Billy on the back of the head once more. "Don't ever disobey orders again!"

"Yes, sir. I mean, no, sir."

"Get your ass in line and stay out of my sight for a few days."

Billy scurried to the platoon where Terrell and Alabama Bob, along with several others, gathered around.

"What was it like?" someone asked.

"It smelled like a barn. I'm not sure why."

"They live underground." Flash elbowed into the circle.

"They have to crap somewhere. What did you think it would smell like? A bouquet?"

"Was LT right?" Alabama Bob asked. "Did you smell them before you saw them?"

"They were dead, so yeah."

"You'll smell them when they're alive too." Flash held his nose. "Whoo-ee!"

"You know the VC can smell *us* a mile away." Deus sniffed Flash. "Whoo-ee!"

Flash's amusement fled as fast as it came, and he shoved Deus. "Even if we eat *khoai mì*, they still seem to know we're comin'."

"What's *khoai mì*?" Billy asked, more to prevent continued shoving than anything else.

"Sweet potatoes," Flash said. "You think they live on rice but not in the jungle. In the jungle, it's *khoai mì*. Maybe snake meat or rats if they're in the shit a long time. You wanna sneak up on 'em you need to eat what they eat so you smell like they smell. That's what Special Forces do."

"How you know what Special Forces do?" Terrell demanded.

"Deus has a buddy in Tiger Force."

"No way! Those guys out-guerilla the guerillas. They badass."

"Tiger Force?" Alabama Bob repeated. "I never—"

"Long-range reconnaissance patrol." Deus lifted a hand to acknowledge LT's order to fall in. "You'll hear them called Lurp. Airborne. Rangers."

"They eat gook chow so they smell like gooks when they're deep in Indian country."

Flash seemed to know a lot about it for someone who was getting secondhand intel.

"We don't get back before dark," Hammer whispered, "we gonna find out more than we wanna about what Charlie smell like."

Without consultation or orders, their pace increased to a

steady jog on the high-speed trail. It didn't stop Alabama Bob from talking.

"Sparky said there are tunnels all over the country. Sometimes they might even run right under a camp."

"Well, thanks for that." Terrell used a long finger to slide his glasses up the bridge of his nose. "Now I'm gonna see little gook shadows darting here and there whenever I wake up."

"Better to be alert than get a bayonet in the belly."

"Bama, if you don't shut the hell up—" Deus began.

"Just sayin'."

From that moment on, Alabama Bob became Bama. He didn't seem to mind that as much as he'd minded Bob instead of Robert.

CHAPTER 9

Jay
"Blowin' in the Wind"

illow Creek—June 1967

Due to various responsibilities—Helen had to help her mom clean the house, then they visited her aunt in Oconomowoc; Ronnie had an orthodontist appointment, then the stomach flu—Jay's life was Musketeer-less for over a week.

But one day, despite a steady drizzle, Jay decided to go to the clearing. By the time she'd showered and dressed, the rain had stopped, and the sun shone. Typical in Wisconsin, where daffodils often withered after a fluke snowfall and snowmen died in a sudden blast of heat. She brought along Billy's drawings, thinking she might share them with her friends if they showed up. Keeping them to herself was making her head feel full to the point of bursting.

Kingo ran ahead; he knew the way, and by the time she joined him, he sat in the center of the lush grass, nose tilted to the sky. They hadn't been there three minutes when the dog sprinted toward the forest, no doubt to perform his favorite pastime—treeing a squirrel, then standing at the base of the trunk barking like a lunatic. Instead, Paul stepped from the shadows, and Jay shoved the envelope containing the drawings into the back of her shorts.

"Three-J." He lifted his hand. "How—?"

"You followed me?" How could she have been so careless?

"Well . . . yeah. I wanted to apologize."

"You need to go." What if one of her friends saw him here?

"All right, but first let me say I'm sorry."

Ringo danced with joy at his side. *Traitor.*

"I should keep my mouth shut about the war, but I have a hard time not telling it like it is."

"Like you think it is," Jay snapped, then wanted to bite her tongue. Wasn't his habit of "telling it like it is" one of the things that interested her? Paul was different in ways she didn't understand but wanted to explore.

"I read, watch the news," he continued. "What is, is. You know? But I should be more careful of my audience if I want to fit in."

"Do you want to fit in?"

He peered at her as if she'd said something fascinating. "Not really. Or at least, not with everyone."

Jay shifted, both uncomfortable with the way he was staring at her and excited by it. She wasn't sure anyone had ever looked at her like that before.

The envelope of drawings slipped out of her shorts and hit the ground between them with a *plunk.* Together they bent to get it, and the noise their foreheads made when they collided sounded exactly the same.

Jay rubbed the bump, the envelope clutched in her sweaty free hand.

Paul rubbed his bump with one hand too, but in his other, he held Billy's sketches, which must have fallen out.

What if he didn't give them back? What if he behaved like every other boy in town and teased, told, made fun?

Paul offered them to her; the portrait of Terrell had landed on top. "Who's this?"

Jay snatched the papers to her chest, crossing her arms over both them and the envelope. "No one."

"Okay." He turned away. "I get that you don't want me here."

He wasn't going to demand that she show him the rest? Grab the sketches from her hands? Question her until she gave in and admitted everything?

Paul *wasn't* like every other boy in town, but hadn't she known that from the start? She'd wanted to share the sketches with someone, maybe she should share them with him.

"Wait."

When Paul turned back, she handed him the first three drawings.

He hesitated, giving her a chance to change her mind, making Jay glad she'd shared a few. "Your brother's?"

She nodded.

He sat, right there in the wet grass, so she did too, fidgeting as he paged through—once, twice, again. "He's gifted. He could change things if he sketched the truth."

"He did."

"With these?" He lifted the portraits. "I'm sure your brother has seen deeper truths."

How did he know?

Jay gave Paul the most recent drawings. He studied them longer than he had the others, spending the most time on the final, fiery one. He whistled low, bringing Ringo to his side, then scratched behind the dog's ears as he stared at that sketch some more. "What would happen if thousands of people saw this?"

As if the wind had shifted from south to north, Jay shivered. She snatched the sheets out of Paul's hands, nearly tearing them, and jumped to her feet. "My *momma* isn't even supposed to see these."

He stood slowly and tilted his head. "Why'd you let me?"

Jay wasn't sure. Maybe because Billy's sketches were pecking away at what she'd believed. Not changing it. Not yet. But she'd started to wonder, and she thought Paul wondered too.

"Did you leave a copy of *Rally!* on the bench in town?"

"You read it?" he asked.

"Is it true?"

"Is what true?"

The grass rustled in that chilly north wind. "Everything."

He lifted his hand, and his fingers brushed her bump. "What if it is? Don't you want to know?"

Something shimmied in Jay's belly, or maybe a few inches lower, a lifetime deeper. It got really hard to breathe. "I honestly have no idea."

"Okay." He smiled so gently the shimmy came back. "Okay."

Then Ringo pushed between them. Jay wasn't sure if he sensed something was happening—something confusing, something real—or if he just wanted Paul's attention on him. Jay could relate. The instant Paul glanced down, patting Ringo and laughing, she wanted those blue-blue eyes back on her. And because she did, because it scared her almost as much as her brother's drawings, she turned away.

Paul caught her arm. "I'll walk you home."

They probably shouldn't be seen coming out of the woods together, smelling of grass, damp spots on their clothes. They'd be married by sundown if Gramps found out. He didn't have much use for her, but he still might dust off the shotgun to avoid embarrassment to the family name.

"I know the way."

"I'm sure you do, but I'd feel better if I left you at your door rather than . . ." He jerked a thumb at the acres of trees surrounding them.

Until this summer no one had ever cared about the looming forest, the dark of the night, or if Jay and her friends were wandering around in either one. But the world outside Willow Creek had suddenly become dangerous, frightening, complicated. Was that why the world inside Willow Creek seemed a little darker, a little scarier, and a lot more confusing too?

She thought of the bruises on Helen's arm, and she wondered if, maybe, for some people, it always had been.

Jay skirted the town, making sure they exited from the trees behind her house. No one should have seen them. No one would have seen them.

If her friends hadn't been waiting in the yard.

Jay quickly put the envelope down the back of her pants yet again, sending Paul, still in the shadows, a glance. Now that she'd shown him the sketches, she probably shouldn't show anyone else.

He gave a slight nod.

"Where have you been?" Ronnie shouted the instant she saw Jay, then Paul stepped out of the trees, and her mouth snapped shut.

"Something wrong?" Jay asked.

"You tell us."

"I'm not the one waiting at your house and shouting like the sky is falling."

"Hi!" Paul held out his hand. "I'm Paul."

Ronnie stared at his palm as if he'd just spit into it, and her lip curled. "The new guy."

Paul let his arm fall back to his side. "Guilty."

"These are my friends, Ronnie Frederick and Helen Murphy."

"Glad to meet you."

"I . . . uh . . . yeah." Helen's eyebrows drew together, and she shoved her hands behind her back so fast it was almost as insulting as Ronnie's sneer. Helen cast Jay a look she couldn't figure. "We gotta talk."

"Alone." Ronnie scowled.

"I'll see ya, Three-Jay." He brushed his fingers across her bump once more. "You're okay now, right?"

Jay thought she might die—from embarrassment and from that shimmy in her gut. She felt both nauseous and hyper, as if she could run five miles, but then she might puke.

"Right," Jay echoed, but he was already gone, loping up the sidewalk and disappearing as quickly as Mags had on sleepover night.

"What the hell, Jay?"

"Nothing happened."

From the way Ronnie and Helen glanced at each other, she'd said that too quickly. But nothing *had* happened. Not really.

"How'd you get that knock on your noggin?" Ronnie asked.

Jay was thankful they hadn't questioned, again, where she'd been or flat-out asked if they'd come from the clearing. Jay didn't want to lie, but she probably would have.

"Accidental headbutt. I'm fine."

"People have been talking about the new kid. He's . . ." Ronnie gazed in the direction Paul had gone. "Different."

"He's vocally anti-war." Helen's voice was clipped and accusing; Jay got annoyed.

"So?"

"Whaddya mean *so*?" Ronnie asked.

"It's America. He can say what he wants, feel how he feels. Right?"

"Not in Willow Creek," Ronnie muttered.

"Anywhere. Everywhere. Isn't that a law or something?"

"My dad says . . ." Helen paused, but when she spoke, her words were both rapid and sure. "He says that the reports on the news are mostly lies. That the soldiers want to be there; the

South Vietnamese are treating them like gods, and the hippies are the ones causing trouble, riling up the stupid people."

As Helen's dad wasn't exactly a mastermind, it was gutsy for him to throw the stupid stone.

"I thought your family believed in the war," Helen continued. "Isn't that why your brother enlisted?"

"It's one thing to support a war you've only glimpsed long distance and heard about from other people and another to support it when you've seen up close what's truly going on."

"When did you become anti-war?" Ronnie demanded.

"I didn't. I was just . . ."

Despite the rampant patriotism of their hometown, they didn't discuss Vietnam, probably shouldn't be discussing it now considering her friends' angry, bewildered expressions. Willow Creek was . . . well, Willow Creek. Frozen in the fifties, if not the forties. Definitely a throwback to a time when wars were black and white—good against evil. Most people around here, including Billy, thought this war was the same, but was it?

Jay wanted to share her uncertainty, would have in the past with the Musketeers because they shared everything. But right now, she was glad she hadn't shown them Billy's drawings.

"Why are you here?" she asked.

Helen whipped a sheet of paper out of the pocket of her shorts and snapped it open. In the center, someone had pasted a black-and-white photo of a rabbit—at the top the word *MISSING* printed in precise letters with black marker, *FLUFF* at the bottom, along with a phone number and the owner's name. The last explained the existence of a poster instead of just asking Jay, the girl who could find anything.

Miss Brecklewait was a math teacher. Math and Jay did not get along any better than Jay had gotten along with Miss Brecklewait. Jay doubted the woman wanted to see her before September any more than Jay wanted to see Miss B. She'd ask if Jay had been doing the practice worksheets she'd given her at the end of the school year. As Jay had thrown them out on the way home, it was best to avoid both Miss Brecklewait and that conversation.

"I can look around," Jay said, confused by Helen's seeming excitement over something not that exciting.

"No! We should all search for Fluff!"

Ronnie nodded frantically behind Helen's back.

"Sure. Yeah," Jay said slowly. "When?"

"At midnight. Tonight."

Jay laughed; Helen didn't.

"You're serious?"

"I'm pretty much always serious, Jay."

Jay glanced at Ronnie, who shrugged. "She is."

"Okay. But tonight?" Momma had said something about Jay cleaning her room, washing the dog. "I'm not sure I—"

"Tonight," Helen insisted so loudly Jay started. "Please?"

Helen was acting strange. Sometimes she did.

"You think our moms are suddenly going to forget our brand-new curfew and let us—?"

"We aren't going to ask; we're just going to go."

"Sneak out?"

"Nothing we haven't done before. It'll be fun. Don't you want to have fun?"

Helen had never been the girl to initiate fun of any kind or to propose outings that might get them grounded for weeks. That had been Mags.

"If we get caught . . . " Helen shook the poster. "We say we're searching for the bunny, and everyone will believe us because you know, you're you, Jay."

"That is true," Ronnie said.

"My momma will still kick my ass if she finds out."

"We'll worry about that if it happens."

Helen was also not a "worry about it if it happens" girl. Helen was more of a "worry about everything all the time, even if it didn't have any chance in hell of happening" girl. Helen did not plan after-hours sneak arounds and instigate lying to their parents.

Just another example of a world gone mad.

And when had Jay begun to think that? While watching the news she wasn't supposed to watch? Reading a magazine she wasn't supposed to read? Or staring at sketches she'd never imagined her brother sketching?

Maybe it had all started when that bus disappeared around the bend in the road.

"I guess we don't have anything else to do," Jay said.

Helen's smile bloomed. "Exactly! And we need something."

"We do?"

"Mags left the sleepover because it was boring." Helen's smile wilted. "We're boring."

"Speak for yourself, toots," Ronnie said in an Edward G. Robinson–gangster voice. When no one laughed, she gave an impatient sigh. "You think running around after curfew is going to be less boring than what we've been doing so far?"

"How can it not be?"

The idea of Helen being bored with them was disturbing. Mags was understandable; she had the attention span of a gnat. However, if Jay thought about it, really thought about it, Helen being bored with them wasn't surprising—that it had taken her this long to become bored was. None of them were stimulating conversationalists for someone like Helen.

"Midnight it is," Jay said.

"Everyone will be asleep but us."

"And the cops," Ronnie added.

"You think the cops in this town are gonna be able to catch us?" Helen asked.

"Maybe," Ronnie said.

"I guess we'll find out."

When she put it like that, Jay got interested. They hadn't had cops chasing them since they'd switched the *Elect Johnson* yard signs with the *Elect Goldwater* yard signs. That had been Billy's idea and hilarious. In that instant, Jay missed him more than ever.

Ronnie and Helen headed home as Jay hurried inside. Once in her room, Jay hid the drawings inside her winter boots instead of behind them. If Momma started snooping, and so far she never had, she'd be distracted by the schnapps. Jay would be grounded but better than the alternative.

Since Momma was working late, Jay flipped to the national news just in time for the daily body count.

More of them than us—a good day—as long as you weren't one of "them." It made Jay sick the way they translated people into numbers and now that one of those dead might be Billy . . .

The TV flickered. Jay adjusted the rabbit ears decorated with tin foil, then gave it a smack; the picture cleared. She lay on the couch, hoping the roll in her stomach and the thud in her head would fade, but unless she turned the channel, she didn't think it was going to. Jay closed her eyes, floating along on the solemn tone of the anchorman.

"Soldiers in-country refer to the Viet Cong as ghosts; getting spooked is to get killed. To say, 'Don't give up the ghost, man!' is cooler than 'Stay safe!'

"Ghosts are rarely seen, and if they are, they disappear —*whoosh*—like magic. They blend into the jungle, the mountains, the grass, the trees, the earth. They can slip through barbed wire, sneak up without a sound, melt into the air on a whisper.

"In the bush, spirits dance in the fog, whirl through the mist. Music plays in places far away from any possibility of there being music as often as the scent of incense—an offering to a hungry ghost—wafts over two dozen kilometers from the nearest village."

A different voice replaced that of the anchorman, and Jay

opened her eyes. A soldier as young as Billy, his face sweaty, filthy, spoke into a microphone.

"Just before dawn, the whole place"—a beep drowned out the next word, but Jay could lipread *fucking* as well as the next person—"shimmers with a mist that swirls and hides damn near anything."

The idea of Billy wandering around in that fog, unable to see where he was going or who might be coming . . .

The screen left Vietnam behind and returned to the newsroom where the anchorman's already-drooping face drooped more. "In other news, the search for the Communist Central Office of South Vietnam, the headquarters of the enemy, has continued. Earlier in the year, an air offensive was launched."

Footage of paratroopers swaying peacefully downward appeared; the sheer number should have been intimidating.

"Military intelligence has begun to suspect that the reason the enemy's nerve center has been so elusive is because the North Vietnamese military and political headquarters in South Vietnam, which has long been thought to be near the Cambodian border, is actually nowhere."

How could something be nowhere?

Jay tried to keep her eyes open, but they were too heavy.

The anchorman's voice seemed to travel farther and farther away, until it was as far away as Billy and Vietnam.

CHAPTER 10

Billy
"What Are You Fighting For?"

*V*ietnam—June 1967

Billy ducked out of his tent carrying his sketchbook and pencils; he avoided the glowing red circles dotting the darkness.

Everyone smoked in Vietnam, both to keep the bugs away from their faces and to give them something to do. But seeing how far a lit cig could be spotted at night in the jungle had made Billy think twice about making himself a target. Sure, guys shielded the glow, but every once in a while, they forgot and then *bam*. Good-bye head.

He settled at a table in the mess tent and put pencil to blank page. On patrol he did his best to keep his mind . . . well, not really blank but open so that when he had to act, nothing kept him from it. However, during downtime, and especially at night, what he saw, what he did, what he didn't think about sometimes appeared. Then he would draw what kept him awake. Once those thoughts, memories, images lived on paper, they seemed to die in his head, at least for that night, and he could catch a few hours' shut-eye before dawn.

But the first time he'd opened his sketchbook and seen what he'd drawn, everything had come flooding back, so he'd torn the sketches free, shoved them into an envelope, and sent everything to Harold. Billy had told his friend it was for safekeeping, so they wouldn't get ruined, but what he'd really been worried about ruining was himself. Since then, Billy hadn't thought about the memories behind those sketches even once. Should he be worried about that or not?

"Johnson." LT stood next to the table.

It was the first time he'd spoken to Billy directly since he'd ordered him to stay out of his sight. The man's gaze flicked to Billy's sketch. "It wasn't your fault."

Billy contemplated the blazing village, gaping hole in the ground, just the hint of a hand with a pistol inside and the body of Alby with half a head. "If I'd been quicker to shoot, the kid wouldn't have made it to the tunnel and then—"

"We wouldn't have found the tunnel and the next patrol down the line could have lost more than one man."

"I think too much, act too little, or too slow."

LT sat on the other side of the table. "Who told you that?"

"My grandfather."

"You can practice shooting for decades, but until you practice shooting the enemy . . ."

"It's not the same."

"No."

"Does it get easier?"

LT sighed and looked away. "Yeah."

"How?"

"Just like everything else, practice makes perfect." LT flicked one finger at the sketchbook. "You're good at that. Really good."

"This I've practiced. I want to attend art school when I . . . if I
. . ."

"Always say *when*, son. Positive thinking never hurt anyone."
LT lit a smoke. "Could you draw what you saw in those tunnels?
The beds, the hospital, the booby trap?"

"Sure."

"What about the cave-in? Could you recreate a pretty accurate rendition?"

Billy closed his eyes, then snapped them open when an all
too accurate rendition appeared. "Yep."

"Do it."

LT stared into space, not seeming to notice when ashes
tumbled off his cig and blew over Billy's sketch, just as the ashes
had drifted over the village they'd burned.

A short while later, Billy pushed the sketchbook across the
table. LT dropped his stub onto the floor, crushing it with his
boot before depositing it in a butt can next to his others. In the
bush, he would field strip what was left by shredding the paper,
filter, and tobacco into tiny pieces so they could flutter away,
then make sure every other guy did the same.

*Cigarette butts are like Hansel's and Gretel's breadcrumbs to
the VC.*

LT turned the pages. "Can I have these?"

Billy tore them free, handed them over, even the first one
with Alby—sending that home to Harold, maybe not the best
idea. The immediate wash of relief upon doing so had become
addictive. Out of sight, in this case, was completely out of mind,
and he needed it.

"I reported a body count of seven on that search and
destroy. But HQ is insisting there had to be dozens in that
tunnel." LT lifted the drawings. "I can use this to back up my
contention that dozens is an inflation I'm not willing to stand
behind."

"You're a good LT."

"Am I? Guys would get more in-country R and R at Vung Tau if I reported a higher body count."

Billy could do without that *atta boy*. Shooting the enemy was one thing—it was his job, his duty—but lying about it didn't seem very American.

"I refuse to order kill quotas or offer rewards to my men for meeting those quotas any way they can. I don't give a rat's butt-hole about promotion."

Billy was tired, they all were, but he thought he was following what LT was saying and—

"That's crazy."

"Welcome to the US Army." LT pulled out another smoke, but he didn't light it. "You should cut some Zs. I have a hunch we'll be headed into the bush again soon."

Since LT's hunches were more like predictions, Billy got some sleep.

By the following evening, they'd marched for miles and seen little in the way of the enemy.

As promised, the monsoon season continued. It poured nearly every night and sometimes all day as well. Billy couldn't decide which he hated worse—dripping with sweat when it wasn't raining or dripping with rain when it was. He couldn't count how many leeches had dropped from the trees onto him or the guy in front of him and had to be plucked off. Talk about having someone's back.

Several soldiers had immersion foot, or jungle rot, even though LT ordered everyone to change his socks whenever they stopped to rest. Itching, burning, blisters, in some cases the skin rubbed clean off. Unfortunately, when it rained multiple inches a day, spare socks did not dry well inside shirts as wet as the whole damn jungle.

"Are my fingers pruney?" Bama held out his hands for Terrell to examine.

"How would I know?" Terrell yanked off his glasses, but

wiping at the steam with a wet shirt only spread more wet around. "I can't see a thing."

"Just shut up and start digging," Deus snapped.

They still didn't have a sergeant. Some in the platoon whispered the army was clean out of them. Scuttlebutt said LT had recommended Deus for the position, but no one at the top had confirmed it yet. Nevertheless, Deus ordered everyone around as if they had. A few guys bitched, but Billy didn't mind. Deus knew what he was doing.

They'd found a flat-topped ridge safe enough for the night, but darkness threatened, and they still needed to dig a foxhole for the watch. Everyone pitched in; the quicker they finished, the quicker they could eat cold C-rations. The coin-shaped tabs of compressed fuel meant to heat the meals were never used in the bush. Releasing the scent of warm food into the jungle wasn't worth the risk, especially since C-rats weren't much better hot.

"I hate ham and lima beans." Nevertheless, Bama shoveled more into his mouth.

New guys got last pick, and all that had been left were ham and lima beans.

"I figured they'd be better than nothing." Billy set aside his half-eaten container. "I was wrong."

Terrell gave up too. "Let's bed down."

"There's no bed about it." Bama grabbed his poncho and so did Billy.

Three by three, men constructed shelters—two ponchos made a roof and sides, one the floor—space was tight. Bamboo poles provided support; extra shoelaces and small sticks pinned the ends. They formed a circle inside the foxhole, facing out, with LT, Sparky, and Bones in the center.

Billy didn't think he'd sleep—the makeshift tents weren't as waterproof as the army made out—but he must have because an unknown amount of time later, Terrell shook him awake, his eyes so wide the whites bobbed like golf balls in the darkness.

"Somethin' rustlin' 'round right outside the perimeter."

Billy grabbed his rifle and followed the line of Terrell's finger past the slope of the ridge on their side of the circle.

"Whoever's on watch ain't watchin' too good."

Either that or Terrell was hearing stuff. Sitting in the jungle waiting for something to happen messes with the mind. Guys heard things that weren't there, or maybe they just weren't there anymore once they got to where they'd thought they were. Made everyone jittery.

One time their gunner, Dutch, woke everyone mowing a path through the jungle with his M60, but in the morning, they hadn't found anything but massacred leaves and sticks. Dutch had sworn he'd heard voices speaking "gookanese," seen tiny shadows flitting here and there, but there'd been no dead people, no blood, not even a footprint.

"Keep your eyes right there," Terrell whispered.

When just a breath of sound traveled in the jungle for miles, talking at full volume was the same as sending up a flare to any VC in the vicinity.

"I'm gonna tell LT." Terrell took off, hunched low, toward the center of the circle.

Bama snorted and turned over. Guy would cut Zs through an air strike.

Camp was as quiet as the whole world before a grenade exploded. All Billy saw were the swaying tips of bamboo and elephant grass, but that didn't mean squat. When you saw the least, that was when Charlie was there the most.

Billy narrowed his eyes. The back of his neck tingled as a shadow shimmied near the foxhole.

Should he shoot? What if one of the guards was taking a leak? Which would be worse, not shooting and allowing the enemy to kill one of his buddies or actually killing one of his buddies?

And here he was thinking too much ag—

A grenade exploded, lighting up the night long enough to determine that the figure at the edge of the foxhole was not an American soldier—too short, wrong hat. Billy emptied his mind on an exhale and pulled the trigger an instant before the flash died.

The night erupted in gunfire.

Terrell dove in next to him, grabbed his rifle, and started shooting too. Even Bama woke up and did the same.

"How many?" Terrell asked.

"I only saw one."

Terrell kept shooting. "There's never just one, and better safe than sorry."

As usual, Terrell summed things up perfectly.

Eventually LT called a halt to the free fire and radioed the watch. The silence after so much noise seemed to amplify his voice. "We clear?"

"Think so."

"Flash," Terrell muttered. "Figures."

Flash might be fast, but he got distracted easy.

"Toss another frag and see what pops."

"Roger that, lima tango."

To confuse any listening VC, LTs were referred to as *lima tangos* over the radio, though Billy thought the VC had probably cracked that code a while back.

Standard operating procedure while on watch was to toss a pineapple-shaped fragmentation grenade in the general direction of any suspicious noise. Couldn't hurt and rifles only gave away position.

The frag went boom, lit up the night. Nothing moved. Didn't mean nothing was out there.

"Keep a sharp eye until daybreak," LT ordered. "Two *clicks* for okay on the hour."

During the night, the RTO *clicked* the Prick once every hour. If all was well, the watch *clicked* twice.

"What if it's not okay?" Bama asked. "Does someone check?"

"Sending guys out in the dark to check on guys in the dark without an okay would be dumb," Terrell said.

"Isn't it dumber not to? I mean, if the watch isn't okay, won't whoever made them not okay make the rest of us not okay too?"

"What the hell you just say?"

Not long after, the clouds blew away. Billy and Terrell played cards by the light of the full moon that shone through a big gap in the tree canopy and into one of the open triangles on either end of their poncho tent. It wasn't like they were going to sleep after all the excitement. No one probably would.

"I wonder who made that." Terrell lifted his chin to indicate the massive tear in a jungle so thick sometimes they heard rain but never felt a drop. "Us or them?"

"Remember our first week in-country when we came across that place where the trees were all shot up, some uprooted, with divots all over the ground?" Bama lay on his back, his arms behind his head so he could stare at the slice of sky.

"Yeah." Billy played a card. "Reminded me of those pictures of the craters that Spacecraft Ranger sent back."

"Except the moon doesn't have trees or elephant grass." Terrell laid down a card too.

"LT said it looked like Peter Pilot screwed up," Bama continued.

"Say what?"

"That's what they call FNGs that fly. Except, according to LT, they don't usually let them do anything but watch the gauges or read the map."

"You saying LT thought a cherry pilot dropped a bomb by accident and moonscaped part of the jungle?" Billy asked.

Considering the craters had still been smoking when they arrived, Peter Pilot could easily have dropped the bomb on them. Talk about friendly fire.

"Either that or a crazed giant left behind footprints when he was pulling up trees."

Billy and Terrell stopped playing.

"LT did not say that," Terrell accused.

Bama grinned. "Ya think?"

"Does it matter why there's a gap?" Billy asked. "We can play cards without a flashlight, which we aren't supposed to use anyway."

Lit flashlights inside poncho tents revealed perfect silhouettes for snipers.

Bama glanced uneasily at the night. "You think the moon's lighting us up for the VC?"

"Cool it. Beej killed the sniper."

"Did he? Snipers hide and pick you off, they don't sneak up on the guard."

"We haven't had any more trouble. Go to sleep."

"If you aren't expecting trouble, why don't you go to sleep?"

Terrell ignored him, and Billy tossed his last card.

Terrell smirked. "You owe me five bucks."

Billy rooted in his ruck and found a five-dollar MPC.

"I thought your momma didn't like gambling," Bama said.

Bama's didn't either, which was why Terrell and Billy were playing cards and Bama was lying there talking about it.

"Momma isn't here."

"I bet she'd smack you stupid if she caught you."

The longer Billy was in Vietnam, the more things he saw, heard, did that Momma would smack him stupid for.

At first light, Billy emerged from his poncho tent and joined LT, Deus, and Flash outside the perimeter.

The bodies appeared to have been tossed to the jungle floor

by that giant Bama had mentioned. Except giants didn't leave bullet holes.

"Looks like a graveyard exploded." Flash pointed at the corpse closest to the foxhole, then winked at Billy. "That one's yours."

Deus hunkered next to the VC, who had been shot through the neck. "This shot's the stuff of legend."

While Billy was thrilled to have done something that caused Deus to speak of him with admiration, if the VC ever figured out he'd been the one to make such a shot, he might as well tattoo a target on his back.

Billy shifted his shoulders, flicked a glance around the perimeter, caught sight of several things he hadn't before. Mixed in with at least a dozen guerrilla fighters lay several dead women and children.

"Shit," he said.

"Who owns the night?" LT asked.

"VC," everyone chanted but Billy.

"Therefore anyone walking around in it, outside our perimeter is . . ."

"The enemy!"

Were they at a pep rally?

Whaddya want?

VC!

What's that?

The enemy!

Billy rubbed his forehead. He was thinking again.

Terrell arrived with Bama. "What could they have been up to out here besides mischief?"

"The enemy uses women and children to keep us from shooting them," Bama said.

"They do," LT agreed.

Except it had been too dark to distinguish women and children, so how did that work?

It hadn't.

"He who hesitates is dead." LT lit the inevitable cig. "Kids and women have firearms and grenades too."

"Did they?" Billy took a step in that direction.

"Leave 'em lie."

Flash punched Billy's shoulder. "They could be booby-trapped, moron."

Billy glanced at LT, who nodded. "If there's another patrol in the area, they've been known to booby trap the dead. Too many GIs have lost hands, feet, sight, lives because they wanted a souvenir."

Bama, who'd been itching to take home an enemy knife, gulped.

"I've done a body count, so let's break camp and gear up. NVA was spotted five Ks east."

A few weeks back, the Army of North Vietnam had engaged with the Fifth Marines near the Que Son Valley. Since Billy's platoon was neither marines nor anywhere near Que Son, that information should have been nothing more than noise.

NVA lost over six hundred men, but they'd killed a hundred marines. The Fifth needed to rest, regroup, resupply, which meant that when the enemy scattered south, resupplying themselves with the rebel VC, or maybe the VC resupplied with them —hard to say since both the NVA and the VC were an enemy that looked a helluva lot like friends—Billy's platoon had been sent after them.

"By the time we hoof it five Ks, they'll be ten Ks gone," Flash complained.

LT rubbed his forehead. "Just break camp, Flash. Now."

Flash opened his mouth again.

"Do not make me tell you twice," LT said so quietly Billy was surprised anyone heard, but they did, and they moved, arriving in front of LT a short while later, geared up and ready for orders.

LT assigned everyone their positions—which of the three Slicks each of them would climb onto, who would be piling out in what order, where they would head when they landed—clock system with the nose of the bird as twelve, fanning from two to five on one side, seven to eleven on the other, no one at six because that would get your head torn off by a rotor.

"Johnson, take point once we're on the ground."

"Roger that."

"We're gonna double time it to an LZ over that ridge." LT lifted his chin. "The Slicks will then drop us at an LZ nearer where the enemy was spotted."

"Why didn't whoever spotted them kick their ass?" Hammer asked.

"I'm gonna kick yours if you don't shut up," Deus said.

"No one told him to shut up when he was lippin' off." Hammer turned his scowl on Flash.

"Move! Out!"

Billy had never heard LT shout quite like that before. From the speed they all moved out, no one else had either.

He couldn't blame LT. Not only was Flash annoying just being Flash, but the bickering between the Negroes and the whites was getting worse. Just yesterday, Ghost, a Negro so light he looked white, and Crazy Joe, a white guy whose real name wasn't even Joe, had to be separated when they ended up rolling around on the ground pummeling each other because Ghost had called Muhammad Ali "the greatest" and Crazy Joe had said he was a draft dodger. Even when they set up camp, the Negroes, who sometimes called one another *Bloods*, were on one side of the circle, the white guys on the other, with Billy, Terrell, and Bama in the middle.

Didn't they all want same thing? Weren't they all fighting the same war?

"It ain't your turn to be on point." Terrell spoke low; Billy barely heard him over the double time thuds of their boots.

"I don't mind." If Billy could make things safer by doing more than his fair share, he was happy to.

Though it was early morning, the sun blazed like late afternoon, so they arrived at the LZ dripping sweat and light-headed from the double time. It felt good to pile on the birds and lift off. The air that blew in the open side door was hot, but it was air, and they needed it. Up ahead, purple smoke curled into a powder-blue sky.

As they got in range, their escort gunships laid down cover fire. Terrell, stuck to Billy's side like a burr, pointed at the figures wearing uniforms nearly the same shade as the uncleared elephant grass firing into the sky while they retreated toward the thicker cover of the jungle, despite its being pounded by mortars and machine gun fire from the gunships.

Everything was chaos below, but during their three-day training course, they'd practiced over and over how to come into a hot LZ.

"The bird will hover above the ground," the sarge had told them. "Could be seven or more feet above depending on the terrain. Pilot needs to keep that tail rotor clear. Step onto those skids and jump. Pronto. That chopper is one big motherfucking target, and ya need to move yer ass so it can get gone. When ya hit the ground, it ain't gonna feel good, but ya need to clear that bird by ten plus feet, ASAP, no matter how much yer teeth or yer bones are rattlin'. Bird's gonna lift off or come down, and you don't wanna be near it either way."

LT motioned in the direction he wanted Billy to head once they were all on foot. Billy acknowledged and stepped onto the skid. From the corner of his eye, he saw one of their gunners recoil from a hit, but Billy only had seconds to jump, and there was nothing he could do for the man anyway. The gunner's monkey strap, attached to his gear, kept him from tumbling out.

Billy's boots hit with enough force for his head to ache. But when a bullet sliced the air in front of his nose, he dove into elephant grass that had appeared six feet high from the air but was really four feet high on the ground. Guys landed and rolled into the grass all around him.

The first Slick lifted and flew away; the second took its place. More bullets whistled from the trees to the east, and Billy returned fire while others dropped, then took up their assigned place on the clock ASAP. They opened fire, too, as the final transport hovered.

Billy glanced up to check their progress just as Crazy Joe stepped onto the landing skid. Ghost had the six, last guy off, eyes on the jungle, M16 trained there too. He stopped firing an instant before Crazy Joe fell like a ton of bricks, hitting the ground and lying still.

Bones and Deus leaped from the grass, each grabbing a foot and dragging Crazy Joe out of the open, as Billy and the others covered them.

Billy felt rather than saw Ghost land; the last Slick lifted and spun away. Dutch set up his M60, and in no time, what remained of the enemy retreated.

Everyone gathered around Crazy Joe, who was covered in blood but didn't seem hurt that bad.

"Head wounds bleed like a bitch." Bones disinfected the bullet crease on Crazy Joe's cheek—in the jungle, infections took root quicker than a blink—then tied a bandage around his head.

"I'm gonna have a scar."

Crazy Joe seemed more upset about that than he needed to be. It wasn't like he was Paul Newman to begin with.

"What the hell happened?" LT demanded.

"One of those peckerwoods got 'im." Ghost didn't look as upset about that as maybe he should've.

"You stopped the cover fire," Crazy Joe said. "I heard you."

"Can't shoot while I'm jumping, can I?"

LT's gaze narrowed. He remembered as well as anyone how Ghost and Crazy Joe had come to blows the day before.

"It's not like I can see every zipperhead in the shit." Ghost jabbed a filthy finger at Billy. "Like him."

"Beej can't see everything," Terrell said.

"Could've fooled me." Flash lifted his upper lip like Ringo did whenever he caught a whiff of skunk.

"Enough," LT snapped. "Move out."

The enemy had fled, but they'd left a trail so obvious Billy checked it for booby traps more thoroughly than usual. The NVA appeared to be long gone. Being small had its advantages out here where the jungle was so thick it could take an hour for the GIs to move a hundred yards.

"Need to feed this crap some o' that weed killer we saw in them orange-striped barrels." Terrell's voice whispered across the back of Billy's neck. "Wash it down with napalm."

As darkness threatened, the Negroes blended into the night in a way Billy envied. Sometimes he thought his pasty white skin glowed like a spotlight.

A single gunshot split the silence, and Billy stumbled, but he wasn't shot. Ghost was. Right through the back of the head.

Everyone panicked, hitting the dirt, shouting, waiting for an ambush that didn't come.

Billy crouched, eyes straining the gloom for a hint of the enemy, but he didn't see anything worth worrying about until he caught a glimpse of Crazy Joe peeking over a fallen tree. In that minute Billy knew why they called him *Crazy*.

His eyes. They weren't quite right.

Billy started to think about what had just happened and what he concluded he didn't much like. One shot, no more, from the rear. Which didn't make any sense unless there wasn't an enemy out there. Unless the enemy was right here.

LT combat-crawled from his hidey-spot behind a thick, low bit of brush. "You see anything?"

"Shot came from . . ." Billy lifted his hand.

Crazy Joe tilted his head, lifted his eyebrows, and Billy indicated the tangle of bamboo that seemed to march on forever, taking the heat off point, which couldn't have seen a sniper over there even if there had been one.

"Anything now?" LT asked.

"No, sir."

Not a lie. Billy didn't see anything because nothing was there. Nothing ever had been.

Slowly, Billy got to his feet, then so did everyone else.

"Probably some baby dink that pissed his pants at the sight of us." Flash puffed out his chest.

The guy was such a dork.

LT let his gaze wander from the trees to the soldiers to Ghost, then back again. "You." He pointed at Flash. "And you." This time he pointed at Crazy Joe. "Pack up that body."

LT definitely had some suspicions.

They made camp soon after, and late that night, when all was quiet and Billy was the most alone he'd ever been, he came to a few conclusions.

Not only had Crazy Joe killed Ghost, but Crazy Joe knew that Billy knew.

And that target on his back just burned all the time.

CHAPTER 11

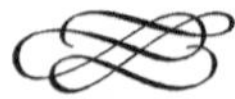

Jay
"I Should Be Proud"

illow Creek—June 1967

Jay awoke with a gasp when Momma stumbled in just after nine. She sat up and cast a quick glance at the television. It no longer played the news, thank God. Still, she feared Momma would start grilling her on why she was so spooked, then she'd spill everything.

Billy's sketches. The day's body count. The plans to sneak out and search for Fluff, or at least pretend to.

Instead, Momma tossed the mail onto the coffee table and plucked an envelope from the pile. "A letter from your brother." Momma kicked off her shoes and sat. "Dear Momma and Jay," she began, absently stroking Ringo when he pushed in close.

My platoon is doing good. I haven't gotten a scratch. Knock wood.

I guess that's not completely true. We all have scratches from the elephant grass—the edges are sharper than a razor, and it's slipperier than black ice if you step on it—and from itching the bug bites that seem to multiply by the minute.

You know how I swell up when I get bit, Momma? Some days I look like I have chicken pox again or maybe the plague. I swear the bug juice they give us is bug attractant and not repellent. I really wish it would work on the leeches.

I'm sure you're both gagging, and they are disgusting. We have to stop when we are on patrol sometimes for a leech check, even if we haven't been slogging through water up to our armpits—which we do often enough, and then you get leeches for sure.

"Tomorrow." Momma's gaze remained on the letter. "I'm going to send him better bug spray."

Jay doubted anything was going to work on leeches, but she kept it to herself. She couldn't believe how different Billy's letter was from the drawings he'd sent. Her brother made Vietnam sound like a camping trip.

Could you send me paperbacks? Sometimes we've got nothing to do but sit around, and then if you're not on watch, you can read. I've finished the books I brought and traded them to other guys, but I read theirs too, so I could really use some fresh stories.

The picture he painted of himself just sittin' out there in the jungle, catching up on his reading made Jay grit her teeth. It was all a lie. Except, maybe, for the leeches.

Momma rested the letter on her lap. "Does Helen have books she's done reading?"

"Helen gets her books from the library."

Her family barely had money for food and clothes, and what was left over, even some that wasn't, went to fill the glass of clear liquid that Mr. Murphy always carried in one hand. For years Jay had thought it was water, but she didn't anymore.

Momma's face lit up. "One of my customers bought a whole box of books at a rummage sale for a dime!"

No doubt most of those had been thin Harlequin romances,

but since Jay didn't want to rain on Momma's parade, she kept it to herself.

I have to sign off. My lieutenant, we just call him LT, says we'll be moving out soon. Here are a few sketches of the land and the people using the colored pencils you sent like I promised.

Momma peered at the first, and tears filled her eyes. What had Billy sent this time?

"He's so good at this." Momma turned the sketch toward Jay.

Oddly, the drawing, now in living—or rather penciled—color, made what her brother depicted less real. Or maybe it was just that Jay had caught a glimpse of the truth, and this wasn't it.

A water buffalo, so dark a brown it was nearly black, stood in the middle of a grayish-yellow stretch of water, shot through with sprouts that blazed bright green against a clear blue sky. Guess none of those clouds she'd been wondering about *had* made their way to Vietnam.

The animal brought to mind a cow, except for the great curling horns clasped by the grungy fingers of a Vietnamese boy so skinny his bones seemed to ripple beneath his skin. His grin revealed several missing teeth, though he seemed too old to be gifting the tooth fairy. Did that swaying grass at the far edge of the water conceal a booby trap, a tunnel, the VC?

What was wrong with her? Was she seeing something that wasn't there? Or had her eyes been opened to the ugly that lurked beneath the surface of everything beautiful?

The next sketch showed mountains vibrant with color, blue and green, beige and yellow, all blended together with wisps of white as clouds—there they were!—drifted along the peaks.

"Almost makes you want to go there," Momma said.

Yeah, if only to drag Billy right back.

"Every time we get a letter I feel better. He was alive when he sent this."

Jay clenched her teeth to prevent *he could be dead by now* from slipping free of her mouth. Momma didn't need to hear that. Why was Jay even thinking it?

"I'm going to write back before I fall asleep. You eat supper?"

"PB and J, supper of champions." Enjoyed by the children of working moms everywhere.

Except Jay had been sleeping, not eating, but Momma didn't need to hear that either.

"You gonna write him too?"

Jay nodded as Momma kissed her good night, taking Billy's sketches, his letter to her room.

What Jay would write in the letter she gave to her mother would be very different from the one she sent on her own. The two faces of Jay to match the two faces of Billy. She barely managed to finish both before she had to meet her friends. Being two-faced was hard!

She placed the bullshit letter on the kitchen table for Momma to include with hers, tucking the other into an empty boot to be smuggled out later.

Ronnie and Helen stood in the yard. Willow Creek was as still as Jay's mother had been when she'd tiptoed past her bedroom.

"Any trouble sneaking out?" Helen asked.

Jay shook her head. "You?"

"A little. My parents are gone, but the morons were home."

Jay and Ronnie exchanged a quick glance. Helen's desire to chase a rabbit after midnight *tonight* made more sense. Her brothers behaved a lot worse when her parents weren't around.

Helen frowned at Ringo. "Maybe he should stay here. What if he barks?"

"If I leave him in the house, he'll wake Momma for sure."

"Fine." From the way Helen's nose crinkled, it was not fine. "Let's go."

"Where?" Jay asked.

"The cemetery."

"Whoa now," Ronnie said. "Why?"

"Why not?"

"Because it's"—Ronnie shifted her shoulders—"creepy."

"Creepy is half the fun."

Was everyone turning into someone they were not?

"I was doing some research," Helen began, and Ronnie groaned.

"Why do you always have to take the fun out of everything by researching it to death?"

Helen wasn't nicknamed "the Brain" for nothing. Her favorite kind of day was rainy, so she could read from morning to night. If she had something to research, to learn, to share even better. She was going to attend Princeton one day, never mind that the school was all male. The news that they'd recently allowed a few women to attend a special government language program only made her more determined to change their admission policy forever.

Everyone needed a hobby.

"Don't you want to know what I found out?" Helen asked.

"No!" Ronnie stomped ahead. "I want to continue in ignorance forever."

Helen glanced at Jay, who shrugged. Sometimes it was hard to tell if Ronnie was being sarcastic or just bitchy.

"Perry Petroski fell at the Battle of Cantigny," Helen said, "in World War One. He was the first man to die in any war from Willow Creek."

"Considering his statue has been sitting in Remembrance Square, smack in the center of town for our entire lives . . ." Ronnie threw up her hands. "We know."

Other towns might boast statues of fallen Civil War heroes, Spanish-American War casualties, and so on, but Willow Creek hadn't existed until 1913.

"What got you going on Perry?" Jay asked.

"His ghost haunts the graveyard."

Ronnie stopped so fast they nearly plowed into her. "Why would Perry haunt the graveyard when he's buried under his statue?"

Helen didn't roll her eyes, but Jay could tell she wanted to. "You can't just bury people in the center of town."

"I think she's right," Jay said.

"Where did you hear about Perry's ghost?" Ronnie asked.

"My brother."

"Which one?"

"Does it matter?"

They *were* interchangeable.

"We snuck out in the first place to do something exciting, so we could be less boring. This is pretty exciting. Not at all boring. Right?"

"Why would you, of all people—?" Ronnie began.

"It's a dare," Helen blurted. "I have to go into the cemetery after midnight and touch Perry's grave."

"And then?" Jay asked.

"They'll stop scaring me."

"How are they gonna do that with faces like theirs?"

Ronnie's question surprised a laugh out of Jay, but Ronnie wasn't done.

"Brain, you need to stand up to them or they'll never leave you alone."

"I've tried." Helen looked down. "I can't."

"Then tell someone who will."

"Tell them what?" Helen's hands fisted. "That my brothers tease and torment me? No one will care."

"I care," Jay said at the same time Ronnie snapped, "If you won't do it, I wi—"

"No!" Helen's voice held a chill they'd never heard from her before. "If you want to stay my friends, you'll mind your own business, both of you." She walked away.

"If we want to . . ." Jay repeated. "Huh?"

Ronnie spread her hands.

That unspoken rule about family matters—private, secret, off-limits—had never seemed more real.

"Come on," Ronnie said, her voice no longer angry but defeated.

They caught up to Helen just outside the cemetery.

"What about that?" Ronnie indicated the Closed After Sunset sign posted at the entrance.

"No gate, no lock." Helen strolled inside.

"Who is she, and what has she done with Helen?" Ronnie asked.

Shrill, girlish laughter split the silent night, drawing Jay's attention to Susan Grant's nearby house. From the multitude of bodies darting here and there beyond the open window, another sleepover was in progress.

"Pssst!"

The only person in sight was Chief Vanderhooven, who'd just stepped out of the station and cast his eyes—

Ronnie yanked Jay behind the hedge lining the cemetery an instant before the chief would have seen her. "You are really bad at this."

Ronnie squinted at Susan's bedroom window where, for an instant, Susan appeared in only her bra and panties.

"Well, that's something I'll never unsee." Jay rubbed her eyes.

"Me either." Ronnie didn't sound as put off by it as Jay was.

"Did it ever occur to anyone that we could get arrested for peeping?" Jay asked.

"If we aren't arrested for trespassing first." Helen's voice was far too jolly.

Suddenly Jay wished she'd stayed home, something she couldn't remember having wished before when she was with her friends.

The white gravestones seemed to hover amid a great big

nothing. Then, out in the middle of all that rippling black and petrified white, something moved.

Jay's breath caught.

"What is it?" Helen forgot to use her graveyard voice.

"Shh!" Ronnie hissed.

The something that had moved . . . hopped.

"Fluff," Jay said.

"That's right," Helen agreed. "We're searching for Fluff."

Ringo barreled in that direction, barking madly, and screams erupted from Susan's window.

Helen bolted, skirting the hedge, Ronnie on her heels. Should Jay go after them or the dog?

The screaming got louder. Jay hadn't thought that possible, considering the ear-piercing nature of the noise already, so she joined her friends just as Mags leaned out the window and flicked her fingers. Whatever she'd tossed wasn't big enough to see in the dark; unfortunately, they were.

"Who's out there?"

They hit the dirt faster than GIs confronted by a VC patrol.

"What's going on? What happened?" the other girls asked.

"I thought I saw someone in the cemetery when I tossed the spider."

"Spider." Ronnie huffed. "Babies."

Helen slapped her hand over Ronnie's mouth and not an instant too soon.

"What's the meaning of all that caterwauling?" Chief Vanderhooven demanded.

As the shrieks rose again, Ronnie and Jay crowded in next to Helen, who peered through a bread-box-sized gap in the hedge.

The girls in their underwear must have ducked below the windowsill or run from the room. Mags, the only one still dressed, had not.

"There was a spider." She dusted her hands. "Gone now."

The chief rubbed his forehead. "I'd hate to hear how you'd scream if anything was really wrong."

"Yeah, um . . . " Mags glanced over her shoulder, then lowered her voice. "I saw something in the cemetery. Maybe someone?"

The chief muttered a curse, then strolled toward the entrance, his overly large belly leading the way.

"We are screwed," Ronnie whispered.

There was only one way into and out of the place, unless they went over the hedge, which would be as good as standing up and shouting they were there.

Chief Vanderhooven, who was big both up and down as well as sideways, wasn't known to move fast, ever. His partially bald head bobbed along at a speed slower than most senior citizens; what was left of his hair sparkled silver in a shaft of moonlight that pulsed through a break in the clouds.

Jay's gaze flicked around the cemetery, hoping to see Ringo before the chief did. Instead, she glimpsed again the hazy white something she'd glimpsed before. She took off, reaching a set of well-kept bushes that flanked—*whattaya know?*—Perry's grave just as that white blob disappeared into one. Jay dove, hands outstretched.

"Jane Josephine Johnson! What in tarnation are you doing here in the middle of the night?"

Jay lifted her arm; from her fingers dangled—

"Fluff!" Helen reached out quick and snatched a Pez dispenser shaped like Frankenstein's head from the top of Perry's headstone.

The chief spun, hand on his gun.

Really?

"Helen?" His hand lowered. "Ronnie?"

"Chief," they said together.

Helen surreptitiously slid the Pez dispenser into her pocket. As one of her idiot brothers collected the things, it must be the evidence she needed to prove she'd touched the grave where he'd left it.

"What are you doing out—?"

Helen whipped the Missing poster from her other pocket, then pointed at Fluff.

"Hmm." The chief's eyes narrowed. "Miss Brecklewait's been hounding me daily about that varmint. Thought the coyotes ate him for sure." He made a "gimme" gesture with his fingers, and Jay handed over the bunny. "Let's go, girls. You're not supposed to be in here."

"Fluff was in here," Ronnie said.

The chief ignored her. "I'll walk you home. The world's not as safe as it used to be."

"Since when has the way the world is had anything to do with Willow Creek?" Ronnie asked.

Since this summer, Jay thought, but she said nothing.

Billy's dog chose that moment to bark from somewhere outside the cemetery. How had he gotten there?

"I have to fetch Ringo."

"We have to help." Ronnie said.

Fluff, bless his heart, began to struggle as if his life depended on it.

The chief bobbled and nearly dropped the rabbit, then sighed. "You three stick together, okay?"

"We always do!" Ronnie said.

"Aren't there usually four of you?"

"Nope."

The chief appeared about to say something else, then Fluff thumped a hind leg against his stomach.

"Go home." He hurried for the exit, managing only a few feet before he bumbled the bunny. "Dammit." His head swiveled right, then left as Fluff scooted into the greenery behind him. "You see where he went?"

Jay lifted her hand to point, and Helen pulled it back down. "No, sir, we didn't."

He wagged an index finger the size of a bratwurst. "Do *not* tell Miss Brecklewait that I lost him. That woman . . ." His lips tightened, and he strode away.

The three of them followed more slowly.

At the entrance, Helen glanced left, then right. "Which way should we—?"

Jay whistled low, and Ringo peeked around the edge of the cemetery that fronted Susan's window for just an instant before he disappeared again instead of returning to Jay's side. That wasn't like him, and the reason became clear as soon as they turned the corner.

Mags stood in Susan's front yard.

"What are you doing out here?" Ronnie demanded.

"What are *you* doing out here?" Mags ignored Ringo as he pranced and begged, yet again, for her love.

Helen held up the Fluff flyer.

"Are you three ever gonna grow up?"

"You first," Ronnie said.

Mags tossed her hair, which gleamed more blond than ever before beneath a moon that danced with the clouds blowing east on a summer wind. "You are so infantile."

"At least I'm not dancing in front of an open window in my undies for everyone in town to see."

Mags's nails, painted a shade to rival the moon, curled inward on her palms. "Neither was I, which I'm sure *you* could clearly see."

Ronnie's freckled skin flamed.

"Pull the shades next time, Mags," Jay said.

"You're just jealous."

Did Mags want to be stared at by strangers? That couldn't be right. Maybe she meant she had the goods to be admired, but being admired for something that wasn't in your control, something you hadn't earned, something that just *was* because of genetics made no sense, at least to Jay.

"Well, it finally happened." Ronnie's face was still flushed, but her voice remained as sarcastic as ever. "Your brain exploded inside your pretty little head."

"Ronnie, come—" Helen began, but it was too late.

"I don't know why I ever bothered with you."

"You know what, Princess, I don't either."

The four of them had fought before, especially Ronnie and Mags, but this was something else. Something permanent.

"Mags?" Susan called from the backyard.

Mags sped around the house and out of sight. "Right here."

"Were you talking to someone?"

"No one at all."

A door closed, and seconds later, squeals erupted above their heads.

"And that's that." Ronnie didn't sound as happy about it as Jay would have thought, considering. "She's gone."

"Hasn't she . . . been gone?" Helen asked.

"There's gone and then there's . . ." Ronnie jerked a thumb over her shoulder at Susan's house.

No one seemed to know what to say.

"Well, this was fun, wasn't it?" Helen's voice had gone high with hope. "We can meet again tomorrow."

"You did your dare, Brain. What's the point?"

"*Fun.* Excitement." Ronnie snorted, and Helen hurried on, words tumbling free. "Something to do besides the usual. And . . . and . . . Fluff escaped; we should probably—"

Ronnie walked away. The two of them stared after her until she turned a corner, headed home.

"Jay?" Helen's voice wavered. "You'll come, right?"

As she gave it two days before Chief Vanderhooven told their parents where and when he'd seen them, and her momma put a stop to it—Fluff or no Fluff—Jay shrugged. "Sure."

Except the chief didn't tell Momma, or anyone else, because the three of them met every night, or every other, for nearly two weeks, and Jay had to admit it *was* fun being out and about when hardly anyone else was.

Ronnie was quiet at first, but that wore off; silence wasn't Ronnie's bag.

They didn't get caught again; they didn't catch Fluff again either. No one seemed upset about that since it gave them reason to continue. The night had become something that was theirs as much as the clearing.

The weather turned hot the week of July Fourth, and they had to stop sneaking out when folks started sleeping on their front porches to catch a hint of a breeze.

Air conditioning was considered a wasteful luxury in Wisconsin, where ten months out of twelve the thermometer seemed stuck well below eighty. The only air conditioner Jay had ever seen was in the window of the previous mayor's house. Momma said that machine had lost him the next election. No one voted for an extravagant civil servant.

Willow Creek's annual Independence Day celebration, complete with a parade, picnic, and fireworks, approached. Even if it was ninety in the shade, so what? There was free ice cream and lemonade.

On July third, a *tap* sounded at Jay's windowsill well after dark. When she lifted the shade to reveal Mags, she very nearly pulled it back down. What if Ronnie or Helen found them together? Mags was pretty much public enemy number one these days, at least to Ronnie.

Except the window was wide open, so Mags crawled inside.

"Where are your new best friends?"

"I'm meeting them aft—" Mags bit her lip. "Never mind. There's something I should tell you."

"I need to pluck my eyebrows." Jay threw herself onto her bed. "Old news."

"No." Her attention went to Jay's bushy eyebrows. "Well, yes, but that's not why I'm here."

"If you want back into the Musketeers, you should probably talk to Ronnie."

Mags drew the shade. "Ronnie's what I want to talk about."

"She's mad. She should be. You were a bitch. But she'll forgive you. She always does, though this is worse than—"

"She kissed me."

Jay sat up. "What?"

"Ronnie kissed me."

"Okay. So?"

Mags rested her butt against the desk and stared at her nails as if she'd find the answer to every question in the depths of their fresh fuchsia polish. "Not the way we've hugged and kissed since we were little."

"The way? I don't—"

"She used her tongue."

Jay's automatic denial died on *her* tongue when Mags lifted her gaze. "Is that why you—?"

"Partly."

"What's the other part?"

Mags went back to examining her nails. "We don't have much in common anymore."

"We never did."

Momma always said: *How you don't fight like cats in a sack I'll never understand.*

Mags dropped her hands. "I thought you should know."

"You think she's going to kiss me? Kiss Helen? I don't care."

"You like boys. She doesn't."

"I don't think Helen likes boys either."

"If you had her brothers, would you?" Mags asked.

"That doesn't seem like the same thing as Ronnie's . . . thing."

"It's easier if I'm friends with Susan now."

"Easier for who?" Jay demanded.

"Ronnie wants me to be someone I'm not."

"The friend you should be?"

"She doesn't want a friend, or at least she doesn't want me as a friend."

What had happened after the kiss? Had Mags pushed Ronnie away? Said things that shouldn't be said, that could never, ever be unsaid? What about all for one, one for all? That shouldn't, wouldn't, *couldn't* end because of this, because of anything.

Jay stood, and her hands were fists. "You tell anyone else about this, and I'll—"

"Are you kidding? It's just as embarrassing for me."

"I doubt that. She likes you; you don't like her."

"I didn't say that."

"What *did* you say?" Jay tried to unclench her fingers, but they didn't want to go.

"I don't like her the way she likes me, and I never will. Isn't it better to know that now?"

"Maybe you should ask Ronnie."

Mags lifted the shade but hesitated before crawling out. "Talk to her, Jay. She's not going to have an easy life."

"Times are changing."

"Not that much. Not that fast. And definitely not here."

"You think she can become someone she isn't?"

"If she can, now's the time." Mags slid out the window and dropped to the ground. "She needs you and Helen both."

"You don't?" Jay waited for a flippant, hurtful answer, but it didn't come.

Mags smiled softly, sadly. "I'll be all right."

She hurried away without a backward glance, but that smile made Jay wonder: Had Mags given them up because Ronnie needed them more?

The Mags Jay knew wasn't that selfless. Then again, this was New Mags. Jay hadn't thought she was Improved Mags, but maybe she was wrong.

Jay leaned out the window, hoping to catch the tiniest hint of a breeze as she tried to figure out what she should say to Ronnie, when she should say it, *if* she should say it, and out in the dark, something moved.

Jay straightened and smacked the back of her head on the window.

Ringo *woofed* and hurried in from the hall. She set one hand on his head and the other on her own and rubbed them both. What had she seen?

Fluff? Bugs? The wind?

What if it was Ronnie? How would she explain—

A man strode into the yard. "Jay?"

"Harold?"

Ringo placed his paws on the sill and slurped Harold from chin to cheek. Harold, ever a good sport, even kissed Ringo back—without the slurping.

"I didn't mean to lurk, but your friend got here a second before I did."

"She isn't . . . " Jay paused. Was Mags her friend? She didn't know anymore.

Harold lifted an envelope. "I'd have come back tomorrow, but I'm leaving bright and early for the cabin."

Harold's family had a cabin on a lake where his family spent their vacation every summer. It would be peaceful and cool. So very not here.

"I thought you should see these."

Jay reached for the envelope, and something in his face made her ask, "What is it?"

"I'll be back in a few weeks." Harold turned away. "Happy Fourth."

His voice sounded anything but happy.

Jay drew the shade, locked the door, and pulled out the first sketch.

Billy had used an everyday pencil, not the colored ones

Momma had sent, to draw a cratered landscape similar to the moon. The trees were all sliced up and fallen down. Smoke trailed skyward.

It disturbed Jay to think of her brother in the middle of all that . . . she couldn't find a word beyond *shit*, and it didn't get any better when she set aside the first sketch for the second.

Zombies crept out of the ground.

No, not zombies. Bodies had been blown apart, making a partial leg appear to be crawling free, when in reality it would never crawl anywhere again.

Then Jay saw the tiny hand, all alone by itself, and closed her eyes, swallowing several times. Maybe she should grab a Coke, kill the taste of ashes on her tongue with all that sweetness. She wasn't sure what she could do about the dull, tin-like scent of blood in her nose.

It wasn't real. Jay knew that. But it *felt* real.

Last sketch. Could she look? How could she not?

A gray helicopter hovered in a white sky. A soldier's foot hung into space, searching for the skid somewhere beneath, his rifle slung over his shoulder, useless. One of his boots was untied, and the shoestring seemed to flutter in the breeze.

Not so bad, his toe had nearly tapped the place he needed to be. Then Jay saw the faint outline of a target on his back, and suddenly—she swore it hadn't been there before—the barrel of a rifle appeared in the tall grass below pointed upward.

CHAPTER 12

Billy
"Born in the U.S.A."

*V*ietnam—July 1967

"I'm so bored." Terrell juggled a football between his big hands. "I almost wish something would explode."

They lay on their bunks inside their tents at camp, waiting for orders. They'd been waiting for days, maybe more like a week—it was hard to tell when every day was exactly the same—and guys were getting antsy. Several had complained, like Terrell, that they'd rather be out there getting shot at than waiting around just thinking about it. Sure, that was weird, but so was patrol because when they went out, they would be assigned to cover a certain area. They would get to know the terrain, the villes, the trails, the locals.

Then their turn would be done, and some other unit would be sent to tromp around the same place, having to learn what Billy's already knew. When Billy and the others returned to the field, they were sent to another area altogether and had to learn new terrain, new locals all over again. Was the army dumb as a box of rocks?

"You'd think I'd like it boring," Terrell continued. "No one shootin' at us; we aren't shootin' at anyone."

After being on constant alert to everything all around, above, and even below them for days and nights at a time, they couldn't just shut off that awareness like a light switch. Billy was starting to wonder how they would shut it off when they went home.

"I like it boring." Bama, not asleep as he'd been pretending, flipped onto his back.

"That's because you lazy." Terrell threw the ball so hard it bounced off Bama's chest and rolled under an unoccupied rack.

"I thought we were playing football!" Flash shouted from outside.

Billy was sick of playing football, sometimes baseball, though that always ended pretty quickly when someone hit the small white ball past the barbed wire into the mine field. Either the ball set one off and exploded into tiny pieces of leather all over the place, or it was left there with half a dozen others because no one was going to go after it and wind up tiny pieces of person all over the place.

Billy had also read every book his mom and the other guy's moms had sent and played enough cards to lose over half his MPCs, mostly to that asshole Flash. Still, doing something was preferable to doing nothing. Too much nothing led to sleepless nights.

How many times had Billy jerked awake, swearing he'd heard something—shouting, screaming, explosions, or monkeys shrieking, tigers roaring, who knows what else chattering in the trees—but all would be quiet; he'd be the only one awake. Was he hearing things that weren't there, or was everyone else not hearing things that were?

Of course, half the guys were high. Terrell had been right

about the easy access to drugs in Vietnam. Some smoked pot in order to rest, then sniffed cocaine to wake up. So far Billy hadn't seen anyone toking or snorting in the field, but he had seen F-Cat—for Fraidy Cat—shaking pills out of a bottle, which he'd insisted had been prescribed by the army.

"Your mind not quite right? Uncle Sam is happy to help."

But wouldn't drugs make someone's mind less right?

The idea of a good night's sleep was tempting. Then again, what if he was sleeping the sleep of the drugged and Crazy Joe decided to frag him like he'd fragged Ghost? The guy stared at Billy all the time, and he wasn't subtle about it neither. Whenever Billy caught him, Crazy Joe would wink or shoot him with a finger pistol. Both responses made Billy's invisible back target burn.

"If you aren't going to play, Slayer, toss me the ball." Flash stood in the doorway.

Flash had started calling Billy "Slayer" after his first kill, but Billy didn't much like the way he said it. However, telling Flash not to do something was the same as telling him *to* do it.

Billy fished the football from beneath the bunk and headed outside with Terrell, Bama, and several other guys who had been lying around too. Sure, they were sick of football, they were sick of pretty much everything right now, but if they didn't release the energy boiling inside them this way, they might release it another, and no one wanted to see that.

The first time they'd played, the teams had been mostly whites against Blacks, and nearly everyone but Terrell, Billy, and Bama had wound up fighting in the dirt.

LT had been forced to intervene. "One of you breaks an arm or a leg fucking around, and I goddamn guarantee I'll break the other one before you get on that chopper! Johnson! Jones! Pick teams. Permanent teams."

Neither Billy nor Terrell were thrilled—they wanted to be on the *same* team—but there was no arguing with LT, unless you were Flash, and Billy had to say that he and Terrell picked fair. The teams were integrated, and for some reason that ended the fistfights, though they still played hard enough that guys walked away with a hitch in their step and a few fat lips.

"It's football, not ballet," Flash retorted when someone complained about his habit of elbowing, hip-checking, or tripping whoever tried to tackle him.

"He's fast enough not to have to play dirty," Terrell said.

"If he was fast enough, no one would catch him," Bama replied.

"I think he lets people catch him." Billy twitched one shoulder. "Just so he can play dirty."

"That sounds like Flash." Terrell tilted his head and scowled at Billy. "There you go again, spazin' like an addict. What is wrong with you?"

Billy dropped his hand away from the small of his back, where he'd been trying to scratch at the itch that seemed to live there all the time. Sure enough, when he turned around, Crazy Joe's crazy eyes were fixed right on him.

The idea of Crazy Joe on the opposite side of the line of scrimmage, just waiting to mow Billy down with his body instead of his rifle, had convinced Billy to pick Crazy Joe for his own team. Unfortunately, that hadn't stopped the guy from staring at him.

"Take a picture," Terrell said. "Lasts longer."

Crazy Joe shot him the finger. "We gonna play or what?"

"If you can take your eyes off Beej long enough. You queer for him or somethin'?"

Crazy Joe made smooching sounds in Billy's direction before he jogged to the secondary.

"That boy is weird."

"Picking on him doesn't make him less weird."

Terrell punched Billy's shoulder. "Got me there."

Deus played quarterback for Terrell's team, which had been his position in high school.

"He makes even me look good," Terrell said.

Everyone had insisted that Billy play QB on their team, though he never had, and it showed, which caused Flash to cackle and shout, "Bart Starr, my ass!"

On the first snap, Deus went back as if he was going to pass, and Billy tensed. He wasn't an athlete, and a lot of receivers got by him. But instead, Deus handed the ball to the running back, and the running back handed it to—

"Reverse!" Crazy Joe yelled as Terrell almost fumbled, then tucked the ball and ran.

He bobbed, he weaved; he nearly went down when one of the D-line grabbed at his foot, but he high-stepped, avoided the tackle, did an awkward spin, and—

"Hell," Billy muttered.

That spin had taken his friend dangerously close to the first stretch of barbed wire. If he bounced against that, it was gonna hurt.

"Terrell!" Billy swept his hands away from the fence like an official calling a receiver out of bounds.

Terrell stormed for the end zone; it was going to take a full-out tackle to stop him, but this close to the wire . . . probably not the best idea, so Billy performed the matador defense, and his friend flew past, grinning ear to ear. Terrell probably hadn't made a touchdown in his life. Something else he and Billy had in common.

Out of nowhere came Crazy Joe, eyes fixed on Terrell.

"No!" Billy meant to shout, but it came out a whisper instead as the horror of what he was about to see choked off his breath.

Crazy Joe planned to tackle Terrell straight into the barbed wire.

Instead, Terrell stopped on a dime—the matador move again —and Crazy Joe flew past, smacking into the waist-high wire so hard he spun over the top. He yowled like a scalded cat as the barbs bit skin, then he landed on his back on the mined side of the fence and . . .

Bam!

Billy didn't have to worry about Crazy Joe anymore.

Terrell's grin faded as pieces of Joe fell all around as well as on him. He dropped the football, then he threw up.

"Fumble!" Flash snatched the ball.

He would have run for the end zone—once an asshole, always an asshole—but Deus yanked the ball out of his hands and threw it as far as he could in the opposite direction, nearly hitting LT in the head when he stepped out of the mess tent.

From his leisurely exit, LT must have thought an animal had wandered into the minefield again. But what was all over the ground and Terrell was a lot bigger than an animal and definitely not furry.

LT crossed the distance in a few strides, his gaze bouncing from soldier to soldier; it didn't take him long to add two and two.

"Crazy Joe. What the fuck?"

"He . . . uh . . ." Terrell threw up again.

"He was going to tackle . . ." Deus pointed at Terrell. "But then Teej matadored him."

"He what?"

"You know . . ." Deus held out an imaginary cape, then theatrically yanked it aside as he stepped to the side too. "Matador."

LT blinked rapidly as if his brain were having a hard time matching the actions and the words. Maybe his brain was just having a hard time. Right now, wasn't everyone's?

"And then?" LT asked.

"Then Joe's momentum flipped him over the top and . . . " Deus made a kaboom motion with his fingers.

"Dammit. The paperwork on this shit is . . ." LT put his thumb between his eyes and rubbed. "Bag and tag him."

"But, LT—" Bama began.

LT dropped his hand. "Bag whatever's left on this side of the wire. We have orders to move out in the morning. So get it done and get some shut-eye."

"You heard him," Deus said as LT stalked away. "Move!"

"But how—?"

"Get a shovel, Bama, and shut up."

CHAPTER 13

Jay
"One More Parade"

illow Creek—July 4, 1967

Independence Day dawned clear and hot. Jay couldn't recall one that hadn't, though Momma told stories of parkas at parades. She always smiled when she said it, like it was a fond memory, but really . . . that would be such a bummer.

Jay had thought a lot about Billy's latest drawings. Who was the soldier with the target on his back? Billy? Someone else? What did it mean?

Jay pulled her red-and-white star-spangled tank top from the bottom of a drawer and yesterday's cutoff blue jean shorts from the floor. At least she'd have plenty to distract her today from things she'd have to think about tomorrow.

Momma sat in the kitchen still in her robe. The Fourth was a rare day off. No one got their hair done on a holiday. Of course, she'd been busy as a honeybee in springtime for the week leading up *to* the holiday.

"See you at the picnic!"

"Hold on."

Jay had her hand on the doorknob. So close.

"Let me braid your hair." Momma frowned at the wild mass tumbling over Jay's shoulders and halfway down her back. "You look like one of those flower children."

Jay looked the same as she had on every Independence Day since she'd gotten this shirt—at least three now—but she kept that to herself. Momma always chose holidays to girlie her up.

"I gotta meet Ronnie and Helen. If we don't get a seat on the curb by nine, we won't get one."

The newest mayor had put a stop to the pitching of tents on Maple Avenue the night before the parade. No one was allowed to even sit along the route until an hour before the festivities started, which only meant there'd be a lot of pushing and shoving this morning.

Momma crooked her finger, and Jay followed her to the kitchen. Arguing with her mother only prolonged the inevitable.

Momma separated, brushed, tugged, smoothed, the motions practiced and sure. She was done in less than five minutes. Jay had to admit the braid was cooler and kept her hair out of her face. If only Momma hadn't insisted on pinning the huge red bow on the crown of Jay's head.

"All I need is a lollipop and they'll let me right back into first grade."

"Watch your mouth," Momma said, but there wasn't any heat to her words, and she motioned for Jay to run along.

Ringo paced at the front door, unaware he wouldn't be joining her. The day would be too hot and too long for a dog. He stared at the bow as if he wanted to eat it. Maybe that wasn't a bad idea.

Jay lifted a hand, then Momma appeared in the kitchen doorway, her eyes sad, her smile melancholy. "You're growing up so fast it almost breaks my heart."

Jay's hand fell back to her side. "See you later." She patted Ringo. "Stay."

Ronnie and Helen had staked out what appeared to be the last open curb space on either side of the street. Ronnie held both elbows wide so she could occupy a larger area than she actually took up.

"Nine o'clock was five minutes ago." Ronnie dropped her arms and scooted sideways as Jay sat between her and Helen, then her gaze caught on the bow, and she started laughing.

Helen, who'd been reading *Much Ado About Nothing*, lifted her eyes and made much ado about the bow. "Oh, Jay, that's . . ." Laughter took over.

Several families in the vicinity glanced at them to see what was so hilarious, then they laughed too.

"Thanks a lot." Jay hunched her shoulders, trying to make herself smaller, but that only made the bow feel larger.

"Like no one was going to see that on their own." Ronnie's elbow came out again and jabbed Jay in the ribs. "Take it off before I hurt myself."

"I'm gonna hurt you."

"Big talk, Shirley Temple."

"If I take it off, I'll hurt my momma's feelings."

Ronnie stopped laughing. "Sheesh, we're seventeen. Not that anyone could tell by looking at you."

"Fuck you."

"Jay Johnson!" Mrs. Luchessi, whose five daughters under the age of seven sat in a row on the curb to their left, shook her finger. "That is not how a lady talks!"

Jay definitely wasn't a lady, but she *shouldn't* talk like that out loud and in public no matter what she was. Or wasn't.

"Sorry. You're right."

Mrs. Luchessi gave a sharp nod. Of course, she was right. "Girls, isn't Jay's hair pretty?"

Ronnie gave a short bark of laughter, but luckily, one of the little Luchessis puked what appeared to be blue cotton candy—where she'd gotten it this early in the morning was anyone's guess—and Mrs. Luchessi turned away to mind some of her own business.

In the distance, the high school band began to warm up in the parking lot of the school, which sat in the center of a former cornfield donated to the town when its owner died without male issue. An oddity in farm country, where parents usually kept trying until they popped out a boy—kind of like Henry VIII from what Jay remembered of history class. It handily explained the five Luchessi daughters as well as the bulge under Mrs. Luchessi's red, white, and blue tent dress.

"I gotta get out of this place."

Jay didn't realize she'd spoken out loud until Helen set her finger beneath the last line she'd read and turned her Coke-bottle lenses in Jay's direction. Though Helen was the one who resembled a bug under a microscope, Jay suddenly felt like one. "This is a good spot."

"I . . . uh . . . yeah. I was . . . um . . . singing. You know. The Animals."

"Hippie song, Jay." Ronnie punched her shoulder. "You're starting to worry me."

"It's just a song," Jay said, but was it?

"I don't think much of anything is just anything anymore." Ronnie stared across the street where Mags sat in the middle of all the cheerleady girls, giggling like she was one of them. Like she'd always been one of them.

"Mags is . . ." Jay shrugged. "Mags."

"Is she?"

"Unless there's been an *Invasion of the Body Snatchers*."

They'd seen the fifties horror movie at the Weber Theater

during Halloween week when they played gems like *The Blob* and *The Mummy.*

"I have been tempted to check her basement for a pod."

"Funny."

"Not really," Ronnie murmured.

Jay nearly confessed that Mags had come to see her, that Mags did still care, was just as confused as the rest of them, but then the parade marshal—always the oldest veteran in town who could still walk—carried the flag around the corner with the band right behind him, and conversations stalled.

Everyone stood until Mr. Galaway passed. It took a while. He'd been a marine in World War One and taken part in the Battle of Belleau Wood in France. He liked to tell the tale of Sergeant Daly, who'd shouted, "Come on, you sons of bitches, do you want to live forever?" before the marines attacked.

As Gramps had fought in the trenches and his stories were not nearly as exciting, though Billy listened to them with rapt attention over and over again, Billy loved Mr. Galaway's account. Even after Jay had looked up Belleau Woods and pointed out that most of those marines had died—Mr. Galaway only lost part of a foot; he was lucky—Billy still couldn't hear the story enough.

"The French renamed those woods *Bois de la Brigade de Marine*, Woods of the Marine Brigade. It was our biggest battle since Appomattox. The Germans called them *holendhunde.* Hellhounds."

Momma and Jay never stood a chance against all that. How could you fight hellhounds and heroes?

The band played Independence Day ditties, one after the other: "This Land is Your Land," "God Bless America," "America the Beautiful," "You're a Grand Old Flag." Would they ever run out?

"Forever in peace may you wave." Jay snorted. She couldn't

help it. How often had America been at peace since it had become America? She had no idea, and shouldn't she?

"Shh." Ronnie gave Jay another elbow.

Jay shushed her mouth, but her mind . . . it continued to wonder. Shouldn't peace be celebrated more than war?

The band marched on, followed by the antique car parade, and then the Little Leaguers strutting proudly in their uniforms.

"I hope this war ends before they're in it," someone murmured, and Jay looked behind them.

Mr. Nattasheim and Mr. Francola, their bright-white legs revealed for the first time all summer in their dad shorts, waved to their sons, who were young enough to wave back instead of being embarrassed by parental attention.

The idea that the war might still rage when those little kids were old enough to be called up made Jay shiver despite the sun's heat baking the top of her head and scalding the back of her neck.

"Why wouldn't it end long before then?" Mr. Francola asked.

"It's a mess. Half our troops are drug addicts." Mr. Nattasheim crossed his arms over a sport shirt only slightly whiter than his skin and glanced at Jay. She quickly turned away. When he spoke again, he'd lowered his voice. "I guess it's better to be high than drunk during a fire fight."

"Where'd you get that?"

Though they spoke softly, Jay listened hard and caught every word despite the mixture of music and laughter all around them.

"Wife's brother just got back from a tour. He's . . ." Mr. Nattasheim breathed in, then out. "Any loud noise and he hits the floor with one hand over his head, the other groping for a rifle he no longer has. He doesn't sleep; he wakes up screaming about VC."

"Shell shock."

"They're call it Post-Vietnam Syndrome now, but yeah. What

seems to bother him the most is that his sergeant was killed by accident."

"Friendly fire?"

"Maybe. My brother-in-law wasn't sure if it was that or if he'd been fragged."

Jay nearly turned around and asked what that was, but Mr. Francola beat her to it.

"It's what they call it when one soldier kills another," Mr. Nattasheim continued. "Someone said something, did something, or didn't. Maybe the sarge was too gung-ho, thought he was John Wayne, led them into danger one too many times and got guys killed. Or maybe he was just a jerk. I don't know."

The wind whispered across the back of Jay's neck. Hadn't Billy's drill sergeant labeled him the most gung-ho individual of all?

"Think about it. You're in the jungle with a rifle, a pistol, a grenade or ten. The guy in the lead is practically panting for a firefight. A buddy gets killed, then another, and pretty soon you figure life would be a lot safer if you made just one guy go away. Bam!"

"Jesus," Mr. Francola said.

Jay heard the rat-a-tat of gunfire followed by an explosion, saw bodies fly up in one piece, come down in a lot more, and she rubbed her arms against a sudden chill, but there wasn't a summer day hot enough to warm her right now.

Helen, whose focus was legendary and had probably heard every word even while she read her book, reached over and laced her fingers with Jay's. Jay tried to smile, but she couldn't manage it while straining to hear whatever else the men might say.

Ronnie stood and took a few steps into the street, shading her eyes as she tried to discover the reason for a sudden gap between the parade participants.

"We'd better get going so we can meet the boys at the fountain."

The men disappeared into the crowd.

"You okay?" Helen whispered.

Jay nodded and took back her hand, but she wasn't sure. It was the first time she'd heard the war talked about in the open, unless it was to say something along the lines of *Kick that commie ass!* and it made her think, it made her see, almost as clearly as Billy's sketches had, what life might be like over there.

It wasn't pretty, it wasn't patriotic; it was ugly, maybe all the time.

Ronnie rejoined them as another band from some other town turned the corner and marched toward them playing a snazzy jitterbug so the tiny dancers from the local dance school could shake their tutus.

"Remember dance class?" Ronnie asked.

"Nope." Helen stuck her nose back in Shakespeare.

"You were the lucky one."

Helen's family had not been able to afford something as frivolous as ballet and tap lessons.

"I didn't see it that way."

Dance was one of the few things the four of them had not done together. Ronnie and Jay had hated it so much they'd envied Helen's escape, never considering that she would feel left out and envious herself.

"You saw me in that tutu, right?" Ronnie scowled as the girls skipped past. "You know the saying about putting lipstick on a pig?"

"The tutu didn't look any better on me," Jay said.

Tutus were not made for the short and stout or for the stick-thin beanpole. Tutus were made for . . .

Mags. She had always stood front row center at the recitals. Did she miss that?

Jay's gaze flicked across the street, where Mags sat cocooned by her new friends. What was there to miss?

Clowns pranced between them, tugging along dogs wearing clown costumes, followed by horses. Wearing clown costumes. What was it with clowns?

The Willow Creek Independence Day parade was always the same, and Jay had loved it. She could depend on this parade never to change—unlike friends, brothers, parents, your body, the world, life. But today she wanted something to be different. One thing, just once.

Come on!

Members of the local VFW post toddled around the corner. Nothing new there.

"Aren't all our wars foreign?" Ronnie asked.

"Not the Civil War." Helen tilted her head. "Hence the word *civil.*"

"Seems pointless to specify that they're the veterans of the foreign war club when all the participants in the only non-foreign war have gotta be dead by now, right?"

"Mmm." Helen pointed at the street. "There's your gramps, Jay."

How could Jay have forgotten that Gramps always marched on Independence Day? Then he joined them for the picnic, returning to the farm right after since "cows had to be milked twice a day no matter what day it is." Would Gramps join them since Billy wasn't here to admire him and, as far as she knew, Gramps and Momma still weren't talking?

"How come he's carrying the final flag?" Helen got to her feet along with everyone else.

While the oldest veteran carried the first flag in the parade, the last was an honor reserved for one who had done something admirable over the past year: paid for a new roof on the VFW post, served drinks while the bartender was out with surgery—because if the bar at the VFW closed for more than a day, the

Earth stood still—mowed the VFW lawn or the lawn of a vet who couldn't mow his own any longer.

Gramps had never carried the final flag before. One thing different! Jay wasn't as excited about it as she'd thought she would be.

"Jay?"

Both Helen and Ronnie stared at her, waiting for . . .

"I . . . uh . . . don't know why he's . . ." Jay swooshed her hand back and forth to indicate her grandpa's placement in the VFW contingent.

Gramps must have thought she was waving at him because he waved back, grinning.

"Wow." Ronnie waved too. "I've never seen him crack a smile."

Jay hadn't either. What had Gramps done to deserve this beyond convince his grandson to enlist?

Shit. He'd convinced his grandson to enlist.

The parade petered out near Perry's statue, its participants scattering like bugs beneath a sudden light.

"Want some?" Helen asked as Old Lady Brown, owner of the grocery store, began to distribute red, white, and blue Bomb Pops.

Why was a popsicle the color of America called a *bomb*?

After that thought, Jay couldn't stomach one, so Ronnie followed Helen, and Jay headed for the shorter lemonade line in front of Pulaski's Tavern. It had to be eighty-five already, so cold and tangy over ice definitely appealed. And there, a few people ahead of Jay in line, stood Gramps, sharing a Polaroid photograph with his buddies.

Mr. Leslie slapped Gramps on the back. "I wish my grandson would send me a picture like that."

Mr. Carmichael snickered. "A little hard when he's studying to be a professional nose wiper."

"Elementary school teacher," Mr. Leslie corrected. "At least he isn't in Canada."

Mr. Carmichael's back went as straight as the flagpole in the center of town. "His fiancée lives there."

"Funny how they got engaged right after his draft notice showed up."

Mr. Carmichael's arthritic fingers curled inward, but they couldn't quite form a fist. He shifted to one shaky leg, maybe to try a swift kick instead, and Gramps handed him the Polaroid. "You wanna hold it for a while?"

What had Billy sent a picture of that was so fantastic?

Jay attempted to see over the shoulders of those in front of her. No luck. Then the photograph slipped from Mr. Carmichael's grasp, skating across the asphalt and landing upside down at her feet. How was that for luck?

She picked it up, then nearly dropped it herself. Her stomach did the same oily tumble of a few moments earlier when she'd considered Gramps was being rewarded for convincing Billy to go to war.

Unless he'd been rewarded for this.

In the photograph, soldiers circled a body, one had his boot planted on the chest of the enemy.

Billy had his boot planted on the chest of the enemy.

He appeared both older and younger, both proud and a bit horrified, strong and yet frighteningly weak, despite the bold *FIRST KILL* written at the bottom.

When she was at last able to drag her eyes from Billy to the enemy, she blinked. "He looks like a kid and not a communist."

"Janey." Gramps yanked the Polaroid from her hand. "What did you say?"

Only Gramps called her *Janey*, and she hated it.

"I believe she said the gook looked like a kid and not a communist," Mr. Leslie offered.

"Where'd you hear that nonsense?" Gramps couldn't tear *his* eyes from the picture any more than Jay could.

"Some hippie, no doubt." Mr. Carmichael's gaze flicked over Jay's shoulder, then narrowed.

She turned, and Paul, halfway up the block and the last in line, waved two fingers in a V. He wore a fringed vest without a shirt and a necklace of red, white, and blue beads. Was he trying to get beat up?

"Janey?"

Jay braced herself for questions. Who was that? Why was he waving? What was wrong with him? What was wrong with her? She should have known better than to think Gramps gave a fig about anyone but himself and Billy.

"What does age have to do with anything?"

Dogs and bones had nothing on Gramps.

"I heard little gook kids juggle hand grenades like tennis balls." Mr. Leslie made the motions of juggling.

"I don't know what that means," Jay said.

Gramps cast Mr. Leslie a glance that very clearly said *shut up.* "It means that you don't know what you're talking about."

"Women should be seen and not heard." Mr. Carmichael cackled like an old hen.

Gramps turned his back, dismissing Jay. "I trained Billy so well that when he walks point, no one dies. I bet he walks it more than anyone."

"Isn't point the most dangerous place to be?" Mr. Leslie asked.

"Facing danger is what makes a man."

The idea of her brother putting himself in more danger than anyone else in order to *be a man* caused Jay's hands to fist.

"How ya doin', Mr. Johnson?" Ronnie licked her Bomb Pop in a futile attempt to keep it from melting all over her.

"Uh . . ."

Gramps had no idea who Ronnie was, even though he had to

have seen her at least once a year, every year since they were three. Then again, he thought his only granddaughter's name was Janey.

"We gotta meet Helen." Ronnie hooked a sticky hand around Jay's elbow and tugged. "Happy Fourth!"

"His buddies call him Slayer," Gramps said before they'd gone five steps. "Isn't that great?"

One of the few things Billy had ever wanted was the approval of Gramps, and now he had it.

For killing a kid.

Jay nearly turned around, though what she would have done or said she had no idea, but Momma stood in the town square. Momma could not see that Polaroid.

"What was he talking about?" Ronnie offered Jay a lick of her patriotic popsicle.

Jay made a face, and Ronnie rolled her eyes, then continued to French kiss it.

"Just Gramps being Gramps."

Jay didn't plan on telling Ronnie what she'd seen. The fewer people who knew about the photograph the better. Though she was sure Momma would hear about it eventually, she wasn't going to hear about it from Jay on her first bonus day off since New Year's.

"What was that Slayer stuff?"

"Billy's nickname, I guess."

"Not a bad one to have." Ronnie continued for a few steps before she realized Jay wasn't at her side any longer. "What? You'd rather he was called something wimpy like . . ." Ronnie tossed what was left of her Bomb Pop, the stick, into a garbage can. "Junior or Skippy or . . ." Her forehead creased, then smoothed out, and she pointed her index finger at Jay like a gun. "Gomer. That would be bad."

"What difference does it make?"

"I'd rather think of myself as Slayer, kicking ass and taking names, than grinning, bumbling Gomer. Wouldn't you?"

Did Billy think of himself as Slayer now? Did Jay want him to?

"You should really take that ridiculous ribbon out of your hair."

Jay's hand went up and almost immediately encountered the hair ornament large enough to be seen from the moon. Too big to forget about, and yet, still, she had. Everyone must have seen it. Paul had seen it.

"You need help?" Ronnie reached for the bow, and Jay stepped back, shook her head as she indicated Momma, now talking to a few clients.

"Why can't you be yourself?" Ronnie made another grab, caught the end of the ribbon, and tugged.

Jay slapped her wrist. "You first."

Ronnie's hand fell back to her side; her freckles stood out against her pale skin like spaghetti sauce splatter on Momma's white tablecloth. "What does that mean?"

"Nothing. Never mind." Jay tried to walk past, and Ronnie grabbed her arm.

"Tell me what you meant."

Her fingers were so icy Jay jerked back, and Ronnie's nails drew pink furrows along her elbow. It made Jay mad. Yeah, she probably shouldn't say anything—here, now, anywhere, ever— but Ronnie had started it.

A lame excuse used by children, but the only one she had.

Jay lowered her voice. "Mags came over last night."

The twitch of Ronnie's eye told Jay louder than words that what Mags had said was true. What Jay hadn't known was that she'd been hoping it wasn't. Not because it changed anything between Ronnie and her, but because it changed things between Ronnie and the world. Secrets had a way of doing that.

"It doesn't matter," Jay said quickly.

Ronnie's face flushed so red her freckles nearly disappeared. "*What* doesn't matter? What, exactly, did the princess say?"

Jay glanced around. They were as alone as they'd ever be in a crowd comprised of the whole town, but no one was paying attention to them.

Jay shifted her shoulders, uneasy. "You know."

"With her, not really. Tell me."

When Jay hesitated, Ronnie shoved her in the chest. Not hard, but it was surprising enough that Jay stepped back.

Ronnie followed. "Did she want you to join her merry band of morons?"

Jay opened her mouth, and Ronnie shoved her again, harder this time.

"Did she want to give you a makeover? I hear your eyebrows need work."

Now they were starting to draw attention.

"Ronnie, maybe we should—"

"What?" Another shove. "Did?" Shove. "She?" Shove. "Say?"

The last shove caused Jay to trip over her own feet, and her cheeks went as hot as the rest of her, but she managed not to lose her temper. She did not shout. "She said you kissed her."

Ronnie pushed with both hands, and Jay landed on her ass. If anyone had missed the huge red bow in her hair before, they certainly saw it then as three-quarters of Willow Creek stared.

Jay met Ronnie's eyes and whispered, "With tongue."

They glared at each other—Jay on the ground, Ronnie looming over her—until Helen arrived, practically tiptoeing. "What's going on?"

What *was* going on? How had what Mags said—truth or not, Jay didn't care—caused this much trouble?

"Ronnie?" Helen's voice wobbled.

Ronnie didn't answer, but she did offer Jay a hand. Jay was so thrilled she grabbed it.

She was halfway to her feet when Ronnie said, "You tell

anyone else, and I'll make you sorry you learned to talk." Then she let go, and Jay fell all over again.

"Hey!" Helen exclaimed, but Ronnie was already striding away.

Helen's wide, panicked eyes met Jay's; her lower lip wobbled. Would Jay ever learn to keep her mouth shut?

"I'm fine." Jay held out a hand, but instead of taking it and helping her up, Helen chased after Ronnie.

Momma appeared and pulled Jay to her feet. "You okay?"

Jay wanted to rub her butt, but everyone was still staring. "I'll live."

Momma adjusted the bow in Jay's hair. "I'm sure whatever it is with the four of you will blow over."

Ronnie might forgive her for repeating what Mags had said, but Jay didn't think Ronnie would ever forgive Mags for saying it, or for anything else that had gone on this summer.

"Jay?"

Jay's throat went tight, and she had to swallow several times before she spoke. Even then her voice was faint, sounding young and scared and so very not her. "You always told me we'd grow apart."

The crease between Momma's eyebrows deepened. "I figured I was wrong."

"Shouldn't friends be friends forever? For always? No matter what?"

"In a perfect world."

"The world's not perfect," Jay whispered.

"No." Momma put her arm around Jay's shoulders; Jay put her arm around Momma's waist. Her mother softly touched Jay's hair. "Let's eat."

The Ladies Auxiliary hosted the picnic. For a dollar each, they could load paper plates with hot dogs, hamburgers, potato salad, corn on the cob, and what else but apple pie?

Sometimes Willow Creek was such a cliché it made Jay laugh. When she felt like laughing.

She played with her food, didn't eat much because she kept scanning the crowd for a glimpse of Ronnie and Helen. Jay wanted to make things right before they went even more wrong. Who was she if she wasn't one of four?

"Billy loves corn on the cob." Momma crunched a bite of her own. "What do you think he's eating today?"

Hopefully not a dirt sandwich.

Jay filled her mouth with enough hot dog and bun so *that* didn't slip out. Where had she heard it?

I left most of my buddies munching on dirt sandwiches in France.

Gramps. Who else?

Jay hadn't caught sight of her grandfather since she'd left him in front of Pulaski's. Maybe he'd taken his Polaroid and gone home.

"Did you see your grandpa?"

Jay choked on the mouthful of hot dog and wondered, not for the first time, if Momma read minds.

She drank some lemonade, grimaced. Lemonade and hot dog did not mix well. "He was in the parade."

Not a lie. Gramps had been.

Momma continued to wait. She definitely read minds.

"I talked to him in the lemonade line," Jay blurted, then bit her lip to stop the rest. She needn't have bothered.

"Where he showed you the photo from Billy?"

Damn small-town grapevine.

Jay nodded.

"What was it a picture of?"

"No one told you?"

"No one saw it—for his cronies' eyes only—but they saw Gramps show the photo to you."

"He didn't, not really. Mr. Carmichael dropped it. You know how bad his hands are now with the arthritis, then I picked it up, and . . ." Jay refused to allow her lower lip to tremble, even though it wanted to. "Oh, Momma."

Momma began to move her food around. She hadn't eaten much more than Jay had. "What did you see?"

Jay could lie, but not only would Momma know, Jay wouldn't put it past her to drive to the farm, knock on the front door, and demand that Gramps produce the Polaroid. It would be easier for them both if Jay came clean.

"American soldiers gathered around the body of an enemy."

Jay was not telling Momma that the enemy had appeared about thirteen.

"Random American soldiers?"

Again, Jay could lie and say yes. For all Momma knew, Billy had taken the picture instead of starring in it. But lies had a way of biting your ass, same as secrets. Weren't lies and secrets the reason the Four Musketeers were down to two? Or was it one?

"One of them was Billy."

Momma remained quiet, studiously separating the potatoes from the onions in her salad. "I've heard that GIs often take pictures with their first kill."

Relief nipped at the heels of Jay's wince. She wouldn't have to say it out loud. Momma already knew.

"Better than the other way around," Momma continued.

Wait . . .

"What?"

"Well, I sure don't want Billy starring in the first-kill Polaroid of the enemy." Momma took a big bite of potatoes, chewed once, then looked around as if she wanted to spit them out.

"I doubt the VC have Polaroid cameras." Unless they'd taken them off a dead GI.

What was wrong with her? With Gramps? With Momma? What was wrong with the world?

Vietnam.

"They call him Slayer," Jay said.

Momma spit the potato salad into her napkin. "Okay."

"That's not who Billy is."

"It's not who he was." Momma set the napkin on top of her nearly full plate.

"Is that who you want him to be?"

"I want him to be whoever or whatever he has to be to come home exactly as he was when he left."

"But he isn't going to be. You just said that."

Momma sighed.

"That dead soldier was some other mother's son." As the words came out of Jay's mouth, she realized how true they were, and her eyes prickled.

"Sometimes, Jay, it's like I don't even know you anymore."

All that she had heard, seen, said, done since the beginning of summer came together to reveal one simple truth.

Jay yanked the bow out of her hair and tossed it on top of Momma's plate. "That makes two of us."

<h1 style="text-align:center">CHAPTER 14</h1>

Billy
"Bungle in the Jungle"

*V*ietnam—July 1967

The line of GIs trailed through the jungle. Some had slept, some hadn't, which made that morning no different from any other, even though it was.

Or maybe it wasn't. They walked through the same overgrown maze, hacked at the same overgrown bamboo with the same three machetes, and when it got too thick or someone heard something, they crawled instead. They listened to the same birds, got bit by the same bugs; they smelled the same stink of sweat and mud and rot.

Billy kept waiting to feel . . . sad? Mad? He shouldn't be relieved, but he was. For the first time in a long time his back didn't itch, and that alone made him feel damn good.

Terrell still seemed shaky. At night he'd stare into space,

rhythmically rubbing his head though he'd showered for a half hour after Crazy Joe went *boom*, and no one had even complained that he was using all the water. If anyone deserved to scrub over and over, it was Terrell.

He often asked Billy to check his hair to make sure *he all outta there.* Billy thought it obvious, given the shorn stubble of Terrell's fro, that there was nothing in there but his own scalp. Nevertheless, Billy would check, then tell his friend *all clear*, but Terrell still stared, still rubbed, still asked.

"We always at point," complained Big Al, a Negro so tiny his back had a hump from the weight of his gear. "Always."

The Negroes grumbled that they walked the most dangerous of positions more than anyone else, but that wasn't true. LT was fair. Since the white guys grumbled just the same, that only proved he was.

About an hour in, a flicker to the right caused Billy, leading flank, to take a knee. Everyone behind him did the same. But the point hadn't seen Billy, or the flicker, so they kept going, and several guys went down the hard way.

Madness followed—rifles firing, grenades flipping end over end all over the place; Dutch and his ammo guy dove behind some trees and lit up the world.

When the gunner paused to reload, and the jungle stopped dancing and jigging from the M60 fallout, Billy was able to narrow the field of enemy position by the sound of their AKs. Then a renegade beam of sunlight pierced the triple canopy jungle and twinkled along what had to be the barrel of an AK. Billy took the shot.

A body hit the ground; he'd been right.

Billy breathed in, then out, he watched, he listened, but he did . . . not . . . think. And . . . just there to the left . . . a sparkle.

Another VC fell. Then another.

His buddies fired where Billy had, and after that, the enemy retreated pretty fast.

Bones inched over to the wounded. He lifted three fingers, then whirled one in the air.

"We got three peanuts, three peanuts." Sparky spoke softly into the handset. "Need a dustoff." He continued with the number jargon used to identify each platoon and command as well as their location.

The army never referred to their wounded or dead as anything but a peanut or Kool-Aid because they didn't want the VC to know a platoon was shorthanded, or that a chopper—always a dustoff—was on the way.

"Keep your eyes peeled." Deus combat-crawled close. "Sometimes they leave a dink or two behind to pick us off when we abandon cover."

Billy lifted his thumb. He'd learned that his first day here.

"I've also seen them hang around and shoot down a dustoff, though I don't know how they manage it."

"AKs," Billy murmured.

"Still a helluva shot. Heard they brought one down last month with a crossbow. I'm not gonna believe that until I see it, but I hope I never do."

Billy hoped he never saw it either, especially on his watch.

Ten minutes later, when Billy's eyes had started to burn from staring into the shifting shadows caused by a blistering sun doing its best to fry both the vegetation and their minds, LT called, "Johnson?"

"Nothing." Billy kept his rifle pointed right where it had been.

Everyone else climbed to their feet as he covered them. When no shots rang out, Billy stood and nearly got sucker punched as what was left of point rushed flank and tail-end. Terrell stepped in the way and took it on the jaw instead.

It wasn't until LT started separating people that Billy realized the skirmish had been Negroes against whites more than point against the rest. This wasn't new; what was new was that it had erupted into physical blows in the field rather than low-voiced insults.

"What's wrong with y'all?" Terrell stood in front of Billy, fists raised. "Beej just saved us."

"He saved *them*." Hammer stabbed a huge finger at the white guys. "Ya dumb, nig—"

Billy had to drop his M16 so he could grab Terrell before he jumped on Hammer and got himself killed. Until today, Terrell had been the most level-headed, relaxed guy Billy had ever known.

"Beej ain't like that." Terrell shifted his shoulders, so Billy released him, though he stayed within grabbing distance; he left his rifle where it lay. "And he's about the only one."

A few guys nodded. LT stood back, letting them work it out.

"Slayer is the best on point," Hammer said. "He sees things no one else does."

Now everyone nodded. Truth was truth, and whenever Billy walked point, no one got killed, no one had even gotten shot.

When Hammer called him Slayer, Billy didn't mind so much. He kinda liked it. The more he answered to the nickname, the more he felt like he should. Slayer was badass, damn near indestructible; Slayer caused fear, he didn't feel fear. When Billy thought about it like that, Slayer was who he wanted to be.

"He always up front for *his* people. What about us?"

"You're all my people."

Hammer snorted. Big Al outright laughed.

"I refuse to fight a man who wears the same uniform as me." Billy remembered what Drill Sergeant Garrett had told them, seemed like a lifetime ago. "If we don't stick together, if we don't have one another's backs no matter what color that back is, we aren't gonna make it outta here."

"He's right," LT said quietly.

"The enemy is them." Billy jabbed his thumb over his shoulder. "Not us." He switched his forefinger back and forth between the two groups, still divided into white and Black, except for Billy and Terrell in the middle. "Okay?"

Begrudgingly, Hammer nodded.

Billy looked at Flash, who always had something to say.

Flash remained stubbornly silent until Deus elbowed him, hard, in the ribs and dislodged a disgruntled, "Yeah."

"I don't care who I walk with."

Total lie. Billy wanted to walk where he had Terrell's and Bama's six, or they had his, except Hammer was right. It wasn't fair, and Billy wanted to keep the peace. They'd wear out on fighting one another and have nothing left for the enemy.

"If he's on point for you, then he isn't for us," Flash said. "Screw that."

"We want him half the time." Hammer's fists not only hit like hammers but looked like them too.

"No way in hell," Flash snapped.

The two groups moved forward, ready to fight again.

Billy held up his hands. "I'll walk in front for everyone."

"Hold on—" LT began.

"You been callin' him the QB," Hammer said, snotty-like. "QB leads the way. You okay with permanent point, Slayer?"

"Sure."

"Works for me." Hammer cast a narrow glance at Flash. "How 'bout you?"

Flash's lips curved—not a smile, not really. "Works for me too."

He put out his hand, but when Hammer tried to shake it, he pulled it back and made the motion of running his fingers through his hair like a fifties greaser, even though he wore a steel pot, beneath which there was very little hair, then he cackled like an idiot.

Deus shoved Flash aside before Hammer hammered him. "You sure about this, Johnson?"

Billy nodded, and Deus grabbed Hammer's hand, pumped it up and down.

"That's all well and good," LT said. "But none of you are in charge. Orders are to rotate point, flank, and tail-end."

"Everyone will." *But me* was left unsaid. "You know I'm the best at point." Billy suddenly saw how things could play out—they'd be safer, they'd do better, maybe they'd all get along—and he didn't want to go back to the way things had been.

"It isn't procedure."

"As if anything's procedure out here," Flash said.

"There's not following procedure because things have deteriorated into chaos, and there's not following procedure on purpose."

"We aren't gonna tell." Flash flicked his gaze at the group, but they were already shaking their heads.

"Point gets shot at the most," Terrell said. "That ain't fair; that ain't right."

"As if anything's fair or right out here either," someone mumbled from the rear.

"Point does get shot at the most," Billy agreed. "But if I was in the lead, none of us would get shot at as much as we do now."

Billy knew it; the others knew it. LT had to know it too.

"If me walking in front helps us work together, won't that mean less of us dead and more of them?"

LT rubbed his nose. "In theory."

"Then what's the harm?"

LT sighed and dropped his arm. "Let's hope there isn't any."

Terrell scowled mightily in Billy's direction, but Billy ignored him. If he was going to do this, and it looked like he was, he wanted something too.

"If I'm the QB, then the rest of you need to be a team. If we wanna get out of here in one piece, we stick together. You wanna go home and kill one another, have at it, but not here.

Here we kill them. I'll lead point, but I want the rest of you to rotate behind me. And you're all gonna be mixed together. Anyone doesn't hold up his position, doesn't defend his brother no matter what color he is, then that guy gets to walk first in line. Agreed?"

Glances, snarls, and a few shoves were exchanged, but they agreed.

"Dustoff on the way," Sparky said. "No LZ near enough to land. We need to hump those peanuts to a break in the canopy about a klick west."

Sometimes dustoffs had to hover over the jungle, lower a basket if the peanut could sit up, a litter if they couldn't, then haul the wounded up and fly away. It wasn't ideal, but it was quicker than finding an LZ in areas where there weren't many or there weren't any that weren't hot.

"Grab those peanuts," LT ordered, and the men closest to the wounded did just that without the usual jostling to assure that white carried white and so on.

Maybe things would get better.

"You an idiot." Terrell pushed Billy forward, and Billy got worried. If he lost his best friend, wouldn't that make things worse?

"Terrell, I—"

"You got a damn death wish." Terrell muscled the soldier nearest the front behind him so that Terrell would have Billy's six. "And now I got me one too, I guess."

Bama shouldered between Terrell and that same guy. "So do I."

"Permanent point, my ass." Terrell seemed more himself, like he'd forgotten the other day in the drama of this one. "Hero complex more like. Folks start callin' you Slayer, and you start believin' that shit. Gonna get us all killed."

"I won't."

Confidence flowed through Billy. He could do this; he would do this. He would not fail. He'd be a hero just like Terrell said. Just like Billy had always dreamed.

How could Gramps not be proud of him then?

CHAPTER 15

Jay
"Talking Vietnam Blues"

Willow Creek—July 4, 1967

Jay awoke in the clearing as shadows flickered across her face. The sun was dying. She'd been here a while.

She'd dreamed of Billy at the head of a long line of soldiers, slogging through a jungle so dense he had to hack at it with a machete to gain a single inch. Wearing raggedy uniforms, the green dulled by dirt and age, their faces as filthy as their hands, everyone blended into their surroundings, except her brother, who sported a target on his back that glowed like neon in the gloom.

Jay lay there a minute, remembering Momma's words. Momma didn't know her anymore? Lately, Jay didn't know herself. So many new thoughts—about the war, Vietnam, her brother, her friends. So many new feelings—about the war, Vietnam, her brother, her friends. Paul.

She had never remained at the clearing this late in the day. Even before this summer's curfew, Momma liked her home, or in the vicinity, before dark. There were bears in these woods, and while most would gallop in the opposite direction the instant they heard or smelled a human, there was always the off chance of running into one that was stupid, deaf, or just in a fightin' mood.

"No, thank you," Jay murmured, and her voice, even at that volume, was so loud in the twilight stillness she winced and got to her feet.

Jay trudged toward town as the sun fell, and while she could still see a blaze of orange to the west, the forest around her went dark as a rainy night. She knew her way; she wasn't frightened. Nevertheless, the familiar *oom-pa-pa, oom-pa-pa* of the same polka band that had played at every Willow Creek gathering for decades was a comfort. Then familiar laughter mingled with the music and drew Jay to the edge of the trees.

Ronnie and Helen sat, shoulder-to-shoulder, on a blanket not a dozen yards away. Seeing them there, like that—two where it had always been four—caused the same drop in her stomach that she'd felt as Billy's bus drove away. Without her brother, without her friends . . . who was she? The fear, the confusion . . . she wasn't certain what to do with them anymore.

Were feelings like these the reason Billy had embraced the nickname "Slayer"?

A hand landed on her arm, and she spun, fists up.

"Hey!" Paul drew back. "Sorry."

"What are you doing here?"

"Waiting for the fireworks."

Fireworks. Right. Independence Day seemed so long ago, even though proof that it was not danced and sang and laughed nearby.

"Why are you waiting in the woods?"

"Everyone's so . . ." He drew a square in the air with his index fingers.

Jay took in his vest, the beads, the sandals and lifted her eyebrows. "You didn't really expect them to—?"

"Admire original thought? Understand freedom of expression? Believe in the right to choose . . . whatever? Whoever? However?"

"Yes," Jay said. "Those."

Paul laughed; his bare arm brushed hers, and suddenly she couldn't breathe. She wanted . . . everything? Anything? All the things? Problem was, she didn't know what those things were beyond a few hints in the school locker room or at slumber parties, and she thought most of that was baloney.

"Three-J, don't you want to learn the truth?" He lifted one shoulder. "I know I go on and on about the war, but you let me, and thanks for that. Even my mom tells me to stow it sometimes." His blue eyes flicked to hers, then away. "From what I've seen, you're you, always. You're not trying to be cool, and because of that, you are."

If not trying to be cool was cool, that was definitely her.

"I saw you earlier with your friends. With your mom."

Jay wanted to crawl in a hole and pull the hole in after her. Paul had seen her get knocked down. He'd seen her visible-from-the-moon red bow; he'd seen her throw said bow on top of Momma's plate like a three-year-old having a tantrum.

That he was still here and talking to her convinced Jay more than anything else that Paul was different. Paul was . . . what? The guy she'd been waiting for all her life?

That was something Mags would think. Not Jay. Not hardly. So why did she want so badly for him to be who she thought he was? Because he seemed to see her, really see her the way no one else did, even herself? Or was it that she needed someone, anyone, to fill that hole where her friends, her brother used to live?

She'd tried to tell the Musketeers what she felt; she'd tried to tell Momma what she thought, what she feared, but no one wanted to hear it; no one wanted to know. They wanted Jay to be the Jay she'd always been—following along, getting along, never making waves, never causing trouble. But she wasn't that Jay anymore; she didn't think she could be.

"You went into the woods," he continued, "and you didn't come back. I was worried."

No one else had worried about her. Had anyone else even noticed she'd been gone?

Jay's gaze cut to the town square where her friends, or girls who had once been friends but now she wasn't sure what they were, seemed just fine without her.

And there was Momma talking to Mr. Jeffries, the school janitor. He was old—like forty maybe even fifty—though his limp, from a wound courtesy of D-day, probably made him seem older than he was. Jeffries touched Momma's arm, and she laughed. Momma seemed just fine without Jay too.

"Let's go." Jay headed back the way she'd come.

Paul had to hurry to keep up. "I didn't think you wanted me there."

"Think again."

The last rays of the dying sun through the leaves shaded the whispering grass an eerie greenish-blue, but when Jay dropped onto it, the familiar swish of the blades against her skin made her feel . . . not all right but better, and that was probably the best she could hope for.

"If your friends come, will they be mad if I'm here too? The clearing's your place, not mine. I dig it."

"They aren't coming."

Jay waited for him to ask *why not*, but he didn't, and she was glad. The reasons were complicated, private, and she would not be the one to spill them to someone who was little more than a stranger. No matter how good he smelled.

Paul sat next to her, then leaned back on his elbows; the vest fell open, exposing more of his smooth, tan chest. Her eyes caught on a thin line of hair below his belly button, which was lighter than his skin but darker than his head hair. Her stomach twirled, slow and warm; her fingers itched to touch. Was it as soft as it looked? Would finding out make her a slut? Did she care?

Jay breathed in. All day in the sun and Paul still smelled like limes.

"Have you heard from your brother?"

The heat, the tingle vanished as the memory of Billy's most recent sketches flooded Jay's mind. The brother who had drawn the cratered landscape, the body-part zombies—the brother now known as Slayer—was not anyone she knew, and it scared her.

The world wasn't the way it had always been; to fix it, things had to change. Jay was starting to think that the only way to do that was to make waves, follow a different path. Not everyone was going to get along. Not anymore. Maybe not ever again. She'd learned that the hard way today.

The only one who seemed to get it lately, to get her, was Paul.

"My brother sent more drawings."

Paul sat up, and his vest slid forward, removing most of his chest from view. Probably for the best, but she missed it.

He lifted his face to the now-purple sky. "You wanna talk about them?"

Jay swallowed the unpleasant lump that threatened the base of her throat. She either shouldn't have eaten the hot dog or she should have eaten more of it.

"Yes. And also no."

"It's cool." He continued to stare at the stars as if he had all the time in the world to do just that.

The whirling inside Jay seemed to ease as she listened to the steady in, the steady out of his breathing. "The drawings weren't the worst of it."

"Okay."

He said nothing else; he didn't push; he sat next to her, and he waited, so she told him about the Polaroid, about Gramps, about Billy's new nickname and his skill at walking point. When she was done, Paul set his hand over hers where it rested on her knee, and it felt better than anything had in a long, long time.

What was it about Paul that calmed her? What was it about him that had made her want to confess everything, even though she probably shouldn't?

"Is your brother as good with a gun as your granddad thinks he is?"

"Yes," she said slowly. "He can hit whatever he aims at, except . . ." And this was what had worried Jay all along, yet no one—not Momma, not Gramps and certainly not Billy—had ever mentioned it. "He's never aimed at anything but a target."

"He's aimed at something other than a target in Vietnam, and he's hit it at least once, considering the Polaroid."

"It's what he's supposed to do."

"I know, but—"

"But what?" Anger sparked, and Jay wasn't sure why. So far Paul hadn't said anything she hadn't thought already.

"That doesn't make it right."

"If he doesn't, he'll be dead, and that is so far from right I can't even see it from here."

"The guy he killed is some other sister's brother."

Had Paul not only seen her argument with her mother but heard it too? So what if he had? Truth was truth.

"Better hers than mine."

Paul withdrew his hand. Jay waited for him to tell her she

was a selfish, evil bitch, then get up and walk away. Instead, he put his arm around her shoulders and drew her close. "I hear you. I get that."

For a moment, Jay let herself sit there with him as if she were just a girl, cooling it in a forest clearing with the new boy who made her want things she'd never much wanted before. Secret things. Forbidden things. Things only a woman should know.

But now was not the time; this was not the place.

"Billy has always wanted to become a man our gramps can be proud of."

"Does killing a man make you a man?"

"In Vietnam? Maybe. Not killing gets you dead, and then you aren't anything at all. You're just dead."

Paul nodded. "The war is . . ." He considered for a moment. Then shrugged. "Fucked up."

Jay had been thinking of other words—*horrible, twisted, frightening*—but *fucked up* was probably the best choice. Even if she supported the war, or at least her brother's role in it, she could still think parts of it, as well as some of the people fighting it, were fucked up.

The distant *whoosh-boom* of the first firework sounded, and above them blue sparkles exploded, then rained like melting wax.

Whoosh-boom, whoosh-boom, whoosh-boom.

White, then red, then gold all tumbled together and then . . .

Boom.

Jay jerked, and Paul's arm tightened. "It's okay."

She laid her head on his shoulder, just because, as colors shot across the navy-blue night. "What do you think it's like over there for him?"

"Hard to say, but I doubt your brother's sitting on the grass with his arm around a girl, watching fireworks."

"No," she agreed. "The grass there isn't like this."

. . . the edges are sharper than a razor and it's slipperier than black ice if you step on it.

"There's probably a lot that isn't like this."

"Definitely no girls."

"Oh, there are girls. Mostly for sale."

Jay might be naïve, but she knew what that meant. "Billy would never. . ."

Did she really know what Billy would do or not do anymore? Before that morning, the idea of her brother killing someone, then posing in a picture of it had never entered her head.

"Never?" Paul asked. "Does he have a girlfriend?"

Billy had barely had *a* friend.

"Never," Jay echoed.

"So he's . . ."

"Shy. Yeah."

Only when Paul made a soft sound of amusement did Jay realize he'd meant something else. Annoyance flared, followed quickly by a trace of fear. Was that how Ronnie felt? If so, no wonder she was prickly all the time.

"Just because Billy likes to draw and is quieter than most doesn't mean—"

"I was just asking."

"Probably shouldn't ask that in Willow Creek."

"Because there are no homosexuals in Willow Creek?"

Maybe one but Jay would never tell. No matter what Ronnie had done and said, no matter who she was or might become, she was still Ronnie, and Jay had spent more of her life loving her than she'd spent not.

"If there are," Jay said, "they certainly aren't going to tell anyone. Not here. Not yet anyway." Maybe not ever. "You must think we're huge hicks."

Paul's shoulder shifted, rubbing the bare skin of his upper

arm against the bare skin of hers, and despite the still, heated night, Jay stifled a shiver. "Not you."

She turned her head; he was smiling. Why did she like him so much?

Because he shoveled no bullshit. He told it like it was. She hadn't realized how much she needed someone to.

Paul draped his elbows over his knees, returned his gaze to the sky.

What had just happened? They'd been staring into each other's eyes, and then they weren't. He'd had his arm around her, and then he didn't. She'd either done something she shouldn't have or not done something she should.

She was so damn bad at this.

Another skyrocket exploded, the glow spreading over Paul's face. Jay wanted to touch it so desperately she sat on her hands. He'd been the one to pull away, to touch him now would be . . . bold? Fast? Pathetic?

Yes.

"I . . . uh . . ." Jay's mind groped for something, anything, to say so he didn't notice her confusion or her longing. "I read in *Rally!* that Hanoi is going to be one of the most air-defensible cities in the world thanks to the equipment China is sending. Russia too."

Paul cast Jay a look that made her think she'd surprised him. She liked that look; she thought she'd like to surprise him again and again for a very long time.

"Commies always stick together."

Silence fell, then Paul gave a short, sharp laugh. "Of course they do."

Jay's cheeks warmed. She'd started out so well; she'd actually said something intelligent, but she couldn't leave it there. No. She had to parrot what she'd heard at home like the child she was.

"I never thought . . ." she began, then tightened her lips.

Obviously, she'd never thought—for herself—or at least she hadn't started to until Billy left and everything seemed wrong. "People talk like the Viet Cong are a bunch of farmers with pitchforks. Maybe some have ancient weapons that barely fire, but they're lucky if they have the ammo for them."

"Even if that were true, and I don't think it is, they're still fighting on their own ground. They know that jungle. We don't."

Jay blinked. "You don't think we can win."

"Do you?"

"We're . . . America."

"So we can't lose?" Paul threw up his hands. "The French fought there for over a decade and got nowhere. Why do we think we can waltz right in and do what they couldn't?"

Jay had never considered that America might lose. All she'd considered was that she might lose Billy.

That no one had mentioned losing somewhere along the line, at least in her hearing, made Jay consider that what they'd been told on the news, in the papers, in school, at home, and in public was being manipulated; at the very least, it was being managed. Which was a new thought, an odd thought, a disturbing thought, like so many others these days.

The world outside Willow Creek seemed to grow bigger and bigger with everything Jay didn't know, every place she'd never seen.

A solitary firework exploded into the stillness that always fell right before the finale's chaos.

"How do you know so much about Vietnam?" she asked.

"Since I want to be an investigative reporter, the editor at *Rally!* lets me hang out, even write a little. Mostly ad copy, but it's something."

"That's . . ." Jay paused, trying to identify the emotion that had risen at his words. She was surprised to discover it was admiration. She didn't know what she wanted to do tomorrow, let alone for the rest of her life. "Cool."

Paul's shoulders, which had been scrunched nearly to his ears, lowered. He turned his head, hope all over his face. "You aren't mad?"

She was struck dumb for an instant by how gorgeous he was. Why on Earth was he here with her?

"Three-J?" Paul brushed his thumb over the place where her bump had been.

"Hmm?" She leaned closer, and he cupped the back of her head as his gaze dropped to her lips.

Her first kiss had been behind the storage shed at school. She was twelve, Tommy Mueller eleven. Tommy had always been ahead of the curve—at least until he'd missed the curve outside town going ninety in his brother's Dodge Charger. As Momma always said, *trees don't move*. Today Tommy was six feet under and would never move again.

Sheesh! Now was not the time for that thought. Or for the one that followed, which was the memory of Tommy's tongue pushing at hers, and the revulsion that had made her punch him in the nose. She felt bad about that, considering.

Paul drew her closer, and a tingling warmth unfurled down low. Nothing like that had happened when she'd necked with Rob Stonecroft at Mags's sweet sixteen party. The instant Rob had set his hand on top of her shirt, on top of her breast, she'd suddenly had an uncontrollable desire for a piece of birthday cake.

All of that flashed through Jay's mind in an instant, the way things did. But then Paul's mouth touched hers, and she couldn't breathe; she could barely think. Thank God.

His lips were warm and soft, gentle. Their breath mingled, and she didn't even worry if hers smelled like hot dogs; his didn't. He tasted like morning rain—fresh, clean, a chill gray-blue. But he smelled green—limes, yes, but something else, too, something of the earth. Not grass but—

His tongue slid along the seam of her lips, and she could breathe again. Faster than before, faster than she should because her chest tightened; her head went light, and she grabbed onto him because she felt like she was falling.

His biceps tightened against her palms, and the warmth down low blazed and danced. When his tongue touched hers, it was nothing like Tommy's had been. Just a flick at the end, and her brain melted; her breasts sizzled.

The earth beneath them trembled. No wonder Therese Madden had gotten pregnant her senior year and ended up living with her aunt in Topeka. Who could stop something like that if it felt like this?

The finale went off like a rocket—many, many rockets—and the kiss ended. They remained nose-to-nose, their breath still mingling, their eyes locked on each other's as so much light flared above that the clearing lit up like . . . well, the Fourth of July.

Jay's fingers still clutched Paul's biceps. His hand now cupped the back of her neck. They might be frozen, except sweat trickled between Jay's breasts, and a drop slid along Paul's neck—slowly over his collarbone, then fast down his chest until it reached that line of hair she'd been so interested in, then completely forgotten about when he'd kissed her.

She reached for it, and he grabbed her wrist with a sharp intake of breath.

"Whoa." His voice wobbled. From the force of the fireworks? Someone had spent a lot of money on fireworks this year. "We should stop. I don't—"

Jay yanked her wrist from his grasp as everything that had been warm went suddenly cold. "Want to. I get it."

He could have anyone; why would he want her?

"Oh, no." Paul laughed and flapped a hand at his shorts, which were a lot tighter than they'd been before.

The sight kind of turned her on, and the tingles that had begun to fade roared back.

"I definitely want to. But I don't have . . . uh . . . anything."

From where Jay was sitting, he had everything.

"I never . . ." Paul sighed and wrapped his fingers around her neck, drawing her near enough to kiss her nose. "Have you ever?"

She blinked once, twice, again as the sense of that settled. What guy admitted that he'd never?

Wide-eyed, Jay shook her head.

The finale ended as it had begun, with a single, tree-rattling boom. The silence that followed seemed as loud as the fireworks had been, the babble of the creek faint and very far away.

Embarrassment swamped her. What did you say after confessing virginity?

Paul stood, and she couldn't see his face; she didn't know what he was thinking.

He offered a hand. "You wanna go to State Street with me?"

Jay had yet to set foot on State Street—a bohemian avenue that led to the capitol building in Madison, a tree-infested thirty miles from where they sat—though she badly wanted to.

However, due to several protests in the area, whenever Jay mentioned State Street, her mother's eye began to twitch. Momma thought the place was dangerous.

Jay should probably say no, not only because of Momma's eye twitch but because spending time with Paul was going to cause trouble eventually, and trouble she had enough of already.

Except she wanted to. And she was getting really, really sick of not doing what she wanted, not being who she was, not saying what she thought.

So Jay put her hand in his and said, "Groovy."

CHAPTER 16

Billy
"The Men Behind the Guns"

Vietnam—July 1967

Within two weeks, an increase in the body counts reported by LT, combined with the decrease in casualties, drew the attention of command, and the platoon was sent to cool their heels at Camp Enari until some colonel showed up to give LT an ARCOM—Army Commendation Medal.

"They actually asked me if I was inflating body counts."

LT blew smoke out of his nose so hard he reminded Billy of a carny game where striking the bull's-eye of a poorly carved wooden bull caused smoke to shoot from its nose as a bell rang and the tail swung up. Billy had wasted three dollars trying to win Jay a stuffed cat. If only he could have used his rifle and a bullet rather than his hand and a softball.

"I should have admitted to body count fuckery rather than telling the truth and having to put up with this."

"You didn't—" Billy began, then bit off the rest at LT's sharp glance.

"I told them we'd found a way to get along." He turned that gaze on the rest of the platoon, which had gathered around on his orders. "I didn't tell them the specifics behind that, and no one else had better either."

"Naw, sir, Mr. LT, we won't say nothin' to the big boss man." Big Al laughed so hard he had to hold his stomach.

"He won't." Deus hip-checked Big Al, who had to straighten up or fall down. "*We* won't."

Others nodded or mumbled agreement, and Billy noticed, not for the first time, that marching together, working together, living, eating, breathing together had caused them to stand together, even at ease. Sure, there were groups of two or three black guys or white guys here and there in the crowd, but mostly, they all just gathered now however they gathered, mixed however they mixed. It made Billy as proud as their reduced casualty rates.

Guys still fought. Hammer and Flash were mad at the world and everyone in it half the time, and Vietnam wasn't making them any less angry, which meant some days they punched someone, but it wasn't as much about race as it used to be.

The distinct *whoop-whoop* of an approaching transport had LT tossing his cig, motioning for everyone to do the same. "Button up, covers on, at attention until told otherwise. No saluting."

They'd been briefed already, but standing around in heat that easily topped one hundred degrees, they'd unbuttoned and uncovered. Everyone hustled into line, straightening and tucking. By the time the bird landed and the colonel hopped off, they were presentable—at least for Vietnam. Their boots weren't shined; their uniforms weren't pressed; they weren't completely clean.

In contrast, Colonel Landis might have flown to Camp Enari

straight from dates with the barber, bathhouse, shoe-shine kit, and equipment sergeant.

The wind kicked up, and Landis, who'd had his hand outstretched even though LT was at attention and could not shake until released, stopped dead. The half a dozen followers that had emerged from the gunship on his heels stopped too, so fast it was almost comical. The colonel's smile faded, and he ran his tongue over his front teeth, then spat the dust that had coated his pearly whites. Guys in-country learned pretty quick not to smile in a high wind for just that reason.

"Lieutenant Welch, at ease. Everyone." The colonel's lips trembled as if they'd thought about smiling again and decided against it. "At ease."

As Billy set his feet apart and lifted his hands to the small of his back, eyes still front and center, he realized he hadn't performed parade rest since he'd stepped onto the tarmac at Tan Son Nhut. There'd been no reason to.

Colonel Landis beckoned the nearest corporal, who didn't appear old enough to shave, and the kid scurried forward, then placed a box the size of his palm into the colonel's outstretched hand.

Landis pulled out a six-sided gold medal, which hung from a green-and-white striped ribbon. "For distinctive meritorious achievement and service, the United States Army awards this commendation to Lieutenant Aaron Welch." He pinned the ribbon to LT's uniform.

Had Billy ever heard LT's first name before today? Why would he?

"Should be giving that to you, Beej." Terrell spoke low, the words garbled since he barely moved his mouth, but Colonel Landis glanced their way.

"Thank you, sir!" LT said loudly enough to tug the officer's gaze from the line back to him.

Deus, on the other side of Terrell, kicked him in the shin.

"How'd you manage this, Welch?" Landis swept his hand to indicate their formation.

"They learned how to fall in at basic, sir. Nothing to do with me."

The colonel chuckled. "Don't be modest. Your platoon works together better than any of the others. It's amazing." The colonel shook his head. "Take a photograph."

Did anyone else feel like an animal in a zoo?

Terrell muttered something Billy didn't catch, but LT shot a narrow glare their way just as a camera shutter whirred, capturing that expression forever.

Terrell had been muttering a lot lately, both when he was awake and when he was asleep, but when Billy asked what he'd said, Terrell would only rub at his head the way he'd been doing since Crazy Joe went airborne in pieces. What if he was muttering or rubbing or thinking too hard about things he should never think about again when he was supposed to be watching the perimeter or Billy's six or anyone else's?

Billy wasn't sure how to get Terrell back to the Terrell he had been. When he'd offered a piece of sketch paper to his friend and suggested he draw what he dreamed, Terrell had looked at Billy like he was crazy, then told him to "mind his own biz." After that, Billy had heard variations of the same—*kiss my ass, fuck off, blow it out your pie hole,* and so on—every time he'd tried to help.

"Your body count increase is unprecedented," Landis continued. "Don't try to tell me that's blind luck. I know better."

LT sighed, then beckoned Billy. "This is Private Johnson, Colonel. He's a crack shot."

"And how much of that shiny new body count is yours, Johnson?"

"I don't—"

LT interrupted. "I'm even more proud of our lowered casualty rate, sir."

The spark in the colonel's eyes at the discussion of enemy dead blinked out, leaving them an eerie ice-blue. "The most important thing, Welch, is to win this war, and we do that by killing more of them than they do of us."

"Exactly, sir. I'm glad we agree."

Behind them in the line, someone turned a laugh into a cough.

Colonel Landis hesitated, uncertain if he'd won that argument or not. "Let's get this matter of your sergeant settled." He lifted his chin to indicate Billy. "How 'bout him?"

Someone—Flash?—said "Sheesh!" from the line, and the dull clunk of a shoe against an ankle echoed in the sudden silence.

"Is there a problem?" Landis stared directly at Billy.

"Um . . . sergeants bring up the rear. Sir."

"I'm well aware of what sergeants do. Once upon another war I was a sergeant myself."

"I belong at point."

LT started rubbing his forehead the way he did when he really wanted a smoke but couldn't have one.

"I believe you belong wherever we put you."

"Yes, sir, bu—"

Landis shot Billy a glance so sharp he bit the end of his tongue, cutting off the word.

"I made a recommendation on sergeant—" LT began.

"Your CO mentioned that. Who was it?"

"Jesús Gonzalez." The colonel frowned, and LT hurried on. "Second tour. Knows more than I do about a helluva lot." LT beckoned Deus.

The colonel's frown deepened when Deus stood at attention in front of him. "Where are you from, soldier?"

Deus, far from stupid, answered the question really being asked. "I was born in southern California, Colonel."

Landis peered into Deus's face as if he could see his every

ancestor back to Cortes. "Welch, how long have you been in Vietnam?"

"Four and a half months, sir."

The army rotated officers into and out of Vietnam every six months instead of every twelve like the rest of them, which meant LT would be gone in another month and a half.

Murmuring began in the line as others did the math, but it was quickly hushed when Deus shot a dark, sideways glance in that direction.

Landis observed that glance and the reaction it had caused. "If you say this man is the man, Welch, and your CO had no objections, I'm inclined to agree."

Their CO, or commanding officer, Captain Fromm was mostly a voice on the other end of the Prick. He'd shown up once or twice in the field, led a mission, went back to HQ. For day-to-day ops, LT was in charge, and that was just fine all around.

"Congratulations, Sergeant." Landis shook hands with Deus.

"Thank you, sir."

"As long as I'm handing out kudos . . ."

The followers scurried to the chopper, returning with armloads of boxes.

"I'm sure you were wondering why I had the entire platoon sent here."

Guys had been bitching, but they hadn't really wondered. The army didn't make a whole lotta sense on a good day.

"Go ahead, Welch, take a look."

LT tore open the closest box, and his lips curved. "Steaks!"

A few guys *wooted*.

The colonel, like a kid on Christmas, tore open another, pulling out a familiar red, white, and blue can of PBR.

The *woots* became whistles.

Landis handed Deus the beer, and Deus bobbled it, face full of wonder. "It's ice cold."

The whistles turned to cheers.

The baby-faced corporal whispered to the colonel, and Landis lifted his hands like a preacher on Sunday. "You've earned this, men. Keep up that good work! You're an example to other platoons."

The colonel made his way back to the transport, waving like the president. His crisp, creased uniform had wilted in the humidity, and his shiny dress shoes, as well as every inch of visible pasty white skin, was covered in dust.

The instant the helo's skids lifted from the ground, everyone bolted for the beer.

As LT assigned some the task of unpacking the steaks and others that of cooking them, Deus stared at the PBR in his hand as if he couldn't believe it was real.

"You gonna drink that or marry it?" Flash took a long swig from his own can, made an *ahh* sound, and did it again.

"Beej!" Billy looked up just as Terrell tossed him a beer. Since Terrell wasn't much of a QB, and Billy wasn't much a of receiver, he bobbled it, and when he made the first hole in the flat top of the can, using the church key Flash handed to him, beer bubbled out the opening, then down the side before he could make the second hole.

Flash snickered as Flash often did. "Slayer, you'd think you never had a brew before."

Billy deliberately took a huge swig of beer; the chill made his teeth ache something awful, but he took another right after, and Flash snorted, then drained what was left in his can before starting back for another.

Deus followed. "Slow down on those."

"Just because you're the sarge now doesn't mean you can tell me what to do."

"Actually, that's exactly what it means."

"What a dumbass." Terrell finished his beer too.

"Always has been." Billy lifted his can.

Terrell *clinked* his empty against it. "Always will be."

Billy waited for Terrell's big grin, but it didn't come, hadn't for a while now. "You okay?"

Terrell shrugged, which was better than the response he'd been giving lately whenever Billy asked. "Where's Bama?"

LT arrived with three PBRs and handed them around. "He insisted no one grills a steak better than a man from the South, so I told him to prove it."

As they sipped the rapidly warming beer, LT's gaze flicked to Terrell, and a crease appeared between his eyebrows. "Bama could probably use some help."

"Yes, sir." Terrell meandered in the direction of the smoke.

"He's . . ." LT's voice drifted off.

"Yeah," Billy agreed, though LT hadn't said anything. They both knew what Terrell was, or rather wasn't.

Himself.

LT guzzled what was left in the can and tossed the empty into the trash. "Sometimes the only way to get back to who you were is to get away from who you are."

"Sir?"

"I'm giving you three days R and R at Vung Tau. Take him with you."

"But—"

"Just go. Drink, play cards, do whatever the hell soldiers do there."

"What about everyone else?"

"They'll do what soldiers do here, or well"—he waved a hand —"out there."

That's what Billy was afraid of. What soldiers did out there, way too often, was die.

"There are a couple new guys finishing up charm school, so we won't be shorthanded." LT lit a cig, his attention on the not-so-distant hump of Dragon Mountain. "Or at least no more shorthanded than usual."

"But I should—"

"We managed to survive before you showed up; we'll be fine without you for a few days. But if Jones doesn't get his mind right and soon . . ." LT shook his head, leaving unsaid what Billy had been thinking far too much.

If Terrell didn't get his mind right soon, something bad was gonna happen.

"You think a few days in Vung Tau will help?"

"Fuck if I know, but it's all I got right now." LT reached into his pocket. "I don't know why this wasn't delivered in the last batch of mail . . ." He handed over an envelope and returned to the others.

Billy recognized his sister's neat, swirling cursive, which had never seemed to reflect Jay in the least. Weird that she'd sent him a letter on her own, usually hers came in the same envelope as Momma's.

He grabbed another beer and found a semiquiet place to read.

Dear Billy,

What the hell?

Billy's eyebrows lifted.

The most unpleasant things you've told Momma are that your rations smell like last week's garbage and the water tastes like dirt. But I know you can't tell her the truth.

"That was the truth," Billy said as if Jay could actually hear.

Or not the whole truth. The real truth. The truth in the drawings you've sent Harold.

They're good, Billy. So, so good. Better than the bogus ones you've sent Momma.

Billy tried to remember what he'd drawn, what he'd sent, but the whole point of drawing and sending was to remove them from his head. Get those images gone so he didn't think about them when he should be doing his job. Apparently, it had worked even better than he'd hoped—he couldn't remember the bogus ones very well either—and while on the one hand he was glad not to dream the dreams he'd dreamed before he'd sketched, then sent them to Harold, on the other hand the hazy hole in his brain where those memories should be was worrisome. Was the way he was coping any better than the way Terrell was?

Billy shifted his attention to Jay's letter and away from questions he couldn't, probably shouldn't, answer.

You know I've always loved summer, but this one is different. Me and my friends started out same as always, but things have changed. They've changed. Maybe I have too.

Billy took a swig of beer. The idea of anything, anyone back home changing . . . he didn't like it. He wanted to remember it all exactly as it was when he left, he wanted it all to *be* exactly as it was when he'd left.

Until he'd met Terrell, Bama—hell, everyone but Flash and Crazy Joe—Billy hadn't understood the bond his sister had with her friends, at times he'd maybe even been jealous of it. But he understood now. There was nothing he wouldn't do for these men because there was nothing they wouldn't do for him. That was how you survived Vietnam, but really, wasn't it how you survived anywhere?

Momma, and everyone else's momma too, it seems, has decided that our hanging out in town after dark is unacceptable and given us a ten o'clock curfew. Remember how we used to play Kick the Can until midnight and no one cared? Sure, you and Harold were with us, but sheesh, nothing ever happens here. Nothing.

As opposed to Vietnam where the enemy had figured out pretty quick that Americans couldn't stop themselves from kicking cans, so they rigged them to explode, then scattered them all over the country like bird seed. One of the first things new guys learned in-country was "see a can, let it lie."

What had caused the mothers of Willow Creek to suddenly worry about something they never had before? Was the turmoil here making everyone there as nervous as an FNG on his first night in-country?

Do not tell Momma, but we plan to sneak out.

Unease flickered, but Billy shook it off as foolishness. Unlike here, the enemy wouldn't pick off his sister and her pals if they were where they weren't supposed to be in the dark. And any cans they might kick would not go . . .

Billy shut his eyes as the dull thud of a boot against a tin can was followed by the *boom*, the screams, and the distant, inevitable *whoop* of a dustoff.

"God," he murmured. A curse? A prayer? Both?

There's a bunny named Fluff on the loose, so finding him is a pretty good excuse if we get caught.

Jay had been finding lost things since she was old enough to toddle—Momma's keys, Billy's shoes, Ringo—and everyone in town knew it.

"Beej!" Terrell held a steak aloft with a fork, and Billy's stomach growled.

He lifted a hand as he read the last few lines of Jay's letter.

Billy, you should draw your truth. Always.

Love, Jay

Billy folded the letter, put it in his pocket, and considered *the truth.*

He'd come to this country to help the Vietnamese, but also to help himself, to make his mark, to become a man that Gramps— no, that *everyone*—would be proud of, and he'd known, in a distant not-really-knowing-it way, that he'd be changed by this.

What he hadn't considered, but did now after reading Jay's letter, was that those he knew, those he loved, would be changed by it too.

CHAPTER 17

Jay
"Lyndon Johnson Told the Nation"

Willow Creek—July 1967

Weeks passed and—surprise!—Paul didn't call. No one else did either.

Momma pretended they'd never argued, and Jay let her. Right now, Momma was all she had.

Jay got so bored she agreed, for a price, to comb strangers' hair from the brushes at Momma's salon before sticking them into the sterilizer. Disgusting, yes, but someone had to do it, and as Momma liked to say: *Money buys things*. Not that Jay had anything to buy since she had nowhere to go and no one to go there with, but what else did she have to do?

After what seemed like decades spent with a never-ending mound of hair encrusted brushes, surrounded by the constant flock-of-geese chatter from the ladies sitting under the driers or in the spinning chairs, Jay escaped.

Someone waited on the porch, and for a second, she thought it was Harold. But the figure that rose to its feet wasn't Harold.

"Hey, Three-J!"

"You didn't call."

Hell. That sounded whiny, like something Susan would say.

"Sorry. I've been helping at *Rally!* Things are heating up, boiling over."

"What things?"

"The riot?"

Jay stared at him blankly.

"In Detroit. Started Sunday, hasn't stopped. Johnson invoked the Insurrection Act of 1807. Do you believe that?"

Jay could only shake her head, wide-eyed. The world was on fire, and she had no idea. That used to be okay. What happened outside Willow Creek didn't affect her. But it did now, really it always had, and she should be more aware of it.

"What does invoking . . ." She waved her hand in place of the words. "What does that mean?"

"The president can use armed forces in any state facing an insurrection against the government. Nothing new for Detroit. They're now the only US city occupied by the federal government three times."

"Detroit's a problem?"

"Or the solution."

"To what?" Jay asked.

"Race equality."

Half the time when she talked to Paul, Jay felt as if she knew nothing about anything. But he didn't mind when she asked questions. He seemed to admire her curiosity. If she didn't ask, if she didn't listen and learn, she'd only continue to be ignorant about things she probably couldn't afford to be ignorant about much longer.

"You think a riot's going to help?"

"Standing there and taking it sure doesn't."

Paul sat on the top step, and Jay joined him. Their hips bumped, their legs too, and when he took her hand, a tingle went up her arm. She hoped he didn't see the hair standing on end.

"The Detroit Police have only a handful of Black officers, so when they march into a Negro neighborhood, a Negro club, a Negro party, what else would the Negroes see but the enemy?"

More and more Americans seemed to see one another as the enemy. Where would that lead? What good could that do?

"You wanna go to State Street tomorrow?" Paul rubbed his thumb over hers, and Jay's heart thundered. "There's something I want you to see."

"Okay."

Paul leaned in close and kissed her, right where they'd once bumped heads, and places that had tingled only with him tingled again. "I'll pick you up at eight."

"Can you make it eight thirty?" Momma left for work at eight fifteen.

"Sure." Then he was gone, waving the peace sign as he went around the corner.

The next morning Jay stared into her closet, tore through her dresser drawers, and wished, for the first time ever, that she saw something else to wear beyond her usual cutoff shorts and washed soft T-shirts. Then again, wearing anything else—if she'd *had* anything else—would only invite questions.

"We need to talk." Momma stood in the doorway holding the half-empty bottle of schnapps.

"That was in Billy's closet." Jay pushed aside any guilt about throwing her brother to the wolf. He wasn't here; she was.

"Then why did I find it in yours?"

No moss on Momma. Hell, what else had she found?

Do not glance at your boots! Do not glance at your boots!

"Why were you in my closet?"

"Since your closet is in my house, I think that makes it my closet, don't you?"

"Yes?"

Momma's eyes narrowed at the question in Jay's tone, then flicked to the yellow and orange alarm clock on the bedside table, which clearly read eight seventeen. "We'll talk about this more tonight."

As soon as the front door closed, Jay sprinted to the closet, stuck her hand into the boot hidey-hole. She went dizzy with relief when her fingers encountered Billy's drawings and the magazine. She needed to find another place to keep them. However, a thorough consideration of her room turned up no better options.

A horn honked, and Jay hurried to the window. A Chevy Nova the shade of old mustard idled at the curb, Paul behind the wheel. While they obviously couldn't ride their bikes thirty miles to Madison, the car gave her a jolt. Jay didn't have a driver's license. None of the girls her age did, except Susan, who had her own car, which was as annoying as she was. A lot of families only had one car. They didn't grow on trees.

Quickly Jay dug out her only handbag, a woven straw monstrosity with a clunky leather buckle and thin leather straps. The drawings and the magazine appeared forlorn inside the seemingly bottomless purse. She looked like an idiot carrying the mini suitcase over her shoulder, but what choice did she have? Momma rarely came home during her shift. She was usually too busy, but with Jay's luck lately, today would be the day. Since Momma had been in Jay's closet once, what was to keep her from going in there again?

Paul gave the handbag a glance—he didn't have much choice given its size—but only smiled and pulled away from the curb.

"Your car?"

"My mom's. Belonged to her dad, but he died."

They motored west toward the capital, the windows open,

Jim Morrison crooning "Light My Fire" from the radio. The wind rippled Jay's hair backward like flag.

The volume of the music, the rush of the wind made conversation impossible, and Jay didn't mind. Sure, if Momma found out about this, she'd be in all kinds of trouble, but she was finally, finally going to State Street, and she wanted to enjoy every minute.

As they entered the city, people clogged the sidewalks, many carrying signs.

WAR IS DARKNESS. PEACE IS LIGHT.

DRAFT BEER, NOT BOYS!

END THE WAR NOW!

"You brought me to a war protest?" Jay *did* want to question, to learn, to know, to *hear*, but she wasn't sure she wanted to hear *that*.

Paul cast Jay a wary glance. "This was supposed to be a civil rights rally."

He pointed to a group where whites and Negroes mixed together more than Jay had ever seen them mixed before, carrying signs that read:

BLACK POWER!

POLICE BRUTALITY MUST GO!

DETROIT IS ONLY THE BEGINNING!

Paul signaled a left turn and waited as another crowd, this one a blend of signs about Vietnam, civil rights, women's rights, voting rights. One man, wearing blue-and-white-striped overhauls with no shirt, carried a poster that read: *IF YOU HAVE FOOD, THANK A FARMER.*

"Sometimes when you hold a rally, everyone comes." Paul completed his turn into a parking lot, slid into one of the last available slots, and shut off the car.

"When who holds a rally?"

He pointed at the cream-brick building rising from the far end of the lot labeled: *Rally!*

"*Rally!* organized the . . ." Laughter bubbled in Jay's throat. "Rally?"

Paul touched her hand where it rested on the seat. "I wouldn't spring a war protest on you. I understand where you're coming from with your brother, your family. I don't agree with it, but what you believe is every bit as valid as what I do."

Momma and Gramps would have a different opinion.

"You believe me, right?"

She did. What good would it do to bring someone who was for the war to a war protest? Would chanting people with signs change her mind?

"We don't have to stay."

The desire to see, to hear, to learn, to *know* what others thought, what others believed was too strong. "I want to."

"Bitchin'!" Paul got out of the car and hurried around to open the door for Jay, but she was already climbing out. He reached for her arm, and his fingers tangled in the leather strap of her handbag. "You want to leave your . . ."

"Suitcase?"

His uncertainty flowered into a grin. "You want to leave it in the car?"

"No." Jay wasn't letting the drawings out of her sight. What if she never saw them again? "I had to bring Billy's sketches. Momma was snooping in my closet."

His grin faltered. "She do that a lot?"

"Never."

"Why now?"

Jay hadn't been thinking about why, and she should have been. Momma had bigger things on her mind than Jay's closet, so why there, *and* why now?

In the distance, someone spoke—garbled but amplified.

"If we're gonna do this," Paul said, "we should do it."

Jay hoisted the strap over her shoulder. "After you."

She almost got swept away in the crowd, but Paul caught her arm, and they matched their strides to the others.

The day was sunny and bright, the sky so very blue. The heat wave had broken, and the breeze off Lake Monona was cool not cold. Perfect.

Someone handed Jay a beer. She stared at the can, uncertain what to do, then Paul took it from her, pulled the tab, downed a swig, and gave it back. She put her lips where his had been. That feeling was almost as heady as the foam that tickled her lips.

"Are we gonna get arrested?" She returned the beer.

"Not for this." He lifted the can to indicate several officers standing in a cross street, monitoring the crowd, their attention skipping right over the open alcohol containers without pause, even when people toasted them.

"Is everyone always so happy at a protest?"

"Civil rights rally."

She glanced pointedly at the sign of the woman in front of them.

DMZ=DEAD MARINE ZONE!

"Okay." He tossed the empty into a garbage barrel. "We'll call it a gathering of like-minded individuals."

Jay's gaze bounced from one sign to another—very few of which seemed like-minded. "You sure about that?"

"Everyone's united in a common hope for what they might be able to change today, right here, together."

Jay thought *today* was optimistic, but who knew?

They turned a corner, and State Street stretched out before them; a wave of humanity extended all the way to the capitol square. A portion of the avenue was a pedestrian mall, but today even the area where cars were allowed was clogged with people from storefront to storefront, any vehicles that had parked there earlier now surrounded, frozen for the duration of the rally.

A Negro man stood on the steps of the capitol, speaking into a microphone. They couldn't hear him any better now than they'd been able to before.

"That's Bayard Rustin." Paul's breath stirred Jay's hair as he leaned in. "I can't believe he's here."

Paul tried to inch them closer so they could hear more than *bwah, de, bwah, de, bwah,* but it was no use; the crowd was packed too tightly.

"He organized one of the first Freedom Rides. He'd probably be on Dr. King's staff except . . . well, he's gay."

"A homosexual Negro?" she whispered.

"They do exist, though most probably aren't as open about it as Rustin. It's caused him no end of trouble, that's for sure."

Jay could imagine, and the spark of worry she nurtured for Ronnie flared.

From Rustin came "swah, ba, swah, de, bwah," and the crowd roared.

"They love him," Paul said.

"You sound surprised." Paul obviously idolized the man.

"He's a wonderful speaker, but he's also an openly gay Negro who agrees with President Johnson's Communist Containment Policy."

"He's for the war?"

"Not the war, or at least not how the war is being fought. He's for keeping communism contained."

Jay considered the man who was the opposite of Billy in so many ways yet believed the same. Rustin had devoted his life to it; not in the same way Billy had, but still. He was trying, and she admired that.

Paul continued to share what he knew about the speakers, pointing to a tall, thin blonde wearing pants as well as Katharine Hepburn. "She's a psychology professor, has some interesting theories on mob mentality, or the 'us versus them' mind-set. And that guy"—he aimed his finger at a clean-shaven young man in rumpled dress pants—"is the head of the local Communist Party."

"Wait. There's a— What?" Jay squinted, trying to see . . . his horns? His tail? His pitchfork? That's what Gramps would be looking for. "Why is he speaking at a civil rights rally?"

"Explaining civil rights, the guarantee not to be discriminated against because of race, religion, political affiliation, and so on."

"He's a communist."

"Yep, and he's got rights just like Nixon."

"Does Nixon know that?"

Paul laughed as if she'd said something hilarious and Jay nearly preened. Very few people thought she was funny. Not her friends, certainly not Momma. Only Billy. But Billy had always seen things in Jay that no one else, not even Jay, did. Odd that Paul, so very different from her brother as well, seemed to see those things too. Maybe differences didn't always keep people from being a lot the same.

Smoke wafted past, but it didn't smell like the Camels Gramps puffed after every meal. Jay sniffed, sniffed again. What was that?

"Grass," Paul said.

"Yes! After it's been rained on for five days and started to turn funky. Although how would anyone get something that damp to—?"

Paul lifted his eyebrows.

"Oh!" It was *grass*!

Jay went on tiptoe to see who was smoking it, but from where she stood, all she could make out was a misty trail rising from several locations.

"You want some?"

Jay landed on her heels with a jolt. "You have some?"

"No, but I could get it."

The word *how* perched on the end of her tongue, but that

was a conversation best had in private, which was also the best place to smoke.

"No, thank you." Jay did not plan to flip out in the middle of a rally in Madison.

"Okay." Paul laid his arm across her shoulders, and they stood together with thousands of others. Jay felt part of something larger than herself, something important, life-changing, world-changing, and she liked it.

"Hey, wait here a sec." Paul's arm slid away; he slid away and into a nearby shop.

Shell necklaces hung in the window. Beaded bracelets, silver rings, silver bracelets, and beaded rings lay scattered across a background of black velvet beneath.

If Jay brought home anything like that, Momma would kill her.

Beyond the window, ribbons in every imaginable color trailed from the ceiling and fluttered whenever the door opened or closed.

Paul stepped onto the street, several ribbons the exact shade as the Good Ship Lollipop embarrassment Jay had torn from her hair on the Fourth clutched in his hand.

"You're . . ." Her heart stuttered, and her eyes burned. "You're making fun of me?"

"No!"

The rally over, people streamed behind them, between them, and Paul flickered—there, gone, there.

"Never. I saw the ribbons, and they're the same color as the one you had on when—" He stopped. "Oh."

Jay didn't speak; what could she say?

"It's just . . ." His eyes were so blue Jay could almost smell the wild violets that grew at the edges of the clearing every spring. "The color was out of sight against your hair, and I thought—"

"That I'd want to wear another just like it?" Her tone very clearly asked *are you nuts?* without her even having to say it.

"Well, not the way you had it."

The crowd broke for an instant, and he snatched her hand, then drew her into the shelter of the building.

"Sometimes if you take something down to where it began, then put it back together a different way . . ." He twisted the ribbons round and round. "What you make is changed for the better, though it's still the same underneath." He lifted the loose band, along with his eyebrows. "Can I . . .?"

Confusion, embarrassment, curiosity, excitement—Jay was too dizzy with their swirl to do anything but shrug.

Paul took that as a *yes* and placed his creation on her head, adjusting it to make a headband. His fingers tangled in her untidy hair, and the usual tingle started up down low. What was he doing? How could she keep him doing it?

He turned her toward the window. Jay didn't recognize the person staring back. He'd secured the headband, then twined the trailing ribbons with the strands of her hair in a way that made the wild, unruly mass less of a mess and more of a style. Or a statement.

"Wow!"

A guy and a girl paused behind them and stared into the glass too.

"You get those in there, man?" The guy pointed at the store.

Paul nodded, and the stranger pulled his girl inside.

Jay continued to peer at the window where the Jay that had been and the Jay that could be were suddenly the Jay that was.

"Is it okay?" Paul asked. "You can take it off if you want."

"No." Jay threaded their fingers together and squeezed. "It's better than okay."

"Just like you."

Their gazes held for several seconds, then Paul grinned quick and pulled her along with him into the crowd. Though they strolled in the middle of hundreds of people, the two of them seemed to exist in a bubble all their own.

"When you said you could take something down to where it began," Jay said, "then put it back together so it's better than before you meant—?"

"America!" Paul bent the elbow of his free arm and made a fist. "Right on!"

Several people around them echoed, "Right on!" So much for their own bubble.

Jay lowered her voice. "You can't take America apart."

"Well, not me personally . . ." Paul laughed.

"That's not—"

"Possible?"

She'd been about to say *funny*, but he'd stopped laughing.

"You don't seem worried about the idea of America coming apart." And now Jay was.

"Haven't you noticed?" Paul paused in front of a window filled with photographs so vivid Jay swayed. The feeling she could be drawn into them, through them, that she could become part of them, became so strong she barely heard his next words.

"It has."

CHAPTER 18

Billy
"The Unknown Soldier"

Vietnam—July 1967

Billy waved off the beer Terrell offered as he approached. "Leaving for R and R at 0600. I don't wanna be groggy."

"You got R and R? Shi-i-i-i-t." Terrell finished his beer and started on Billy's.

Billy took the can from Terrell and set it aside. "You're coming with me."

Terrell blinked a few times, then grinned the grin Billy had missed more than he realized. "Beej and Teej loose in Vung Tau? Watch out!"

Terrell offered his palm, and Billy gave him some skin, and for just a second, the guy Terrell had been the day Billy met him returned.

Then distant gunfire erupted, and New Terrell—jumpy and sarcastic—was back.

"I guess killin' enough gooks to become *Slayer* has its privileges."

Billy sighed. Maybe Vung Tau would help; it sure couldn't hurt.

At 0600, the camp was silent. No one stirred. The rest of the guys had stayed up drinking until all the beer was gone. The colonel had brought a lot of beer.

"How far to R and R?" Terrell asked as they climbed aboard the Slick.

"This bird takes you to Xuan Loc where you'll catch an aircraft to Vung Tau, which is about six hundred Ks that way." The gunner pointed south.

"Wish I knew how far that actually is," Terrell muttered as the chopper lifted up and away.

Billy dozed, waking up when Terrell came to his knees, gaze riveted to something he could see through the open side door.

Billy sat up, fingers curling around his M16.

Terrell leaned close so Billy could hear him over the roar of the Slick. "Don't sweat it, man. We ain't close enough to be much help, even with your Superman vision and godlike skills with a rifle."

Lately, Terrell sounded a lot like Flash. Which meant, lately, Billy had considered punching Terrell almost as often as he'd considered punching Flash. Since Billy had been the one to insist they fight the enemy and not one another, he said nothing, did nothing beyond imprinting bright-red half-moon indentations across both palms.

Ahead of them a mountain rose, deep purple against a blue sky. A wave of men flowed over the peak, then down the other side, like ants spilling from an anthill. The Slick was too loud for them to hear any rat-a-tat of gunfire, even the boom of artillery was faint, but bursts of smoke here and there told the tale. Why didn't they call in an air strike?

Before the question made it from his head and out his mouth —not that Terrell could have heard him anyway unless they were closer than close—the ants swarmed over everything in their path, devouring it. The Slick continued south, the lost battle, the lost hill disappearing behind other lost hills. Leaving Billy with an aching sadness he really needed to shake. This trip was about getting Terrell back to the Terrell he'd been, not dragging him into the shadows even more.

In Xuan Loc, dozens of Vietnamese kids tried to sell them all sorts of things. Terrell nearly bought a Coke from one sweet-faced . . . boy? Girl? Hard to tell when they were all skinny with bad haircuts, gaps in their teeth, and worn-out clothes with no shoes.

"Sorry, kid." Terrell pulled an MPC from his pocket. "No dough."

They would change their military currency for the local— piasters—in Vung Tau, but right now they had nothing legal to use.

The kid shouted something that sounded like *number ten* and flipped them off as they hurried for the plane.

The GIs already aboard were asleep, testament to how much real rest anyone got in-country—not much—and Billy dozed again as well, coming awake what seemed only moments later when Terrell exclaimed, "The beach!"

Through the window a tiny spec of blue-green grew and grew into the South China Sea. A city lay nestled between two mountains on a strip of land jutting into the water.

Terrell slapped Billy on the back. "Righteous!"

Maybe everything would be okay. For them. For now. The guys on that hill, however . . .

Inside the small terminal at Vung Tau, they were directed to a bus that would take them to the R and R center at the beach.

The town flew by in a blur—narrow streets, which brought the businesses and dwellings close to the road where almost everyone drove a motorcycle or scooter like they had a death wish.

"I wonder how many gooks a day get creamed by a bus?" Terrell murmured when the transport lurched as yet another local darted in front of it.

At the R and R center, the sergeant on duty greeted them. "Gotta check your weapons."

He possessed the largest ears of anyone Billy had ever seen. They were so big, in fact, it was hard not to see anything *but* them. The sun seemed to have had the same problem since the tips had been burned bright red so many times that tissue-thin peels of skin fluttered in the sea breeze.

They handed over their M16s and sidearms. It wasn't easy. Sure, they were in a "friendly" city, but how friendly was friendly?

"Knives? Brass knuckles? Grenades? Claymores?"

"Say what?" Terrell asked.

"Anything in those rucks that could kill someone?"

"I might commit murder with my toothbrush. You want that?"

The sergeant grunted. "Rules are rules."

"Who we gonna kill here?"

"No one, 'cause I got your weapons." The man heaved a tired sigh. "Look, in Vung Tau you can drink, you can smoke, you can gamble, shoot the shit, listen to music, swim, surf. I don't give a fuck."

"Hey, what about that?" Terrell rubbed his hands together.

"What about what?"

"Fucking."

Billy winced. "Terrell, let's—"

"There are girls in town. What you do with them is up to you and to them. Enough"—the sergeant rubbed his forefinger and thumb together—"you can buy anything. Three square hot meals a day and all the showers you want here at the R and R. Free bus to town. Air-conditioned hotels, bars, shops. You can get a room there, but curfew is at eleven p.m. MPs will bust your ass if they find you out on the streets after that. Here's your passes. Exchange your MPCs. You can pick up your weapons in three days."

"My man!" Terrell held out his hand for some skin.

The guy stared at Terrell's palm. "Yeah, I'm not gonna do that."

Terrell shoved his hand into his pocket.

"You can wear what you got on." The sergeant waved at their fatikees, which literally could have stood up without the two of them inside. "Or buy beach stuff." He pointed to a thatch hut nearby.

"Laundry?" What Billy had on smelled nearly as bad as what he had inside his ruck.

"Buy new clothes and they'll wash your old ones."

After he received piasters for his MPCs, Billy headed straight for the hut where an ancient, shriveled man folded shirts and shorts so brightly colored Billy's eyes hurt.

"Where you think the old gook gets this stuff?" Terrell asked. "China?"

"No gook! Friend! From here." The man pointed to the city of Vung Tau, then grabbed a pair of swim trunks from the wild array and displayed the tag sewn inside. *Janzen*.

Billy had swim trunks at home, which were plain, boring blue and labeled *Jantzen*. He didn't point out that *Janzen* was an obviously cheap imitation because he wanted clothes that weren't army green and smelling of things he didn't want to smell for the next three days so badly he didn't care if they were made on the moon, let alone China.

Billy chose yellow swim trunks, an orange Hawaiian print

shirt, a purple tank top, a pair of shorts the shade of the ocean nearby, and some flip-flops. "How much?"

The old guy named a ridiculous number of piasters, but the exchange rate to the American dollar was about 400 percent, which made the purchase price quite a deal. Billy counted out the money as Terrell chose a new wardrobe.

"You got this any smaller?" Terrell held up red swim trunks so large they could have fit two Terrells inside.

The man shouted in Vietnamese, and a minute later, a young woman pushed through the curtain serving as a door.

Terrell dropped everything in his hands. Billy nearly did too. Was she as beautiful as he thought, or was it just that he hadn't seen a female younger than a crone since he'd left the States?

The girl handed the swim trunks to her father—maybe her grandfather—bowed, and hurried away, never once lifting her eyes from her tiny slippered feet.

"Take off stink clothes. Granddaughter wash." He snapped his fingers. "*Mau!* She waiting."

"He wants us to strip right here?" Billy asked, but Terrell was already handing over his pants.

In short order they headed for the beach wearing swim trunks, tank tops, and flip-flops, carrying their boots in one hand and the rest of their new clothes in the other. The old guy had taken their rucks too. He said he could get out the smell and repair the holes.

Terrell kept looking over his shoulder, nearly falling on his face a few times because the sand shifted the way the jungle did not. "You think I got enough piasters?"

"For?"

"You heard the sergeant. With enough money we can buy whatever we want. I want her."

The only *her* they'd seen had been—

"Do *not* offer that man money for his daughter."

"Granddaughter."

"There are girls in town so just . . . don't."

Terrell didn't argue, but he glanced over his shoulder one more time before they reached the beach where GIs dotted the sand, some in cutoff fatigues, others in brightly colored clothes like Billy and Terrell.

The two closest guys, one with hair so red it had to be hard to miss in the jungle and another with very little hair, played checkers and drank beer. They were dressed exactly like Terrell and Billy, but they'd kicked off their flip-flops, no doubt to relieve pressure from what had to be mighty painful cases of immersion foot.

The redhead tossed them both a beer from a cooler at his side. "I'm Opie. That's Crash."

"I'm Teej. This here's Slayer."

While Billy had gotten used to answering to the nickname, he'd also liked that Terrell still called him Beej. Or at least he had until now.

"Where you come from?" Crash jumped two of Opie's black pieces, then picked them up—*click, click*—and set them on his side of the board.

"Chicago." Terrell pointed at Billy. "Wisconsin."

"I meant where you stationed?"

"Central Highlands. You?"

"Long Binh." Crash frowned impatiently as Opie stared at his checkers like he expected them to get up and dance. "How many days until your DEROS?"

"Three hundred and fifteen," Terrell said without pause.

That drew the man's attention from the board at last. "How'd you get R and R so soon? You the goddamn soldier of the month or something?"

"Slayer is the goddamn soldier of the year."

Billy cast Terrell a glance but said nothing.

"Must be." Opie jumped four of Crash's red pieces.

Crash cursed and stood. "SOB never loses. I'm gonna hit the surf."

"Surf?" Billy's ears perked. "Where'd you learn how?"

"I was born on a wave off the coast of Malibu. Want me to teach you?"

"Wanna come, Terrell?"

"Where's a Negro gonna surf in Chicago?"

Billy opened his mouth—wasn't Chicago on the lake?—and Terrell shook his head. "Not a real question. Run along, choirboy."

Billy ran along. By the time he learned to stay on the board for more than ten seconds before he ate sand, then returned tired and hungry, Terrell was gone.

"Where'd he go?"

"Not his mom," Opie said.

Billy hunted around, but there wasn't much to the place, and what there was did not contain Terrell. He was hurt his friend had gone into town without him, but there was nothing to do about it except head to Vung Tau with Opie, Crash, and a few others.

"There are like a hundred bars," Opie said. "Most of 'em named after American cities."

Billy walked into what he swore later was called *Dallas*, though it might have been *Detroit*. As soon as he stepped past the threshold, a Vietnamese girl in a very short skirt and low-cut blouse grabbed his hand and led him to a table. She asked him to buy her a "Saigon Tea," which, when it arrived along with his beer, resembled Kool-Aid in a shot glass.

She said her name was Mai, which meant "apricot blossom" in her language. She did smell like apricots, or maybe it was just the tea, and while she appeared about sixteen, Mai insisted she was nineteen. She spoke very good English, and they talked about American TV shows. She wanted to know if Beverly Hills was as pretty as it appeared in *The Beverly Hillbillies*, and he had to say he'd never been out of his home state until he enlisted.

"You live in place like *Green Acres*?" Mai asked.

"More like Mayberry, but it snows."

Her face creased. He waited for her to ask about snow, but instead she asked about his family. He showed her the picture he carried of Ringo, then the one he'd received recently of his mom and sister. Mai smiled vaguely at both. When Billy asked about her family, she ordered more drinks.

Opie and Crash disappeared with their girls at some point, but Billy was distracted, on the lookout for Terrell, increasingly worried about his friend and guilty about having left Terrell behind—happily, considering Terrell's behavior lately—to surf.

When curfew arrived, Mai dashed off. Billy, drunker than he'd ever been, managed to wobble to the nearest hotel. The next morning he caught the bus back to the R and R center, hoping to meet up with Terrell in the buffet line.

"Joe? Joe?" The clothing salesman beckoned from his hut. "You come now, Joe."

Billy still felt drunk. "Why are you calling me Joe?"

"GI he say 'Joe! Joe!'" The man frowned at Billy. "Joe not you?" He lifted his chin to indicate the mess hall. "Which one Joe? You get. Bring here."

Billy didn't remember any of those guys being Joe either.

"Never mind. What's wrong?"

"You come." The man disappeared inside.

Billy followed, curious.

Sobs from behind the curtain between the shop and what must be the old guy's living quarters warred with the crash of the waves. Billy pushed through the divider to find Terrell lying on the floor, his head cradled in a woman's lap. Billy feared it was the beautiful young girl, and there would be trouble. But the woman turned her head, and she was not beautiful; she was not young.

"She not supposed to be here," the old man said.

"Crazy Joe." Gasp, gulp, sniff. "Crazy Joe, he—"

"See? He ask for Joe. You get him gone. I make her gone. All good, not bad." He grabbed the woman's arm, but Terrell had his arms wrapped around her waist, and he would not let go.

The woman lifted her gaze. Billy didn't know what he'd expected, but it wasn't the boredom he found there.

"Terrell." Billy squatted in front of his friend. "Time to sleep."

Terrell smelled like the floor of Pulaski's Tavern after *Everyone's Irish on St. Pat's Day* landed on a weekend.

"When I sleep, I see him." Terrell released the woman and grabbed Billy's elbows, almost tipping him on top of them both. "I don't wanna see him no more."

"Okay." Billy managed to hoist both himself and Terrell to their feet, and the woman followed the old guy out the rear door without a backward glance.

Terrell swung his long, skinny arm around Billy's shoulders. "He was such an asshole!"

"Shh," Billy whispered, though Terrell was where he belonged and the woman—how the hell had he found her?—was gone or near enough, and they should be okay. Still, he didn't want anyone to see Terrell like this. *He* didn't want to see Terrell like this. Terrell, like this, was disturbing.

"He was probably gonna kill you eventually."

Billy started to walk, arm around Terrell's waist, and Terrell walked, too, but not well. He was a helluva lot heavier than he looked. Like everything else in Vietnam.

"Everyone knows the bastard killed Ghost."

They did? Billy had thought he was the only one who suspected, who *knew*.

"I should be glad he's dead, right?"

They reached the sand, and Terrell went to one knee, dragging Billy with him. Billy tried to hoist him up, but it was like trying to climb a muddy hill. They just slid back down.

"Fuck it." Terrell let go, landing on his back.

It was early yet, and only a few GIs lay on the beach. Those who weren't asleep or passed out appeared as hungover as Billy, maybe still as drunk as Terrell. None of them even glanced their way. Since Terrell had given up walking far enough away from anyone to hear, even if they were awake, Billy sprawled next to him. At least the day was overcast, so the sun wasn't frying their eyeballs like eggs on a griddle.

"Right?" Terrell nudged Billy with his bony elbow.

Billy tried to remember what Terrell was asking, got nothing. He'd thought the sight of his friend sobbing on some foreign woman's lap—except she wasn't foreign, they were— would have sobered him up, but no.

"I should be glad Crazy Joe is dead, aren't you?" This time Terrell didn't wait for Billy's answer, and that was good because his answer was yes.

And didn't that make him as much of an asshole as Crazy Joe?

"But all I can think about is his eyes right before . . . you know . . ." Terrell's long, usually clumsy fingers made a graceful upward *boom*. "He knew, in that one instant, and then he . . ." Terrell started rubbing his head.

"Then he didn't know anything anymore."

"I hope not." Terrell dropped his hand. "I understood we could die. We all get that. But to see the light go out, right in front of me, so damn fast, so damn easy . . ."

Wasn't dying fast and easy a good thing? If you had to die.

This is what Billy told himself whenever memories of those he'd killed tried to jitterbug through his head. A bullet to the brain, to the chest—fast, easy—and if he didn't do his duty, people still died. His people.

"I thought if I could just get through one night without thinking about him, maybe he'd stop . . ."

Billy knew he should ask *stop what?* but he was afraid of the answer.

"Drinking didn't help; dope didn't help."

Terrell had been smoking dope? How had Billy missed that? The stuff smelled like the bottom of a ditch after a week of rain, and while in Vietnam that shouldn't be easy to distinguish, it was.

"So I figured I'd . . . you know?"

"Drink and smoke at the same time?"

Terrell tried to snort, but his nose was full of snot, and that wasn't pretty. He wiped his lip with the tail of his shirt, then made a circle with one thumb and forefinger so he could poke the other forefinger through the middle.

Billy rubbed between his eyes. Why hadn't he figured it out, considering the woman, without the cringeworthy hand signal? He blamed the booze, if not his terminal virginity, which he should probably be more concerned about, but he just . . . wasn't. He had better things to worry about, and if that made him "queer" as Gramps had hinted whenever he'd seen Billy drawing—oh well, that was a worry for another time.

"Where'd you find her?" Billy asked.

She hadn't looked like one of the girls in the bar; she'd looked like their mother, maybe an aunt, even a young-ish gramma.

"I went to the clothes hut, tried to buy the granddaughter."

"Oh, Terrell," Billy began. "She's just—"

"A gook."

No gook. Friend. From here.

Deus had advised them to think of the enemy as gooks, dinks, slants, whatever name allowed them to do what needed to be done. But what Billy hadn't thought about, because he'd been doing his best *not* to think, was this: If the enemy were gooks then, by definition, their allies weren't.

"She isn't a gook," Billy said.

Terrell blinked blearily.

"There are two kinds of Vietnamese. The ones that want to kill us and the ones that don't. Shouldn't there be a different name for the people who want us dead?"

"Huh?" Terrell asked.

Billy decided the gook, not-gook conversation was better left for a day when both he and Terrell weren't wasted, so he moved on.

"What happened after you offered the old man the money?"

"There was a lot of shouting in Vietnamese."

"I bet."

"Then he sent the granddaughter away, and she came back with the boom-boom girl."

"The what?"

Terrell smacked his hands together in a rhythm that was becoming familiar, even though Billy had never done that rhythm himself.

"You think Boom-Boom got his name from hittin' hisself in the head?"

Well, *yeah.*

"He got it because he whacks off so much."

Billy nearly asked how Terrell knew that but decided to add it to the long, long list of things he did not want to know.

"Old dink is one smart mo-fo. Dangles the pretty one in front of the GIs, then pulls the switcheroo and takes a cut of the money."

Billy didn't think the old guy had done any dangling but—

"So sex," Terrell began, and Billy's ears perked up, "Not as great as I been hearin' about."

Billy frowned. How could that be?

"I thought I'd feel less alone." Terrell's breath hissed out like a tire stuck with a nail. "Instead, I never felt more alone in my life."

"But you aren't alone. You got me."

"When we first came here, I had Beej, but Slayer . . . he belong to everybody."

"I'm still Beej."

"No," Terrell said. "Ya ain't."

Billy wasn't sure what to say. That he'd go back to who he'd been? No way. Beej was a kid who hid in a ditch and couldn't fire his rifle because he couldn't stop thinking too much about what had happened, what was happening, what might happen. Slayer was a man of action who used his talents to save his friends and non-friends, a man who convinced everyone to get along, who got them steaks and beer, commendations, atta boys, R and R.

"Who wouldn't want to be Slayer?" he asked.

His only answer was a snore.

A soft intake of breath had Billy grabbing for the rifle that wasn't there, even as he spun from back to front, then sprang to a crouch. He no longer felt drunk.

The girl from the clothing hut hovered a few feet away, wide-eyed.

Billy held up his hands, palms out, showing he had no weapon, he meant no harm, even as he came to his full height, towering over her so that she had to tilt her chin to see his face. What was she doing here?

"Friend okay now?"

"You speak English?"

"So-so."

Billy smiled at the slang. She no doubt spent her days listening to the soldiers talk as they bought clothes from her grandfather, but it would take someone both smart and determined to learn even so-so English.

She continued to stand there, so Billy continued to look at her. She really was pretty, and he hadn't seen pretty since . . . he couldn't remember past all the ugly.

"What's your name?" he asked.

"Bian." She bowed her head, and he did too. "You are *kẻ giết người?*"

Billy spread his hands.

"It mean . . ." She lifted her face to the sky for a few seconds before returning a gaze, filled with admiration, to his. "Slayer. I hear you best at *pac-pac.*" She pretended to sight down the barrel of a rifle, pull the trigger. "Everyone afraid."

The idea that those he had feared, even those he had not, were now afraid of him made Billy throw back his shoulders, lift his chin, and claim the name with pride. "That's me."

Rapid fire Vietnamese exploded from the clothing hut, and between one blink and the next, Bian was gone.

CHAPTER 19

Jay
"2 + 2 = ?"

*M*adison and Willow Creek—July/August 1967

Jay peered through the window, her gaze riveted to the photos displayed beneath the words: *America in Chaos.*

A half a dozen Negro men, palms against a white wall graffitied with a black fist, feet apart, one looking over his shoulder at the three white cops behind them.

Soldiers wearing riot helmets, rifles trained on a crowd waving protest signs as a young couple draped garlands of flowers over the muzzles.

A man wearing a black shirt, his lack of a hat glaring in the presence of so many on the heads of the suited men surrounding him, several clutching his arms on either side with fingers as tense and tight as their faces.

"That's Albert DeSalvo," Paul said.

"Isn't he the Boston Strangler?"

"Maybe. They weren't able to prove the murders, so they arrested him for a series of rapes. Then he escaped from a mental hospital in February. Crazy."

What was crazy? The escape? Or that a man could rape and maybe kill so many women before he was caught?

"What about that?" Jay pointed at a lone color photograph in the center of the others, the orange, red, yellow explosion brilliant against every imaginable shade of green.

"Napalm in Vietnam."

"Are there . . .?" Faces danced in the flames just like . . . Jay set her hand on the suitcase-purse, but in the next blink, the faces were gone. "That isn't America."

"Isn't it?"

Not as she saw it, then again . . .

Soldiers in the streets. Protests. Race riots. Multiple murders. Napalm.

Chaos.

Maybe she hadn't been looking.

Paul took her hand, and either his was on fire or hers was frozen. He didn't seem to notice.

Dazed, Jay didn't realize where he was taking her, where they were, who that window belonged to until they stepped inside where *Rally!* was splayed across the far wall in four-foot-high black letters just as it had been outside the building.

Paul led her through a room full of desks occupied by a few older men in white shirts and black pants, as well as student volunteers, like Paul, distinguishable by their complete lack of white shirts and black pants. He rapped on the open door labeled with a handwritten EDITOR sign.

"Come."

The man behind the incredibly messy desk sported a white shirt and black pants, too, but his bushy, light-brown hair stuck out from his head like a halo, and when he stepped around to greet them, he did so with bare feet.

"You must be Jay." He enveloped her hand in both of his. "I'm Sam Laughlin."

"Nice to meet you, Mr. Laughlin." Jay moved her arm up and down, like a shake, hoping he'd release her, but he didn't.

"Sam, please." He sat on the front edge of the desk, dislodging a stack of papers, which scattered into the air, skating gently to the floor. No one seemed to notice but her. "I hear your brother is an amazing artist." He released her at last. "I'd love to see his work."

She touched the bag that still weighted her shoulder, and Sam's gaze sharpened. "You have some of it with you?"

Between Momma finding the schnapps, the rally, the ribbons, then the chaos photographs, Jay was so mixed up she nodded before she thought, then cast a glance at Paul, who smiled, oblivious to her concern.

Hadn't she told him the sketches were a secret? She thought so. Although maybe she'd said they were a secret from Momma. That hadn't meant she wanted a stranger to know about them, but it was too late to stop the downhill train that was Sam Laughlin.

He used his forearm to sweep the contents of his desk onto the floor, where it mixed with what was already there, then rubbed his hands together, attention pinned to her purse.

Should she show him or shouldn't she? She hadn't even shown her friends, back when they'd still been friends. She hadn't shown Momma. However, for some reason, she wanted to show Sam Laughlin, so Jay pulled Billy's sketches free, but instead of placing them into the man's outstretched hands, she sidestepped and laid them on the desk herself.

"Holy fuck," Sam said.

"Right?" Paul asked.

In the other room telephones rang, typewriters clacked,

voices muttered and murmured. The world moved on, while here, in the office, even the air seemed to still.

"I'll bump everything from the next issue."

"Wait," Jay said. "What?"

"The whole issue." Sam made a Moses-parting-the-Red-Sea gesture. "For these."

"That's amazing, Sam." Paul grinned. "Wow! Tha—"

"No!" Jay found her words, or at least one of them. The important one. "Hell no."

Maybe the important two.

Showing Sam was one thing, showing the world quite another. She stacked the sketches and returned them to her bag, then latched it and set her palm on top before heading for the door.

Paul made a grab for her elbow and missed. "But don't you want to—?"

"No." Same word, why wasn't he getting it? She'd try two all over again. "Hell no."

Sam turned a laugh into a cough. "I think she means no."

"Yeah, okay. But I thought you were digging the rally; I thought the photos in the window opened your eyes."

If that were the case, wouldn't she have seen this coming?

She felt dumber than a new guy in Vietnam, the kind who, no matter how many times he'd been warned, still stepped on a land mine. She'd certainly stepped in it here. Why had she wanted to show Sam the sketches? For confirmation they were good? She knew that. Had she wanted an adult to tell her the drawings were the product of an active imagination and everything would be all right? That would be total crap, but she knew that too.

"The sketches are my brother's," Jay said. "They aren't mine to give."

Sam nodded. "Maybe you could ask him?"

"He won't—"

"Just ask."

The idea of Billy giving permission for his drawings to appear in a magazine like *Rally!* was so far out there, she blurted, "Sure," then fled. She managed to walk almost a block before Paul caught up with her.

"Where are you going?"

Jay had no idea. She couldn't walk home. She couldn't call Momma. None of her friends had a license, let alone a car, and even if they did would they come? Once upon a time they would have. Somehow.

Jay followed Paul to the parking lot.

"I'm sorry," he said once they were out of the city and traveling the highway headed home. "I thought—"

"You were wrong." Jay hoped he'd take the hint and shut up, but he didn't have to. She was a captive audience, unless she wanted to jump from a car traveling fifty miles an hour.

"I don't think I am. Wrong."

"Men never do." She'd heard that from Momma. Jay had no idea about men. Obviously.

"Your brother's sketches could make a difference."

Had Paul become her friend, had he become something more, because of the drawings?

"My brother's making a difference."

"Is he?"

"Fuck you."

Jay refused to speak another word, and eventually Paul stopped using them. The idea that Billy wasn't making a difference as a soldier, that he could die and *still* not make one was an idea she did not want to examine. She would *not* examine it. She would also not share her brother's drawings with anyone who did not understand and support the sacrifice Billy was making, that her whole family was making.

Her gaze slid to Paul, then away. She'd already done that enough.

He stopped in front of her house, and she got out, slammed the door, went inside, where Ringo greeted her as if she'd been gone a lifetime. It probably seemed so to him. Right now, it seemed so to her too.

She'd left that morning happy to be doing something – anything—after the boredom of the last few weeks. She'd been excited to see Paul, to visit State Street at last. Even the rally had intrigued her. A few hours later, State Street and the rally were old news, and boredom was far preferable to this . . . this . . .

Jay yanked the headband out of her hair, considered tossing it into the trash, but Momma might find it there, so she thrust the thing to the back of a drawer, then spent the next ten minutes trying to decide on a better place to hide Billy's drawings.

There wasn't one. The best hiding place was right where they were, at the bottom of an item Momma would never suspect that Jay would touch—the suitcase-purse—something she'd been very vocal about loathing. Besides, Momma had already found the schnapps. Would she search for anything else?

Jay glanced at the drawer with the hippie headband. She hoped not.

Hours later the TV was talking, but Jay wasn't listening. She was still thinking about the contraband in her room, along with . . . everything else, so when the phone rang, Jay jumped. She was as bad as Helen.

"Hello?"

"Jay, hey."

Helen. Weird.

"You wanna come over? Maybe sleep over?"

Sleep over? At Helen's? Even weirder. Though maybe Helen was trying to bring them all together, work things out. Jay's mood lightened.

"Is Ronnie coming?"

"I asked her but . . ."

Jay's mood deflated like a leaky balloon. "When you told her I might come, she said no."

"She said she was busy."

With who? Jay thought. *Doing what?*

"Can you?"

As she wanted to avoid the schnapps conversation as long as possible, Jay agreed. She scribbled a note for her mother, then strolled through Willow Creek as darkness fell and shades were lowered, curtains drawn. The night held a chill far ahead of its time.

A car turned the corner, and its headlights splashed over Jay before it stopped, idling in the center of the street.

Mr. Maxwell from the service station rested his arm on the open window and the *Semper Fi* tattoo he'd gotten in World War Two shimmied. He'd tried to get Billy to enlist in the marines, but Billy would not be swayed from following the family footsteps straight into the army.

"What're you doin' out here, kiddo?"

Where was Helen and her *Missing* poster when she needed her?

"I'm . . . uh . . . searching for Fluff."

Mr. Maxell frowned.

"There's a bunny. Missing for a while now."

"Doubtful it's missing anymore. Coyotes gotta eat too."

Jay winced. She should have kept searching for Fluff. Truth be told, she'd forgotten all about him, and that wasn't like her, but lately what was?

"How's your brother?"

"He's . . . um . . ." What was Billy? Not fine. Not really. But should she tell Mr. Maxwell?

Definitely not. In this town, grown-ups stuck their noses into any old kid's business just because they could, then blabbed whatever they learned to whoever might listen. Telling Mr. Maxwell would be as dumb as broadcasting it on WISM 1480.

Mr. Maxwell revved the engine, impatient.

"Billy's good," Jay blurted.

"I doubt he's good, young lady." Mr. Maxwell sighed. "But he's alive?"

"Yes." Jay nodded like the bobble-headed dog Gramps kept on the dash of his Chevy pickup. "Alive."

"Good," Mr. Maxwell echoed. "You better get on home, quick-like. Wandering around after dark isn't something good girls do."

Why, all of a sudden, was everyone so concerned about how things looked instead of how things *were?*

A light drizzle began to fall as Mr. Maxwell pulled away.

"Crap." Jay's hair was going to expand until it resembled a Brillo pad, but at least it kept anyone else who might have trolled the damp semidarkness inside and saved Jay from explaining—lying—anymore. For some reason, the residents of Willow Creek, who would not only dance in a snowstorm but drive in it too, avoided rain as if it were droplets of fire falling from the sky.

Fog swirled in, brushing her face like damp fingertips. Jay stared into it, but instead of Willow Creek, she saw Vietnam, where the fog was a sinister, slinking monster, a living, breathing being that surrounded her brother in a bubble of danger he could not escape. He would die there, and then what? Would communism die too? No. Would it die if a thousand, ten thousand, a hundred thousand Billys bled out into the soil of that place? Hell no

Why didn't anyone see that? Why hadn't she?

She wanted her brother out of Vietnam. Yesterday. He didn't . . . they didn't . . . *America* didn't belong there.

Billy didn't believe that, neither did Gramps. It wasn't what she had even a few weeks ago. But if she voiced this opinion in Willow Creek—Patriotic Small Town, USA—she'd only hear . . .

What is wrong with you? Don't you love America?

She *did* love America. It was the best country on earth, and *because* it was America, she should be able to say what she thought to anyone, whenever she wanted to.

"Jay?" Helen sat on the top step of the Murphys' crooked porch.

Jay had been so deep in thought she barely remembered walking here.

"What's wrong?" Helen asked.

Should she tell Helen her conclusions? Maybe not yet.

"Nothing's wrong." Jay was getting far too good at lying. She turned up the sidewalk, avoiding the areas of broken cement without even looking down.

"I saw you in the hippie kid's car this morning."

Jay tripped. Maybe she didn't know the cement—or anything—as well as she thought.

"Where'd you go?"

Jay paused at the foot of the steps. Nothing moved but the breeze. "Promise you won't tell my mother?"

"What did you do?"

Jay didn't answer, and Helen's breath hissed out, exasperated. "Of course, I won't tell."

"I went to State Street."

Helen's eyes widened. "To the protest rally?"

"How'd you know about that?"

"It was all over the news."

"But it wasn't a protest rally. Not really."

Helen came to her feet. Standing on the top step, she towered over Jay still at ground level. "How dumb are you?"

Jay stepped back as if Helen had shoved her. Sure, Helen was smarter than everyone else, and she'd often pointed out the stupidity in the world, but she'd never, ever pointed the stupid finger at one of her friends. That she was doing so now, over this, made Jay mad.

"How can we ever discover the truth if we don't hear both

sides? Isn't that what they do in court? Isn't that why they do it? So a judge can hear everything before making a decision?"

"Did *Paul* tell you that?"

"No. I came up with it all on my own." And she was proud of herself too. "Maybe I'm not as dumb as you think I am."

"It sure isn't smart to spend so much time with him. He's—"

Before Helen could say something Jay might regret, she jumped in. "Nice."

"To you." Helen's gaze sharpened behind her glasses. "People wonder why."

"People wonder why a cute boy is nice to me?" Jay shouldn't feel hurt—who cared what "people" wondered—but she was.

"The consensus is more along the lines of 'dirty hippie' rather than cute."

"Mags thought he was cute."

"You really want to use Mags as a defense?"

"I didn't think I needed a defense," Jay said. "Especially with you."

The silence went on for a long time before Helen broke it. "Let's just . . . just forget it, okay?"

"Okay." Jay was happy to forget about it if Helen would. She followed her last friend inside. "Where is everyone?"

"Mom's working. Dad's at his brother's place. The morons are at a party."

Well, that explained the invitation, along with the desire to forget the angry words that had just passed between them. That Helen was still spooked by the dark meant her brothers either hadn't stopped tormenting her, despite her completion of the cemetery dare—big shock—or the damage was already done, and Helen would be afraid of the dark forever.

Jay wanted to know which one, but from past experience, she knew that Helen would deny everything. She wasn't sure of the best way to demand the truth from anyone she thought was lying. If she could figure it out, she should knock on the front of the White House and talk to good old Lyndon B.

Helen drew the curtains. "You wanna watch *Andy Griffith?*"

Jay sighed. "Sure."

They spent the rest of the night in their usual sleepover pursuits of watching TV, munching on junk food—at Helen's this meant popcorn washed down with Kool-Aid—then playing Yahtzee until after midnight when Jay could no longer stop yawning, and they headed for Helen's room.

Jay fell asleep, only to awake an unknown amount of time later.

Something was wrong.

CHAPTER 20

Billy
"War (What Is It Good For?)"

*V*ietnam—July/August 1967

Terrell seemed almost himself as they rode a Slick back to their platoon. He'd insisted on buying a shotgun—available in Vung Tau for no earthly reason that Billy could understand—and hauling it along with them.

"You don't have any ammo," Billy pointed out.

"Sure do." Terrell laughed like a loon.

For the rest of their R and R, they had stuck together, swam, slept, ate, gone into town, drank, smoked, gambled. But neither one of them had taken a woman back to their hotel. Billy already felt alone enough.

Flash and an FNG he introduced as Magoo—thick glasses and perpetually blinking eyes made no explanation necessary—met them at the LZ. "This here's Slayer and Teej. As you've already heard, they're special."

Terrell flipped Flash the bird, and Flash laughed. "So how special was it?"

"Damn special!" Terrell winked, and the two snickered like they were best friends.

Maybe Terrell *wasn't* back to his old self. The niggle of worry that had crawled along the back of Billy's neck now and again since Crazy Joe had rained down on Terrell in pieces returned. If Terrell continued to be the short-tempered, twitchy, insomniac Terrell, did Billy really want him watching his six? Did he want Terrell watching anyone's?

Flash led them into the bush. Billy didn't like not walking at the head of the line, but he had no idea where they were going.

"What'd we miss?" Terrell asked.

"Nothin' much. Sugar Bear bought the farm."

Sugar Bear was dead?

"Seems like something much to me," Billy said.

Flash cast a quick glance over his shoulder. "What'd you expect? We're down our permanent point and his fruitcake pal, makin' do with two cherries. The other one's an even bigger dumbass than this one."

Magoo's shoulders hunched.

"What the hell's his name?" Flash snapped his fingers—once, twice. "Mayberry," he said at the same time Magoo mumbled, "Floyd."

Billy saw the connection—Floyd was the barber in Mayberry, America's favorite fictional town.

"Anyway," Flash continued, "we're lucky we weren't wiped out."

"I had sex," Terrell said.

Billy stumbled.

Flash hooted. "How'd you manage that?"

"Ain't hard."

"If it ain't hard, you aren't doin' it right." Flash paused to hack his way through some bamboo, which blessedly shut him up for a second.

Billy poked Terrell in the shoulder, and when he turned, Billy mouthed: *Why?*

For an answer, Terrell gave Flash's back the double bird.

Apparently being called a *fruitcake* filled Terrell with the irresistible desire to prove he wasn't. And guys that had something to prove often wound up dead, along with their friends.

Billy muttered a curse. Everyone's eyes turned his way. "Uh, what happened to Sugar Bear?"

Flash lowered the machete, kicked at the bamboo he'd hacked, and enough of it fell for them to continue. "You remember the AK Sugar Bear took off the baby gook you wasted your first day?"

"The first day?" Magoo asked.

"Like I told you, Cherry, he's special."

Anyone else calling Billy *special*, and he might believe it, or at least be flattered. But Flash was trying to get his goat. It was what he did best.

"We got in an itty-bitty firefight," Flash continued.

"That was itty-bitty?" Magoo echoed, voice faint.

Flash ignored him. "AK worked fine. Better than a piece of shit Mattel."

Some guys had taken to calling their M16s *Mattels*, as in toy, plastic weapons. They weren't, obviously, but guys had to bitch about something.

"Sugar Bear was at point. Got pinned down and ran out of ammo."

"Too far away for any of us to give him some," Magoo said.

"Shit for brains, you can't share M16 ammo with an AK." Flash shook his head. "Remember that."

Terrell flicked Billy a glance. "Was his own fault."

Though Terrell's noticing Billy was upset, actually caring, was an improvement on how he'd been, his words didn't do anything to make the tug of guilt go away. Billy wasn't sure anything could, except maybe a time machine.

"If I'd been here, he wouldn't have been there."

"He still would have run out of ammo."

"But if he were with the others, he wouldn't have needed it."

Sure, Sugar Bear would have looked like a moron, regardless; he'd have been razzed about it for a week, but he'd still be alive to get razzed.

"Don't do nothin' dangerous or stupid to try and make up for this."

Did Billy's thoughts show on his face, or was Terrell a good guesser? Because Billy *had* been thinking along those lines. Well, not about doing something dangerous and stupid, just that he'd have to try harder to be more Slayer than ever before. Which he could do. No problem. The more he thought of himself as Slayer, the more Slayer-like he became.

"I know what I'm doing," he said, and Terrell frowned. Had Terrell begun to worry about Billy as much as Billy had been worrying about Terrell?

Flash whistled the distinct high-low warble of a cardinal, which was repeated from beyond a six-foot-high stand of elephant grass to their left.

It had been Billy's idea to use the cardinal call as a signal. There were plenty of birds in the jungle, but none of them a cardinal, eliminating any confusion except in soldiers from the South who had never heard the trill of a bird that lived year-round in the North. Luckily, the sound was as easy to learn as ABC.

They pushed through the grass and in a gully on the other side lay the camp.

"How was it?" Boom-Boom approached with Big Al and a few others.

"What'd you do?" asked a small, dark-haired, jittery kid Billy had never seen before.

Must be Floyd, a.k.a. Mayberry.

Flash slapped Terrell so hard on the back, he took a step forward. "Teej is now a man."

Terrell began to share how sex was life-changing, man-making. Not what Terrell had shared with Billy. But according to the army, the truth was what they said it was—inflated body counts, expanded occupied territory, fighting the good fight to preserve the American way. Why should Terrell be any different?

Terrell drifted off with the others, leaving Billy behind.

"How is he?"

Billy started. Three days away and LT was able to sneak up on him. What had happened to being more Slayer than ever before?

"Johnson?" LT snapped his fingers in front of Billy's face. "You in there?"

"Uh . . . yeah. He's better." Billy debated telling LT about the meltdown and decided against it. If Billy'd been crying in some stranger's lap, he wouldn't want LT—or anyone else—to know. That was basic friend code. Even Billy knew that much.

But what about army code? LT needed to know if Terrell was fit to go back out there, and *that* Billy wasn't sure about.

"Sometimes he seems like his old self and other times . . ."

"You're not sure who he is."

Billy gave a shrug-nod.

"Well, unfortunately, not being yourself isn't a good enough reason to go home." LT lit a smoke. "Otherwise, we'd all be outta here."

"Sir?"

"Are you the same man you were when you came?"

Billy hadn't been a man, at least according to Gramps, which made him wonder what Gramps thought of him now.

"I was a kid."

"Weren't we all?" LT drew on his cig.

"Not you."

"You'd be surprised." Smoke spurted from LT's nose in a dragon-like puff. "When I got here I was green as fresh grass."

"Then what happened?"

"Vietnam," LT said quietly.

Flash hooted, drawing their attention just as he slapped Terrell's back. "Big man!"

LT crooked an eyebrow. "Having sex does not make you a man."

"I know."

"Neither does killing."

Billy frowned. "But then . . ."

"What are we doing here?"

Billy knew that answer by heart. "Stopping the spread of communism, protecting those who've been invaded."

LT heaved a long sigh that smelled of smoke and disappointment. "Fighting another man's war doesn't do it either."

"I stood up, volunteered; it's my duty."

"You're getting warmer."

Billy tried to think, but he'd been trying not to for so long, his brain was a big, blank sheet of nothing.

LT's gaze remained steady on the men; he was the definition of patience, a picture of calm. He set his hand on Billy's shoulder. "It'll come to you," he said, then walked away.

Billy wanted to be like him more than he'd ever wanted to be like anyone in his life.

"Catch!"

A steel pot bounced off Billy's chest. He managed to grab the thing before it fell to the ground. "What the hell, Bama?"

"I missed you." Bama threw his arms around Billy's neck.

Luckily the helmet was between them, or it might have gotten awkward.

Billy shoved him away. "I missed you too."

Bama was annoying, but he was Bama. One of Billy's

buddies, his pals, his brothers. Someone he would die for.

"I made this for you." Bama tapped a finger crusted in something that was too red to be dirt and not red enough to be blood against the pot.

Billy thought longingly of the daily showers he'd taken in Vung Tau, then pointed to the pot he already wore. "I have one."

"This one's better." Bama took it back, turned it around.

SLAYER had been printed across the cover; black hash marks climbed up the dome and over the top. One, two, five, ten.

"That's your kill count."

Billy could do nothing but stare. There were too many marks. Weren't there?

Bama removed the graffitied cover from the helmet, plopped that one onto his own head, then motioned for Billy to hand over his. When Billy just stood there—his brain kept counting those hash marks, then whirling round and round—Bama removed Billy's steel pot and exchanged the dirty but unmarked cover for the one Bama had made before setting it back onto Billy's head. "There you go."

He waited for Billy to speak, and when he didn't, Bama's grin wilted. "You don't like it?"

Billy lifted his hands, palms up. Bama took that as an invitation to keep talking, as Bama often did.

"The whole platoon got together to figure out how many slashes you've earned. It was hard because they're just dinks, right?"

"Just dinks," Billy repeated, a little dizzy.

"We wanted to thank you for, you know, doing what you do."

"Killing."

Confusion filtered over Bama's face. "Well, yeah."

Billy took off the helmet, considered the marks again. If they were true, why didn't he remember?

Would Slayer remember? No, because to Slayer, they *were* just dinks. That was how Slayer got the job done.

But Billy *was* Slayer. Wasn't he?

Slayer was who he needed to be to get out of here alive. To get all of them out of here alive. So while it bothered him that he didn't remember killing all those people—*dinks!*—he was also glad he didn't remember if not remembering allowed him to kill more.

"If you don't wear it, Deus is gonna shit a brick. It's bad luck not to wear a cover with your name on it. He's really superstitious." Bama glanced furtively at the others. "Lately, we all are."

Since Bama kept staring at him all worried-like, Billy set the pot on his head. He wasn't superstitious. Then again, what did wearing it hurt?

That night it started to rain and continued for several days. Then the fog came in, so thick it seemed to whisper. Everyone was jumpy. Even Billy, at the head of the line, shot up a tree that looked a lot like a VC, until it didn't die.

Flash laughed so hard he almost dropped his M16. "Be cool, Slayer. Can't make a new slash on your pot for a tree."

Billy didn't make new slashes on his helmet for anything. He didn't need to. Every time he added to the platoon's body count, the next morning when he put on the helmet, new marks had mysteriously appeared.

Terrell denied it; Bama denied it. Hell, everyone denied it, but someone was doing it, and that, combined with the way half the guys were staring at his cover, at him, like they were magic or something, made Billy more determined to do his job.

LT had said killing didn't make you a man, but as the days went by and his kill count climbed and the guys around him treated Billy more and more like he was invincible, he started to believe it. Who else could boast this many marks on his helmet without a single mark on himself?

The morning of the fourth, or maybe the fifth, day—between the rain and the fog and the mysterious appearing helmet slashes, Billy'd lost track—they were on patrol, and Magoo, who'd begun following Billy around like Ringo, collapsed as if he'd been shot.

Everyone dove for cover; a few started firing even as Magoo stood, then immediately hit the dirt when a friendly bullet whistled too close.

"I stepped in a hole! A hole!"

The shooting stopped. Guys got to their feet.

Deus strode up from the rear and smacked Magoo in the head. "Didn't I tell you to step where the guy in front of you steps?"

"Yes, Sarge."

"Did Slayer fall in a hole?"

"No, Sarge."

"Then what the fucking fuck?"

Magoo blinked even more than usual, uncertain what to say to that.

"Looks like an air hole," Billy said. "Gotta be a tunnel entrance around here somewhere."

"Spread out," LT ordered. "Find it."

They did not find it, which only made everyone skittish again. Was the enemy crawling along beneath them? Had they crept topside up there, over there, or behind? Would an ambush blaze from the depths of the fog?

They had no choice but to continue, and while Billy did so as if he hadn't a care in the world, hoping his confidence would leech into the others, secretly he worried that someone might be jittery enough to shoot him in the back, and then where would he be?

Dead. Which, oddly, bothered him a lot less than the thought that everyone else would be.

Late in the afternoon, the sun finally came out, and the jungle steamed.

"It's worse than the fog." Terrell squinted at the rising wisps. "Fog don't hiss."

"It'll stop soon," Billy said.

"Well, if you say so, it must *be* so." Flash's tone was singsong, meant to annoy, but when didn't he?

"You know . . ." Terrell got up in Flash's face. Lately he'd been turning his snotty sarcasm on Flash rather than Billy, and that was a change Billy could get behind. "You been more of an asshole on this patrol than usual, which is pretty hard to do, considering."

Flash bumped his chest into Terrell's. "Oh yeah?"

Terrell seemed to be returning to the Terrell he'd been "before," lessening Billy's concern his friend might be distracted enough to get himself, or someone else, killed. Sure, he smiled less, and when he did, the smile wasn't as bright, wasn't as wide, but whose was?

Had Terrell forgotten Crazy Joe or just gotten past it, found a way to live with it? Billy wanted to ask how, but he didn't. Because they didn't talk about stuff like that. Not here, not now, maybe not ever.

"Knock it off," LT ordered, voice quiet, attention on the jungle.

Everyone knocked it off, staring where LT did as they lifted their rifles, fingers poised.

Something was coming.

The trill of a cardinal split the silence; they relaxed as LT whistled back, and Win, the Kit Carson scout, emerged from the brush. Win often slipped off, returning hours, sometimes days later, with intel. He was always able to find them, even though half the time they were just wandering around with no specific place to go.

"I saw LT talking to him last night," Terrell said. "Blinked once, and poof, the guy was gone."

Bama snorted. "He ain't a genie."

"No." Terrell's gaze remained on the scout, who'd hurried to LT and begun yammering. "But he's somethin'."

"*Con ho!*" Win said that word louder than all the rest.

"What's *con ho?*" Terrell asked.

"Tiger." Deus slipped past to join LT and Win.

"I heard a marine got killed by a tiger near the DMZ." Boom-Boom smacked himself in the head. "That's messed up, man."

"We aren't anywhere near the DMZ," Billy said.

"There's more than one tiger in Vietnam." Flash thumped Billy on the back. "You kill that thing, Slayer, and you'll be goddamn legend."

"He already is," Terrell murmured.

For some reason that murmur made the back of Billy's neck tingle.

"All right, listen up." LT approached. "A ville two Ks north lost a water buffalo and five chickens in the past week. Last night a kid disappeared."

"Probably joined the VC," Bama said.

"*Con ho* tracks at stream. Blood." Win made a dragging motion, then pointed to the ground. "Not VC."

"Does he seem to know more English than he's let on?" Terrell asked.

"Or else he's learned some along the way," Billy said.

"We're gonna give it a look-see," LT continued. "Goodwill mission."

"What does that mean?" Flash asked.

"If we kill the tiger"—Deus slid past them in the other direction—"the ville will think twice about harboring VC."

"A tiger hunt?" Bama shifted from one foot to another in excitement or with his seemingly constant need to pee. "No way, Jose! My brother isn't gonna believe this."

"I don't believe it," Terrell said. "And I'm right here."

"Win's gonna lead us to the ville." LT rolled a smoke between his fingers. He didn't seem to realize he hadn't lit the thing.

Billy stepped back so the scout could take his place, and Win gave Billy a great big smile, patted his shoulder.

"What was that?" Terrell whispered.

The scout had never seemed to notice Billy before; he never noticed anyone. He kept to himself, did what he was told, and reported to LT.

Billy rubbed the back of his neck. "He's warming up to us."

"Warmin' up to you maybe."

"I didn't come here to shoot no tiger." Boom-Boom clapped his hands once, the sound almost as loud as a gunshot in the steamy stillness. "Aren't they like extinct or something?"

"Extinct means they're all gone, forever." LT rubbed his forehead. "So, no."

"Still, he's just bein' a tiger."

"My daddy always told me 'a killer is a killer,'" Bama said. "'Always.'"

They'd gone nearly two klicks when Win started to mutter in Vietnamese, the words a cadence, almost a song, a chant, maybe a prayer. He seemed nervous, which made Billy nervous, and he glanced at LT, who left his position to join Billy.

"Does he always do that?" Billy asked.

LT shook his head, eyes narrowing.

"Can you understand him?"

LT, who was good with languages and had caught on to quite a bit of Vietnamese just by dealing with the scout, tilted his head. "Behind. First. Fire? No shoot. Maybe."

Win turned his head slowly to the left, set his finger to his lips, then lifted his arm in the signal for *freeze* before he crept in that direction.

"He's probably never hunted a tiger before," LT said softly.

Who has? Billy wondered.

Suddenly Win shouted several words in Vietnamese. One of them—*kẻ giết người*—made Billy move forward—Bian had uttered the same phrase on the beach in Vung Tau—but LT set his hand on Billy's arm.

"He said *slayer*."

LT frowned and slowly lifted the smoke he'd never lit toward his mouth. "He also said *now*."

Win hit the ground.

LT yanked Billy behind him as a shot rang out.

Everything seemed to go silent, even the birds. No one breathed as LT slowly fell and fell and fell.

Billy stepped toward him then, up ahead, something twinkled. The last time Billy had seen such a twinkle it had been the sun glancing off the barrel of an AK. Like then, he took the shot.

A VC tumbled out of a tree and landed with a boneless thud. The only sounds were the birds suddenly scolding and the platoon suddenly breathing.

LT's unlit cigarette lay in the center of the dark, slick circle of blood that had created a bull's-eye around the hole above his heart.

Bones set his fingers to LT's neck and cursed.

Billy could not stop staring into LT's eyes, which would not stop staring back. He wanted to shake him, shout at him, plead with him to *get up*, to *please, please, please not be dead*. But he couldn't speak, and that was probably for the best. If Billy let out all he was keeping in, he might never stop screaming, and if he lost it now, wouldn't everyone?

"What the hell happened?" Deus asked, and when no one answered, when Billy continued to stare, Deus snapped, "Slayer!"

Billy blinked. Right. What would Slayer do? He would not shout or plead; he would not cry or whine or stare. Slayer got the job done.

"Ambush," Billy managed, his voice not his own.

"For the tiger?" Deus asked.

Billy's gaze flicked to Win as the scout gained his feet.

Kẻ giết người!

"No," Billy said. "For me."

Then he shot Win in the chest.

CHAPTER 21

Jay
"Child in Time"

Willow Creek—August 1967

The room was darker than the blacktop leading out of town. Jay's eyes strained, ears too, but all was quiet, nothing moved. Had she imagined the creepy certainty that something was wrong, someone was there?

"Don't," Helen whispered.

Jay heard breathing other than hers. Other than Helen's. Breathing that was getting faster. Louder.

The sound of skin violently meeting skin cracked the night like a gunshot.

"Please." Helen's whisper now held a hint of tears. "Don't."

Smack. The bed shook.

Suddenly Jay understood so many things, and her hands curled into fists. "Get out."

A quick, indrawn breath followed her words before she sensed movement again.

The bedroom door opened, and a shadow slid through; the light from the bathroom threw a silhouette across the far wall before the figure melted into the darkness. Nevertheless, Jay recognized a brother. But which one?

Guess assholes *didn't* stop being assholes. Ever.

She leaped up, shut the door, fumbled for a nonexistent lock with fingers that shook, then leaned her forehead against the cool wood.

They'd all thought Helen was just high-strung, smarter than they were so the world, life, anything, everything bothered her more than it did the rest of them, and others preyed on that. They'd suspected bullying. They'd been right, but who could have figured on this?

No wonder Helen was so twitchy; no wonder she was afraid of being alone in the dark. No wonder she tried to find excuses to stay out late and rarely asked anyone to sleep over. Why had she asked Jay?

Jay joined Helen on the bed. "How long has he been touching you?"

"He hasn't."

"Bullshit, Helen." Fury rolled over her like a red-hot wave. She wanted to punch something. Someone. "You didn't scream; you weren't shocked." As Jay had been. "This has happened before."

"Danny's always in my room."

"I bet." At least Helen had narrowed it down. "We need to tell your mom."

"No!" Helen grasped Jay's arm. "Whining to my mom about Danny in my room isn't going to do anything except get me yelled at for whining."

"It will if you tell her he's touching you."

"Will it?" Helen asked.

A chill settled over Jay. "What does that mean?"

"My mom is not going to believe that her son has any interest in his sister's body."

"Ick."

"Exactly. She told me I was disgusting, and if I brought it up again, she'd send me away."

Jay laughed. Helen didn't.

"Wait, you're serious?"

Helen didn't answer.

"Then I'll tell her."

Helen's grip on Jay's arm tightened. "Promise you won't."

Jay took her arm back. "Why not?"

"They'll send me to my aunt's in South Dakota."

Jay couldn't make out Helen's expression. "They'll send *you*?"

"Yes."

"Helen, that's—"

"No one ever blames the boy. You know they'll blame me. They'll say I led him on; what was he supposed to do?"

"Jesus, Helen—" Jay began.

"Why make trouble? It's not like he touched you."

"Got that right." Jay's fingers curled into fists again.

Would he have if he'd known she was there? His sharp intake of breath and the way he'd beat feet hinted that good old Dan hadn't known his sister had company.

The idea of waking up with someone touching her in the dark, the way Danny touched Helen, made Jay's skin all prickly and not in the good way it prickled when Paul touched her. She couldn't imagine what Helen's must feel like.

Jay took her friend's hand. "It's only going to get worse if you let it." Jay squeezed. "Promise me you'll tell, Helen, or I will."

The breath Helen drew wobbled. "Have you ever been afraid of anything?"

"Me?" A single bark of laughter burst from Jay. "Of course. I'm afraid Billy won't come back. I'm afraid Paul's going to realize I'm not the greatest girl in town. I'm afraid the friends I've had all my life are going to desert me, then I'm going to be more alone than I've been since I was three. But right now, I'm really afraid my last friend on earth is going to spend her life fucked up because her brother—"

"Stop!" The word cracked into the nighttime stillness, and Helen slapped her hand over her own mouth. When she lowered it, she continued on a whisper. "You have to promise me you won't say a word. Not to anyone. Not even to Billy. This is my business, Jay, no one else's."

Jay thought it *was* her business now, and for an instant, she wondered if Helen had invited her over, had smacked Danny hard enough to shake the bed just to make certain Jay was awake, so Jay could back her up if she needed it. But if so, then why was she behaving like this?

"I'll do it. Just promise me you'll let me do it my way."

"I'll promise if you do."

Helen turned her hand in Jay's, changing the gesture of comfort into a handshake before she lay back down and seemed to fall instantly asleep.

For the remainder of the night, Jay waited for the door latch to click open. Every sound made her flinch. Every time she began to nod off, she jerked awake wondering what she'd heard, *if* she'd heard anything. Was this what it was like for Billy when he was on watch in Vietnam?

When sunlight tinted the curtains, and the rest of the household began banging doors and tromping like elephants, Helen didn't move.

A tap came on the door, then it opened. "We're leaving for work," Mrs. Murphy whispered.

Since when did the Murphy boys have jobs?

Jay kept her eyes shut, her mouth too, afraid if she opened either one, everything she'd promised not to say would spill free. But she'd promised Helen, and Helen had promised her.

Promises meant something, so she'd give her friend the chance to keep hers.

Mrs. Murphy waited a few seconds, then shut the door; her footsteps faded.

Jay crept to the window and peered out a tiny opening in the curtain as they all piled into a station wagon older than Helen and putt-putted away.

Helen's eyes opened. "Remember, Jay, you promised."

And because Helen was her friend and she *had* promised, Jay nodded. "So did you."

Helen closed her eyes.

Jay waited, thinking Helen might want to talk more, and if so, she should be here, but again her friend seemed to fall asleep. The reason for Helen's crashing first at sleepovers was now obvious. She spent every night waiting, wondering, worrying. When she didn't have to, when she was safe . . . out went the lights.

Jay changed into the clothes she'd brought, picked up her bag, and left her friend to sleep.

In Willow Creek, anywhere could be reached from anywhere in almost no time, so Jay entered her house pretty early. If she could just make it to her room before Momma—

"Jay?" Momma's voice came from the kitchen.

Jay sighed and gave in to her inevitable grounding for life.

Momma sat at the table, a mug of tea in front of her. She motioned to an empty seat.

"I should have had a conversation with you years ago, but you always seemed . . ." She took a breath, let it out, stared hard at the Formica tabletop. "Young for your age. Your friends too. Except Mags, I suppose. I'm sure Peggy already talked to her daughter."

"About schnapps?" Jay hadn't said she'd shared the bottle. She hadn't even admitted to drinking it, but Momma knew. Momma always knew.

"Never mind that. I overreacted. I'm surprised you haven't tried booze before."

"Okay." Jay started to get up.

"Sit," Momma said so forcefully Ringo, who'd just pranced into the room, sat too. "We need to talk about sex."

"I'd rather talk about schnapps."

Momma's eyes narrowed. "You know what goes where?"

Jay sat there trying to catch up, trying to find sense. They'd had a sex talk when she was . . . twelve? Thirteen?

"Boys have a—"

"Know that," Jay blurted.

"And it goes—"

"Sheesh! I know that too."

Now that she thought about it, the first sex talk had been more of an explanation about getting her period, most of which she'd already heard from Mags, who'd gotten hers at the age of eleven and been the envy of everyone. Jay's envy had ended when she *became a woman*. Having your period was not fun. Ever. Talk about gilding the lily.

"*How* do you know that?" Momma asked. "From experience?"

"No!"

Momma let out a long, relieved breath.

"Wait a second," Jay said. "Why *are* we having this conversation now?" She wanted to add *or ever* but knew better.

"Someone saw you go into the forest with the new boy on July Fourth."

In this town, *someone* was probably more like *everyone*.

"Then you didn't come back for a very long time."

"We watched the fireworks."

"I'm not stupid, Jay. You can't see fireworks through the trees."

Jay almost explained about the clearing, but she'd kept it a secret this long, she wasn't going to blab now. Besides, where they'd gone wasn't the issue; the issue was—

"So you immediately jump to the conclusion I'm boning the new boy?"

"What?" Momma's head came up.

"It means—"

Momma held up her hand. "I know what it means. Where did *you* hear it?"

"In the locker room where I heard everything else."

Momma's hand lowered; her fingers curled around her mug. "That's where I got my information too, which made my wedding night quite the surprise."

"Ew."

Momma ignored her. "Your father—"

"Oh, hell no," Jay began.

"Watch your mouth." The words didn't have much heat. "Well, he knew what went where."

"Fabulous."

"Nope," Momma said. "But it got better."

Momma's expression made Jay think it *had* gotten better. Maybe even as good as it had been when Paul kissed her. She'd barely been able to think; she hadn't remembered her name. Scary, really, to be that much of a slave to a feeling. So why did she want to feel that way again, even though she was still angry at him?

"I was glad I'd waited for marriage," Momma continued. "The idea of fumbling around, naked, with someone I didn't love—"

"You loved Dad?"

From the way Momma had talked about him—which wasn't much, this was the most she'd said about Jay's father in a lifetime of conversations—wild horses couldn't have dragged her to the altar if she'd had a second chance to make the first decision.

"Why else would I have married him?"

"You had to?"

"Honestly, Jay!" Momma gave an exasperated huff.

"You never talk about him! What was I supposed to think?"

"I . . ." Momma frowned. "I was afraid bringing him up would only make you miss him more."

"Can't miss what you never had."

"I thought maybe your searching for lost things was your way of searching for him."

"Did you misplace him like your keys? Is Daddy in the junk drawer?"

Momma let go a surprised burst of laughter. "It would be a good place for him." Her eyes widened. "Whoops. I try not to talk ill of the . . . well, he's not dead. But—"

"I'm not looking for Dad when I look for lost things. I promise. I'm just good at it."

"What about Billy?"

"He's not good at it. He's probably misplaced his combat boots at least a dozen times already."

Momma smiled. "I meant, do you think he misses his father?"

"He never said that. Doesn't mean he doesn't, but I don't think so. You did a good job Momma. We're fine."

"Okay. Great. Where were we?"

"All done here." Jay tried to make a quick getaway.

"I remember now." Momma pointed to the chair and Jay returned to it. "Becoming a woman is both frightening and wonderful."

Those were the exact words Momma had used when they'd had the last "becoming a woman" talk. But Jay had not felt any differently once she'd crossed that threshold, unless she counted feeling "differently" once a month, and she didn't. And here was why . . .

The first talk had been BS. Getting your period didn't make a girl into a woman. Did sex make a woman out of a girl?

"I know they're calling this the Summer of Love." Momma rolled her eyes. "Free love. Love, love, love. But sex isn't love. Don't fool yourself into thinking it is."

Now Jay was really confused. If you got married for love, and you waited for sex until marriage, didn't it follow that sex was love?

"You know about rubbers?"

"I know what goes where," Jay said dryly.

Momma appeared relieved. She got to her feet.

That was the sex talk part two? Jay didn't know much more now than she had ten minutes before.

Momma kissed the top of Jay's head. "You know you can tell me anything?"

Helen's brother is touching her. Ronnie likes girls. Paul smells like limes and sunshine; he tastes even better. I went to a civil rights rally. The war is not what we think it is.

And the revelation that she'd come to on the way to Helen's last night.

Even if we win this war, if thousands die, communism won't. So what's the point?

She couldn't say any of that to anyone, especially not Momma.

"Sure, Momma, sure," she said instead, then escaped to her room.

CHAPTER 22

Billy
"The Sound of Silence"

*V*ietnam—August 1967

Win hit the ground and did not move.

Guys crouched, rifles poised, gazes on the jungle around them. But if there'd been more than a single sniper, more of them would be dead.

"Sparky, get us a dustoff," Deus ordered. "Now."

"No need to rush," Bones said. "They're all Kool-Aids."

Billy continued to stare at the dead sniper, the dead scout. He wasn't sure why. They weren't going to get up and run off any more than LT would ever get up or run off again.

"Beej?" Terrell stood at Billy's side. "What did you just do?"

Billy didn't answer; the question, considering the bodies, seemed rhetorical.

"What about the tiger?" Magoo's voice wobbled, on the verge of tears.

Billy heard several other guys take breaths that hitched in the middle. Should he be crying, or at least fighting not to? Probably, but Billy's eyes were as dry as his mouth.

Maybe he'd cry later, alone. Although if he started, would he be able to stop? And then what? He'd be sent home; he wouldn't be able to protect LT's men, and wasn't protecting them the least he could do considering LT had just died for him?

Crying wouldn't bring his lieutenant back. Nothing could.

"There isn't a tiger," Billy said, pleased that *his* voice didn't shake. The way he sounded—calm, cool, controlled—settled the whirl in his stomach. "There isn't even a village."

Terrell blinked, his eyelashes dragging tiny windshield-wiper-like streaks in the steam that fogged his glasses. "But—"

"If there were, we'd smell it."

Without plumbing, without sewers, the mixture of shit and piss and jungle near a village produced a scent similar to gasoline but a lot less appealing.

"We'd hear . . . something." Billy's hands were so cold his thumbs were falling asleep. How could that be when it was hotter here than any place he'd ever been in his life?

"Maybe." Deus joined them. "Maybe not."

"We can look but . . ." Billy flexed first one hand, then the other. "I don't feel it."

Deus and Terrell exchanged a glance.

Terrell put his hand on Billy's shoulder. "Whatchya talkin' about, bro?"

Terrell's fingers were scalding, or maybe Billy was just cold all over. Like LT soon would be. Dizziness fluttered, and Billy shook his head hard enough to stop the invasion of dancing black spots in front of his eyes.

"Beej?"

"Hmm?" Everyone stared at him, waiting. "Oh, right. It's the reason I'm so good at point."

"You see the field." Terrell's hand slid away, but the imprint of his fingers continued to burn.

"It's more feeling than seeing."

"Whatever you say." Terrell patted him.

Deus drew Billy away from the others; Terrell followed. Flash checked the enemy for booby traps, then began to go through his pockets.

On the surface everything seemed slow, muted, foggy—blues and greens and grays—but under that raged yellows, oranges, reds. Scream, rage, cry, kill. All of which needed to stay where they were.

Below.

"This was a trap," Billy said.

"Considering the dink in the tree, yeah. But how is that Win's fault?"

Billy shared LT's translation of Win's muttering and his own knowledge of the Vietnamese word for *slayer*.

"How'd a girl in Vung Tau hear about Slayer?" Terrell asked.

Why hadn't Billy wondered about that then? Because he'd been too busy being proud that she had.

Shame was the shade of banked coals in a fireplace, pulsing like a heart—*ba-boom, ba-boom.* Would it ever go away?

"Word must have gotten around gook-land that the douchebag who's killin' more than his fair share is called *Slayer*."

Deus cast Flash, who'd started going through the dead scout's pockets several feet away, an irritated glance. "Do you have ears like a fucking bat or something? Mind your own business."

Flash saluted with his middle finger.

"The only way word could have gotten around," Deus said, "is if Win told them."

They went silent as the truth of that sunk in. Yes, the scout had been a traitor, maybe to both sides, but if Billy hadn't been such a hotshot, would it have mattered? What would the guy have had to report?

Guilt, horror, embarrassment, sadness dropped atop scream, rage, cry, kill, and shame, mixing together to make a foul mash the shade of vomit and pus. Billy's stomach rolled again; he swallowed that mash back down where it belonged.

Below.

"If I wasn't Slayer, LT would still be alive."

"If you wasn't Slayer, no one would be." Terrell patted Billy again.

While the gesture did nothing for Billy but make him wish Terrell would stop, doing it seemed to help Terrell.

"He's right." Deus set *his* hand on Billy's other shoulder, squeezed once, and let go, leaving another set of fiery prints in its wake. "You've saved all of us, over and over again."

"Except now he's got a big-ass target on his back." Flash dropped what he'd found in Win's pockets into a plastic bag and secured it to the scout's wrist. "He's Slayer; they know it; they want him dead. Anyone near him is gonna end up like that." Flash pointed to LT being wrapped in his own green poncho by Monk.

Billy's stomach swirled faster, slick and greasy.

"If the VC knew which one of us was Slayer, there'd have been no reason for a trap, no reason for Win to point anyone out," Deus said. "But Win isn't going to be able to tell anyone anything anymore, and neither is that guy."

"All they gotta do is read his brain bucket," Flash said.

"Most of them can't read their own language," Deus pointed out, "let alone ours."

"You think they're too dim to understand he's got more hash marks than anyone else in the whole goddamn war?"

All eyes flicked to Billy's helmet like magnets.

"Gimme that." Terrell grabbed Billy's pot and made as if he'd throw it into the trees.

"Don't," Deus said. "He can't walk around out here without one."

"He can't walk around out here with this one."

"Here." Bama stood beside them, LT's dirty but non-graffi-tied helmet cover clutched in grubby fingers.

Terrell took off the *SLAYER* cover and replaced it with LT's, then handed the old one to Billy. Billy stuffed it into his pocket. "Slayer is dead."

He *should* be dead. Instead of LT.

"Beej—" Terrell began.

"No," Deus interrupted. "He's right. Everyone call him Beej. If they're looking for Slayer, let 'em look. They won't find him. Eventually they'll give up."

Billy didn't think the VC gave up on much of anything, but since Deus was agreeing with what he wanted, he kept it to himself.

"Who died and left you in charge?" Flash asked.

Deus lifted his hands in a "who do you think?" gesture.

For the first time ever, Flash colored, eyes flicking to LT's poncho, then back to them. "Sparky's in command now, not you."

Terrell straightened as if he'd been goosed. "The fuck you say?"

Deus rubbed his forehead. "Following the death of an officer, the RTO takes command."

"No thank you." Sparky didn't even glance up from the PRC-25.

"It isn't up to you. We need orders."

Sparky continued to fiddle with the gadget. Eventually he lifted his eyes, which widened at the realization everyone was waiting on him. "Uh . . ." His gaze bounced from one guy to the next as if someone, anyone, might help him out. No one did. "I . . . uh . . ." He stared at the LT-shaped poncho. "Grab LT and bugout."

"What about Win?" Deus asked.

Sparky appeared lost again.

Terrell spat in the scout's general direction. "That Kit Carson SOB can rot here with the butthole that shot LT."

"Win is considered US Army." Deus tossed his own poncho at Terrell. "Bag him and bring him along."

Terrell appeared like he might argue, but when Bama grabbed the covering and headed off, he followed. As Flash had already bagged Win's pocket contents, Bama removed the heavy items—canteen and ammo belt—from the body and set them next to Win's fallen rifle. Then they worked together to wrap him tight.

Sparky hoisted the Prick onto his back. "Move out."

It should have been disturbing how little things changed after LT's death. The loss of someone who had been so very good at his job should have made more than a ripple, but it didn't. And that it didn't kept Billy awake at night. He tried to draw that day so he could send it away, but how could he draw the absence of someone? How could he sketch the ache he felt every time he looked for LT and he was gone, yet Billy just kept on breathing?

They continued as they always had. Sure, their RTO was in charge, in theory. In practice, Deus made suggestions; Sparky followed them.

Often Billy caught Terrell and Deus, sometimes Bama, staring at him, frowning. They asked him way too often if he was okay. He said he was because, wasn't he? He walked point. No one died. But he saw the world, and everyone left in it, through a haze he couldn't seem to shake.

"Intelligence reports a troop build-up on the Cambodian border," Sparky said. "Rumor has it the Chinese Communists have sent men. Thousands of 'em. We're goin' on night patrol."

"Last time it was the Soviets. Now it's the ChiCom." Big Al

rolled his eyes. "We didn't see jack shit then, and I bet we don't see it now either."

"Because y'all can't see yer hand in fronta yer face durin' night patrol," Monk drawled.

"But you can hear everything." Boom-Boom smacked his palms on both sides of his head. "For miles."

"What's night patrol?" Magoo asked, and everyone hooted.

"It's the night life, Cherry!" Flash punched Magoo's arm. "You're gonna love it."

Billy had heard about the night life. Everyone made it sound like a party. It wasn't.

The Slicks dropped them at an LZ several klicks from the border as close to nightfall as possible.

"We sleep in daytime, walk in the dark," Deus instructed. "We never set a foot on the main trails. Strict field discipline. This is an LP."

Magoo opened his mouth.

"Listening patrol," Deus said, and Magoo's mouth closed.

"Pretend you got no tongue, new guy." Flash elbowed Magoo. "That way when the VC cut it out, you'll be all set."

Magoo didn't blink for a change; his eyes had gone too wide for that. "What do we do if we run into thousands of Chinese soldiers?"

"Die?" Flash asked cheerfully.

Deus cast him a disgusted glance, which only made Flash more cheerful because . . . Flash.

"We do not engage. We get out of Dodge and call in Arty."

"Who?" Magoo asked.

"Artillery strike, dipshit."

Deus rubbed his forehead. He'd been doing that a lot since LT had died, oddly in almost the same way LT had.

"Fall in. Single file. Follow the man in front of you. Don't lose him. If you have to, hold hands." Deus put his finger to his lips, pointed one arm toward the dense jungle, and made a semicircle with the other up and over his head, indicating they should move out.

Clouds had blown in the day before on a tepid breeze that smelled like last year's campfire. Then the breeze died, but the clouds stayed. Combined with the triple canopy jungle, not a speck of light remained.

Billy lifted his hand before his face, waved it around. He felt the tiny current of air, heard his wrist crack, but he didn't see a thing. What if he walked into a tree?

That would be embarrassing but not as deadly as falling into a punji trap or tripping the trigger on a mace. Under these conditions, he wouldn't even know he'd done the latter until the weighted ball flew in from above and stuck its spikes into his head.

Leading with his rifle, Billy avoided the trees, putting one boot in front of the other, slowly, deliberately—heel rolling toward toe—he imagined a personal shield, like the one he'd read about in *Foundation*, an old Isaac Asimov book Momma had sent, which repelled any weapon in the universe.

He listened so hard the world started to buzz; the hum along his skin made him twitchy, and he didn't like it, hadn't missed it while he was busy being Slayer. Slayer didn't get nervous; Slayer's entire reason for being was to make *them* nervous.

Of course, he'd made them *so* nervous he'd gotten the best man he knew killed, and Billy wasn't sure how to live with that.

CHAPTER 23

Jay
"The Times They Are a Changin'"

Willow Creek—August 1967

There came a morning when Jay woke with a desperate desire to see the clearing, to feel again the peace she'd always felt there, so she meandered downtown with Ringo.

Harold stood at the gas pumps, filling it up for several cars at once. He didn't wave; he didn't seem to see her. Jay thought it odd he hadn't come by, but unless he had more sketches, what would be the point?

She'd written to Billy, but she'd hadn't told him about the rally or about *Rally!* She also hadn't told her brother about Paul. Did that make her a liar? Maybe. But she was starting to think everyone lied, it was just a matter of how much.

Ringo paused at the intersection of Maple and Elm, then woofed. Halfway down on the right, Mags, with several cheer-leady girls, climbed the steps to the McBride house and disappeared inside. A wave of sadness swept over Jay, so strong she considered going home. Then Ringo sprinted past, sliding to a stop in front of Helen as she exited the Ben Franklin.

Jay hadn't tried to contact her friend. She kept waiting to hear through Momma's beauty salon grapevine that Danny Murphy had been sent away—whether it was by his parents or the chief, Jay didn't care as long as he was gone—but she hadn't.

Jay took a step in Helen's direction, and Ronnie came around the corner of the café with Eileen Puccio. Eileen ran hurdles for the track team, had graduated in spring, and would soon be headed to Mt. Mary College, an all-girl school in Milwaukee. Their heads tilted together; they were laughing. Jay hadn't seen Ronnie that happy since . . .

Ronnie stopped laughing when she saw Helen. Her smile remained as if forgotten until she saw Ringo, then Jay, and it died.

"Hi, Ronnie." Helen glanced nervously behind her, then quickly toward Jay.

Ronnie nodded but didn't speak; she tugged Eileen's sleeve, and they disappeared in the direction they'd come.

The barely discernible swoosh of Ringo's tail reflected his confusion. He slunk to Jay's side, an illustration in dejection. Jay could relate.

What had she expected? That the past two months would be forgotten and everything could return to the way it had been? Even if they were the same people they'd been in May—and they weren't—things had been said, things had been done, things had been discovered, and there was no putting any of that back in the box it had burst out of.

"You wanna go to the clearing?" Jay didn't plan to ask Helen what was going on with Danny in the middle of the sidewalk, in the center of town.

"You should go." Helen stared at the corner around which Ronnie had disappeared.

"Come with me."

"I mean, you should go away." Helen's gaze flicked to the Ben Franklin again, and something about the way she did it made Jay twitchy too.

"Helen, what—?"

Danny Murphy came out of the store, stopping dead at the sight of Jay.

The world all around them kept moving, but Jay, Helen, and Danny seemed frozen in time.

Then Danny smirked, and Jay took a step toward him, hands balling into familiar fists. He backed up—good choice—but Helen shook her head at Jay and said, "No."

And Danny strutted down the sidewalk like he owned it.

"Are you kidding me?" Jay glanced at Helen, but her friend was pointedly not glancing at her. "You promised you'd tell."

"I can't. I'm not like you. I . . . Just let it . . . let it be. If you ever cared about me, please just let it be."

Helen ran around the corner, leaving her brother behind. The look Danny threw Jay's way before he followed . . . he thought he'd won. But hadn't he?

Jay hugged herself against a sudden chill. What should she do? What *could* she do?

For the first time, the clearing did nothing to help. The babble of the creek did not solve Jay's dilemma; the wind through the trees didn't whisper a single answer. By the time she and Ringo went home, the only decision Jay had made was that being an adult . . . she didn't wanna.

Momma sat on the couch, feet up. How long had Jay been in the clearing?

"My last appointment—a perm—came down with a summer cold."

As a permanent wave took at least two hours, it wasn't as late as Jay had feared.

"Okay." Jay started for her room.

"You want to tell me what's wrong? You've been off ever since—"

"If I exchanged promises with someone, but they didn't keep theirs, do I have to keep mine?"

This was a question that had been rolling in her head all day. Jay wasn't sure of the answer because she couldn't recall any of the Musketeers ever breaking a promise before.

"A promise is a promise." Momma rubbed at the third finger of her left hand. "Just because a person is untrustworthy doesn't mean you get to be."

"Okay." Except . . . "What if keeping my promise means another person could get hurt?"

Maybe more than one person because people like Danny Murphy . . . she didn't think they stopped at one.

Momma's gaze had shifted from curious, a bit concerned, to downright worried. "What do you think?"

Jay sighed. She didn't want to be an adult, but she needed to be. Right here, right now.

Jay told Momma everything. When she was done, Momma didn't look worried anymore. She looked mad.

She shoved her feet into her shoes, then crossed the room, and gently touched Jay's face. "I'm sorry this summer's been so tough."

It had been tough, and Momma didn't even know all the reasons why.

"It's not gonna get any easier because you know what we have to do."

Jay nodded. Together they went to see the chief.

* * *

THE NEXT MORNING, Jay called Helen. No one answered.

Though she'd done the right thing—both her mom and the chief had agreed, and Jay knew it, too, deep down where such things lived—Jay had still broken a promise, and she wanted to . . . apologize? Maybe. She definitely wanted to explain.

Right was right, truth was truth, and didn't the truth set you free? Wasn't Billy fighting to free people he didn't even know? How could she do any less for someone she loved?

Jay called again an hour later. Still nothing. When she'd called three times more with the same results, Jay headed for the Murphys'.

She ran into Helen three-quarters of the way through town. The instant Helen saw Jay, she hurried in the opposite direction.

Considering Helen's much shorter legs, Jay caught up easily. "Please, don't be mad. You know I had to. I think . . . I hope you'd have done the same if it were me."

Of course, the idea of Billy ever . . . just wasn't gonna happen. But the principle remained.

Helen stopped so fast Jay had taken three steps before she realized it. "He might go to Wales, Jay."

Wales was what everyone called the Ethan Allen School for Boys, also known as the reformatory, located in a former TB sanatorium in Wales, Wisconsin. The idea of Danny being sent there, away from Helen, away from everyone . . . Jay wanted it.

"I'm sorry I broke a promise but not sorry about that. He belongs there, and you know it."

Helen didn't agree. She didn't disagree either. Instead, she threw a quick, twitchy glance over her shoulder the way she always had. The way Jay had thought she wouldn't have to anymore if her secret was out, if her brother was gone.

"You should go."

"Didn't we have this conversation already?"

They'd been standing in front of the Ben Franklin. Now they were in front of . . . Crap! The police station. And Mrs. Murphy, wearing the beige, sack-like uniform-dress that flattered no one who'd ever worked at the café, stared at them through the glass door.

Helen's mom had always liked Jay for some reason. From her expression, that was no longer the case. Nevertheless, Jay forced a weak smile. Mrs. Murphy did not smile back.

"My parents won't let me hang out with a hippie."

"You don't have to hang out with Paul."

"They meant you."

"Me?"

Jay felt like they were having two different conversations. The one with words and the one going on without words, beneath. Jay was tired of those conversations; she wasn't going to have them anymore.

"That's not really why they don't want you to hang out with me, is it?"

"It doesn't matter. Like I said, the girl always gets blamed."

She had, but Jay wasn't quite sure who "the girl" was in this case or what any of them could be blamed for in this situation.

"You're not making sense."

"Things are bad. Really bad, so please—"

"Helen!"

They both jumped at the volume of Mrs. Murphy's voice. Jay didn't think she'd ever heard Helen's mom shout, and considering Helen's brothers, that was saying something. Helen scurried inside the police station without glancing back.

At home, Jay shut the door behind her, then leaned her forehead against the wood. Ringo pressed his body to her leg and whined.

"I know, boy." She set her hand on his massive head. "I know."

Had she really thought Helen would thank her? She'd been wrong. Why'd the right thing have to feel this bad?

Someone knocked on the door, right on the other side of her head, and she reared back. Ringo barked.

Paul stood on the porch. "I'm sorry," he blurted. "Can we talk?"

Jay was sad enough, friendless enough to join him outside, but when he reached for her hand, she stuck both behind her back. She wasn't that easy.

"You're still mad at me. I get it. I should never have told Sam about your brother's drawings, but . . . They say a picture is worth a thousand words; his are worth twice that. They're . . ."

Jay thought of Billy's sketches, of how they had made her look at things differently than she ever had before because seeing the truth was—

"Powerful," she murmured.

"Yes! Forgive me."

No one had ever asked Jay to forgive them before.

"They made me feel, they made me wonder, and I wanted everyone else to wonder too. I got carried away. I won't do it again. I swear."

"Your doing that made me . . ." Jay paused.

Relationships were so confusing, but if they were going to have one, she needed to be able to trust him, to believe in him. They needed to drag the conversations that were beneath into the light.

"It made me think you liked me just for my brother's drawings."

"But I met you before I ever knew about them, and I . . ." He peered at his hands. "From the minute I saw you staring down the road leading out of town, you seemed thoughtful and . . . I don't know, deeper than everyone else." He twitched a shoulder. "I was interested. Before I even met you, Three-J, I more than liked you." His bright-blue gaze met hers; his expression open and searching. "I thought you got that."

He brushed his fingers over her forehead, and she remembered the first time he'd done so, before he'd ever seen the drawings. She thought of how they'd met, of each and every time they'd been together. Had he asked to see the drawings? Ever?

No, *she'd* shared them; she'd wanted to. And when she'd shared them with Sam, she'd wanted to as well. It was only when Sam saw in those sketches the same thing she and Paul had—maybe he'd seen even more—and he'd wanted to do something about it that Jay had gotten scared.

"I blamed you for something that wasn't entirely your fault," Jay said. "I'm sorry too."

Paul wrapped his fingers around Jay's elbow, then rubbed his thumb over her biceps, right where the sleeve of her T-shirt ended, and her bare skin began to hum.

This time when he reached for her hand, she let him take it.

CHAPTER 24

Billy
"Have You Ever Seen the Rain?"

*V*ietnam—August 1967

"Hear that?" Terrell's words, released on a breath, tickled Billy's neck, and he fought the urge to slap that tickle like a mosquito. "Bzzz."

The maddening noise hadn't been in his head? Billy wasn't sure if he should be happy he wasn't hearing things or concerned that he didn't know the difference between real and imagined. He should definitely be concerned that he was thinking too much about LT and what had happened and—

"What the hell *is* that?" Terrell continued. "Frogs? Bugs?"

Staring into the abyss of night, Billy did his best to ignore the sound. His toe caught on nothing—something?—and he froze. Terrell bumped into him, Bama bumped into Terrell, and so on, but the darkness did not erupt with gunfire and grenades.

Billy remained still; he barely breathed, and the buzz faded as dawn announced herself not with a blaze of sunrise but with gray, swirling shadows that danced amid the galaxy of black.

"That is some weird shit," Terrell murmured.

They made camp, tried to sleep in the twilight of day.

Billy's sketchbook only had a sheet or two left before he reached his DEROS calendar. What would he do if he dreamed something he could actually draw, not a ghost or a whisper, and he had no paper left?

Except he didn't dream because he didn't sleep. It was daytime, for crying out loud!

When the strange buzzing began the next night, Billy still didn't know what it was, but if it came every night, it must be something of the earth, the trees, the air, and not the Chinese, or even the Soviets. Same went for the shadows that flitted and floated at dawn.

He volunteered for guard duty that day and the next, but there were only so many days a guy could volunteer before questions were asked. Deus was already giving him the side-eye more than usual.

On the fourth day, Billy sat in the hooch while Terrell and Bama slept. As he waited for the sun to set, he unfolded a letter from Gramps that he'd read many times before.

Dear Son,

Gramps had taken to calling him *son* after he'd received the Polaroid. Billy didn't like it; all he'd ever heard from Gramps had been how worthless and useless his son was. When LT had called Billy *son*, it had meant something.

How many have you kilt?

His grandfather's handwriting had never been very good, and a lot of his spelling was just a guess, but Billy figured it out.

You git promoted yet? Only a matter of time.

Billy didn't think so. If he got promoted, he'd most likely be sent to another platoon. No one wanted that, especially Billy.

Have to be honest. Didn't see this coming, but I'm proud of you, son. Keep up the good wurk!

Billy stared out the open triangle made by the ponchos and wondered why, when all he'd ever wanted was to hear those words, now that he had, he didn't feel the way he'd thought he would. In fact, they made him feel sticky. As if he'd fallen in mud or maybe horseshit, then walked around in the jungle until it dried.

The cry of "Tiger!" erupted from somewhere in the camp.

Terrell sat up, rubbed his face. "F-Cat is losin' it. Last night, he babbled a bunch of crazy, and Monk nearly gagged him. Some guys can't take the night life."

Some guys called out for their mothers in their sleep, which was better than when they called out for them as they were dying.

"Didn't think F-Cat would be one of them, considering his peace-out pills," Terrell continued.

"Maybe he needs better drugs."

"Maybe we all do."

That night, the monkeys started screeching, and from somewhere at the back of the line came the shout of "Tiger!"

"Fuck!" Terrell snapped. "I almost blew off my foot."

"Shhh," Bama hissed.

"Ain't no one gonna hear us over them goin' apeshit." Flash gave a single snort of laughter. "Apeshit. Ha."

Billy tried to determine what had set the monkeys off; it had to be something, but as Flash had pointed out, he could distinguish nothing beyond the ear-splitting shrieks. Then they stopped, and everything went so very, very still.

"It's a tiger! Tiger!"

Someone whooshed past. Billy made a grab, and his fingers brushed the tail of F-Cat's shirt before the man was gone into the night.

Deus let out an exasperated huff. "Idiot is going to run into a boo—"

The rest of the word was drowned out by one short, sharp burst of an AK.

Everyone crouched. No one seemed to breathe, not even the monkeys. Billy suddenly understood Bama's constant need to piss because he really, really had to.

Then into a silence that seemed as deep as any silence had ever been came the soft swish of careful footsteps. The night was too black to see, too dark to signal, too long to survive.

Air wafted across Billy's face, left to right, as the enemy passed so close he could have reached out and touched them. Billy felt their heat, smelled their sweat, heard the rush of blood through their veins; their heart beats seemed to echo his own.

Boom!

A frag lit up the night. Billy dove onto his stomach as bullets whistled over his head in both directions. The monkeys started screaming again, or maybe it was men.

The light from the grenade died, but people kept shooting. Bodies kept hitting the ground. The rat-a-tat of an M60 rose above the rifle fire. Another frag went whoosh. This time the burst of light revealed very little but the swaying trees now empty of monkeys.

The free fire slowed. Every few seconds someone shot off a few rounds to make sure the enemy stayed where they were. What would happen when the night died?

Billy kept his gaze on the place he'd last seen movement. Nevertheless, he jumped when Bama murmured, "Holy fuck."

Even though he knew the ghostly whirls were merely fog lit by approaching dawn, the way they danced and swayed above the too-still bodies gave Billy goose bumps.

"Whaddya see?" Deus asked.

Nothing moving. Except for that fog.

Billy balanced his helmet atop the barrel of his rifle and slowly, slowly lifted it. When nothing happened, he put the pot back on his head, then whispered, "Cover me," before he rose from prone to his knees, then slowly to a crouch. He stood and counted to ten. Silence was his only companion.

The others came to their feet in the same way. From the rear, the radio crackled as Sparky called in a dustoff for four peanuts. One of them was Mayberry, which was probably for the best. He *had* turned out to be a dumbass. Bones moved among them—slow and easy—surprisingly, no one was hurt too bad.

"We killed 'em all in the dark?" Terrell asked. "We's amazing."

Billy inched forward. Something was off.

Terrell snatched at his arm, but Billy pulled away, and Terrell cursed, then came along too. "Ya know ya ain't Capt'n America?"

Billy crept through the bodies, around the perimeter once, then again in a wider circle, and again.

"Keep traipsin' around and you're gonna hit a landmine," Flash called.

Billy approached Deus, who stood in the center of the spray of bodies, eyes sharp on the jungle. "We didn't kill them all."

Deus flicked his dark gaze to Billy, then back to the trees. "How you figure?"

"Anyone see F-Cat?"

No one spoke for several seconds, then Deus spat, "Fucking fuck!"

"Maybe he was wounded." Sparky, on his knees next to the radio, didn't even look up. "Wandered off, dazed and confused."

"I found a blood trail," Billy said. "Three men across, the one in the middle wounded. Tracks to the front and the back. Maybe a half a dozen. Any sign of them ends twenty yards north."

Everyone knew what that meant.

VC didn't drag dead GIs into the jungle. They wanted the US to know how many they had killed. The only GIs they dragged away were live ones so they could make them wish they were dead.

"This is going to get me an ass-chewing." Deus sighed. "Right after the one I get for engaging and not calling in Arty."

"You mean I'm going to get an ass-chewing," Sparky said, though he didn't seem worried. "We were told not to engage, but what are we supposed to do if they start it?"

"Did they?" Deus asked, and Sparky shrugged.

"We were told not to engage *Chinese* troops," Billy said. "They weren't Chinese."

"How can you tell?" Boom-Boom tapped his knuckles above one eye. "All slants."

Billy had never seen a Chinese person. There certainly weren't any in Willow Creek. And in Vietnam, all he'd seen were Vietnamese. However . . .

He used his rifle to tap a body clad in black pajamas. "Wouldn't the Chinese Army be in uniform?"

"Maybe," Deus said. "Maybe not."

"What difference does it make?" Flash asked. "We count 'em, then dump 'em in a hole the way we do when we're too far in-country to drag anyone out. We cover it up and see ya." He waved bye-bye. "You think the North Vietnamese are gonna ask General Westmorland where their Chinese pals are?"

"He's got a point," Sparky said. "There's a dustoff incoming two Ks south for those peanuts. I'll request some lime be put on the transport with our water resupply."

"Whatta we need limes for?" Magoo asked.

"Shit for brains," Flash muttered, even as Deus said, "Lime goes on top of bodies for quicker decomposition. You"—Deus made a sliding motion with one hand as if pushing the eight guys closest to the peanuts even closer—"get them there. Bones, go along. Wait for the re-sup and bring everything back here. The rest of you start digging."

Billy had never considered how he might feel after digging a mass grave in the middle of the jungle. Who thought about that?

What he discovered was that he didn't feel much of anything beyond glad when it was done.

Was that normal? He considered asking others how they felt, but *that* would not be normal. Discussing the intimate details of sexual acts—real or imagined—as well as bowel movements—how often, how big, their appearance—and a long, disgusting list of symptoms for any and every type of VD . . . well, that was fine. But feelings? You were just asking to get your lights punched out.

They didn't make camp until almost noon. Bama and Terrell were half asleep as they helped set up the hooch.

"I'll finish," Billy said, and they didn't argue. He heard them cutting Zs as he secured the final corner of a poncho wall with a sharpened stick, then crawled inside.

Minutes, hours, days later—who knew?—Billy dozed with his back against his ruck. Not sleeping, not really, so he couldn't be dreaming of a striped tomcat stalking prey through long autumn-yellow grass. The cat leaped, landed, yowled, then lifted his head, mouth full of—

Billy sat up. He knew what came next. Tomcats ate their young.

He opened his ruck, rooted for his sketchbook, then stared into space as he reached for the wispy threads of memory. The only sounds were the *scritch* of his pencil in syncopation with the in-and-out whistle of breath through Bama's nose.

"Jesus H. Christ, what the hell?"

Billy dropped the pencil.

Terrell continued to stare at the drawing, eyes wide.

"It's not that ba—" Billy glanced down. Instead of the tomcat horror show of his dreams, he had drawn a crouching, stalking tiger—with his own face—surrounded by a field of skulls.

"Huh."

"Huh?" Terrell shoved his fingers in his now half-inch-long Afro and yanked. "Is this what you've been drawing?" He grabbed the sketchbook, but the only sketch inside was the one of the Billy-ger amid the skulls. "I've seen you scratching in here since we met. Where are they?"

"I send them home."

"I hope to Christ they didn't all look like this."

"I don't think so."

"Think? Don't you know?"

Billy didn't clearly remember drawing this one, but from Terrell's expression, he should probably keep that to himself. He should also probably be more worried about what he'd drawn and forgotten, though forgetting it *had* been the point.

"I drew the things that happened, that wouldn't get out of my dreams, then I sent them away so I wouldn't dream them anymore."

Terrell blinked as if his glasses were foggy, but they weren't. "The hell you say?"

Bama shifted. Terrell's question had been pretty loud. But, as usual, their hooch-mate didn't wake up.

"It worked."

"There wasn't a tiger." Terrell lifted the sketchbook. "This didn't happen."

"Not exactly."

"You're gonna need to explain better than that."

Billy wasn't sure if he could, but he'd give it a whirl. He held out his hand for the drawing. Terrell hesitated but, after another glimpse, gave it back.

"I dreamed of a tomcat."

"Not followin'."

"Tomcats are the dirtballs of the farm world."

"I'll take your word. I never been to no farm, never seen me no tomcat."

Billy closed his eyes, tried to make a connection. The dream cat had been a striped marmalade. Orange cats were typically cuddly and cute, very affectionate, but this one had been—

"A killer." Billy opened his eyes. "A killer is a killer. Always."

"Since when did you start listening to Bama?"

"Since he started making sense."

"That boy has never made sense a day in his life." Terrell sighed. "Yeah, you've killed. We all have. But you're not a killer. Not for always."

The skulls dotting that field would probably beg to differ. If he counted them, would the total match the hash marks on the *Slayer* helmet cover he'd burned when no one was looking?

Yes, this was war; the marks were for the enemy. But the enemy still bled; the enemy still died. And because of how good Billy had been at killing, so had LT.

"Did LT know about this?" Terrell flicked a long finger at the sketchbook, then answered his own question. "Of course not. He'd have sent your ass home."

Billy had been staring at the drawing again, thinking he should write something on the bottom to explain. But what?

Terrell's words made his head come up. "Sent me home? Why?"

"This is a little crazy."

"We're all a little crazy."

"Are we? I don't think LT was. Deus isn't. Or Sparky."

"What about Flash? Boom-Boom? Crazy Joe? What about you, after Crazy Joe?"

Terrell's face went still. "What about me?"

"You were . . ." Billy wagged his hand back and forth.

"I had good reason to be."

"Everyone who's crazy does."

Terrell made a soft sound of amusement. "Got me there. You think this drawing and mailing thing gonna work till you go home?"

It has to, Billy thought.

What he said was "Sure."

CHAPTER 25

Jay
"Signs"

Willow Creek—August 1967

"I brought you something." Paul dangled a plastic bag, which held two thin, short, wrinkled cigarettes.

Joints.

"Are you nuts?" Jay snatched the bag out of his hand, stuffed it into her pocket, peered up one side of her street and down the other. As far as she could tell, no one was watching. Maybe.

"You said you wanted to try it."

Jay had always figured she'd smoke marijuana for the first time with her friends. But that wasn't going to happen.

"Let's go." She tugged him down the steps.

On Maple Avenue, they passed the Willow Creek Dairy, where a group Jay's mom referred to as the Gossip Gals—five Willow Creek women who had become fast friends while running the elementary school PTA like the Nazis had run Germany—occupied a single outside table.

Every eye turned their way. Several pairs dropped to their joined hands; several mouths frowned. It wasn't until Paul's fingers tightened on hers that Jay realized she'd tried to pull away, so she lifted her chin, tightened her hold, and marched past. The dope in her pocket burned like hellfire.

"It's the hippie," one murmured.

Paul didn't even look that hippie for a change—T-shirt, cutoffs, the tennis shoes he'd been wearing the day she'd met him, not quite as white anymore—although the peace sign necklace was a dead giveaway.

Once upon a few months ago, Mags had said that what you wore revealed who you were. Jay had sneered, but now she wondered.

People in Willow Creek thought this was true. Probably a lot of people outside Willow Creek did too. But wasn't being a hippie—actually being anything—more about what you believed, how you behaved?

The questions? They just kept coming.

"What do you think she sees in him?"

"He *is* pretty."

Paul *was* prettier than Jay. But the longer she knew him, the less she noticed. The more they talked about things that mattered, the more he listened to what she had to say and thought about it, the more she understood their attraction.

Paul saw in Jay the person she wanted to become. Strong, brave, a true friend, someone who never gave in, never backed down, someone everyone wanted to be around, always. Billy had been the same, and she missed it, missed him.

"Do you think her mom knows?"

Jay stopped, prepared to turn around and give them a piece of her mind—she was seventeen, old enough to choose . . .

whatever, whoever, however. Definitely old enough to choose him and—

Paul tightened his hold. "No."

Jay sighed and kept walking.

"Hear about Danny Murphy?" one of the Gals asked. "His parents are sending him to live in South Dakota."

Jay deflated like a burst balloon. She should have known Wales was too much to hope for.

"You okay?" Paul had noticed her reaction; Paul seemed to notice just about everything.

The Gals didn't know the details of the Murphy situation since things had been hushed up as these things were. And Jay wasn't going to tell Paul; she'd done enough telling for now.

But Danny was gone, or soon would be. Maybe, if the world was lucky, the next time Danny entered a bedroom in the dark of the night he'd meet a better justice. But here, now, Jay had done all she could.

"Is it bad that I hope all those small-minded, gossipy women get lice?"

Paul hooted, then pulled her along faster. "We can hope, right?"

"Didn't they make you mad?"

"If I got mad about every person in this town who called me a hippie, I'd be mad all the time. I don't wanna be."

"How many people have called you that?"

"It would probably be easier to count the ones who haven't. Honestly, Jay, I don't care what anyone thinks in this town, unless it's you."

"I wanna be you when I grow up." If Jay didn't care what others thought, she wouldn't be hurt when they thought it.

"I'm not going to let anyone's opinion ruin my day or change what I know to be true."

"What's that?"

"Nothin' wrong with bein' a hippie."

In the clearing, she pulled the two marijuana cigarettes from the bag. It took longer to get the joints lit than it had taken to light the Marlboros Jay had once smoked right here with the Musketeers, and for some reason, they didn't want to stay lit, which was annoying at first and later hilarious.

The smoke burned her mouth, her tongue, her throat. Her eyes watered as she fought not to cough and lost. She sat on the ground before she fell.

"Try smaller drags. Like this." Paul sat too, drew in a short puff, and held it a while before letting it trail out.

This time when Jay tried, she didn't cough; her throat didn't burn.

"How do you feel?" he asked.

"How am I supposed to feel?"

He lay back. "However you want."

"Okay." Jay lay back too. Everything was so bright and clear. Had she been walking around in the fog all her life? Why couldn't she think of a word to describe the sky's amazing blaze of blue?

"Your eyes," Paul murmured, and she turned her head. "They're the color I smell in fresh-cut spring grass."

"Oh!" Jay said. "Yeah!"

In third grade art class, Billy had drawn a bowl of fruit unlike anyone else's bowl of fruit, with a cotton-candy-pink apple, grapes the hue of Cheeto dust, and a banana the shade of a green M&M. When he'd tried to explain how colors had a smell or a taste, he'd wound up at the hospital getting tested for a brain tumor. After that, Billy drew a lot of things in black and white.

Now Jay got it because the sky smelled like a SweeTart, and she thought the clouds would taste like meringue.

The scent of the pot smoke, both musty and sharp, as ancient as the earth and as new as . . . what? One instant Jay thought it stunk, and the next it was . . . she lost the thought, and it didn't matter. Right now, not much did. She felt . . . mellow. Maybe President Johnson should legalize weed, and then everyone could all get along.

"Yeah," Paul agreed.

Had she said that out loud?

She watched a cloud drift, and she drifted too. It was so nice to . . .

"Jay?" Paul leaned over her. Jay smiled and touched his face. "We should probably get back."

"We just got here."

"You fell asleep for a few hours."

Jay shifted her gaze to the sky. "Huh." The sun caressed the tops of the trees.

She drew her fingers down Paul's cheek; the light stubble made her skin tingle, so she soothed it against his soft, soft lips.

He took her wrist, kissed her palm, then he kissed her. His tongue tasted like grass. Both kinds. And while she'd imagined the taste would turn her off, instead it turned her on.

They made out for a long time; she didn't want to stop. When he set his hand on her stomach beneath her shirt; she arched into him.

More, she thought. *Now.*

And he stilled. His hand stayed on her stomach; his lips hovered over hers. "We can't."

Jay looped her ankle over his calf, which shifted them together enough so she could say with all certainty . . . "I bet we can."

He let out a burst of laughter. "Not here, not like this. You're high."

"Am I? I can't smell colors anymore. Can you?"

"No."

"Cool." Jay lifted her lips, but Paul shook his head, came to his feet, and held out a hand.

"I'll walk you home."

Jay wasn't sure if she loved him just a little or hated him quite a lot.

They didn't speak as they meandered through Willow Creek. Suppertime, so they didn't see another living soul until they reached Jay's house.

Harold sat on the steps. He stood as they approached. Had he brought more drawings? A letter? News?

"Hi." Jay waited, but Harold said nothing. "I . . . uh . . ." Still nothing. "This is Paul. Paul, my brother's best friend, Harold."

Paul held out his hand. "Nice to meet you."

Instead of shaking, Harold stepped closer to Jay; he seemed really interested in her hair.

"Is everything all—?"

Harold plucked something out, stared at it for two seconds, then flicked it. The leaf bounced off Paul's chest as Harold punched him in the nose.

"Hey!" Jay grabbed Harold's arm when he hauled it back again. "What the hell?"

Paul wiped a trickle of blood from one nostril. "Nothing happened."

"You smell like dope," Harold said in a voice Jay had never heard before, then yanked his arm loose. "People are talking, Jay. About you. About him."

"I heard."

"Is that what you want?"

"I can't stop people from talking."

She felt rather than saw Paul glance at her.

"You could stop giving them something to talk about."

"I could." Her gaze touched Paul's. "The question is: Do I want to?"

Harold made a sound of disgust, then strode between Paul and Jay, knocking his shoulder against Paul's like a second-grade bully before spinning back.

Paul flashed him the peace sign.

"Jesus," Jay muttered. "That's like showing red to a bull."

Paul lowered his hand.

"I thought I knew you." Harold tossed an envelope onto the sidewalk at Jay's feet.

She watched him walk away. "What just happened?"

"He likes you," Paul said.

"He's my brother's best friend, of course he likes me."

"I mean *likes* you."

Her friends had teased her about Harold. She hadn't thought anything of it then, but now . . . "I don't see it."

"I do." Paul touched his nose, gingerly. "I also feel it."

"I'm sorry." She kissed that nose.

"It's fine." He smiled at her kind of goofy. Had Harold's punch loosened his brains?

Paul scooped up the envelope Harold had thrown to the ground, then handed it to Jay before moving off a few feet to give her space. Jay pulled out a single sheet of paper and unfolded it. Suddenly she couldn't breathe.

Paul said her name, worried, almost panicked, and she drew in a desperate lungful. She held up a hand, and he stopped.

Jay had done the best thing for Helen. She knew that, even if everyone else, including Helen, didn't. It hadn't been easy, and she'd probably lost her friend forever, but if Jay had to pay that price to change things for the better, it would be worth it.

This was no different.

"Can you drive me to Madison?" Jay asked.

CHAPTER 26

Billy
"Eve of Destruction"

Vietnam—August 1967

A week later, Billy still wasn't sleeping.

They'd returned to camp on stand-down; he'd mailed Harold the Billy-ger, then immediately regretted it and sent a letter telling his friend to destroy the thing. Harold definitely shouldn't show that sketch to Jay. But even after he'd sent it, he'd continued to dream of the tomcat and the field of skulls. Apparently blabbing about his secret weapon had been a mistake.

After a few days of digging latrines, playing cards, eating three hot meals a day, back into the bush they had gone. Command still had a bug up its ass about the ChiCom, but they didn't find any Chinese Communists this time either; they didn't find anything.

"Get a few hours' shut-eye," Deus announced as they shoveled their C-rats just after dawn of the fifth uneventful night patrol. "Then we're back to camp. New LT on the way."

"But we're doin' just fine without one," Bama said.

They were, and then again, were they?

Since they'd lost F-Cat, guys had gotten jittery. No one wanted to be a POW. The tales of US prisoners held at Hỏa Lò, dubbed the Hanoi Hilton, would make anyone prefer death.

"They beat on guys with broken bones," Bama said. "With bayonets!"

"Gook torture chambers are the worst." Boom-Boom clapped his hands. "They stick bamboo where you do not want it stuck."

"Who'd want bamboo stuck anywhere?" Terrell asked.

Flash snorted. "I hear solitary is flooded, and they keep guys there for years. The water's full of poisonous snakes and fish that eat feet.

"Jesus Christ," Deus finally snapped. "No one who's gone into Hỏa Lò has come out!"

Everyone went silent, and Deus threw up his hands and walked away.

"What's he so mad about?" Bama asked.

"If no one's come out of Hỏa Lò," Billy said, "then no one knows what's going on inside Hỏa Lò."

"But the stories—"

"Are made up. Like the boogeyman."

Everyone still appeared confused. Sleeping all day and walking around a pitch-black jungle all night was making them stupid.

"What if the new LT won't let Slay—?" Bama pressed his lips together.

Since Deus had ordered everyone to stop calling Billy *Slayer*, for the most part they had. He didn't want to hear the name that had gotten LT killed; he didn't want to be that guy anymore. Sure, he did his job, it was what he was good at, but he no longer wanted the world to know. He no longer wanted anyone to.

"What if . . .," Bama continued, ". . . you know . . . what if he won't let Beej do what he does best?"

"Then we all gonna die," Terrell murmured.

Magoo's eyes went wide. "What?"

"We'll deal with that if it happens," Billy said.

In the hooch, Billy didn't even bother to try and cut Zs. Instead, he decided to write his mother, but his eyes burned, so the paper he'd bummed off someone because his sketchbook was nearly empty swam, and the pencil kept falling out of his fingers.

"Come 'ere." Terrell pulled out the twelve-gauge shotgun he'd brought back from Vung Tau, then opened the chamber as if to load it.

Billy stepped over a snoring Bama and sat at Terrell's side.

The breech chamber contained something green and seedy, which made no sense until Terrell flicked his Zippo, shielding the glow with his big left hand even though it was the middle of the day, and lit the stuff on fire before blowing the smoke up the barrel. It wafted across Billy's face, smelling both musty and sharp, as ancient as the earth and as new as the metal that encased it.

"You're just wastin' it. Put your mouth over the end and inhale."

Billy hesitated.

"Go on. You'll feel better if you do."

"I don't—"

"Do drugs. I know. But, Beej, maybe you need to start."

"I was gonna say I don't feel bad." Easy to do when you didn't allow yourself to feel.

"Then why ain't you sleepin'?"

Billy didn't answer; he didn't need to.

"You thinkin' too much on things you can't change. You

wanna stop? You wanna sleep?" Terrell offered, again, the shotgun.

Billy put his mouth on the barrel and drew.

Not long after that, time got funky. It seemed as though they'd been puffing on that shotgun for hours, but when the load ran dry, Terrell said, "Burned out quick."

This struck Billy as hilarious. He laughed so hard he had to lie down, then he stared through a hole in the hooch at the small shaft of sun that managed to eke past a million and two trees, and he missed the navy-blue night.

"Mostly I miss the stars I always took for granted more than I've ever missed anything in my life," he murmured.

"I miss hot water, cold water, soft beds, hard liquor, clean sheets, well . . . clean anything," Terrell said, "and you miss the fucking stars?"

"Yep." Billy breathed in, then out. "And my sister."

Silence settled between them, and Billy nearly fell asleep. Then Terrell spoke. "Probably shouldn't tell anyone else how much you miss your sister."

"Jay's my best friend. Besides you and Harold."

"Who's Harold?"

Billy blinked, and the stars blinked back. Why hadn't he told Terrell about Harold? Because survival of the fittest was the law of the jungle, and in the jungle, you ran with a pack. Admitting you'd never had a pack?

"Pass." Billy started laughing again.

"I never heard no one say their sister was their best friend."

"You never met my sister. When we were kids, my mom had to work; my dad . . . he took off."

"I wondered," Terrell said. "You never mentioned him."

"Never knew him, don't care to. Momma is the one who stayed up all night when we were sick. She went without— lunch, new shoes, and clothes—so Jay and I could have them all. Being there is what matters more than . . . well . . . anything. It's been me and Jay and Momma against the world for so long I don't remember much else. We depend on one another."

"Like you and me. We ain't blood, but we're brothers anyway. Forever."

"Yeah." Billy nodded slowly. What he felt for Jay and what he felt for Terrell was similar. He'd do anything for them, and they'd do the same for him. "Jay has this knack for finding lost things—dogs, cats, keys, my sneakers—it's weird."

"She psychic or somethin'?"

Billy'd thought Jay found stuff because she didn't stop looking, ever, but—

"Maybe. She's stubborn and gutsy. She has these three friends, and they've been like this"—Billy held up his crossed fingers—"since they met in a sandbox tussle."

"The hell does that mean?"

Billy smiled at the memory. "Momma took us to the park. Jay was maybe three or four? We hung back because we'd never been there before. There were these girls in the sandbox. One threw sand in the other's face, and that kid began to scream." Ronnie and Mags had been oil and water from day one.

"A girl with glasses thicker than yours wandered over to see what the excitement was, and that first girl picked up another handful of sand. Jay tackled her. By the time the mothers got them separated, they were wearing most of the sandbox. They've been inseparable ever since."

Or at least they had been when he'd left. Billy hoped they'd worked out whatever was wrong between them the way they always had before.

"That's one of the reasons I could leave and not worry so much. Jay's one of a group, a clan, a . . ." He searched for a word that fit. Not platoon, which was close, but not quite. More like . . . "A pack! That counts for something in Willow Creek, same as it does here."

"I gotta meet her."

"Okay."

"Beej." Terrell drew in what seemed a very long breath and let it out just as slow. "If something happens to me . . ."

The shine went off the stars. "Don't be a downer."

"Just promise me you'll go tell my family, in person, how goddamn awesome I was and how I saved your ass a hundred times."

"Sure." Billy started to drift.

"I'll do the same for you."

The next thing Billy knew, he woke up. He'd slept hard for what seemed like days, and he hadn't dreamed. Then he checked the time. Less than an hour had passed.

Terrell dozed, his back against his ruck, the twelve-gauge nowhere in sight. If not for the grungy grass taste of his mouth and the prickly pear tingle of his hair, Billy might think the shotgun bong had been just another dream.

He suddenly understood the doping, the drugs. Right now, he wanted the black hole of the last hour back more than he wanted to see the stars. Was death a dreamless sleep?

If so, why did anyone fear it?

Jay
"I-Feel-Like-I'm-Fixin'-to-Die Rag"

Willow Creek—August 1967

Woof!

Ringo lifted his head, and an instant later, someone knocked on the front door. Since Jay had been waiting for Paul—they were going to the Henry Vilas Zoo in Madison—she opened it with a smile.

Gramps threw the magazine in his hand so hard it bounced off Jay's chest with a *thwunk*, glancing off Ringo's head on the way to the floor.

Ringo yelped and ran away.

Jay wanted to, but she stayed where she was. She'd known from the minute she'd handed Billy's sketches to Sam Laughlin that something like this was coming, though she hadn't expected Gramps to be the first. A less likely reader of *Rally!* did not breathe on this earth. So where had he gotten it?

"Are you a commie?" he demanded, giving her no time to answer before continuing. "You're definitely a hippie." He wagged his finger. "I've heard how you've been traipsing all over town with that radical boy, bold as brass. Don't deny it!"

"Okay."

"I blame him for this." Gramps picked up the magazine.

"Don't." Jay was proud of how calm she sounded, really, how calm she was. "It was my idea."

Not originally, no, not even unoriginally. But in the end, when it counted, yeah.

Her grandpa's face turned bright red. "Are . . . are . . . are . . ."

"You should probably breathe," Jay said.

He filled his lungs, and then he erupted. "Are you on drugs?"

Jay shook her head. *Not at the moment.* Though now she wished she was.

"Are you crazy? Stupid?"

Jay shook her head again.

"The only other explanation is a brain tumor."

"Nope."

He ignored her. "I told your mother if she didn't put a stop to that artsy-fartsy stuff Billy would wind up a faggot."

"Whoa!" Jay's voice was no longer calm. "You need to cool it."

"I am not going to *cool it.*" The last two words dripped with disgust. "I can't show my face in this town."

"Yet here you are."

Jay had no idea where her guts were coming from, unless it was from the knowledge that she had done what was necessary. Twice. Someone had to.

"I never had much use for you."

"Really? I didn't notice."

Gramps frowned. Sarcasm had always been wasted on him.

"Jay?" Momma barreled around the hedges and into the yard.

"What are you doing here?" She'd said she was booked straight through lunch.

"What do you think?" Momma tossed her hand toward the street, where the neighbors stood at windows and doors, on their porches and the sidewalk.

Someone had called the salon.

"The least you two could do is go inside."

"If you think I'm stepping foot in your house ever again, you're as dumb as your kids."

"Did he have a stroke?" Momma asked.

Jay spread her hands; if he didn't calm down, she thought he might.

Gramps threw the magazine at Momma. It made the same *thwunk* as it hit first her chest, then the ground. The copy opened to page two without any help.

"Look familiar?" Gramps asked.

Momma's eyes lifted, and for the first time, Jay felt a trickle of unease. "He sent these to you and you didn't—?" Her voice broke.

"You didn't know." Gramps laughed. "Wonder what else she's been up to?" He indicated town with a lift of his chin. "So has everyone. That's what happens when you let her run wild."

"I've gone for a walk in view of the entire town, eaten ice cream, seen a movie. Paul took me shopping. Today we're going to the zoo. Yeah, I'm a wild one."

"Someone saw you and your friends gadding around in the cemetery!"

"No telling what trouble we got into there."

Momma cast her a quick "shh" glance, then picked up the magazine. She paged through the sketches as Gramps continued to rant.

"Billy's more of a disgrace than his father ev—"

"Billy had nothing to do with this," Jay snapped.

"This . . ." Gramps tapped the magazine in Momma's too-pale, too-tight hands. "Came out of his head. Only a commie sympathizer, a traitor, an anti-American embarrassment would draw those things, which is exactly what I told him."

"Told him?" Momma echoed.

"In the letter I sent along with another copy of that radical piece of trash."

Jay had planned to explain to Billy; she just hadn't yet. Maybe she *was* stupid.

"How did this happen?" Momma asked.

"Her beatnik boyfriend works at the place."

"Oh, Jay." Momma's lip trembled. "How could you?"

"How couldn't I, Momma? Look!" She turned over the cover, and Momma flinched at the sight of the tiger with Billy's face. Jay tapped the caption. "He's not Billy anymore; he's Slayer, and he's going to die over there if we don't do something."

Momma's face had gone as pale and tight as her hands. Jay reached out, but Momma stepped away.

"You think this is going to do anything?" Gramps plucked *Rally!* from Momma's hands.

"Yeah," Jay said. "I do." Otherwise, she never would have done it.

She was no longer a kid, uncertain, without purpose, but a woman with the courage to say what she thought, share what she believed, fight for what was right. Shouldn't everyone?

"All it's done is show your true colors, his true colors. Which I told him are coward yellow and commie red."

Paul pulled up to the curb, got out of the car, saw them standing there, and hesitated.

"Is that what this is all about?" Momma asked. "Him?"

"It's what *he's* all about," Gramps said. "Just look. He's wearing a bracelet, and he doesn't even cut his hair."

"Neither do I," Jay said.

"When boys don't, it's a statement."

"About hair?"

"About everything."

"Oh my God."

"See!" Gramps pointed at Jay. "Lord's name in vain. What next?"

"Anarchy."

Paul took a step in their direction, and Jay frowned and held up a hand. Talk about showing red to a bull.

She hopped off the porch, started toward the car, half-expecting Momma to call her back, but she didn't, and Jay was glad. Paul was the only friend she had left. And she was maybe a little in love with him.

"I take it your grandpa and your mother have seen *Rally!*," Paul said when they were both in the car. "You wanna talk about it?"

"No."

Paul pulled away. "You still wanna go to the zoo?"

"I need to write a letter to my brother."

"Okay." He turned onto his street. "We'll go to my house."

"Your parents . . ." She wasn't sure she was up to meeting them for the first time today. Paul had wanted to introduce her, but so far, it hadn't happened.

"They drove to Door County to see a cottage that's for sale; they won't be back until after supper." Paul parked in the driveway of a white-board-and-blue-trimmed Colonial.

Old Jay thought: *If anyone sees you going inside while his parents are away, your reputation will be—*

New Jay interrupted with: *Exactly the same as it is right now. Might as well earn it.*

The house was huge compared to her own and so immaculate Jay left her shoes in the front hall and tried really hard not to touch anything.

Paul trotted up the stairs. His room was not immaculate.

"Uh, sorry." He snatched a pile of wrinkled clothes from the floor, revealing a wilted jock strap, which he kicked under the bed before tossing the armload into an open closet filled with other piles of the same.

Momma would murder Jay if she left her room like this.

Jay's eyes suddenly burned. Momma might murder her anyway.

She pulled out the desk chair and sat as Paul dug through an equally messy drawer to find a pen. At least the paper he produced wasn't crinkled like his clothes.

Dear Billy, was as far as she got before her mind filled with so many words she became dizzy with them. She laid her head on the blotter, hoping her brain would settle, but it didn't.

Paul laid his hand on her shoulder. "It'll be okay."

"How?" Jay straightened and placed her hand over his.

He tangled their fingers together, then perched a hip on the edge of the desk. "I haven't figured that out yet."

Jay gave an unladylike snort. "Lot of help you are."

"I want to be." His gaze flicked to the letter. "Can't find the words?"

"No, well . . . yes. There are so many." She whirled a finger in the air, fast, like a tornado. "Which ones should I use first? Which ones should I use last? Which ones should I use at all?"

"Maybe . . ." He let out a breath, and a crease appeared between his light-brown eyebrows. "Maybe you start with I love you."

"I love you?" Jay repeated, and he let go her hand, then brushed his fingers along her face.

"I love you too."

Jay stood, and the chair nearly tipped over. "You mean . . .?" She flicked a finger back and forth between them.

When Paul stood, they were very close. "Didn't you?"

She managed to nod before he kissed her, and it was like the first time when her entire body had come alive for . . . the first time.

He smelled good; he tasted better. She wanted to kiss him forever; she wanted to do more than kiss him.

Jay inched back; he appeared as dazzled as she felt. "I'm not high."

"Okay." He tilted his head. "Me neither."

Jay waited until he caught up.

"Oh!" He flicked his finger back and forth between them. "You mean . . . ?"

"Didn't you?"

"Uh . . . yeah. Sure!" He tripped over a book as he hurried to shut the door, then *clicked* the lock.

Jay sat on the bed, leaned aside to pull a shoe out of her butt, and dropped it to the floor next to its mate.

"My mom always said I'd be sorry one day that my room was such a mess." He laughed nervously.

Funny, Jay had always thought she'd be the nervous one.

"It'll be okay." She patted the bed at her side.

He joined her, and for the first time in a long time, Jay didn't feel lost. She felt loved, and everything else melted away.

Later, when they lay all tangled together, her head on his shoulder, his cheek against her hair, he turned on the radio next to the bed.

"By popular request, here's the new single by The Beatles."

"Must be fate." At Jay's curious glance, he continued. "You haven't heard it?"

Jay shook her head.

Paul kissed her nose. "It's perfect."

Jay closed her eyes as *love, love, love* swirled from the radio, then John Lennon began to sing, and she had to admit, it *was* perfect.

Momma had said "Sex isn't love," and Jay could see now that she was right. The only thing that was love *was* love, and sometimes, maybe, that was all you needed.

By the time the song ended, Paul was asleep, and Jay still wasn't sure what to write to Billy.

"And now ladies and gentlemen, Country Joe McDonald and his 'I-Feel-Like-I'm-Fixin'-to-Die Rag' or as I like to call it 'What Are We Fighting For?'"

The music swelled; Jay didn't even realize she was listening until the chorus echoed the DJ and she sat straight up, blinked a time or two or five as her mind whirred, then, finally, settled. She crawled free of the covers, got dressed, and sat again at the desk.

This time when she put pen to paper, she knew exactly what to say.

CHAPTER 28

Billy
"Waist Deep in the Big Muddy"

*V*ietnam—August 1967

At camp they had mail, and everyone perked up.

Billy received an envelope the size of a notebook. Had Momma or Jay, even Harold, sent him a new sketchbook? But the return address belonged to Gramps, and while he'd been complimentary lately, that didn't mean he'd changed his mind about Billy's *pansy-ass hobby.*

Curious, Billy tore open the envelope, and a magazine fell out. Weird. He'd never known Gramps to read.

Billy picked it up. Beneath a masthead that shouted *Rally!* was his sketch of a Billy-ger in the field of skulls, and beneath that were words he did not remember scrawling but must have: *I'M THE TIGER NOW.*

When Billy turned to page two, as instructed, he found an

array of sketches beneath the headline: *A GI'S VIEW OF VIETNAM.*

Trees with eyes. A jungle with teeth. Zombies crawling out of the ground. The faces of the enemy, of women, of children, of old folks, soldiers, and friends dancing amid the flames of napalm.

He didn't remember them, but hadn't that been the point?

He recalled being so proud when he sent the Polaroid of his first kill to Gramps, but now Billy felt sick. Nevertheless, he pulled out the letter.

Paragraphs canted sideways. Punctuation was nonexistent. Several words had been underlined so forcefully the pen had torn the page. Considering those words were *commie-sympathizer, traitor, anti-American embarrassment,* that made sense. There was some gibberish about colors that Billy couldn't untangle, and a crunch of letters at the bottom that tumbled all over one another. *Hippie, Janey,* and *child* or maybe *wild* were all he could decipher. But he didn't need to read every word, or even half of them, to sense a theme.

Billy was a disgrace.

All he'd ever wanted was his grandfather's approval, and he'd had it for about a minute. Now it was gone, and he waited for the sad. Instead, he was mad. How could one "aw shit" erase a hundred "atta boys"?

And how had those sketches ended up in front of . . . hell, if not the whole world, then a much larger portion of it than he'd planned? The answer had to be Harold, though . . . how? Why? Even though Harold had gone to college, avoided the draft, he hadn't gone to college *to* avoid the draft. Or had he?

He'd always supported Billy's enlistment, but maybe college had changed his opinion. Harold had a right to his own mind. What he didn't have a right to were Billy's sketches.

Billy shoved the magazine into his ruck, pulled out his last sheet of paper before the DEROS calendar at the end of the sketchbook, and asked his oldest friend a few things. He didn't ask nicely.

"Johnson?" Another soldier from another platoon stood in the doorway. "William?"

"Billy."

The guy pulled an envelope from his back pocket. "I got this by mistake. I'm Johnston, William. Will."

Billy accepted the envelope. "I can understand that mistake."

"As long as they only confuse our mail and not our death certs, dog tags, next-of-kin notification." At Billy's frown, Will held up a hand. "Sorry to be a drag. We just, uh"—Will hunched his shoulders, jerked his head in the direction of the bush—"lost a few, you know."

Billy knew. Everyone here knew.

"You're . . . uh . . . lucky to have a girl." Will's gaze flicked to the envelope where Billy's name swirled across the front.

"Sister."

"That too."

"Slayer!" Flash shouted, and Billy winced. Every once in a while someone still forgot—and by someone, he meant Flash— and called him by the old nickname. "Get your ass to the Slick."

Hell, he hadn't even gotten a meal.

"Fucking ChiCom again," Flash said from the doorway, though Billy hadn't asked. "New LT, McDaniel, came in with better intel and a great big hard-on to use it."

"Swell."

"Swell!" Flash made an obscene gesture. "Good one."

Flash was annoying, but Flash never changed, and that was . . . also annoying. How could you come to a place like this, do all they had to do, and remain exactly the same?

"Let's go!" Flash hurried off.

"You're . . .?" Will's eyes were wide. "My sarge said the VC aren't ever gonna stop looking for Slayer until— " He pressed his lips together.

Billy had been foolish to hope that rejecting the nickname he had once embraced would magically cause everyone to forget the existence of Slayer. But hope was often foolish and magic only found in fairy tales.

"Thanks for bringing the letter." Billy shoved the one he'd been writing and the one he hadn't read yet into his pack with the magazine. Then he hustled to the pad, getting there just in time to climb on the last of the three Slicks as the first lifted and flew away.

They hit the ground a few klicks from the place they'd last left it, and everyone fell into the line where Lieutenant McDaniel had apparently assigned them during the chow Billy had missed.

"Man so new he shines, don't he?" Terrell asked.

Billy followed Terrell's gaze to where McDaniel, uniform still green and not gray, his boots carrying only one layer of dust, like his face, urged everyone to "Move it!"

"Flash already started callin' him McLoot. Loot instead of LT 'cause . . ." Terrell's bony shoulders shifted, and his eyes slid to Billy, then away. "And Mc because—"

"McDaniel?"

"Well, yeah, but also 'cause the army go through so many LTs they all start to look the same. Like McDonald's. Flash be pretty funny sometimes."

As funny as a screen door on a submarine.

"Did the new lieutenant think this was as hilarious as Flash did?"

"He did not. I'd say he don't seem the laughin' type."

"Not surprised." Billy headed for point.

McLoot—hell, now Billy was going to have a hard time not calling him that out loud—stepped in front of Billy. "Where do you think you're going?"

"To walk point, sir."

"Did I assign you there?" The man *had* only been with the platoon a few hours. Too soon to remember names or faces.

Billy glanced at the others, who nodded, but Billy didn't want to start off their first day on a lie. However, before he could answer, Deus did.

"It's Johnson's turn, sir."

The lieutenant took off his helmet, scrubbing his fingers through hair as red as Ronald McDonald's.

Flash choked, so did several other guys. With that hair, the nickname McLoot was never going away.

"Is that so, Johnson?" McLoot plunked the steel pot back on his head.

"Yes." Not a lie. It was always Billy's turn.

"Fine." McLoot snapped his fingers—one, two, three, four times—in a jazzy, syncopated rhythm. "Get there and let's move."

In the first half hour, McLoot stared at his compass so much he tripped and nearly fell several times. He corrected Billy's direction almost as much.

"No one can walk a straight line in this mess. Only way to get where we're going is to keep correcting."

"Yes, sir. Where *are* we going?"

"The Chinese were seen due north of the LZ."

If the Chinese were even here—and Billy had doubts that the third time would be the charm—it was highly unlikely they'd stayed right where they were. But let McLoot figure it out.

When they paused to rest on the west side of a waist-high line of brush, Billy stood at the perimeter with a canteen and his sister's letter.

It was unfair of me to share your drawings without asking.

Harold hadn't been guilty after all, but to discover Jay was . .
.

His sister had always been behind him 100 percent. She'd

had his back in a way that no one else ever had, until he'd gotten here.

I'm sorry you found out the way you did, but I'm not sorry for what I did. I don't think it was a mistake.

Your sketches, Billy, they mean something. They can change things, maybe everything. They certainly changed me.

The idea that his little sister had been changed because of him . . . he wasn't sure what to think about that.

Before I saw your drawings, I believed whatever Momma and Gramps said, whatever I saw in the papers or heard on TV, but they're lying, Billy, and you aren't. The truth matters, maybe now more than it ever has. People need to hear it, see it, know it, and it isn't easy when truth seems to be covered by a mountain of lies.

Your drawings make me wonder: What are you fighting for? Who have you become?

"The tiger," he whispered.

A killer is a killer, the jungle whispered back. *Always.*

Maybe a better question is the one I asked myself before I gave your drawings to Rally!: Who do you want to be?

If you want to be Slayer because that's who you have become, fine. But if you want to be Slayer because it impresses someone who will never be impressed enough . . . well, I wouldn't bother, Billy. Who you are is enough for anyone who truly knows and loves you.

For me, I want to be someone who stands up for what's right even if everyone thinks I'm wrong. I want to be the kind of sister, the kind of friend I'd like to have. Someone who would do anything, even lose the most important thing, if doing it, if losing it, might make things better.

I hope you understand that's what I did, and I did it because I love you.

Jay

Billy stuck Jay's letter in his ruck, then he pulled out the not-very-nice one he'd written to Harold and tore it into teeny-tiny pieces as he watched the fog creep out of the trees thirty yards to the east and swirl across the elephant grass in their direction.

Suddenly he missed the white birch in the forest back home, along with the weeping willows that bent and swayed along Willow Creek and the evergreens that smelled like Christmas even when it wasn't. Here the trees were thin but so close together in some areas the forest became impassable, and they smelled like mold and rot and a particular shade of gray-green he remembered from a paint-by-number kit Momma had given him when he was four.

He'd come here to prevent the spread of communism, to protect a way of life he believed in, the people and the country he loved. But didn't the Vietnamese have every right to fight for the way of life they believed in, the people and the country they loved?

If that were the case, then what was he fighting for now? Who *did* he want to be?

Something moved at the edge of his vision. Though it had to be a hundred degrees, a chill rustled over Billy at the sight of the solitary figure in black pajamas, carrying an AK-47 and slipping from tree to tree amid the fog.

He'd been thinking again. Too much? Too long?

Billy lifted his hand to his waist, then took a knee, lowering that hand along with his body to the ground behind the brush. Everyone hit the dirt.

The approaching soldier beckoned, and more black-clad figures slid free of the mist. A lot more.

Billy put his hand on his wrist. *Enemy.* He pointed to Deus, then McLoot, then scooped air toward himself.

They slithered to his side, gazed where Billy did, and Deus drew in air sharply through his nose.

McLoot tapped the back of his helmet with his palm several times. *Head count.*

Billy opened his hands, palms up—trees, elephant grass, fog and they were all dressed the same—who knew?

McLoot tapped his helmet harder, and a spurt of annoyance made Billy give the signal for *ten*.

McLoot smirked, until Billy gave it again and again and again. He shouldn't have enjoyed the way McLoot's smile faded, but he did.

The first VC paused at the edge of the mist-shrouded field of elephant grass that stretched from there to where his platoon lay concealed.

Billy lifted his M16 and peered through the scope.

McLoot put his lips near Billy's ear and breathed, "Snipe that little fucker."

The little fucker turned, and Billy's heart went *bu-bum*. The kid appeared no more a communist than the first one he'd shot.

Gook, gunky, slant, dink.

He ran through the litany in his head, but all he could see was a kid. All he could think of was that this kid wanted the same thing Billy did, and how was that wrong?

The enemy, what appeared to be a whole battalion, began to pour from the low-hanging fog. Time seemed to slow, but Billy's mind went very fast. A battalion could contain thousands of soldiers. Even if there were only hundreds, Billy and his platoon would be overrun; they would all die. He didn't want that more than he'd ever not wanted anything in his life.

Billy heard his sister's voice as clearly as if she were there: *What are you fighting for?*

Suddenly he knew. He was fighting for the guys he'd laughed with, learned with, those who'd walked at his side; he was fighting for his friends. And sometimes you had to live for your friends instead of dying for them.

. . . the VC aren't ever gonna stop looking for Slayer until . . .

They found him.

Billy laid his rifle next to his ruck, glanced over his shoulder at Terrell and Bama, then forced a smile, along with a thumbs-up. They both seemed like they wanted to puke, but Billy had never been so calm. Because he knew what he had to do; he knew who he wanted to be, or at least who he had to be to do what needed to be done.

He mouthed *go* to Deus, pointing both thumbs over his shoulders, back the way they had come, then he stood and pushed through the cover, one hand held high above his head while the other patted his chest as he shouted, *"Kẻ giết người!"*

CHAPTER 29

Jay
"San Francisco (Be Sure to Wear Flowers in Your Hair)"

Willow Creek—September 1967

On Labor Day weekend, two days before school would start, someone knocked on the door early in the morning, and Jay hurried to answer before they woke Momma.

Momma hadn't forgotten that Jay had shared Billy's sketches with the world and not with her, but she had forgiven it.

"It's what he asked of you. I understand."

Momma had even accepted Paul. She could see that Jay loved him, but more importantly . . .

"He loves you."

However, she couldn't stop herself from offering to cut his hair—which was now long enough to tie into a stubby pigtail—free of charge, every time he came over. Paul laughed like Momma was kidding, but Jay wasn't so sure.

The two men on the porch wore clean, pressed uniforms; the sun sparked off their shoes and nearly blinded her.

"Laura Devries Johnson?" asked the one with crosses pinned to both lapels.

Hearing Momma's full name was always a shock, and it took Jay a second to answer. "No, I'm—"

"May we speak with her?"

"Why?" Jay asked, but she knew.

They hadn't had a letter from Billy in weeks, and Jay had taken comfort in Harold's words, which she heard now as if he were right there, even though he'd left for college without saying good-bye.

If something happens, Jay, they come to your door.

"Something happened," she said.

The men exchanged a glance, then the one without the crosses said, "We need to speak to Mrs. Johnson."

Jay left them on the porch with Ringo—he was thrilled to have new shoes to smell—and hovered in the door of her mother's room. Jay didn't want to wake her. Once she did, everything was going to change. Again.

Momma's eyes opened. She went from "dead to the world" to "what's wrong?" in two point three seconds, the way mothers did.

"There are men asking for you. They're wearing—" To her horror, Jay's voice broke, and Momma flinched. "Uniforms," Jay managed.

Momma vaulted out of bed and headed for the front door quicker than Jay had seen her move in a decade. She marched up to the visitors so fast they took a step back.

"Mrs. Johnson?" the non-cross-wearing version of the two asked.

They gave way as Momma stepped onto the porch and made a shooing motion. "Mind your business."

Jay got to the window in time to see the neighbors melt back into their houses.

"Please come in." Momma shut the door behind them and led the way to the living room. She did not seem aware that she was entertaining a chaplain and an army officer in Billy's old gym shorts and a once-white, now grayish T-shirt without a bra. Momma did not own pajamas.

"Tell me." The words were strong, but Momma's voice was shaky, scared; she looked old.

"We regret to inform you," the officer began, and Momma started to cry.

Jay had never seen her mother cry. Uncertain what to do, she lingered near the window.

"William Michael Johnson is missing in action, most likely a prisoner of war."

"What happened?" Jay asked.

The officer frowned at Momma, who was crying harder and louder, so Jay crossed the room and patted Momma's shoulder, keeping her steady gaze on the men.

"We aren't supposed to . . . You see we're . . . uh . . . here for notification and comfort, information on where to call for details but . . ." He exchanged a glance with the chaplain, who nodded. "Your son surrendered to the enemy."

"That doesn't sound like Billy." For an instant, Jay held out the hope that they were notifying the wrong family.

"By doing so," the chaplain said, "he saved his entire platoon."

That sounded like Billy.

"They were outnumbered. It would have been a massacre, but William Johnson, known to his friends and the enemy as Slayer—"

"Dammit!"

"Language!" Momma snapped.

"Yeah, my language is the problem here."

"Go on," Momma said, and she seemed more herself.

"He identified himself as the sniper the VC had been looking for, and the enemy, understanding the prize they had captured, retreated, allowing his platoon to do the same. William Michael Johnson is an American hero."

"For killing people," Jay said.

"Well, ye—" the officer began.

"No." The chaplain held up his hand. "For saving them."

"Will there be a prisoner exchange?" Momma asked.

"We don't know."

Jay's fingers clenched. "What *do* you know?"

Neither one of them answered.

"That's what I thought."

"Jay." Momma reached out, but Jay backed away.

She went into her room, closed the door, began to pace. Billy had become an American hero, just what he'd always wanted, but did it matter? The war still raged, and he was just . . . gone.

Had he received *Rally!*? Their grandpa's letter? Hers? Had any one or all of them caused him to do what he had done?

She couldn't stay there any longer.

Quickly she changed clothes, threw some others into her huge straw suitcase-purse, along with all the money she had, then climbed out the window.

"What in Sam Hill are you doin', girl?" Gramps strode up the sidewalk; his ancient pickup sat at the curb.

If only she'd scanned the street before she'd made her escape, she could have huddled in her room until he . . . Wait—

"Why are you here?"

His scowl deepened. "I was at the Feedbag, and Bernaducci came in."

The Bernaduccis lived across the street and three houses north. Mister had to have broken a land-speed record to get to the Feedbag and blab, which meant the entire town would know very soon.

"He said there were officers at your place, and I . . ."

Gramps's scowl faded as did the fiery shade of his cheeks, leaving them a mottled pink and white. "Is Billy—?" He swallowed, tried again. "Is he—?"

Maybe Gramps really did care about Billy more than his behavior had ever indicated. Jay felt bad about some things she'd said and thought.

"He's missing." She stepped closer in case Gramps needed her to help him inside. "They said he surrendered, saved his entire platoon. Isn't that—?"

"He what?" Color flooded his face again.

"Surrendered," she said more loudly. His hearing wasn't the best, but she was right next to his ear.

"I heard you! I just can't believe it. I thought he'd finally become a man I could be proud of."

"If you aren't proud of him, that's on you, not Billy."

Gramps continued as if he hadn't heard. "After all that nonsense with his drawings, front and center in that radical piece of trash." His lips curled. "I was hoping he'd died a hero."

"Hoping he'd died?" Jay repeated.

"Nothing like a hero's death to erase any embarrassment."

"Anyone can die." Right now, Jay almost wished Gramps would. "It takes more courage to live. The *army* thinks Billy's a hero."

"Then the army's gone namby-pamby too."

Jay's mouth opened, shut, then she turned away. Why even try?

"You aren't going to walk through town in that getup, are you?"

"No." Jay began to run. She didn't stop until she stood on the highway at the far side of town.

A car approached, and she stuck out her thumb, but it flew past without stopping. A short while later, so did the next one, and the next.

"Where you going?" Helen emerged from the woods.

Nosy neighbors spread news like rats spread the plague.

"Anywhere but here."

"Okay." Helen climbed the embankment and offered her thumb too.

"I thought you weren't allowed to hang out with the hippie," Jay said.

"We aren't hanging out."

"What *are* you doing?" Ronnie emerged from the trees as well.

"Hitchhiking," Helen said.

"Groovy." Ronnie's thumb joined theirs. "Why?"

"You know why." Jay continued to stare at the horizon, willing another car to come by, but none did.

The wind ruffled the trees. No one said a word.

"Billy stood up for what he believed in," Jay said. "I should do the same."

"What *do* you believe in?" Helen asked quietly.

The wind whispered Billy's name, though she hadn't needed any hint. "I believe in my brother. Always have, always will. But the war needs to end; we need to bring everyone home."

"What about communism?" Ronnie asked. "Didn't Billy enlist to stop it?"

"He did, but in the end, he gave his life for his friends, not for the army, not for a cause. But for the ones who stood at his side."

"Okay." Helen nodded, thoughtful. "I see where you're coming from. I get it, but what are you going to do about it 'anywhere but here'?"

"I don't know yet. I gotta think some more."

"You can't do that here?" Helen asked.

"Here I'm just the hippie."

"Hate to break it to you." Mags stood at the edge of the ditch. For the first time in the history of Mags, she was a mess. Uncombed hair, no makeup, her blue jean bell-bottoms had a stain, and her yellow midriff top looked like it had spent the last week in her purse. "But dressed like that, you're gonna be a hippie everywhere."

Before she'd climbed out the window, Jay had donned the cream-colored macramé-fringed halter top and necklace of shells nearly the same shade that she'd found while shopping with Paul. She'd been feeling rebellious when she bought them, but the feeling had faded, and she hadn't found the guts to put them on, along with the red-ribbon headband, until today.

"I won't be a hippie in San Francisco."

Mags's lips quirked. "Oh, you'll still be a hippie, you just won't be the only one."

She did her best to clamber up the embankment, but she kept sliding back down on her ridiculous shoes, which resembled sandals but had a chunky two-inch heel.

"Honestly, Princess!" Ronnie stomped halfway down and offered a hand.

Helen and Jay held their breath, waiting for everything to explode all over again.

Mags contemplated Ronnie's hand. She looked at Jay, then Helen before her lips curved just a little, and she smacked her palm against Ronnie's. Ronnie hauled her onto the gravel at the side of the road to join them.

Mags tossed her tangled hair and stuck out her chest along with her thumb. "Now we'll get some action."

Behind her, Ronnie rolled her eyes, and Jay laughed. It was almost like it had always been but—

"Why?" she asked.

"Because a car that would fly past you three would probably stop for me."

"Sheesh," Ronnie muttered. "Because if you're going to San Francisco, Jay, we are too."

"I thought that was over. I thought—"

"Yeah, yeah," Ronnie interrupted. "So did I, but I learned

something while chumming around with other people." She took a deep breath. "A friendship like ours is worth something; it's worth everything."

"Billy taught us that." Helen looked down, twisting her fingers together until the knuckles went white. "I'm sorry for how I behaved. You were right to go to the chief when I couldn't."

"She was," Ronnie agreed, and Mags nodded. The two of them knew about Helen's brother, though how, why, were questions for another time. "You should have told us, Brain."

"So you could punch Danny?"

"Well . . ." Ronnie flexed her fingers. "Yeah."

Helen smiled. "Thanks, but it'll be okay. I'll be okay."

"I still don't understand why all of you are here when you don't agree with . . ." Jay swept her hand down her body, and the fringe on her halter top swayed.

Mags threw her arm over Jay's shoulders. "You do look ridiculous, but I love you anyway."

"Me too." Ronnie put an arm around Jay on the other side. "Sure, we got stuff to talk about, to work out, but what's important right now is you."

"Exactly," Helen said as Mags nodded.

"We don't have to agree on everything," Ronnie continued.

Helen curved one arm around Ronnie and the other around Mags, completing their circle. "We don't have to agree on *anything* to be all for one . . ."

"One for all!" the rest of them shouted, and they laughed.

"God, that felt good." Ronnie dropped her arms.

"The motto or the laugh?" Helen asked.

"Yes."

Jay remembered what Paul had said on State Street when he'd crowned her with the ribbons she now wore.

Sometimes if you take something down to where it began, then put it back together a different way . . . what you make is changed for the better, though it's still the same underneath.

She and her friends had been stripped down to where they'd begun all those years ago, before the sandbox. Had putting the Four Musketeers back together in a different way changed them for the better, even as it kept them—or at least their friendship —the same underneath?

At four, they hadn't known each other; they hadn't known themselves yet. They were so different, yet they'd fit together just right.

And now . . . now they'd reached another point in life where they didn't know each other anymore; they were still getting to know the selves they would become. They were so different, but could they fit together again just right?

She hoped so. And sometimes hope was all you had.

"You okay?" Mags asked.

Jay shook her head. "Billy's missing, maybe dead, maybe in prison, soon-to-be-dead. I don't know if I'll ever be okay again."

Everyone went silent, and while Jay should have felt bad that she'd killed the joy, all she felt was scared. She wanted to cry, but if she started, she might not stop, so she glanced away, tried to get a grip, and her attention caught on a blob of white nestled in the tall grass at the bowl of the ditch. There was something about it that drew her.

"Where you going?" Helen asked again.

Jay pointed.

"Damn litterbugs."

"Not litter." Jay picked up—

"Fluff!" everyone exclaimed.

"I thought he was dead," Mags said.

"Me too," Ronnie agreed.

"It's a sign." Helen patted the quivering bunny when Jay brought him close.

Ronnie made a soft sound of amusement. "Oh, boy."

"No, really. Everyone thought Fluff was dead, but he was only missing. Like Billy."

Even though signs were bullshit, Jay felt slightly better.

"You could find Billy," Helen continued.

"In the middle of a war? I don't think they'll let me."

"You could make other people look."

"I . . ." Jay lifted her gaze to the sky. The thought of actually doing something . . . "I could try."

"Your try is better than most people's," Helen said.

"I think this car is stopping." Mags shaded her eyes with one hand, waggled her thumb with the other. "We getting in?"

The car did stop. The driver leaned over and peered through the open passenger window. "Need a lift?"

Jay got in, along with the others.

"Where to?" Paul asked.

Everyone's eyes were on her, and Jay knew that if she said *San Francisco*, they would all settle in for the ride.

Jay thought maybe, just maybe, the four of them might be all right. Not completely, or immediately, but eventually, and that was okay.

"How 'bout we get this bunny home?" Jay asked.

CHAPTER 30

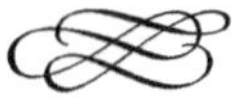

Jay
"Bring the Boys Home"

San Francisco—January–March 1973

"The establishment wants the families of the captive and the missing to stay quiet. To be good, to behave." Jay made a *what can you do?* gesture. "But I haven't behaved since 1967."

The crowd—several thousand strong—went wild.

"My brother is still in Southeast Asia, along with a lot of other brothers, fathers, sons, and husbands, be it in a hut in the darkest parts of Laos or Cambodia, the Hanoi Hilton, or a shallow grave."

Jay had to pause, sip water, swallow after those words. She hated to think of Billy in any of those places. But he had to be somewhere, despite the army's and the enemy's seeming confusion on the subject.

"Right now, in Paris, our delegation is hammering out terms

for an American withdrawal. Will one of the conditions be the return of all US prisoners? They've made unkept promises before, and you know what? I'm done with that shit."

Jay glanced at Momma, who stood at the side of the stage. Even though she was twenty-three, Jay still expected her mother to ground her for swearing, but Momma had given up on that in 1967 too. Instead, Momma smiled the smile she smiled now —more vague than happy. She wouldn't ever be happy again unless they found Billy.

"I will not give up until we all have the answers we need," she continued. "No matter how long it takes."

Billy had been missing for six years, and the hope that had caused Jay to wear flowers in her hair the first time she'd spoken in San Francisco—circa 1969—had dimmed, but it wouldn't go out. Jay wouldn't let it. She hadn't come this far, sacrificed so much, to quit.

"My brother's sketches . . ." Jay indicated the poster-sized copies hanging to her left, a mixture of the ones he'd sent to Harold and the BS ones he'd sent to Momma. "They made people think; they led to questions. Picture's worth a thousand words, right?"

Jay remained silent so the crowd could gaze some more at the sketches they'd probably gazed at a dozen times since the *Rally!* article had been picked up by the wire services and broadcast all over the globe.

Instead of going to college, Jay had gone on the road, telling her brother's story to anyone who would listen. Then came the letters, the phone calls, the visits from other families of the lost, and Jay began to advocate for the release of not only her brother but for all POWs, as well as an accounting—even if it was a stab in the jungle—for all MIAs.

Paul had traveled with her, freelance reporting on the movement, selling articles and photographs to any place that offered.

"I'm getting a better education than I ever would have in journalism school."

He'd been a lot of help writing speeches, booking venues, begging interviews. Then one day he'd disappeared, the only explanation the draft notice he'd left behind.

She wasn't surprised; he'd always told her if he got drafted, he would leave, and he'd known she couldn't. Still, she'd been hurt; she'd thought it was love. But she'd thought a lot of things back then.

A svelte blonde in a dove-gray, cap-sleeved sheath strode in Jay's direction on three-inch-high, needle-heeled ankle breakers the exact shade of her dress.

Mags was a producer for CBS. No one had seen that coming. She'd been runner-up in the Miss America pageant of 1970. Instead of the meltdown the Musketeers expected over second place, she'd shrugged and asked Jay if she could travel with her for a while.

"Maybe having a Miss America runner-up on stage will bring in more people."

Weirdly, it had. But the weirdest part had been Mags deciding that she wanted to report on the war, that she wanted people to know the truth, that she was the one who was going to tell it. And she had.

Mags had come to San Francisco this time to support Jay, not report on Jay, yet in her hand she clutched what looked a lot like a press release. Mags always managed, somehow, to be first in line for any news.

Jay took the paper. At first all she saw were squiggles and dots. Then she realized she wasn't breathing, and when she did, the squiggles and dots became words.

"What is it?" Helen approached with Ronnie and Momma. The three of them had traveled here together to be with Jay at this, her largest engagement to date.

There'd been protests, even at Princeton, and while Helen, as one of the first women ever admitted in 1969, hadn't wanted to make waves, she'd also been unable to ignore facts. Helen was, first and foremost, smarter than the average bear, and she'd used her smarts writing op-ed pieces for the *Princetonian*. Since she'd graduated in May, she'd been writing Jay's speeches. Eventually she wanted to go to law school and fight for kids, women, really anyone that had been abused as she had.

Ronnie had run the 1500 meter in the '72 Olympics in Munich, had been there when Palestinian terrorists stormed Olympic Village and killed two Israeli athletes in their rooms, then nine more at the airport a day later. The world didn't seem to be getting better but worse, and Vietnam was part of that.

Since the day the Four Musketeers had stood on the side of the road vowing friendship, no matter what, they'd had their issues. They'd fought, separated, reformed, and fought again, about little things and bigger things. But as Ronnie had said, they didn't have to agree on everything. Sometimes, in fact, it seemed that the *only* thing they agreed on was that always and forever they would have each other.

For all of them, leaving Willow Creek had opened their eyes, showed them the world, allowed them to become who they wanted, who they needed to be. But they'd all gone back, eventually, maybe not for good or for long, but Willow Creek was home; it always would be.

"Jay?" Momma was ghost pale, Ronnie and Helen not much better.

The audience shifted and murmured, uneasy.

From the beginning, Jay had ended her speeches by reading from an unsent letter to Billy. Now everyone expected it, and she would not disappoint them.

Jay stepped to the microphone, and the crowd hushed.

"Dear Billy." Jay looked at her mother, her friends, and she smiled. "I hear that you're coming home."

* * *

OF COURSE, it wasn't simple; it wasn't fast. After dealing with the army, as well as both the US and the North Vietnamese governments, Jay should have known better.

"The POWs will be released in the order they were captured," Mags said. "Except for the injured and sick; they'll be on the first C-141 out of Hanoi in a few weeks."

"His name was never on any of their lists," Momma said.

"It's on there now." Jay checked the press release one more time. Yep, still there, about midway down in black and white.

"But what if . . ." Momma bit her lip. "What if it isn't him?"

"It's him," Jay said. It had to be.

Still, neither one of them slept until they spoke to Billy on the phone.

"How's Ringo?"

Definitely Billy. Unfortunately, everything else . . . not very Billy at all. Sure, he answered their questions.

Where had he been?

No idea.

Who had been holding him?

VC.

Why hadn't he been on the list of the captured?

Ask them.

His voice was a monotone, and the silence that pulsed between their questions made Jay wonder if the Billy they'd known would ever come out of that jungle.

Two months later, they stood on the tarmac at Travis Air Force Base, waiting for Billy's transport to arrive. Jay could barely stand still. She'd been working single-mindedly toward this goal for so long, now that it was happening, she felt lost.

Momma took Jay's hand. Her fingers were far too cold considering the California heat.

"You okay?" Jay asked.

"No. You?"

"No."

They exchanged wan smiles as the plane taxied in. The mood all around them was electric—both excitement and fear creating a static that tickled along the edge of Jay's last nerve.

The plane door opened, and the first pale, thin ghost of a man stepped onto the rollaway stairs. He wore a uniform so new the sunlight bounced off the fabric, the creases as sharp as the man's cheekbones.

A tiny sob escaped Momma—air force uniform, it wasn't Billy. Jay tightened her fingers around her mother's as more POWs came down the staircase, stepped to the podium, said a few words into the microphone. The majority of them were air force, reflecting the more than 50 percent ratio of air force captives to all the rest. The VC had shot down a helluva lot of aircraft.

Several men wearing army uniforms appeared, descended, spoke, then disappeared in a flurry of shouts and hugs from their families.

Then finally, finally . . .

"Billy," Jay said, that single word holding every hope and every heartache that had fueled her for so many years.

CHAPTER 31

Travis Air Force Base—March 1973

A breeze blew in the open door and across Billy's face. Could the air really smell like freedom? Why not? Captivity certainly had an odor all its own.

Daylight beckoned, and Billy stepped into it. He saw Momma right away, her gaze riveted to the top of the staircase. At the sight of him, she winced and put out a hand as if suddenly afraid she might fall.

Did he look that bad? Thin? Sure. Pale? Check. His hair had been shorn close to his head because of the lice. But lice died; hair grew back; thin and pale went away. What probably wouldn't were the eyes of a stranger that stared back from the mirror instead of his own, the eyes of a man that had seen, done, endured too much. But Momma couldn't see that guy from there.

In an attempt to make sure she *never* saw that guy, Billy smiled, waved. Momma started to cry. Billy shoved his hands behind his back and his teeth behind his lips. Both of them looked a lot different now than they had before.

The woman next to Momma touched her shoulder, said something, lifted her face.

"Jay," Billy whispered in both shock and awe.

No longer a kid—had he really expected her to be?—Jay had grown into her legs, her nose, her skin. She'd cut her hair as short as Mia Farrow's—or at least as short as Mia's had been the last time Billy saw a photo—and her green eyes loomed large. She wore a pantsuit the shade of sunlight; the bell-bottoms fluttered in the breeze. In his memories of her, she wore frayed cutoffs that displayed her scabby, knobby knees and a T-shirt that revealed all her mosquito bites. When he got closer, would he discover that the Jay he'd once known was as gone as the Billy she once had?

Someone prodded him from behind, and he descended the staircase, did his turn at the microphone. What he said? No idea. He no sooner stepped away from the podium than Jay broke, running straight toward him and throwing herself into his arms.

Billy staggered. He wasn't that strong anymore. But Jay held on, hugging Billy so hard his ribs crackled. A lot of his bones crackled these days; he tried to ignore them.

"Oh, Billy." She drew back. "Your hands."

His fingers cupped her elbows. Some of them had healed crookedly, the rest sported lumps. "They work."

"What ha—?"

He shook his head. Not now.

Billy let Jay go and wrapped Momma in his arms, startled by how fragile she seemed. If he hugged her as tight as he wanted to, would she break in half?

"You're home," she said.

"Not yet."

"Soon." Momma reached for Jay's hand, then Billy's, connecting them.

Billy glanced away as the joy of that connection threatened to overwhelm him, but he forgot about it just that fast when he saw—

"Flash?" Of all the people Billy wanted to see, Flash was pretty near the bottom.

"Slayer!" Flash clapped his hands on Billy's shoulders. He'd put on weight, grown out his hair, neither of which made him any more attractive. Or less annoying.

"Don't call me—"

Flash yanked Billy into a hug. "You saved my life, man. I'll never forget it."

He punched Billy in the arm, his usual jackass laugh spewing free, but the expression in his eyes, the shimmering sheen of tears, made Billy's eyes moist too. That happened a lot lately—sometimes for no reason that Billy could figure. He really wished it would stop.

"Remember me?" A second man approached. His face had been burned in quarter-sized spots, the skin alternating between shiny and smooth; his eyebrows were gone along with most of his hair. The guy smacked himself in the forehead. "I knew you wouldn't."

"Boom-Boom?"

Boom-Boom's smile blossomed. He still had all his teeth, and it was a nice smile, one Billy aspired to once he spent some quality time with a dentist.

"You do know me." Boom-Boom seemed unreasonably thrilled by that, as if Billy had recognized his face and not his tic. Billy was just happy to find him alive.

"Is Deus—?" he began, and Boom-Boom glanced helplessly at Flash.

"Sorry, man." Flash actually seemed to be. Maybe *once an asshole, always an asshole* no longer applied.

"Bama?"

Flash and Boom-Boom shook their heads, looked down. They didn't elaborate, and that was good. Billy didn't need to know how they'd died, only that they had. He tried to force another name past his lips and couldn't.

In battle not thinking had saved him, in captivity, thinking had. For the past six years he'd fought despair by imagining his friends happy, healthy, alive. But right now, despair hung over him like that damn triple canopy jungle that had blocked the sun and the rain and the rest of the world for what seemed like eternity.

"Beej!"

Suddenly Billy could breathe again.

Terrell dropped a kiss on Jay's head that only Billy seemed surprised by and pulled Billy into his long, skinny arms.

His fro was huge and waved in the breeze, brushing against Billy's nearly bare head, tickling like a feather as Terrell leaned back. Glasses rimmed with gold wire sat where the Buddy Holly frames used to be. His dark eyes searched Billy's, then he gave a quick smile. "My man!"

A forgotten slice of the Billy that was slid into place when Terrell held out his hand for some skin, and Billy actually laughed as he gave it to him. The sound was more "puking cat" than "happy fellow," but it felt good. Maybe the more he laughed the better it would sound, the easier laughing would get. It could happen. At least his laugh made Momma smile.

"Where's Gramps?" he asked.

Momma's smile died. His friends shuffled their feet.

Jay's lips tightened the way they always had when she was seriously teed off. "Did you . . . uh . . . get a letter from him before you . . . uh . . . ?"

"The one where he called me a traitor, a commie, and an anti-American embarrassment?"

"Fucking old man."

Billy's eyes went wide. Momma didn't swear. What else had changed while he'd been gone?

"I thought once he heard what I did, how I . . . you know . . ." Billy waved a hand at his buddies.

"Saved us," Terrell said as both Flash and Boom-Boom nodded.

"I thought he'd change his mind."

"Have you ever known Gramps to change?" Jay asked.

What did he have to do to earn that man's approval? The only time he'd ever had it was when he'd been Slayer—kicking ass and taking names. But it was because he was Slayer that he'd been able to save so many. Wasn't saving lives more impressive than taking them?

"I'll talk to him," Billy said.

Everyone exchanged glances.

Shit, Billy thought.

"He's dead," Momma said. "Stroke."

"Because of me?"

"No." Jay set her hand on Billy's arm. "Most likely because of me."

Gramps had never given two hoots about Jay.

"He wasn't thrilled with Jay's occupation," Terrell said.

What could Jay possibly do that would make Gramps have a stroke?

"Your sister draws bigger crowds than Abbie Hoffman," Terrell continued.

"I don't—" Billy managed.

"Tom Hayden? Jane Fonda?"

"Like . . . Henry Fonda?" The number of things he didn't know after being held captive in a foreign jungle for six years had to be epic.

"His daughter. They're all anti-war activists."

"You're an anti-war activist?" He could see where that might give Gramps a stroke, right after the heart attack he probably had when Jay brought Terrell home.

"Not exactly." Jay's gaze shifted to Terrell.

"Jay, of course, wanted the war to end, sooner rather than later. We all did. But she refused to be a lightning rod against a conflict you'd supported. She became an advocate for the missing and the lost; her cause is not only the return of all POWs but the release of all information regarding them, as well as any MIAs. She even went to Hanoi once."

His sister had been in Hanoi?

"She wanted answers, so did a lot of other people."

"And asking for answers gave Gramps a stroke?"

"It was probably the way I asked for them. Loudly, in front of hundreds."

"Thousands," Terrell murmured, and Jay gifted him with a very fond smile.

"Over and over again," Jay continued.

"On TV, on radio, all over the country." Terrell did his *Power to the People* punch; this seemed like the perfect time for it. "She wouldn't let anyone forget you, or any of the others."

Not only did Jay look different, dress different, she was different. The idea of the little sister Billy had left at home accomplishing all that they were saying amazed him. He was proud of her; he could see that Momma, that Terrell, were too.

Over the next few days, until Billy mustered out, his friends took every opportunity to tell him, before they returned to their lives, that everything they had was due to him.

"I've got a hot wife, man." Flash grinned as behind him Terrell shook his head, then crossed his eyes and stuck out his tongue.

Billy choked on a laugh that sounded a lot more like a laugh than the last one had.

"And I have a little boy." Boom-Boom tapped his forehead. "Smartest little fucker I ever saw. He's gonna be president."

Billy had wondered on a few very bad nights if what he'd done had been worth it, and he knew for certain now what he'd known back then.

It had.

"I'm in my last year at the University of Chicago Law School," Terrell said.

"Only occupation where he can talk almost as much as he wants to." Flash cackled—same way he always had, at least one thing hadn't changed—then waved as he and Boom-Boom headed off to catch their planes, vowing to *stay in touch*.

"Just 'cause they passed those civil rights acts don't mean anyone's readin' 'em," Terrell continued. "My people need help."

"And my sister?"

Terrell tilted his head. "What about your sister?"

"You been helpin' her?"

Silence fell; the two friends eyed each other.

"You gonna hit me?"

Billy shook his head. He couldn't think of anyone he'd rather have in love with his sister, but . . . "It won't be easy."

"Nothin's been easy since that draft notice showed up." Terrell took a breath and lifted his gaze to the blue-blue sky. Billy still hadn't gotten used to how bright everything was. "You remember when we promised we'd go see each other's families if we . . . ?"

"Died? Yeah."

"You weren't dead, but we didn't know that, and not knowing was almost worse. I shouted your name in my sleep a lot." Terrell lowered his gaze to Billy's. "So did Jay."

Billy didn't know what to say to that, so he said nothing

"I'd die for her, man."

"How about you live for her instead?"

"Already do."

Silence again.

"We good?" Terrell finally asked, and Billy nodded. "My man."

Expecting Terrell to offer his hand for some skin, Billy nearly got clocked in the nose when Terrell hugged him. There'd been a lot of hugging since he'd returned, and a lot of times—like now—Billy didn't see it coming. Maybe, eventually, he'd get used it.

"When will I see you again?" Billy asked.

"Bro, I spend a lot of weekends at your place." Terrell's smile dimmed, and he set his big hand on Billy's too-slim shoulder. "You sure you're okay?"

"Did I say I was okay?"

Terrell sighed. "If you want to talk or drink or . . . whatever, I'm there."

"I know. I . . . Maybe, but not yet."

Terrell searched Billy's face, then he let him be.

The next day Billy, Momma, and Jay got on a plane headed east. Momma fell asleep before they reached cruising altitude.

"She hasn't slept well since . . ." Jay's voice drifted off.

"1967?"

Jay shrugged.

"Me neither."

"Billy?" Jay put her hand over his. "You wanna talk about it?"

Everyone wanted him to talk—the army shrink, Momma, Terrell, Jay, even Harold, who had called from Georgia where he was living with his wife and three-year-old daughter—but talking had never been his strength, even before he'd spent six years mostly alone in the dark.

He pulled out the sketchbook he'd asked for, then received the morning after he'd been released by his captors. With every drawing he'd made, he'd felt more like himself. Maybe that was the way back to the person he had been.

"I used to draw what I dreamed and then send it away. Once I did, I forgot."

Jay frowned.

"I know that's strange, maybe even crazy."

"We do what we gotta do."

The truth of that had set the course of Billy's life. Since enlisting, he had done what he had to do. Did he regret anything? Sure. Probably always would, but no one got through a lifetime without regrets.

"Slayer didn't think; Slayer acted. That was how he had to be, to be who he was."

"Wasn't *he* you?"

"Sometimes." Billy's lips curved. "I went to prison as Slayer, but Billy's the one who . . . well, let's just say there's a lot of time for thoughts in prison, and thoughts kept me sane. Or sane enough."

At least he hoped so, and his hopes these days were turning out to be less foolish than the ones he'd had so long ago.

The images inside his sketchbook flickered along with a whole lot of others. He handed it to Jay. "Do *not* show Momma."

Jay opened the cover and paged through. Hut, captor, hut, captor. One broken finger, then two, and three. He'd given up drawing those when he reached four. If you've seen one broken finger, you've seen them all.

"Oh, Billy," Jay whispered, and she lifted eyes brimming with so much sorrow he had to glance away.

"I can still draw. I win."

"I doubt they did that to keep you from drawing."

"No." They'd done that to keep him from slaying or maybe to punish him *for* slaying. The result was the same. It could have been worse, had been for a lot of guys. He wasn't complaining. The doctors said they could fix most of his fingers just like the dentist had said he could fix most of Billy's teeth. Six years without a toothbrush or fresh fruit was not DDS recommended.

Jay continued to turn pages. The jungle, the captors, the huts began to look as similar as the broken fingers. They *had* all blended together near the end.

"I was held in a lot of different places. Moved around at night. Handed off to others so many times I lost count."

The last sketch showed Billy, blindfolded, standing in front of Tan Son Nhut Air Base, the dust cloud left from a retreating truck billowing around him like Pig Pen's cloud of dirt.

"When I took off that blindfold, I expected to see the Hanoi Hilton."

"That must have been scary."

"After sleeping every night in the dirt or the mud, eating rice flavored with bugs and not seeing a round eye in years, I wouldn't have been that upset about it."

Jay didn't appear convinced, but she said nothing.

"They were shouting something . . ." He tapped the guards in front of the gate. "Since I hadn't heard more than a word or two of English in quite a while, it took me a few minutes to understand that the war was over, and I could go home."

It had taken him longer than a few minutes to believe it.

"Funny how I ended up right back where I started."

"You have a strange idea of funny."

"And probably always will."

Jay's fingers clenched. "How can you be so calm?"

He'd learned the hard way that getting upset didn't do a damn bit of good.

"I volunteered. I asked for it."

"No," Jay said. "You did not ask for any of this." She lifted the sketchbook.

"I surrendered. I kind of did."

"Oh, Billy," she said again.

"There were good times, too, good people." He pulled out a second sketchbook that he'd started to fill last week. "Those I want to remember. This one I'm gonna keep."

On the first page, LT stared back, cigarette hanging off his lip. On the second, Terrell held his shotgun bong with one hand while the other punched *Power to the People*. The third reflected Sparky and his precious radio. Then Deus, Flash, F-Cat, Hammer, even Magoo and Bama, plus several more.

"Tell me about them," Jay said.

So he did. And the more Billy talked, the easier it got.

"I went to Vietnam because I believed in the war, but the longer I was there, the more fucked-up things I saw, the less the war mattered; the more *they* mattered." He tapped the sketchbook. "I'll never forget them. We were . . ." He tried to think of the best way to explain what those men had meant to him, what they still did.

"All for one?" Jay held out her hand, and Billy took it.

"Yeah." His fingers tightened around hers. "And one for all."

The End

BOOK CLUB DISCUSSION QUESTIONS

1. *Suddenly That Summer* begins as Billy Johnson says goodbye to his adoring, seventeen-year-old sister Jay and their hard-working "Momma" as he leaves Willow Creek, WI behind to enlist in the Vietnam War. How did the dual settings and alternating points of view between Billy in Vietnam and Jay in Willow Creek deepen the reader's emotional investment and understanding of this confusing time in U.S. history?

2. *Suddenly That Summer* revolves around a close-knit brother and sister who must figure out life on their own as Billy fights in Vietnam and Jay struggles with her beliefs about the war while back home in Wisconsin. Whose story did you identify with more—Jay's or Billy's? Why?

3. Each chapter of *Suddenly That Summer* starts with a song from the 1960s and '70s. How did the music of that era reflect the social and political climate in the United States at that time? Which songs might be on the soundtrack of your youth?

4. Because of his only son's desertion, as well as his refusal to

enlist despite military service being a Johnson family tradition, Gramps pushed Billy to be stronger, quicker, smarter, better, *more* than the father who had come and gone before. How does a parent's failure or expectations shape a child's future? Have you ever done something you didn't believe in to please or gain the respect of an authority figure?

5. In a never-ending quest to earn the respect of his grandfather, Billy enlisted rather than wait to be called up to Vietnam in the newly implemented draft. A veteran of The Great War, Gramps valued action—not thought—admonishing Billy throughout his life for being soft and thinking too much. How did the generational divide between men who served in the world wars or in Korea and young men facing the Vietnam War affect society's view of what it meant to "be a man?"

6. While race relations were strained in America, drill sergeants in Vietnam reminded soldiers "In 'Nam, everyone bleeds red" and "If you wanna live through Vietnam, you need to be as color blind as VC bullets." How did Billy and Terrell's friendship illustrate the color-blind bond that comes when people share experience and trauma? How has a friendship with someone from a different background enriched your life?

7. The connection that Billy and Terrell formed was unique but powerful. How important is it to have unique friendships or connections with people beyond those in our inner circle?

8. The Vietnam War was the first time in history that journalists used television to bring the horrors of war into the public's living rooms. Jay struggled with shifting views about what was really happening in the world as journalistic accounts from various sources challenged beliefs and ideals. How does jour-

nalism and media shape our perspectives? Is journalistic integrity as strong now as it was during the Vietnam War?

9. The jungles of Vietnam were described as "a monster that will devour you." How did the jungle become a character in its own right?

10. "The Four Musketeers" are pulled apart by issues of abuse, questions of sexuality and the confusion brought by differing beliefs in a divided country. But, in the end, they conclude that "a friendship like ours is worth something; it's worth everything." Have you ever been part of a friendship like that?

11. Compare and contrast the friendships of "The Four Musketeers"; Jay, Billy, and Harold; Billy and Terrell; and Jay and Paul.

12. Billy copes with the extreme mental, physical, and emotional stress of the war by drawing what he experiences and sending the drawings to Harold—out of sight, out of mind. Do you think this was a healthy way for Billy to deal with his trauma? What outlet do you use to get by when everything is too much to handle?

13. How did your opinion of Billy change as he went from "Beej" to "Slayer" thanks to his crack shot and fearless leadership among his platoon?

14. Which secondary character in *Suddenly That Summer* was your favorite? Why?

15. Was it difficult to read the coarse and racially charged language and graphic depictions of war portrayed in *Suddenly*

That Summer? How did your own experience and perspective shape your understanding of the characters and their reactions to the stress of the times?

16. Was Jay right or wrong to have shared Billy's drawings with *Rally* magazine? Explain your answer.

17. How did you feel about the author's final romantic choice for Jay in the last chapter? Did you expect Jay and Paul to stay together?

18. What pivotal quote or scene from the novel was the most memorable for you?

19. How thought-provoking did you find the book? Did the book change your opinion about anything, or did you learn something new from it? If so, what?

20. From your point of view, what were the central themes of the book? How well do you think the author did at exploring them?

21. How would you adapt this book into a movie? Who would you cast in the leading roles?

22. Would you call the ending of *Suddenly That Summer* "happy?"

23. If you could ask Lori Handeland one question about this book, what would you ask and why?

JUST ONCE

What if you could start over--right at the moment where it all went wrong?

Twenty-four years ago, Frankie's marriage ended. Now, her ex-husband—Charley Blackwell, a world-famous photojournalist—has walked through the door as if no time has passed. And for him, it hasn't. Illness has stolen his long-term memory.

Once upon a time, Frankie and Charley were the perfect couple—utterly, completely, sickeningly in love. They shared a passion for photography, but where Frankie saw the way the world came together, Charley only saw how the world came apart.

The cards of fate dealt them a hand that broke their marriage. Yet, Charley is the only man Frankie ever truly loved, and in Charley's mind they are right back in that era of complete marital bliss.

But Frankie has moved on to a new life, Charley to a new wife. One he doesn't remember at all. Three people trapped in a collision of love, life, and loss.

**What do you do when you are forgotten?
What do you do if you
are the one who is remembered?**

From the voice of New York Times bestselling author Lori Handeland, this heart-wrenching but ultimately uplifting novel contains the humor, depth of characterization and fast paced plot lines she is known for while showcasing the author's incredible range.

DEAR READER/FREE STORY

Dear Reader,

I have been a huge Stephen King fan since I picked up CARRIE in college all those years ago. But one of my favorite King tales is "The Body," even before it became one of my favorite movies, *Stand by Me*. So when I began to mull over what my next women's fiction novel should be, it wasn't a surprise when that chatty little voice in my head asked, "Why not do *Stand by Me* with girls?"

Indeed.

Though I was in elementary school in 1967, the Vietnam War didn't end until I was in middle school. The news coverage of the conflict both overseas and at home permeated my world and the world of my friends, aiding in my creation of the Four Musketeers. I hope you enjoyed my trip down this near-history memory lane.

Reviews are critically important to authors, so if you enjoyed this book, please consider putting up a Review (it can be as short as you'd like) on the platform where you purchased it. I would appreciate it very much!

If you would like to keep up to date on my upcoming

releases, and receive a free short story, please sign up for my newsletter. (You can also do this on my website.)

I love hearing from my readers and can be contacted via my website (LoriHandeland.com), through Facebook (Lori Handeland Books) and on Instagram (Lori Handeland Books).

Best Wishes,
    Lori Handeland

ABOUT THE AUTHOR

Lori Handeland is a five-time nominee and two-time winner of the prestigious RITA™ Award from Romance Writers of America, as well as the New York Times and USA Today bestselling author of over sixty novels spanning the genres of paranormal romance, urban fantasy, contemporary romance, historical romance, historical fantasy and women's fiction. Her novel *Just Once* received a coveted, starred review from Library Journal and was optioned as a feature film by Catalyst Global Media.

Lori lives in Southern Wisconsin with her husband of over thirty-five years. In between writing and reading, she enjoys long walks with their rescue mutt, Arnold, and visits from her two grown sons, awesome daughter-in-law and perfectly adorable grandchildren.

ALSO BY LORI HANDELAND

Women's Fiction Standalones

JUST ONCE

SUDDENLY THAT SUMMER

Midnight Madness

(Nightcreature Spin Off)

Paranormal Women's Fiction

STALKING AFTER MIDNIGHT (e-short story)

NOTHING GOOD HAPPENS AFTER MIDNIGHT

BLAME IT ON MIDNIGHT

IN THE MIDNIGHT HOUR

Nightcreature Novels

Paranormal Romance

BLAME IT ON THE MOON (e-short story)

BLUE MOON

SHADOW OF THE MOON (e-short story)

RED MOON RISING (e-novella)

HUNTER'S MOON

CHARMED BY THE MOON (e-short story)

Found in: MY BIG, FAT SUPERNATURAL WEDDING

DARK MOON

CRESCENT MOON

MIDNIGHT MOON

RISING MOON

VOODOO MOON (e-novella)

HIDDEN MOON

THUNDER MOON

MARKED BY THE MOON

MOON CURSED

CRAVE THE MOON

Sisters of the Craft Trilogy

(Nightcreature Spin Off)

Paranormal Romance

IN THE AIR TONIGHT

HEAT OF THE MOMENT

SMOKE ON THE WATER

The Phoenix Chronicles

Urban Fantasy

IN THE BEGINNING (e-short story)

ANY GIVEN DOOMSDAY

DOOMSDAY CAN WAIT

APOCALYPSE HAPPENS

CHAOS BITES

DANCES WITH DEMONS (novella)

THERE WILL BE DEMONS

(short story)

Found in: HEX APPEAL

Shakespeare Undead Duet

Historical Fantasy

SHAKESPEARE UNDEAD

ZOMBIE ISLAND

The Luchettis

Contemporary Romance

THE FARMER'S WIFE

THE DADDY QUEST

THE BROTHER QUEST

THE HUSBAND QUEST

A SOLDIER'S QUEST

THE MOMMY QUEST

Luchetti Prequels

LEAVE IT TO MAX

A SHERIFF IN TENNESSEE

Once Upon a Time in the West Trilogy

BEAUTY AND THE BOUNTY HUNTER

AN OUTLAW IN WONDERLAND

THE LONE WARRIOR

The Rock Creek Six

Western Historical Romance

REESE – by Lori Handeland

SULLIVAN – by Linda Winstead Jones

RICO – by Lori Handeland

JED – by Linda Winstead Jones

NATE – by Lori Handeland

CASH – by Linda Winstead Jones

Historical Romance

SECOND CHANCE

CHARLIE AND THE ANGEL

(sequel to SECOND CHANCE)

BY ANY OTHER NAME

AN OUTLAW FOR CHRISTMAS

JUST AFTER MIDNIGHT

LOVING A LEGEND

WHEN MORNING COMES (novella)

Lori's Classic Love Stories

Contemporary Romance

OUT OF HER LEAGUE

FRIENDS TO LOVERS

WHEN YOU WISH

MOMMY FOR RENT (novella)

Contemporary paranormal

D.J.'S ANGEL

Historical paranormal

FULL MOON DREAMS

DREAMS OF AN EAGLE

Paranormal novellas

WHEN MIDNIGHT COMES

DEAD MAN DATING

(in DATES FROM HELL)

COWEBS OVER THE MOON

(in MOON FEVER)

Romantic Suspense

SHADOW LOVER

Collections

The Luchettis Books 1-3

The Luchettis Books 4-6

Luchetti Series Prequel Duet

Lori's Classic Love Stories

The Rock Creek Six: The Complete Set in One Bundle

The Nightcreature Collection Books 1-3

Nightcreature Shorts

COPYRIGHT